CHRISTMAS IN CHARMINGTON
SPECIAL EDITION

MADDIE JAMES

SAND DUNE BOOKS

A CHARMINGTON CHRISTMAS

A Christmas village. Three unforgettable love stories. One magical gift edition.

Welcome to Charmington, a snow-dusted Christmas village nestled in the Adirondacks of upstate New York—where twinkle lights glow all season long, hot cocoa flows freely, and love finds its way home.

From the Apple Festival in autumn to the Christmas Jubilee in December, this picturesque town celebrates community, kindness, and second chances. At the heart of it all stands the historic Holly Hill Inn, where snowflakes, nostalgia, and romance intertwine.

This special collector's edition brings together three sweet, small-town Christmas romances—stories of hope, healing, and the magic of believing in love again. Perfect for readers who love Christmas movies, second chances, and cozy holiday happily-ever-afters.

A star-crossed holiday romance about the power of holding on...and letting go.

When Jenny Anders meets Ben Matson on a North Carolina beach the summer before college, it's love at first sight. They dream of forever—but her disapproving father and a snowstorm threaten to derail their plans to elope on Christmas Eve.

Stranded in the mountains, Jenny and Ben find shelter with an elderly couple whose enduring love reminds them what commitment truly means. As Christmas morning dawns, Jenny must decide whether to follow her heart—or let it go.

Sometimes all it takes is a little Christmas magic.

Christmas blogger Ariana Estrella lives for all things holly and bright. When her search for the perfect Christmas village leads her to Charmington, she finds a town bursting with cheer—and one very grumpy hardware store owner who wants none of it.

Matt Matson may be the Scrooge of Main Street, but when a snowstorm strands him and Ariana together at the Holly Hill Inn, the holiday spirit—and a certain optimistic blogger—start to melt his frosty heart.

Can a couple on the brink of divorce rediscover love at Christmas?

Five years after their fairy-tale wedding, Broadway star Ava Cohen and her husband Will have grown apart—her spotlight in the city, and his career in medicine pulling him away. They've agreed to end their marriage...after one last family Christmas together at Holly Hill Inn.

But surrounded by the warmth and wonder of Charmington's Christmas Jubilee, the couple begins to question everything. Between gingerbread house building, family dinners, and a terrifying accident, Ava and Will rediscover the spark they thought was gone forever.

Is it too late to save their marriage—or is this the Christmas miracle they didn't see coming?

CHAPTER 1

HOME FOR CHRISTMAS

*S*unday, *December 23, 1989*

JENNY ANDERS SHOVED HER BACKPACK THROUGH HER BEDROOM window and peered out over her parents' front lawn. The bag was a lot fuller than she had expected, since she'd tucked a couple of Christmas gifts inside at the last minute—but she'd manage. The night was crisp, clear, with a near-full moon shining down from behind the house, casting shadows and dancing light across the neighborhood. She'd waited for the old grandfather clock in their entryway to chime midnight, then made her move.

She felt rather silly, honestly, sneaking out of the house. She was an adult, for goodness' sake—she'd turned nineteen in October. But here she was, sneaking all the same, and avoiding the inevitable confrontation with her parents.

In particular, her father.

The backpack tumbled and slid a few feet down the incline of the steep porch roof, making a snake trail in the skiff of snow on the shingles. One leg through the window, followed by the other, Jenny sat on the edge and studied her surroundings, wondering how many of her neighbors had seen their Philadelphia neighborhood from this vantage point.

She didn't worry about the house alarm. The security lock on this window had never worked. She'd discovered that years ago, and of course, had not divulged that information to her parents. She'd snuck out occasionally during her teen years. Tonight, it made her escape easier than walking out the front door, avoiding disarming the alarm and waking her parents.

It was a pretty view up here, she decided. Serene. She took a moment to gather into herself, knowing that this peaceful feeling might be her last one for a while—that is, until she and Ben got on their way, and she had a wedding ring on her finger. Until then, she'd likely be a nervous wreck.

But right now, sitting in the dark, high above everything but the treetops, she breathed in frosty air and welcomed the silence and the tranquility. Inhaling deep, she sighed, letting the breath out long and slow.

She'd like to freeze this moment in time—just for a few minutes. The previous few weeks had been too stressful with all the family drama. Up here, on the roof, things were simpler and, well, nice.

Calm before the storm?

She didn't want to consider another storm. She was ready for peace.

And she was ready for Ben.

The lights twinkled on the fresh-fallen snow, winking between the branches. The streetlights provided a soft, blueish glow to the tree-lined street. Tastefully trimmed for the season, the colonial houses of her neighborhood sported candles in the windows, and traditional wreaths on the doors, with spotlights shining up on them from the lawn. Christmas trees sparkled in the windows of a few dark houses. And to her left, her closest neighbors, the Garrison's, went all out with a Santa and sleigh on their roof.

"Well, hello there, Santa," she whispered. "Fancy meeting you up here."

Scooting off the sill, she turned to lower the window. Carefully. Simultaneously, her sock snagged at the ankle on a nail sticking out from the roof.

"Shoot." She plucked at the sock, tearing a hole in it. Oh well, she'd change it later. Closing the window with a soft click, she sat on the cold asphalt shingles. Exhaling, she shivered and snatched at the backpack, scooting her way to the edge of the roof, and the ivy-heavy trellis attached to the side porch.

She'd done this a dozen times or more—snuck out after her parents were fast asleep—but this was different. Her previous excursions were because she was a semi-rebellious teenager, tired of curfews and her parents' disapproving notions about all her friends, and what she should, or should not, be doing on a Saturday night.

Now, her sneaking out seemed ridiculous. She should have simply told them she was leaving and walked out the front door—but that seemed logical.

And nothing, lately, had been logical.

By daybreak, she expected to be in the small town of Charmington in upstate New York—with Ben, the love of her life.

Breathing deep, she exhaled. *Her Ben.*

It was the right thing to do—for her and for Ben. She had a good head on her shoulders. She'd graduated high school with honors in May and was now a freshman in college. She was smart and knew what she wanted in life. She was acting in her own best interest—living her life how she wanted to live it. What she wasn't doing was deciding blindly, as her father had suggested weeks earlier.

She and Ben had thought it through.

She was ready to push herself from the nest—just not in the direction her parents wanted.

For them, college followed by law school was her future, and then a position in her dad's law firm. Her parents had worked hard and created healthy college funds for her and her older sister, Candy. That they would graduate from a university, and continue to graduate school, had always been the expectation.

But it wasn't Jenny's dream.

In time, she would get that degree. But when she did, it would be on her own terms, on her own dime, and in her own time. And she would study art, not law. The money her parents had saved for her college would be a nice nest egg for them. She loved her parents—not that she didn't. They'd been good to her growing up, if not overly protective and stricter than the parents of most of her friends. She didn't want to appear disrespectful at all. She just wanted to live her own life, make her own decisions.

Her father had made that impossible with his demands and ultimatums. She knew that living her life to please her father was neither healthy for her, nor in her best interest. He'd forced her hand on the issue and her mother had gone along with him.

A letter she'd left behind explained her plans, where she was going, and who she was with. She'd call them later. After.

They could take some of that college money and do something nice for themselves. She hoped so. They rarely took time off from work to spend time together. Perhaps they could take that cruise they'd bantered about for years.

It made her happy to think about that.

The thing she knew for certain, though, was that Penn State and a Philadelphia law firm were not her destiny.

Ben was her future, and tonight, she was going for it.

Vehicle lights rounded the corner at the end of the street. She watched as the older model red pickup truck drove slowly and approached the front of her house. Scooting toward the edge of the roof and the trellis, Jenny slid the backpack over her right shoulder and slipped over the side to climb down the trellis.

Her stomach erupted in a tumble of nervous and happy butterflies.

Ben stopped his truck at the end of her driveway, killed his headlights, the engine rumbling.

She reached the ground, running toward the truck.

CHAPTER 2

*S*ix months earlier, June 1989

BEN MATSON TOSSED ANOTHER SIDEWAYS GLANCE AT THE GIRL IN the pink bikini with the sheer white coverup as she strolled down the shore. He'd watched her for the past fifteen minutes as she made her way back up the beach. Pausing in front of his beach house, she stooped to pick up something in the sand, glanced his way, then righted herself and wandered on. A stiff breeze raced off the ocean, swirling her long hair around her head and teasing at the coverup, playing peek-a-boo with flashes of pink and tanned skin.

Ben shifted and stood, watching her, his twenty-year-old libido getting the best of him.

It wasn't the first time he'd seen her. She'd caught his eye the morning he and his family arrived at their beach rental. Seemed they both were early risers—he liked to watch the sunrise from the rambling front porch of the beach house with a cup of coffee, and she liked to walk the shore and pick up pretty little objects—rocks and glass and seashells, he assumed.

Truth was, this was the third morning he'd watched her, and he wondered why he'd not yet introduced himself. Summer beach week only lasted so long, right? Why waste time?

He set the coffee mug on the wooden deck rail.

Now or never.

As he strolled down the boarded walkway leading away from the house, his mind drifted, but his gaze still flicked back and forth to her. He was glad about this vacation week with his parents. His job responsibilities working for his uncle would gear-up soon, after they returned home, and he wasn't sure when he'd get another week off. Until he graduated from high school a semester early last year, he'd worked at the hardware store part-time—evenings, weekends, and summers. This past eighteen months, he'd worked full time. And in a couple of weeks, he'd take over as the manager. He was looking forward to an increased paycheck and was glad to work in the family business, especially now that his uncle was talking about retirement.

His future was bright, and he was grateful for that.

One day Main Street Hardware will be his.

Not sure why his head went there now, he shook off the thoughts. Perhaps looking at the young woman made him think about the future—work, eventual marriage, kids. He wanted that one day. He'd always dreamed of a family. So far, though, none of the girls he'd dated in Charmington held his interest long enough to think about courting one for a long-term deal.

And he really didn't want to think about the hardware store right now. He wanted to fixate on the girl ambling ahead of him on the beach—the pretty brunette who just stooped to pick at something in the sand.

He continued walking. She bent and plucked up an object with her forefinger and studied it, a waterfall of shiny coppery-brown hair sliding over one shoulder.

"What have you got there?"

She looked up and Ben was suddenly awestruck by her eyes—round as sand dollars, deep brown with gold flecks. She held his gaze for several seconds, while his heart kicked up a cadence and every inch of his breath exited his lungs.

He grew a little dizzy.

She batted her long lashes twice and slowly straightened.

Ben thought he might pass out from lack of oxygen.

"Hi. I, uh…" She looked at her sandy fingertips where she held a small piece of blue glass. "Sea glass, I think. See?" She held out her hand.

Ben thought his chest might explode with pent-up energy inside that he didn't know what to do with. He took a deep breath, felt a little steadier, and exhaled.

She reached for his hand—small sparks zinging up to his elbow when she did—and laid the sandy object in his palm. Her fingertips lingered over his.

Ben lifted his gaze to look into her eyes again. "I think you're right. It's sea glass." He hadn't even really looked at it.

"I've been collecting all week."

"I know."

"You know?"

"Well…" Ben looked away and shuffled his feet in the sand. "I've seen you."

She said nothing, but the hint of a smile raced across her lips.

"I'm not a stalker," he blurted out.

Her puffy lips stretched into a smile then. "I've seen you, too. Was wondering when you'd come off that porch."

Grinning, and silently relieved, he handed the sea glass back to her. "For your collection."

But she folded his fingers around it. "Keep it. Maybe you'll think of me next time you see it."

She turned and took a few steps toward her beach rental, two doors down from his, pausing once to glance over her shoulder and send him a teasing grin. He stood there soaking up every bit of her lingering gaze until she swiveled back and jogged toward the beach house, while he stared after her like a needy puppy craving attention.

Palming the glass in his hand, he shoved it into his pocket. Somehow, he didn't think he needed the sea glass to remember her.

JENNY'S HEART POUNDED AS SHE RUSHED UP THE WIND-AND-SALT battered steps of the beach house and crossed the porch. As she opened the wooden screen door to slip inside, she glanced down the beach to where the boy was crossing the walkway, two houses down.

She had finally lured him off that deck. After two days, it was about time. He looked her way and Jenny ducked into the house, not wanting him to know that she was watching him, too.

"Finally meet porch boy?" Her sister, Candy, looked up from her magazine. She sat in an overstuffed chair upholstered with a beachy fabric of turquoise shells and seahorses. It was a bit much, to Jenny's liking anyway, but screamed vacation beach rental.

"None of your business." She headed for the stairwell.

"What's his name?"

Well, shoot. Neither one of them shared names. Did they? "I didn't ask."

Candy stood, the magazine dropping to the chair. "Oh, my God. You didn't even get his name?"

Jenny shrugged, tossing off her response. "No biggie. I'm sure we'll run into each other again. I'm headed for the shower."

Candy rolled her eyes. "Whatever."

Taking a few steps up the stairs, Jenny smiled. Yes, they would run into each other again. She was sure of it. She'd *make* sure of it. No boy had ever looked at her like he did—that deep, longing, satisfying, and fulfilling stare that made her heart nearly jump out of her chest, and sent icy shivers all the way to her toes on this scorching summer day. Not to mention the spark that traveled from her fingertips to her core when she'd touched him. That had nearly taken her breath away—and the sensation had taken her quite by surprise.

Sighing, Jenny reached the landing and stripped off her coverup.

She might just marry that boy.

HOURS LATER, THE GHOST CRABS SCRAMBLED AS THE LAST SHRED OF light in the day dissipated, and Ben made his way down to the surf for a late walk. Flashlight in hand, he played the light over the beach in front of him, watching for the critters. As he moved closer to the girl's rental, he paused and looked up, hearing loud voices.

"I'll only be gone a minute, Dad." It was the girl from earlier.

"Jennifer, I'm warning you." Her father? Obviously. His voice was gruff. So, her name was Jennifer. "Don't make this worse than it is," he added.

"But you told us we'd be here until Friday."

"Things change, honey. We have to go."

The light on the porch backlit the pair, and Ben watched as she turned and faced the beach. Had she seen his flashlight?

"I'll be right back!" She tossed the words over her shoulder,

11

tripping down the steps of the house and onto the sand. Obviously, she paid little attention to the crabs—but they skedaddled in her wake. Ben lifted the light to make a path for her, hoping she was coming to him.

Toward him, he corrected himself. Because yes, she was coming his way. Making a direct beeline. For him. To his heart?

"Hey!"

She rushed closer, almost too close, and he caught the glimmer in her eyes and the faint scent of her shampoo. Lemon.

"I hoped to see you," she added.

"Hey there. What are you doing?"

"Came out to catch you." Her face lit up with a grin. Out of breath, she paused for a moment, and danced back and forth in the sand on bare feet.

"You're brave."

"Why?"

Ben pointed to her toes. "Crabs."

"Oh!" She hopped a little more and snickered. "They don't scare me."

Ben liked this fearless girl. "Like I said, brave!"

She glanced back at the porch, and Ben followed her gaze. Her father stood there, watching. Turning back, she said, "We're leaving tomorrow. My father must get back to work. Some emergency, or something. Who knows? Anyway, I...."

Suddenly, she turned shy on him, glancing away. The half-bashful, half-embarrassed look was charming. She took another deep breath and blew it out.

"Anyway," she started again, making eye contact, "I couldn't go without knowing your name. I'm Jenny."

That's progress. Names were good. "I'm Ben. Ben Matson."

"Jenny Anders. Where are you from?"

"Oh, upstate New York."

She frowned. "I'm from Philadelphia."

Ben shrugged it off. "Better than Oregon." Maybe a few hours drive for him. Heck, what was he thinking?

"True."

Her father barked her name, and she jerked toward the beach house.

"Coming, Dad!"

Looking at Ben, she said, "Goodness. I'm eighteen and going to college in the fall, but he still wants to *daddy* me."

"I imagine he always will," Ben told her.

She nodded. "Perhaps."

"Jennifer!"

But instead of paying attention to her father and moving away, she crowded up closer to him. Ben's thoughts went haywire, and he feared his body might implode. This girl—this Jenny—was exciting and energetic and pretty and well... He wouldn't mind if she crowded up even closer.

Or whispered in his ear, like it appeared she was about to do. Her warm breath fanned out across his cheek. "Meet me at the pier at midnight? Can you sneak away?" She pulled back, her eyes big and expectant.

All Ben could do was nod his head and say, "Sure. Midnight."

"Good." Grinning wide, she leaned in and placed a kiss on his cheek. "Good."

Then she ran away again, this Jenny, giggling and tossing an occasional glance over her shoulder, while her father braced himself with his hands on the porch rail of the house, still watching.

"Midnight," he whispered, and glanced at his watch. Two hours. An eternity.

JENNY'S KNEES WERE LITERALLY KNOCKING. THERE WERE STILL plenty of people milling about at the pier, and she wasn't frightened at all, even though it was late, but her insides were twittery and jumpy. It wasn't chilly out either, so that wasn't it. The June night was balmy and pleasant. Yet, she wanted to hug herself to keep her teeth from chattering.

She stood on the pier, waiting for Ben. A half-moon shone behind her, casting a faint triangular beam from the horizon to the shore, and nicely lighting up the area. Of course, most of the pier lights were still on, too, and the lights from the houses.

She'd sneaked out early so she would have plenty of time to make her way several beach houses north. Most of the pier was closed off this time of night, but she stood near the steps looking out over the shallow waters and sand, watching. She'd been sure her parents would be in bed by now when she left, but they were still up packing and cleaning out the refrigerator when she'd sneaked out the back door.

That, was partially why she was nervous. The other reason was Ben, and how he had made her feel this afternoon.

She'd done nothing like this before—be boldly defiant of her father—but something told her she couldn't let the opportunity to see Ben one more time slip away. She had to get to know him a little better before she left.

"Jenny?"

She turned, and he approached from the opposite direction she had expected. He stood there, hands shoved into the pockets of his baggy swim trunks. A light from the pier illuminated his face, and the stiff ocean breeze blew his shaggy chestnut brown hair away from his forehead.

"Hi, Ben."

He stepped up. "Hey."

"You came."

"Yep. I wanted to."

"Why?" She looked at the deck of the pier, then back up again. "I mean, you must think I'm crazy asking you to come here. We've barely even met."

Ben shook his head and moved in closer. His hand searched for one of hers, found it, and he tugged her closer. As he leaned in, Jenny's outward nervousness subsided, sending all her butterflies skidding off to her belly. She looked up into his face—feeling so drawn to him—wondering what his next move was going to be, waiting.

He whispered. "I need to give you something."

"Oh?"

Nodding, he nuzzled his face next to hers and left a soft, lingering kiss on her cheek. "You left an unanswered kiss behind."

Jenny pulled back. "I did?"

"Um-hm. I decided to give it back."

"But maybe I wanted you to keep it?" She was feeling bold, and obviously, he was too. That made her insides happy and her heart full.

"Did you?"

She felt herself grinning. "I did. Hey. Want to take a walk?"

Easing back a bit, Ben smiled broadly and took her hand. "I'd like that."

They left the pier and walked north, away from the beach houses where they were staying, settling on the steps of a walkover leading to an unoccupied house. Nestled there, sitting shoulder-to-shoulder between the dunes, they faced the ocean and watched the surf roll in. Ben still held Jenny's hand.

"What do you do in Pennsylvania, Jenny." He looked at her and smiled, then glanced back to the ocean, waiting for her response.

She studied him. She liked his smile. One corner of his mouth hiked up a little higher than the other. "I'm working a summer job at a craft store. I start next week. In the fall, I'm off to Penn State."

He turned back her way. "Wow. Impressive."

She shrugged. "It's what my parents want."

"What do you want?"

"Honestly?"

"Sure."

"I'd rather they save the college money or blow it on themselves. I'd rather draw or paint or throw pots. I'm an artist."

"Really?"

"Yes. I have this need to create stuff all the time. The more I do, the better I get."

"But they want you to get a college degree."

"Yes. Except, Dad wants me to major in something besides art. Pre-law."

"But you don't want to?"

She shook her head. "No, I want to set up a small studio. It's not going to happen though."

Ben's gaze caught hers and held, and she sensed he was really listening to her. "Because your parents think a degree in something besides art will serve you better in the long run."

"Yeah." She nodded. "Dad wants me to follow in his footsteps. Join the law firm he founded back home. It's just not me."

"And art is you. I get it."

Jenny paused and searched Ben's eyes. He was genuinely interested in her. "I think you do get it."

A half-grin crossed his face. "Yes, but sort of the opposite. My parents were on the college bandwagon too last year when I graduated. I finished my senior year early, and they thought it would be a great idea for me to get some courses out of the way. But I convinced them they needed me in the family business more than I needed to go to college."

"Oh?"

He nodded. "Yes. I run the family hardware store up in Charmington. You know, the famous Christmas village? The hardware store has been in the family for about eighty years now.

My uncle has been running it for a couple of decades, but he is close to retirement. I'll inherit it one day."

Jenny thought for a moment. "I think I've heard of Charmington!"

Laughing, Ben tipped his head closer. "Probably. It has been on TV a few times, you know, those holiday romance movies? And featured in magazines."

"What a lovely place to live."

Ben squeezed her hand tighter and shifted, gazing into her eyes. "Yes, it is. Perhaps you can visit sometime."

Suddenly, Jenny wanted to, very much. "Maybe so," she whispered. "I would like that."

The butterflies that had balled themselves up in her tummy took flight as Ben leaned in to give her a kiss—this time, on her lips. When his arms went around her and held her tight, she felt warm and safe and, well, as impossible as it sounded, kind of loved.

He broke the kiss and pulled back a little, staring into her eyes. With a forefinger, he brushed a few wayward strands of her hair away from her eyes, his fingers lingering at her temple. His words came on a whisper. "I rarely do this—kiss a girl this quickly after meeting her. But, Jenny, I feel so drawn to you."

Gazing into his eyes, Jenny felt his sincerity. "I know. Me too. I feel the same."

"You're leaving tomorrow?"

"Yes. I'm afraid so."

"Can I get your number? Address? Can we keep in touch?"

Jenny's heart sang out with joy. Yes! "I would like that very much."

Ben gently kissed her lips again. "Good. Me too."

CHAPTER 3

*S*eptember, *Penn State*

JENNY PUSHED THROUGH HER DORM ROOM DOOR, CROSSED THE room, and let her heavy backpack slide off her shoulder and onto the bed. She followed the trajectory of the bag with her body, plopping onto the mattress, kicking off her shoes, and throwing an arm over her forehead.

"Long day at the office?"

Her roommate, Claire Baker, whom she met the first day she moved into her dorm at Penn, asked from across the room where she sat on her own bed.

Jenny kept her eyes closed and blew out a quick breath. "Yeah. Sort of. Headache."

"You know this is not what you want to do, Jenny."

"I know that."

"It's tearing you up inside."

Claire was right. She'd known her for a few short weeks, and already she got her. Just like Ben had gotten her so quickly. Sitting up, she looked at her roommate. "I know. I would love to go to the pottery studio, but I simply don't have the energy. Algebra and World History and that stupid Psych class are seriously stifling my creative muse."

"Then get out of it."

Jenny shook her head. "Can't."

"Then just wallow in it, I guess. I don't know what else to tell you." Claire rose and headed for her closet, pulling out a sweater. "I'm off to the library." She hooked her arm through a backpack strap. "Oh, I picked up the mail downstairs. You have a letter."

Jenny's mood suddenly lifted. She hopped up. "Thanks!"

Claire smiled. "Now, there's the Jenny we all know and love. Your face lights up when you think of Ben. You need to re-examine your priorities, girl."

Jenny barely paid attention to Claire's leaving as she picked up the letter with the Charmington Christmas postmark sitting on her dresser. Her heart sung with the anticipation of reading Ben's words.

DEAR JENNY,

I miss you! I hope your classes are going well, even though I know you dread them. Just hang in there and get through the semester. Maybe things will take a turn for the better as we get closer to the holidays.

Speaking of the holidays, we are already gearing up here for Christmas in Charmington at the hardware. We've started stocking up on Christmas lights and decorations, because we know as people get into their attics and drag down their decorations, they discover broken lights and frayed cords and then they all head over here for supplies. We are coming up on our busiest season of the year, and I need to be ready.

Uncle Herb is not doing so well, and he's stepped back to only working one day a week now. I'm loving managing the store and know this was what I was meant to do but I miss having him around. He is such a wealth of knowledge about hardware in general, but also about the history of the old place and the community. I feel I should carry that on, for the family and for the town. I have a lot of ideas for the future. I can't wait to show you the store when you visit. Are you still planning to get away for fall break in early October? I will come get you. I've mapped it out. It will take me about five hours to get to you. Let me know.

I love you, Jenny. I miss you so much. Hope to hear from you soon. I will call you on Saturday, like normal.

Love,

Ben

JENNY LOWERED THE LETTER, TEARS IN HER EYES, AND SIGHED. SHE loved and missed Ben. How this had all happened so quickly, she would never know, but she was happy it had. She and Ben truly fell in love at first sight that day on the beach last summer.

She'd not been looking forward to her days at Penn State—not at all—but meeting Ben, and their summer letters and phone calls, had helped her to wrap her brain around the idea. They'd also managed one brief meeting in the summer, in late August, before she headed off to college. She'd told her parents she was going on a day shopping splurge for college things with her friend, Pam, but drove a couple of hours to meet Ben at a state park in northeastern Pennsylvania. They'd picnicked and hiked the trails, but mostly just enjoyed holding hands, talking, and being together. It was during that day that Jenny knew she was over-the-moon in love with Ben.

And that was the day he'd told her he loved her, too.

He'd helped soften the blow about college somewhat, too, that day, and encouraged her to do her best for now, to give it a try. It was his idea to find some place in State College where she could do her art, and she'd loved him for that. If she could only make time to get there. He understood, but he knew she was unhappy, deep down.

She also knew he didn't want their relationship to be the reason she didn't succeed at college. That was why he wanted her to hang in there and complete the semester.

Even though she was miserable.

Jenny gazed out the window over the campus with unseeing eyes, then heaved a thick sigh. She wasn't happy here, and one day she was going to have to break it to her parents. But as Ben said, the best thing she could do now was finish the semester and go from there. That was her plan.

In the meantime, she'd write to him and visit. The thought of seeing him in just a couple of weeks made her insides giddy with happiness and contentment.

Dear Ben,

I miss you too! I can't wait to see you and to see Charmington. I've heard so much about it I have pictures in my head. Now, I'll soon see it all for myself. I wonder if Charmington really looks like what I think it does? Five hours is a long trip for you to make one way and turn around to drive back. And then to bring me back to college again! Should we come up with a different plan? Would it be better if I took a bus to Charmington? Maybe even part of the way?

I wish Dad would let me have my car here, but he won't budge on that. Not until I'm a sophomore. He didn't let my sister have her car her freshman year, either.

I've never taken a bus outside of the city, but I can look into it. What do you think? We can talk about it on Saturday. You may not get this letter before we talk, though.

You always make me feel better when I get your letters. I was having a rough day today, then your letter perked me up. I must be honest, though. I really dislike my classes. I feel I'm wasting precious time. I am tired and don't feel like going to the studio at the end of the day. But I *need* to do those things occasionally, so I can remember who I am.

Geez, sorry for the downer. I'm fine. I truly am. I'm just so happy we are going to see each other soon. I can't wait to see Charmington and the hardware store and the gazebo and everything else you've told me about. I think I am already in love with the town, just as much as I love you. Talk soon, Ben.

Love you bunches,

Jenny

CHAPTER 4

ctober

"Jennifer, this is not a good idea. We really don't know these people. It's dangerous."

"Mom, it's Ben. I'm staying with his family."

Staring out her dorm window, Jenny listened to her mother drone on about all the reasons she should not go to Charmington for the fall break. Her voice prattled in the wings of her brain while Jenny pulled back the curtains and watched for Ben's truck to pull up to the sidewalk.

The day was Friday, and the sun was just barely poking its head up in the east. Claire was in the shower, belting out a song. Jenny had cleared her classes for the day, turning in all her assignments early, and didn't have to be back on campus until a week from Monday.

She'd been responsible when making her plans. Mostly. But none of that seemed to matter to her parents.

"This makes me very uncomfortable, Jennifer. We only have your best interest in mind. What I don't understand is why you are not coming home for fall break? We would love to see you."

"I'm coming home for Thanksgiving. We already talked about that, right? Most people stay on campus during fall break. I'm just going to Charmington to see Ben. It's not a big deal."

"Well, I don't like it."

"Well, I suppose I could stay on campus and party my ass off all week instead. Would you like that any better?"

"Jennifer!"

Jenny blew out a breath, stepped closer to the window, and peered down the street. That comment was probably out of line— probably nothing. It was out of line. But her mother was being ridiculous.

Time was ticking away, and she expected Ben soon. He couldn't get here fast enough. Her stomach was suddenly in knots, her insides jittery. She searched the traffic for his red truck—a 1980 Ford F100 pickup, he'd told her once—like that would mean anything to her. She knew nothing about vehicles other than they got her to where she was going. But the red part, that would be easy enough to spot.

"Do you hear me, Jennifer?"

"Yes, Mom." She let the curtains fall back into place. "But I don't understand your reasoning. Besides, I really wasn't calling to ask your permission. I was calling to let you know my plans in case you called this week and couldn't get in touch."

Dead silence met her ear from the other end.

Jenny rolled her eyes and let out a shaky breath. "Mom?"

Her father responded instead. "Now, Jennifer, look. Listen to your mother. You've met this boy one time and now you think you are in love. That's ridiculous. You need to stay in State College this week. Work on your classes. Besides, we don't even know his family."

"Two times, and we've exchanged hundreds of letters and talked on the phone every week."

"Two?"

Crap. She hadn't meant to let that out of the bag. "Ben and I met for the day back in August. No big deal."

Silence again. "Jennifer, when did you start lying to us? Is that boy influencing you? Telling you to lie?"

That angered her. Ben was the sweetest, most kind and thoughtful young man she'd ever known. "Absolutely not. And if you got to know Ben, you would see that."

"I saw him only the one time."

"Yes, you met Ben at the beach, but you barely gave him the time of day. The morning we left, remember? And you met his parents, too. You said they were nice people."

Her father didn't miss a beat. "We met them. We don't know them."

"Well, how am I supposed to get to know them if I don't visit?"

"It's not safe."

"It's Charmington! The Christmas village. How could it not be safe?"

"Jennifer. Don't push it."

"Dad, please understand." She didn't, wouldn't beg. But she could feel the tears welling up in her eyes and she'd be damned if she'd let him hear her cry. She didn't want to defy her parents. Yet, they were forcing her hand. She was nineteen, and wasn't that old enough to make her own decisions?

"I've heard enough."

"Dad, the last thing I want is to make you and mom mad, but this is not your decision."

Her father cleared his throat. "Jennifer. I am sending you to college to get an education. Not to go gallivanting all over the eastern seaboard meeting boys."

"Man!" she shouted back. "Ben is a young man, not a boy. An

adult, and for that matter, so am I. I am not gallivanting. It's Ben and I am going. Oh, and for the record? I am not thrilled with the college plan, and you know that—college was your idea, not mine. So, excuse me if I am not as excited about it as you are, but we will discuss that another time. I have to go now. I'll talk to you when I get back."

"Jen—"

She hung up the phone and immediately felt panic well up inside her. Great. Now she'd royally ticked off her parents. That had not been her intent. She'd wanted them to like Ben and hadn't wanted to do anything to make him appear unfavorable in their eyes.

Had she screwed things up?

The phone rang again—she ignored it. Picking up her backpack, she glanced quickly out the window, saw the red pickup truck pull up to the curb, and headed for the door.

"Bye Claire. See you in a week!"

BEN'S HEART SWELLED THE MOMENT HE SAW JENNY RUNNING DOWN the steps of the old dorm building. He shoved the truck into park, cut the engine and grabbed the keys, and threw open his door to run and meet her. Her infectious smile warmed his entire body as she flung herself into his arms. He caught her up and swept her around, holding her close.

She hugged him back so tightly, then pulled back to gaze into his eyes. "Oh, Ben. You're here. I've missed you so. Did you come to rescue me from this horrid place?"

"Absolutely." Then he kissed her. Fully kissed her on the mouth, and then raining little kisses on her face like he needed her lips to breathe, to live. He probably did. Her mouth tasted like a sweet cherry lollipop—her lip gloss, he guessed. And the sensation sent him spiraling. Holding her close after all this time made his chest hurt, so full of love for her.

"Oh Jenny. I feel like I'm about to burst open inside. I am so happy to see you."

She looked up into his eyes and stroked his face with her fingertips. "I can't believe it's you, that we are finally together again. And we have a whole week! Oh, Ben. Let's get out of here."

He nodded. "I can't wait to get you home to see everyone, and to see Charmington."

She pulled back. "Are you tired? That was a long drive."

He shook his head. "No, I'm good. The trip didn't take me as long as I thought. I started out yesterday after work and spent the night in a hotel off the interstate, about an hour away. I figure we have plenty of time to get to Charmington by late afternoon. Oh, there's so much I want to show you, and Mom can't wait for you to meet the rest of the family. She has all sorts of things planned before the week is over."

"Oh, how sweet of her. But I don't want to think about our time together being over yet."

Ben's entire body trembled with happiness, but his heart ached at the same time. "Me either," he whispered, kissing her again. Then he grabbed her backpack and swung it over his shoulder. "Let's get going."

Jenny smiled and hooked her arm in his. "I am so ready. Let's get out of here!"

They chattered for an hour—Jenny more than him, but he didn't care. He loved hearing her sweet voice ring inside the cab of his truck and loved her sitting close beside him on the bench seat. He was thinking he always wanted her there, and that made his soul sing.

DURING THEIR RIDE, JENNY FELL ASLEEP, CUDDLED UP AGAINST BEN'S side. The sensation of being safe and happy had lulled her into a state of contentment, Ben's warm body next to hers. More time had passed than she had imagined as she blinked awake.

"Jenny, wake up, sweetheart. We are almost there. I want you to see this."

Stretching and sitting up, she looked out the wide windshield and saw a big sign on the right side of the road.

"Welcome to Charmington," she read. "New York's Christmas Village."

She turned to Ben. "We're here already?"

"You slept for a while."

"I'm sorry! I should have stayed away to keep you company!"

Ben's big smile captured her heart. "I was perfectly fine with you snuggled up against me." He pulled over and parked in front of the sign. "I think I might always want you next to me, Jenny."

"Oh, Ben. There is no place else I want to be."

Wrapping his arms around her, he nuzzled her cheek. "I love you, Jenny Anders. I'm so happy to have you home with me."

"I love you back, Ben Matson. It feels good here. It feels right."

He gazed into her eyes, and Jenny knew she never wanted him to stop staring into them.

"Are you nervous?"

She nodded. "A little. I only met your parents briefly and I haven't met your sister, so I don't really know if they like me in your life. What if I mess up? What if I say something wrong?"

Ben laid a fingertip on her lips. "Sh. Not happening. They love you already. Everything will be fine."

"You're sure?"

"I'm positive."

Jenny relaxed a little. Maybe he was right. She'd trust his word. She just couldn't image how it would be if the opposite were happening—if Ben was coming to stay with her family for the week. She wasn't sure how her parents would deal with that.

Looking again at the Charmington sign, she felt better, though. "I am happy to be here," she mumbled.

Ben wrapped his arms tighter about her and nuzzled her neck. "Welcome to Charmington, Jenny. I hope you come to love it as much as I do."

"I already do," she said, and then kissed him.

CHAPTER 5

The Christmas Village of Charmington

BEN'S MOM CLASPED HER HANDS TOGETHER AND SQUEALED AS THE
front door to the Matson's home swung open. Her expression was
priceless, so inviting and full of cheer, and Jenny immediately
knew she could come to love this woman. Mrs. Matson reached
for her son and waved him and Jenny inside.

"Come in here, you two! We've been waiting for hours. Oh my,
Jenny. You look prettier than you did last summer. Fall agrees with
you…which is good. Fall is sort of our thing around here."

"Unless it's Christmas." Mr. Matson nudged past his wife.
"Hello Jenny. Welcome to chaos, er, our humble abode. It's good to
see you again." He leaned in and placed a peck on her cheek.

"Oh, thank you for having me, Mr. Matson. I'm so happy to be
here."

Ben's father grasped her hand. "Now, we'll have none of that

Mr. and Mrs. Matson stuff. We're family. I'm Calvin." He squeezed her hand.

"And I'm Maureen." Ben's mother leaned in for a hug too.

Jenny's lips stretched into a wide smile while being steered into the Matson's home, greeted not only by Ben's parents but also his Uncle Herb—Calvin's brother, she learned—and Ben's older sister, Charlotte, and her husband, Brian. In fact, she smiled so big and so long, her mouth hurt.

But she didn't care. She was glad to be with Ben's family, and of course, with Ben—secretly relieved they were so welcoming.

Suddenly, her attention diverted when two young boys galloped in from the kitchen and halted in front of Jenny.

"Boys! Slow down." Charlotte sighed. "I'm sorry, Jenny. They are a train wreck."

Jenny took in Charlotte's harried expression, then crouched a little to make eye contact with the youngsters. The taller boy had an orange sugar cookie rim around his mouth, and the smaller one had chocolate smeared on his T-shirt. "Well, hello there, you two. So, which one of you is Liam and which is Logan?"

"You know our names?" The taller boy's eyes grew wide.

Nodding, Jenny said, "I do. Your Uncle Ben has told me all about you."

An alarmed look crossed the boy's face.

Ben stepped closer. "Yes, I told her everything."

"Everything?"

Leaning down, Ben whispered, "Yes, even about the farting incident."

"Uncle Ben!"

Jenny rolled her eyes and elbowed Ben. "He told me no such thing. Now, I'm going to guess. You're Liam, right?"

"No." He pointed to the younger boy. "He's Liam. I'm Logan. I'm the oldest."

She stuck out her hand. "Well, of course. Hello, Logan. I'm Jenny. Happy to meet you."

He eyed her and tentatively touched her hand. "You, too." He paused for a couple of seconds, then added, "I'm six and in the first grade."

Jenny tilted her head. "Wow. That means you are really smart. I bet you are learning how to read already."

Logan nodded. "I read all the time!"

"That's outstanding, Logan." She put her hand up for a high-five and Logan slapped it, grinning.

Little Liam held up three fingers. "I'm three." Suddenly shy, he turned his face into his brother's side.

Jenny put out her fist. "Well, that deserves knuckles. Three is an awesome age." She pushed her fisted hand forward a little. Liam studied her, then laughed and gave her knuckles back.

Jenny stood, catching Charlotte's eye. "I imagine you have your hands full."

"I absolutely do, but I love every minute." Charlotte stepped forward and tucked her hand into Jenny's elbow, drawing her closer. "You have an easy way with children."

That surprised Jenny. "I do?"

"Yes. Seems natural."

"I've always liked younger kids. I worked in an after-school program in high school. Kids are fun."

"You'll make a good mom one day."

"You think so?"

Charlotte nodded. "I do."

Being a parent wasn't even on Jenny's radar. "Well, college first, and then maybe down the road…" But her mind wandered a bit, thinking about what it might be like to share parenthood with Ben. She glanced at him as he talked with his dad a few feet away.

"Well, of course." Changing the subject, Charlotte continued. "Do you mind coming with me for a minute?"

Jenny noticed Ben, his father and uncle, and Brian heading toward the den. Ben tossed her a smile and a wink, and Jenny waved back.

She turned to Charlotte. "Of course. Ben appears occupied."

Charlotte rolled her eyes. "Get used to it. It's football day."

"Oh?"

"Didn't Ben warn you about that?"

"About football? No. But I'm familiar with football day."

Charlotte glanced at her watch. "It's nearly kick-off time. Once the game starts, there will be lots of yelling and cheering in the family room. Do you like football?"

Jenny stopped up short as they stepped into the kitchen and looked at Charlotte head-on. "I live in Pennsylvania and go to Penn State. What do you think?"

Charlotte grinned. "It's Boston College day, today. You, my dear, are going to have to pick a team if the Eagles play the Nitany Lions this year."

"Oh. Competition. I love it!" While Jenny's own family wasn't sports, she had always loved spending time with her friends at their homes on game days.

Charlotte grinned. "Good. I love you already. But first, we have a few things to take care of in the kitchen."

Jenny paused and gave Charlotte a semi-serious look. "Please don't tell me this is a 'men in the den, women in the kitchen' sort of thing. Is it?"

Charlotte's eyes rounded. "Oh, good Lord, no! Mom raises as much hell at the television screen as the men. She's more diehard football than any of them. And Brian knows his way around the kitchen better than I do. Smell those wings in the oven? He'll be coming in to check on them soon. Now, if it's hockey, though, that's a different story, and one we won't introduce you to this weekend."

"Hockey? Seems I need to do some homework."

"Just whisper the word and watch the guys' eyes glaze over."

A bubble of laughter tickled up Jenny's throat. "I think I love your family already."

"Well, that's a good thing." Charlotte took her arm again, and they moved on into the kitchen. "Because Ben sure loves you, and that's enough for the rest of us." She slowed then and turned. "And I think you love him back just as much. Am I right?"

Charlotte's eyes darted back and forth as she studied her, waiting for a response. Jenny saw the concern and love there that Charlotte had for her brother. She laid a hand on Charlotte's. "I do, Charlotte."

Ben's sister placed her hand on top of Jenny's and squeezed. "I'm so glad."

Her throat about to close with emotion, Jenny continued. "I've never been in this much love with anyone. I know it's sort of whirlwind, and the distance thing isn't easy, but Charlotte, I love your brother so much. If you or your family worry that it's too soon, or that I would hurt him...."

Charlotte cut her off with a wave of her hand. "No. Not worried at all. Ben is a grown man, and we all trust his instincts. We love him and we love you too, Jenny."

The tension in her chest eased a little, and she exhaled a breath she hadn't realized she was holding.

"But enough of that." Charlotte slipped her hand into Jenny's and led her through the kitchen. "I actually need your expert advice for something. Ben tells me you are an artist and, well, I'm in charge of signage for the apple festival in a couple weeks. I have some ideas, but I'm not artsy. I need to get a design to the printer by Tuesday at the latest. I'm already past my deadline. Could you peek at my meager efforts?"

Jenny slowed her steps and turned toward Charlotte. "Me? You want me to give you art advice?"

She nodded. "Of course. Ben says he's seen your drawings and that you are fabulous."

"But I'm not sure I am the person to advise on this...."

Charlotte studied her, holding Jenny's gaze steady. "I value your opinion, Jenny. If Ben says you're good, it's good enough for me. Please?"

Jenny was momentarily taken aback. That Charlotte would take her art seriously was overwhelming. Of course, Ben was always supportive—she'd sketch pictures and send them to him in her letters periodically—but Charlotte was practically a stranger. To have that kind of blind trust placed in her was not only refreshing but also a little intimidating. What if she gave the wrong advice?

"Please?" Charlotte tugged her forward. "All of my stuff is in Dad's office off the kitchen. Just a quick look?"

What can it hurt? Jenny squeezed Charlotte's hand and pushed her self-doubt aside. "Of course. I would love to. Lead the way!"

A rowdy cheer went up in the den, then Liam and Logan raced into the kitchen. Jenny glanced back as Ben's mom playfully slapped at their little hands as they scrambled up on bar stools at the island, grabbing for cookies. The oven timer went off and Brian burst into the kitchen, muttering something about his wings. Another cheer exploded in the den.

Jenny swiveled toward Charlotte.

"We better hurry. The festivities have begun."

Nodding, she followed Ben's sister into the office, her chest swelling with the fullness of family. For a split second, she thought of her own family back home in Philadelphia. Her sister would be in her room, in her own world, looking at magazines for apartment decorating ideas, or makeup tips. Her dad would watch CNN in the family room, perhaps with an Old Fashioned on the side table. Her mother would be meal planning in the kitchen, and then later grocery shopping for the week.

"Woo-wee! Run! Run! Run!"

"He's going all the way!"

"Touchdown!"

Jenny looked at Charlotte while Ben and his dad shouted from the den. "Should we table this until after the game?"

"Exactly my thoughts."

The two women passed through the kitchen, grabbing food trays with sandwiches from Ben's mother on their way. Brian followed up with the wings. Jenny couldn't stop smiling. She loved this. All of it.

"Go Eagles!" she shouted, entering the room, and then setting the tray of sandwiches on the coffee table. She laughed when Ben grabbed her hand and tugged her down onto the sofa beside of him. She settled in next to him, feeling happily giddy. He grinned wide as he put his arm around her and squeezed.

ON WEDNESDAY, WHILE JENNY WORKED IN THE HARDWARE'S backroom, sketching some ideas she had for Charmington Christmas Festival posters, Ben waited on customers out front. She could hear him chatting with the locals as they came in looking for such things as toilet plungers, or nails to fix the gutters on their hundred-year-old house, or screen-repair kits to keep the flies off the screened-in porch. Every need had a story, and Jenny smiled while listening.

Being with Ben at the hardware for the two previous days, she'd picked up the habits of the locals quickly.

Back in Philly, people ran in, plucked an item off a big-box store shelf, then hurried to check out and get home. She was as guilty of that as anyone. But here in Charmington, a trip to the hardware store was more of a linger. First, there was the declaration of what the customer needed, followed by the story about why they were looking for that item. Further amended by a related anecdote—perhaps the customer's cousin once had the same problem and said a *fill-in-the-blank* item would work. Did they have one of those?

More discussion ensued about the varieties of said items in stock, why this type was good for that, and the other one for something else. And so on. Finally, there was the official selection and purchase of the thing, a bit more conversation about random people and upcoming events or maybe the weather, and then the farewell and, "See you next time."

Whew! Just thinking about all that made her tired. But Ben—she was so proud of him—handled it all with ease and expertise. He had advice for everyone and a tool or gadget or solution to fix just about every dilemma. He was good at what he did.

The door slammed. Someone left. And another person entered. More chatter.

"Hello, Gabby. Did that chicken wire work for your pen?" Ben's voice rang out in the store. "What can I get you today?"

Gabby Harper, who lived one farm down from the Matson's place, just outside of Charmington, Jenny had learned yesterday, needed supplies for her new baby goats—kid feed and formula and a couple of bottles, too, since one kid wasn't taking too well to her mama. Gabby worried she might not make it.

Yes, the hardware store stocked feed supplies for small animals, too.

Jenny listened to the conversation and smiled. She liked this town, the people, and she loved this place. The lifestyle was simple and the folks hardworking. It suited her laid-back approach to life and her artsy style—quite the opposite from the fast-paced lifestyle her parents maintained in Philly. Her dad was constantly on the go with his clients and court cases, and her mother flitted from one community project to another, while also teaching comparative literature courses part-time at Bryn Mawr.

Candy had just graduated from Villanova and was circulating her resumes, while preparing to move out and get her own apartment.

The week so far had been pure bliss. On Monday evening, she and Ben explored downtown Charmington after work, and he'd given her the grand tour of the Christmas shops. Tuesday, they headed out to the country, and he'd shown her the Christmas tree farm, the pond where everyone ice skated and played hockey, and then they'd hiked around Lake Charm. Each evening, his mother had fixed a lovely dinner and afterward, they'd settled in family-style in the den, and either watched television or just chatted.

She was so grateful for Ben's caring and understanding family. They had welcomed her with open arms. Already, she felt right at home. Every day, they made her feel wanted and accepted. No tension. No judgmental commentary. In fact, they valued her opinion about things, which was nice.

She found it all very refreshing.

Glancing about, she eyeballed her surroundings in the back room. While it was dusty and the shelves held decades of long forgotten items, she found beauty in the worn and aged wood beams, the paint-chipped shiplap walls, and the huge dust-streaked windows.

Laying her sketch aside, she went to the windows and looked out into the alley behind the hardware. The back of the building faced north. The light was diffused by buildings and trees but cast reflected light through the windows to brighten up the room— perfect for painting. Glancing back at the table where she'd been working, she noted the sunbeam highlighting her work, and had never felt happier or more fulfilled. She loved doing art, and this was, honestly, a perfect place to work.

She was grateful to Charlotte for giving her another project to work on this week. She'd loved her ideas for the apple festival, and now she'd moved on to Christmas. More than anything, she was happy to be helpful and contributing and filled with a joy she hadn't felt for a while, happy that they valued her talent.

With a forefinger, she smudged the dust on the window, then glanced about for rags and cleaners. Finding none, she asked Ben, and turned back into the room.

He stepped in, smiling, crossed the room and gathered her into his arms. "Finally, she left," he said. "I've been dying for a kiss."

His lips were soft and played over hers gently, then with more urgency. Jenny's arms went around Ben's neck, and she pulled him closer. The kiss deepened as their bodies aligned, and their hearts beat in tandem against each other's chests.

Jenny pulled back. "Whew. I think you missed me."

Grinning, Ben leaned in for a second taste of her mouth. "Definitely. I know I missed you. How's it going back here?" He glanced about. "Man, I should clean this place up."

"Oh no, it's perfect. I like the ambience. Except, I would like to clean the windows if you don't mind, and dust a little. Perhaps rearrange a few things."

"Is that all?"

She smiled. "I think so. Do you mind?"

"Of course not. But you don't have to do it. Let me call someone."

"No. I don't mind. Honestly. I like working back here."

Ben eyed her. "In this dusty old storage room?"

She nodded. "Umm hmm. It has great potential."

"For..." Ben arched a brow.

"For creating. I like the old stuff. The beams. The soft, warm tones of the wood. The northern light filtering in... Just need to get those dirt streaks off the windows, tidy up a bit, get some supplies—with your permission, of course—and it will be perfect."

"Perfect? Supplies?" Ben continued to study her. "What are you thinking?" One corner of his mouth turned up into a grin.

Oh heck. Have I put my foot into it? I don't want him to assume that I am presuming I have a place here, yet....

Jenny opened her mouth to speak, closed it again, then finally said, "I'm just saying, Ben, that I enjoy being back here. For one, it's close to you. And when you are working, I might use this as a studio? To create, sketch, do projects for Charlotte, or whatever. You know, when I'm visiting."

Ben pulled her closer.

"Just when you are visiting?"

She cocked her head. "What do you mean?"

"What if you lived here? You know, with me."

Blinking, Jenny stepped back a little and looked at Ben. "Here? You mean, here in the hardware?"

He laughed. "No, silly. In Charmington. In my apartment upstairs. I mean, potentially, in the future. After some time has passed."

"Potentially?"

"In the future."

She glanced about. "With you?"

"Could you ever see yourself living in Charmington, Jenny?"

She studied Ben. What was *he* thinking? After a moment, she whispered. "Ben, I see myself here every day. I see myself with you, your family, the people. I see myself creating art back here in this room while you are selling nuts and bolts out front."

A smile raced across his face. "Really?"

She nodded. "Yes, Ben. I hope you don't think I'm being presumptuous or rushing things, but...."

Ben stepped back. Jenny swallowed hard because she didn't know what he was doing or thinking. Oh, God, she'd said the wrong thing. She was talking about the future too much. About being here with him. And he wasn't ready, obviously, and it was just too soon. Now she was pushing him away.

"Ben, I'm sorry. It's too soon for that kind of talk. I know that. I...."

He put a finger to her lips. "Sh." Then, reaching into his pocket, he lowered to one knee and looked up at her. "I've been carrying this around in my pocket since I picked you up on Saturday, waiting for the most romantic moment I could find to give it to you. I almost did when we pulled over at the sign at the edge of town. I guess this is as romantic as I could hope for because I can't wait any longer." He popped the lip on a black ring box. "Jenny, I love you. Will you marry me? I mean, of course, I need to ask your father for your hand, and all that, but...."

A huge breath whooshed out of Jenny's mouth. "Ben! What?"

"Marry me. Please? I don't mean today, but one day. Of course, we'll need to wait until you finish college, and I need to save some money for a house, but I don't want to wait to make the commitment to you. I love you, Jennifer Anders. Marry me?"

Jenny went down on her knees too, eye level with him. "You don't think it's too soon to get engaged?"

"No, I don't. Not for me. I love you. I want to be with you forever."

"Oh, Ben... I love you too."

"Marry me?"

"But what about the distance?"

"We will find a way. We have so far. And it won't be forever. Now, what do you say?"

"Of course. Yes!"

Every tummy butterfly known to man—or woman—flitted through Jenny's gut as Ben pushed the engagement ring on the ring finger of her left hand. Her entire body erupted into some sort of dizzy happiness, and she couldn't stop the bubble of giggle gurgling upside while looking at the ring on her finger. "Oh, Ben, it's so beautiful."

The sunbeam pushed through the dusty windowpanes, glinting off the diamond.

Footsteps sounded through the hardware and a voice met their ears. The two scrambled to their feet, standing close together, holding hands.

"Ben? Jenny? Where are you two? I just stopped by to see how the Christmas poster designs are coming. Anybody here? Yoo-hoo?"

Charlotte burst through the storage room door, chattering away. "Ben? Jenny?" She halted at the door, gawked at the pair, and clasped a hand over her mouth. "Oh. My. God." She rushed forward, took a lingering look at Jenny's hand, then faced her brother. "Ben?"

Was Charlotte surprised or upset? Jenny wasn't certain.

Ben squared his shoulders. "Yes. You see right. I just asked Jenny to marry me, Charlotte. And she said yes. Not right away, but when we're ready. In the meantime, we're engaged."

He glanced at Jenny and gave her a cockeyed smile, still holding her hand, and tugging her closer.

Charlotte's gaze passed between them. In one swift movement, she rushed forward and wrapped her arms around them both. "Oh, my God. This is incredibly good news. I can't wait to tell Mom." Then she pulled back. "No wait. That's your story to tell, Ben. Yours and Jenny's. I promise I won't, but you must tell her soon because you know I can't keep secrets."

Ben chuckled. "We'll tell them at dinner tonight. I'm going to make reservations at De Luca's. Can you come? Brian and the kids too."

"I wouldn't miss it. But I'll get a sitter for the boys. That place is too fancy for those monsters!"

Dismissing her brother, Charlotte turned to Jenny. "My goodness. I've always wanted a sister. Now I have one. Welcome to the family, Jenny." She embraced her with a strong, quick hug. "I'm so glad it's you."

Slightly overwhelmed, Jenny didn't quite know what to say. Her heart simply ran over with happiness, and contentment.

She was engaged. To Ben. They were getting married.

DE LUCA'S ITALIA, AN UPSCALE ITALIAN RESTAURANT, SAT ON THE edge of Lake Charm about fifteen minutes as the crow flies from downtown Charmington. Ben reserved a table inside, since it was October, instead of on the deck. The scene looking out over the lake was spectacular, with the beginnings of fall foliage.

Jenny sat with her hands in her lap, looking out the window. The dinner was yummy, Italian was her favorite, and she'd ordered the eggplant parmesan special. The company and conversation with Ben's family were equally lovely. She enjoyed being with them all very much.

Beneath the table, she nervously fiddled with the ring on her left hand—Ben put it there earlier and she wasn't taking it off—turning the diamond into her palm. She didn't want Ben's parents to see the ring until he was ready to tell them they were engaged.

In her heart of hearts, she already felt welcomed into the family —but honestly, she didn't know them that well and their reaction worried her a little. She could only imagine the look of shock on her own parents' faces when they would tell them, and the subsequent line of questioning and doubt. She sure hoped that was not the scenario they were facing with Ben's parents.

Quit going down that rabbit hole, Jenny. Ben's parents are nothing like yours.

Shifting a little in her seat, she nodded toward the window, changing the direction of her thoughts. "It's so beautiful here. This view looks like a picture in a magazine," Jenny commented. She glanced up as the server started clearing their table. "I don't believe I've ever seen anything so pretty in all my life."

Ben leaned closer. "Charmington is known for Christmas, but the fall weather brings a lot of tourists too, just to see the leaves."

"That's right," Charlotte added. "Oh, I wish you could come back for the apple festival in a couple of weeks, Jenny. It will be peak season then. You would just love it."

Again, she stared out over the lake. "I know I would. Wish I had my paint box—I would love to capture those colors out there right now. Even though it's evening, the light is near perfect."

Ben leaned into her shoulder. "Maybe you could come back for a long weekend for the festival? I'd come get you. Remember to bring your paints."

She grinned and nudged him back. "I would love that, but we will have to see. It's such a long drive for you." She turned to Ben's family. "My father has a rule about me having my car at college—not in my freshman year. I understand, but it's inconvenient."

Charlotte interrupted. "Oh, my goodness." She gave her father a nod. "Doesn't that sound familiar, Daddy?"

Calvin chuckled. "I had the same rule for Charlotte."

"Except you caved over Christmas vacation my first year."

He nodded. "That I did. I decided if I wanted my daughter coming home to visit, she needed her wheels." His gaze lingered on Jenny. "Perhaps your father will come around."

"Maybe." She paused for a moment. "The thing is, really, I just want to make it through this semester. I'm not sure about going back to Penn State next semester. I'd like to explore other options. That's the hard conversation I need to have with my parents that I'm dreading—but in the end, I know it will be better for me."

Ben squeezed her hand under the table.

His father studied her, then leaned forward. "I'm not sure what the issue is with Penn State, Jenny, but whatever it is, stick out the semester and think it through. It's good to finish what you start, and you'll have a semester behind you. If pursuing other options is truly what you want to do, then perhaps have a solid plan for doing that to present to your parents."

Jenny smiled at Calvin Matson. "That's good advice, and pretty much exactly what Ben suggested, too." She glanced at her fiancé, suddenly feeling so glad that she had him in her life. "Ben has been very supportive, and I appreciate it." Then turning back to his father, she added, "My father wants me to go to law school, so I can become his partner in the firm after I pass the bar."

"And that's not what you want?"

"No. I want to open an art studio. If I stay in college, I want to major in art."

Charlotte cleared her throat. "Jenny, you are so talented. Can you find a way to do that?"

"That's what I need to figure out. The thought of law school makes my stomach turn. It's just not me."

Ben put his arm around her, pulling her closer. "You know I want what you want, Jenny."

"I do know that."

"And we're supportive of that too," Maureen added. "Not that we are encouraging you to go against your parents' wishes. I'm not suggesting that. Just know that whatever you decide is best for you," she glanced at her son then, "and Ben, we support you, too."

Jenny had to wonder... Did they know already about the engagement?

She gave Ben's parents a smile. "Thank you. Everyone. But let's talk about that another time. I didn't mean to bring my current dilemma to the dinner table tonight."

"We're happy to help. Besides, you are family!" Charlotte grinned, then glanced off as if she'd said too much. "So, do you think you can come back for the apple festival, Jenny? We would have so much fun."

"I don't know if I can get away. I don't have another long weekend until Thanksgiving." She paused, searching Ben's eyes. "Which, by the way, I had hoped you would come that weekend to visit my parents with me." Turning back to his family, she added, "Could you spare him this Thanksgiving for a day or so?"

Maureen grinned. "Oh, we might suffer through it…."

"Under duress," added Calvin.

Ben chuckled. "Don't mind them. I would love to. And then I could—" But he cut off his words and glanced from Jenny to his mom and dad. "Actually, I'm really glad you all could come tonight."

Maureen shifted in her seat and fidgeted with her napkin on the table. "It was a lovely dinner, Benjamin. So unexpected and quite a surprise. Thank you for taking us all out."

He grinned. "My pleasure, Mom. You've been cooking all week, and I thought it would be nice to give you the night off."

His mother eyed him. "Well?"

His father smirked a little and glanced away.

Jenny wasn't sure what was going on. She glanced at Ben, who appeared to be tongue-tied.

"Well, Ben?"

"What, Mom?"

"Quit beating around the bush and get on with it. What do you want to tell us?"

Jenny watched Ben's gaze shoot to Charlotte, whose face immediately went *deer-in-the-headlights*. Then he looked at Jenny.

She nudged him under the table. Goodness. Had he changed his mind?

"Benjamin? Good Lord. When in the world are you going to tell us about that diamond ring on Jenny's left hand?"

A long breath whooshed out of Ben's mouth, and he grasped Jenny's right hand tighter. His palm was sweaty. Ben was nervous about telling his own parents. How would he handle telling hers?

"Mom. Dad," he began. "This afternoon… Well, I asked Jenny to marry me. Now, we know it's rather sudden, so we're not planning anything right away. She has some decisions to make, of course, as you heard. And I need to save money, and…."

Both Charlotte and Maureen burst from their seats and ran

around the table to Jenny, hands clapping, their faces beaming.

Maureen got to her first, hauling her out of her seat. "Jenny! Welcome to the family." Her arms went around her in a tight bear hug.

Charlotte bounced beside them, then dove in for a hug too. "I'm so happy for you and Ben," she whispered. "Oh, the ring!" She grappled for Jenny's left hand.

Jenny quickly twisted the ring back, and both women oohed and ahhed over the diamond.

"My goodness, but the young man has good taste," Maureen said.

"It's beautiful, Jenny."

"I love it."

Charlotte looked into her eyes. "You are perfect for him, you know."

Pulling back, Jenny studied the women. "I wasn't sure either of you were ready for another addition to the family, yet."

Maureen clasped both her hands around Jenny's. "Honey, I knew from the moment Ben introduced us to you and your family at the beach that you were the one. I couldn't be more pleased. And neither could Calvin."

She turned and reached for her husband. Chairs screeched as they pushed back, and the three men stood, shaking hands and patting Ben on the back.

The server came back with dessert menus. "Looks like a celebration," he said. "What can I get you for dessert?"

"Champagne all around." Ben's dad took the menus from the server. "And whatever else this crew wants. Bring the check to me." He looked at Ben. "My treat. It's not every day your son decides to get married." Turning to his family, he added. "Jenny, welcome. I'm so glad Ben found you."

Ben gripped Jenny's hand tighter. Turning, she looked into his eyes. "Me, too," she whispered. "Me, too."

CHAPTER 6

N *ovember, Thanksgiving in Pennsylvania*

JENNY DRUMMED HER FINGERTIPS ON THE SOFA END-TABLE WHILE staring out the living room window of her home in Philadelphia.

Please, Ben. Don't do this to me.

She'd caught a ride home from State College the night before with a high school friend she rarely saw anymore, but who also attended Penn State.

Giant dancing inflatables danced across the TV screen as the Macy's parade droned on in the background. Her mother twittered about in the kitchen with dinner preparations. That was her mother's thing—scurrying about, appearing busy while she prepared, not cooked, the holiday meal. Mostly, she ordered the turkey already roasted from a local grocer and catered in the rest. She picked up the pies at the bakery around the corner. Her order was in by mid-October to ensure she would not have to bake. Her preparations comprised making a couple of family-favorite side-dishes—deviled eggs, a salad, green beans with almonds.

Every. Year. The same.

Jenny's father sat at his desk in his study, going over notes for a court case on the docket for Monday. He cleared his throat often, paced the room approximately every ten minutes, then returned to his desk to add some notations to his paperwork.

Candy was...somewhere. Probably fiddling with her new makeup or trying on the clothes she bought yesterday at the mall.

The older she became, Jenny felt she didn't fit in with this family. Had she been adopted?

No. She'd seen the pictures of her mother pregnant. This was definitely her biological family. She guessed she was simply the oddball of the group.

Where *was* Ben? He was supposed to arrive mid-morning, and it was already pushing noon. The family meal wasn't until six o'clock that evening, so she wasn't worried about him missing that —but with every minute that ticked by, she grew increasingly anxious that something had happened during his drive, or that he'd chickened out.

But Ben wouldn't chicken out. Would he?

Her fingers halted their drumming.

No.

She knew him better than to think that. *He will be here, Jenny.*

Biting her lower lip, she resumed drumming.

They'd discussed this day, and how best to approach her parents—especially her father—when she'd gone back to Charmington for the apple festival a couple of weeks ago. She'd hated Ben having to drive so far again, especially since she knew he was coming to Philly for Thanksgiving, but he had insisted.

Besides, she'd wanted to see him badly, missing him like crazy ever since she came back after the early October trip.

They'd had another fantastic long weekend together, and

neither of them had wanted to part. One of the best things about the weekend was that she and Ben were free to just be themselves, sharing their engagement news with his friends and others in town, without worry or concern. Everyone—Ben's friends and especially his family—had been so excited for them. She'd felt so good there, welcomed and happy.

Philadelphia wasn't her happy place any longer. Her happy place was with Ben in Charmington—and always would be.

Another reason she was so antsy now, she supposed. That kind of support and excitement was likely not what would greet them this weekend once her family heard the news. Still, she was so glad Ben was coming here to be with her. She needed him—needed his arms around her to make her feel safe and loved.

She needed his moral support as well.

There. A flash of red caught her eye down the tree-lined street. The familiar pickup truck pulled around the corner and slowed as it approached her home and angled into the driveway. A smile burst across her face so quickly she could feel it. She twisted on the sofa to watch him pull in and park behind her mother's Lexus. His truck looked ridiculously out of place in her upscale, manicured neighborhood—but not in her heart. That red pickup truck symbolized so many things to her. Love. Home. Ben.

It fit her, and that was all that mattered.

She flew off the sofa and headed toward the front door. Her father looked up from his desk as she passed his office.

"Jennifer, slow down. That boy has driven all this way. He can wait another minute or two. You don't have to fling yourself at him."

She halted. "That boy, Dad, is Ben. My boyfriend. Please be nice to him."

He arched a brow and stared. "I will be cordial."

"And make him feel at home, please?"

Her father lowered his pen to the desk. "Jennifer. This

infatuation with this young man—you know it will not last. He's… Well, he's a small-town boy—I'm sure he and his family are nice— but they aren't our kind of people. You know that. Right?"

Jenny stared back. His words had taken her off guard, nearly cut her off at the knees. It took her a minute to respond. "No, I don't know that. What does *our kind of people mean*? I love him, Dad. You need to understand that. Ben and I are a couple, and we have plans."

"Plans?" He laughed. "Jennifer, it's puppy love. Please realize that for what it is." He picked up his pen and looked back at his paperwork. "Think about it."

She'd been dismissed.

"Well, excuse me while I go fling myself at my small-town, country, redneck boyfriend."

She glanced once more at her father—who didn't look up— then hurried toward the front door and yanked it open. Crossing the wide porch, she skipped down the steps, her stomach a jumble of nervous energy and disappointment with her father, and jogged across the lawn toward Ben, gathering speed all the way.

He was only half out of his truck when he caught her up in a bear hug embrace and planted a long, sloppy kiss on her lips. He threaded his fingers into her hair and held her face tight. "Oh, I missed you," he uttered between nibbles.

"Oh, Ben. Me too. I was so anxious. I thought you'd gotten cold feet!"

He pulled back, studying her. "Jenny, you know I would never do that."

She knew that. "I guess I just had to voice my fear. I know."

"We are going to get through this."

Nodding, she looked up. "You're confident all of this is going to work out. Aren't you?"

His head dipped. "One way or another, it will." He smiled.

Suddenly everything seemed all right. *One way or another.* Ben always made everything all right. Jenny leaned in and nuzzled his neck. "Um, you smell good."

"That's probably the apple cake Mom sent."

"Oh!" Jenny placed her hands on either side of his face and kissed his lips. "No, it's you. Oh God, it's only been three weeks, but I've missed you so."

"Me, too, sweetheart."

"This distance thing is so hard—harder than I thought it would be."

Ben nodded, a serious look crossing his face. "I know, Jen. Maybe it will get easier. Or maybe it won't and...."

His pause gave Jenny a moment of concern. "Maybe what? Oh Ben, have you changed your mind about us?"

Ben cupped her face in his big hands. "Changed my mind? Never. I would marry you tomorrow and sweep you away to my meager apartment above the hardware store, if you'd agree. Today, if that were possible."

His gaze danced over hers, and she knew she would do the same. "I'd marry you this minute. I...." Her words trailed off, thinking about the conversation with her father.

"Are you okay?"

She nodded. "Yes. I just had a weird conversation with my dad. I'll tell you about it later."

He studied her face for a moment. "Okay. If you are sure."

"I'm fine."

Ben leaned in and placed another sweet kiss on her lips. He reached for her hand then, and she knew instinctively he was feeling for her ring. He'd done that often during apple weekend. She'd loved the way he fiddled with the engagement ring absentmindedly when they were holding hands. He pulled back. "Jenny?"

She exhaled. "I'll wear it after you've talked with Dad. I didn't want to take it off, but I knew they would see it if I didn't. My sister would make a huge scene. She expects to be the first one to get engaged, and honestly, she's nowhere near that. I didn't want to tackle the subject of our engagement by myself." She clasped his hands. "I hope you understand. I need you beside me for this."

He gazed into her eyes. "I understand. So, do you think our plan is still a good one? To approach your father after dinner?"

"I'm not sure." She shrugged, hesitating. "I've been thinking—maybe too much. Let's gauge that by how the day goes. We may want to get through today and then discuss it all with them tomorrow."

"That gives us today to get comfortable with each other—me and your parents, I mean."

"Yes. I hope so."

Again, he studied her face. "Jenny, you're worried."

"I am a little," she admitted. "My family is not like yours, Ben. Your family, and everyone in Charmington, opened their arms and let me in without hesitation. My family keeps people at arm's length until they get to know them."

"How do you get to know someone by keeping them at arm's length?"

"That's exactly the point...and the problem. My parents keep small circles with few friends. They are not hugely social beyond their work lives. And inviting new people into their small circle is uncommon. I swear. Sometimes I think I was born into the wrong family." She laughed.

He chuckled. "Maybe. What about your plans for next semester? Have you brought that up yet?"

"No. I've been thinking that's also a discussion to approach tomorrow…. Or it may be one of those situations where I just know when the timing is right."

Biting her lip, she glanced off. She'd decided about Penn State, had talked with her advisor at school, and now just needed to share the news with her parents. She was all set up for online coursework next semester, part-time. All she needed now was to get a job. She had some leads lined up.

"Well, there's your dad at the door. I suppose we should go in."

She glanced toward the house. "I guess so. Can you tell I'm procrastinating?"

"A bit."

Jenny glanced back at the house, then at Ben. "What can I help with?"

He pulled out the cake box. "Apple cake?"

"Got it." She gave Ben a smile.

His gaze skittered over hers for a moment, lingering, then he leaned in for a kiss. "It will be fine," he whispered. "I love you."

"I love you too, Ben. So very much."

Cake in her hands, she turned for the house. Ben followed, but after a couple of steps, stopped her with a touch to her arm. "Jenny?"

Turning, she studied him. "Yes?"

"I just want to say something."

"Okay?"

"I've been thinking and want to say this before we approach your parents with everything. There is going to be a lot coming at them, with your leaving school full-time and me asking to marry you. If things go south, if things get out of control, I want you to know that I am by your side, no matter what. I love you, and we are going to be fine. Even if your parents aren't. Like I said, I'd marry you tomorrow, if you wanted. I want your parents' blessing, but I'm prepared to do whatever is best for us. I hope you are too."

Tears stung her eyes. "Oh, Ben. I'm about ready to ditch it all and run off with you tonight, and I wouldn't look back. But let's try to get through this, and then we'll see what kind of Plan B we need to come up with."

Ben nodded his agreement and hugged her tight.

"Jenny!" Her father's voice boomed from the porch.

She pulled back and whispered, "I love you so much. It will be fine." Then over her shoulder, she shouted, "Coming, Dad!"

They approached the house together, stopping as they reached the front porch steps. Jenny stole a glance at Ben, who looked up at her father, put his hand on the small of her back, and guided her up to the porch landing.

Ben sat his bag down on the porch, then extended his right hand. "Good morning, Mr. Anders. It's nice to see you again. Thanks so much for having me."

Her father stared at Ben's outstretched hand and after several seconds, gave it a limp shake. Embarrassed was too mild a word to describe how Jenny felt at that moment. Angry was more like it. She knew her father, and she also knew what a weak handshake meant to him—disinterest. She'd heard him say it a million times. Now, he was obviously sending a message to Ben and to her. He didn't take her, or her relationship with Ben, seriously—and that made her doubt the wisdom of this weekend, entirely.

"No problem," her father said, eyeballing Ben. "Jennifer is happy you are here." Then he turned and silently walked into the house.

Jenny heaved a massive sigh. Ben caught her eye and gave her an uncertain grin.

PLAN B CAME QUICKER THAN EXPECTED.

Thanksgiving dinner was nothing short of a disaster. Ben sat in the middle of it all at the Anders' dining room table and immediately understood the depth of Jenny's dilemma. The family couldn't get through the salad without confrontation or judgement.

Mr. Anders complained that the salad wasn't crisp enough. Did Mrs. Anders make it fresh or buy it from the grocery?

Then, when carving the turkey, his commentary turned to the lack of attention to detail from the meat market. He was unhappy with the size of the bird. Why had she ordered a twenty-pound bird? She knew he didn't like leftovers.

Worse, Mrs. Anders picked at Jenny. How long had it been since she'd had her nails done? She could use a visit to the hair salon—she'd make an appointment for her during Christmas break. And couldn't she have found something nicer to wear to dinner this evening? After all, it was a holiday.

Candy glanced at Jenny, tossing a smirk, and rolling her eyes.

Jenny hid her embarrassment by lowering her gaze and looking down at herself.

Ben reached for her hand underneath the table and squeezed it. "I think she looks beautiful." He studied her profile.

Jenny slowly turned his way, and he noticed the mist gathering in her eyes. Her beautiful, bronze eyes. She latched onto his hand. "Thank you, Ben."

Candy rolled her eyes again. He still had to form an opinion of her, but at this moment, it wasn't super favorable.

Ben swung his gaze across the table to look at her parents, both of whom stared back with blank expressions and no words.

He thought about his own family back in Charmington. By now, they'd have settled in the den talking football or hockey, watching a game, or talking about an upcoming one. The atmosphere would be rowdy and energetic and fun.

Here, at Jenny's parents' home, he thought he might suffocate in the stuffy mood and the lack of kindness exhibited by her parents. He couldn't even fathom what an evening in the family room of this home might be like.

He sorely doubted they even gathered and wondered where they would all drift off to after dinner.

Mrs. Anders spoke up then, turning the subject to her other daughter. "So, Candace, have you thought about furnishings for your new apartment? What style are you thinking? We could go shopping tomorrow if you like."

Candy sat up straighter in her stiff, straight-backed chair, and smiled. "I've been looking at some lofts. Contemporary, for sure. With perhaps a touch of industrial for that upscale, urban look. What do you think, Jenny?"

Jenny cocked her head. "I think it could work. Maybe add a spot of Boho for interest. You know, splash of color here and there. Something unexpected."

Candy scrunched up her face. "No Boho. Definitely not. You're the artsy-fartsy girl. That's not me."

"It could be stunning."

"Everything is not an art project, Jenny. This will be my home."

"All the more reason to personalize it with things you love, rather than a carbon-copy of some picture you saw in a magazine. As I recall, you love those scarves you picked up in Mexico last year. Those would be lovely as decorative accents."

Candy stared. "They're scarves, not decorations."

"But—"

"No. Jenny. Thanks for the tip but I'm sticking with straight lines and monochromatic neutrals. It will be lovely."

"Of course. But you asked my opinion. I was just giving it." Jenny glanced at Ben and blew a thin breath through her lips, dismissing the subject.

He felt for her. Jenny was only trying to contribute, but once again, had been shot down.

"Whatever..." Candy waved her off. Obviously, she enjoyed being the shining star of the family.

Her parents doted on her, discussing her recent graduation from college and her pending job interviews. Mr. Anders talked with her about where she should look for her apartment and that he would subsidize it for the first six months until she got on her feet.

The plan for Candy was to get a job with a law firm somewhere in the city—for experience, you know, and to step her foot into the field. As her awareness and experience grew, she'd move over to her father's firm.

The conversation droned on between them for quite some time. Past the main course and into the pumpkin pie.

That same plan, he assumed, was what they expected of Jenny.

He glanced at her, sitting quietly to his right, and gently nudged her knee with his under the table. She peeked his way and moved her left hand to his thigh.

Was he wrong in wanting to marry her so quickly? Should he hold back his feelings and let her explore the ideas her parents had about her future? But she really didn't want that future, did she? Or was she just saying that for his benefit?

Somewhere between pie and coffee, Jenny's father switched his focus. "So, Jennifer, let's discuss your class load. How are you doing?"

Her hand jerked. Ben noticed the startled look on Jenny's face and felt her sudden anguish in his heart. "Oh, fine, Dad. Everything is going fine."

Her father dropped his chin. "Just two more weeks and you'll be back home for Christmas break. Have you registered for next semester's coursework? Let's go over your schedule. I'd like to see you step it up. Take a few more hours now that this semester is under your belt. You can handle more. Let's move through those prerequisites. Thoughts?"

Jenny looked stunned, staring at her father, and then dropped her gaze to her plate. Her tongue ran over her lower lip. Ben could tell she was contemplating exactly what to say. He had the idea that she didn't confront her father often, and he wondered if she could do it now. Her fingers wrapped tighter around his fingers. Ben held on, hoping she realized he was on her side. Always.

"Jennifer?"

She looked up. "Yes. I have thoughts on that, Dad. I'm happy to talk to you about them, and I'd planned to do that tomorrow." She plunged ahead, the words spilling out of her mouth, as if she had to say them all now or forever hold them. "I suppose now is as good a time as any. I've spoken with my advisor, and we've created a new plan. I'm not going back full-time next semester. I'm taking some distance classes, and I've switched my major."

"To?"

"Art, with a minor in business."

Jenny's father stood, tossing his napkin on the table. He looked directly at Ben and pointed. "This is your fault. She never had these crazy notions until she met you."

"Dad, that's not true." Jenny let Ben's hand go and bolted up.

But Mr. Anders' stare bored into his. Ben was pretty sure he felt the depths of that stare deep in his gut.

"I want a word with you in my den. Now." He glared at Ben, then stalked away.

The confrontation between Jenny and her father was over in a flash. Ben watched him leave the dining room, swallowing the suddenly dry lump in his throat.

Fine.

He'd follow him to his den, and he'd take the brunt of his anger if it took the heat off Jenny. Any day of the week.

Glancing toward the love of his life, he took in Jenny's terrified expression. He stood, reached for her hand, and squeezed. "It will be fine. I will be fine. And so will you."

Kissing her on the cheek, he left the table and followed the path her father had taken toward his den.

JENNY STOOD OUTSIDE HER FATHER'S CLOSED OFFICE DOOR. SHE'D lean in occasionally to see if she could hear anything more than the exchange of low voices. Occasionally, her father's voice would rise, and she heard his and Ben's muffled together, then nothing. Turning away, she'd pace the entryway from the front door back to the office door, and then in reverse.

She'd banned her mother and her sister from joining her as soon as Ben had left the table.

"Stay here," she'd told them then, looking at the two. "Clean up from dinner… And I'll clean up the mess with Daddy."

"You'd better come straight with him immediately, Jennifer," her mother ordered, "because you're walking on thin ice right now. I hope you know that."

"It's not fair to blame Ben. He had nothing to do with this."

"Your father won't see it that way."

"Well," Candy said, "at least I'm not the one in trouble."

"Oh, can it!" Jenny pushed away from the table and followed Ben. When she entered the entryway, the door to her father's office slammed.

She knocked.

"I'll deal with you when I'm through here, Jennifer," her father shouted.

She jiggled the doorknob. Locked!

That's when the pacing began, her heart galloping inside her chest, keeping time with her steps. Her hand literally shook, so she clasped them together as she walked the room.

After a few minutes, the office door abruptly opened. Jenny spun toward it. "Ben!"

A sheepish Ben stepped into the entry and took a step toward her, then stopped. He took one look at her, shook his head slightly, then moved toward the door.

Her father followed him out of his office.

"Dad?"

"Get his bag, Jennifer. Ben is going home."

Anger now replaced the worry in her heart. She rushed toward her father. "No!"

She felt Ben's hand on her arm and turned his way.

"It's okay, Jenny. If you could grab my bag, I'll meet you at the truck. Everything is going to be fine." He winked, then reached for the front door.

Confused, she glanced from him to her father and back again to Ben.

"Then I'm going with him!"

"Go get his luggage, Jennifer. That's ridiculous. It's for the best. Ben and I agreed."

All she could do was stand there and shake her head. "Would someone tell me what is happening?"

"Later." Her father pushed past her and opened the door, ushering Ben out.

Ben glanced her way, then without a word, moved onto the porch. Her father shut the door before she could watch him descend the steps.

Her mother stepped into the entryway. "Here is his bag, Jennifer. Take it to him, please, then help me clean up from dinner."

She whirled. "Wow. Are you serious? You're sending him on his way just like you're putting out the cat? Let him go and then help with the dishes? Does anyone here have any empathy at all for Ben's feelings, or mine?"

She glanced at the small bag Ben had brought, sitting at her mother's feet now. Lifting her gaze, she panned the entry and her family, making brief eye contact. She moved forward and snatched up the bag. "*This* is ridiculous."

Her stare caught her father's as she headed for the front door. "You are wrong to make him leave. I'll never forgive you for this."

"I've done you a favor."

Her heart literally ached at those words. For a moment, she

held his gaze, her head shaking. "You've broken my heart. I'm so disappointed in you." She turned toward her mother. "And you."

"Jennifer...."

"No, Mom. Don't do that. I'm not ten years old. I'm a grown woman. And I can make my own decisions."

"Not when we are footing the bill for your college expenses." Her father's matter-of-fact demeanor broke through her hurt.

She swung back. "So, it's about money, then. Makes sense. Because you sure are not concerned about me as person."

"That's not true, Jennifer." Her mother stepped forward. "We love you."

"You both have an odd way of showing it."

She didn't wait for a response. Tonight, she was done. With all of it. She yanked the front door open and rushed out onto the porch. Ben waited in the cab of his truck, the light on inside. When he saw her, he pushed his door open and met her halfway on the lawn, taking the bag.

"I want to leave here right now. Take me with you, Ben."

He put his arm around her and led her closer to the truck. "Let's talk about this."

"There is nothing to talk about. I can't live here anymore. I won't have them treating you this way."

He faced her. "Jenny, it's okay."

"No, it's not. Nothing is okay."

"It will be."

She studied his face. "What did he say? What did *you* say?"

Ben exhaled, pushing out a long breath. "I did most of the talking. He listened, sort of, but he already had his mind set. I asked him for your hand, to marry you."

"And?"

"And he flat out said no. That you weren't ready."

"And he thinks he can decide that?"

Ben clasped her hands. "Yes, he does. But Jenny, we know better."

Sighing, she held his hands tighter. "What do you mean?"

"We know we love each other. We will get through this."

"Really?"

He tipped his head toward hers, touching foreheads. "I love you. I asked him, he knows my intentions. I told him I would prefer to marry you with his permission, but if he couldn't see his way to grant that, then you and I would find another way."

"And what did he say to that?"

"That's when he stood, crossed the room, opened the door, and told me to leave. You heard the rest."

He put his arms around her and pulled her closer.

"I don't want to go back into that house."

He pulled back, cupping her face in his hands, peering into her eyes. "Go back inside. I'm leaving."

"Jennifer! Your mother needs you."

She gave the front porch a slight glance, noticing her father standing there, then looked back to Ben. "What are we going to do?"

"Listen to me, honey. Look. I'm going home. You're going to go back inside and mend some fences with your family. Smooth it over about your school plans and help them see that what you are doing is best for you. Focus on getting them to warm up to the new college plan."

"But what about us?"

"That's for us to decide, Jenny. I'm all for making our own plans. Is that okay with you? Take the weekend to smooth things over with your parents about school—it's important to me that you do that—then go back to Penn for the last two weeks as planned to finish your classes. I'll call your dorm room Sunday night at ten, and we will make a plan."

"You still want to marry me?"

He grinned. "More than ever."

"I love you, Ben Matson. I want to be with you in Charmington."

He grinned. "Soon, sweetheart. Soon."

"Jennifer!"

She blew out a hard breath, nuzzling closer to Ben. "This was not how I pictured this weekend."

He kissed her nose. "Me, either. But in some ways, it's been good. Everything is out in the open. Now, we just need to deal with the fallout, smooth it over, and decide our next steps."

Jenny thought about that. "You're right." Tipping her head up, she touched her lips to his and burrowed her arms around his back, under his jacket. "I'm going to miss you. I can barely stand for you to leave."

"I always miss you, Jenny." He stepped back, glanced at the house, then focused solely on her. "I love you more than my life. I'll see you soon."

She nodded. "Soon, Ben. I love you, too. Drive safe. Talk with you on Sunday."

CHAPTER 7

*S*unday, *December 23, 1989, 11:46 p.m.*

THE ANDERS' LIVING ROOM HELD A SOFT GLOW. THE LAMPS WERE turned off, but tiny bulbs twinkled lights on the tree and electric candles lit up the windows.

Closing her eyes, Jenny inhaled, held her breath for a moment, then let it out slowly. After a moment, she blinked, spanned the room, and sat alone in the room on the overstuffed chair next to the fireplace. On the opposite side of the hearth stood their trusty Christmas tree. She was pretty sure they'd had the same one for at least fifteen years.

And there it still stood. Tall. Plastic. Silver balls. Red bows. And all that.

Boring.

Where did she get her creativity? It obviously didn't come from either of her parents. Had that bit of genetics skipped a generation or two?

She'd likely never know. Her father had been on the outs with most of his family for several years—she'd never really understood why.

"Maybe now I do," she whispered.

All the family gifts were under the tree. Her family had never been one to go overboard with decorations, or gifts. Her father's big thing was to put money into their savings account each Christmas—for their future, he'd always said. Her mother would stock her girls up on their favorite hair, makeup, and bath products. Then there was another gift from the two of them— something practical yet memorable, like a designer coat, or an expensive charm bracelet. There were also gifts from the girls to their parents, and to each other.

The room was pretty. The Christmas tone was obviously set. And she'd always loved how everything looked at Christmastime in her home. But this year, everything just looked—sterile.

Clinical. Empty.

Boring.

Sighing, she blew out another breath. This one was quicker, whistling through her pursed lips. She longed to be in Charmington. With Ben. Where she could smell the pine or cedar Christmas trees. Where whiffs of cocoa hung in the air and where homemade wreaths graced the front doors of most homes. Where kitchens were messy with flour and sugar while the cookies were baking. And where cinnamon candy and peppermint sticks tempted her with their sugary sweet-hot sting to her tongue.

Soon, Jenny. Soon.

Standing, she crossed the room to the tree, perused the packages there, and glanced at a side table where a basket full of Christmas cards sat. Her mother was still very traditional in her holidays, and she religiously sent out the cards annually. They received an equal amount in return.

Jenny thumbed through the cards. The Johnson's down the

street sent one with a family photograph. Tom Doolin, from her dad's office, sent a one with a manger scene on the front. There was one from the bakery, where her mom shopped faithfully during the holidays. One from the minister at their church. And on and on....

Reaching into her sweater pocket, she pulled out a homemade card—one she'd made earlier that day from construction paper, snips of wrapping paper, and some leftover ribbon. She'd used Sharpies to draw the Christmas scene and for the Christmas poem she'd written inside.

She opened the card once more to read the poem, then secured the piece of stationery on which she'd written a letter to her parents and tucked it inside. Without another thought, she put the card in the front of the stack in the basket.

Turning back to the tree, she crouched there and debated her next move. Earlier, she'd placed gifts under the tree for her family —one for Candy, a Boho pillow for her new apartment, and a joint gift for her parents, a framed picture she'd created from the beach artifacts she'd gathered last summer, and a sketch of their beach house.

There were three gifts under the tree with her name on it. One, was the basket full of personal products. It was too big and bulky for her to carry. One was from Candy, and the other from her parents. Both were small gifts and would fit into her backpack.

She took them.

DEAR MOM AND DAD,

I know you both will be unhappy when reading this letter, and I am sorry about that. I hope in time you will come to understand the choices I've made, and why.

I am moving forward with my plans to go to art school next

semester. I am taking distance courses for the time being. This feels right, and it is what I want to do. In time, I'll open a small studio and teach classes, or just create. I'll figure that out in the future.

I realize you want a more definite plan, Dad, but this works for me, and that's what I need right now.

While we have had a very nice few days since I've been back home from school, you know I am not happy since you forbade me to see Ben. I honestly don't want to choose between you and him, but you are forcing my hand. And choosing between you is not what I am doing. I am choosing, today, to be with Ben. But that doesn't mean that I'm cutting you out of my life.

I love you both, and Candy. You are my family.

I also love Ben. He and I want to be together, build a life together. Get married. We want to have a family one day. And we want to live in Charmington and raise our family there.

I want you to be part of that, too.

I know this is not your dream for me—but it is the dream I have for myself. I hope you can come to accept it in time. I want that and I hope you will.

In case you haven't realized yet, I'm not upstairs in my room. Ben and I are heading to Charmington, and we plan to get married as soon as possible. Please wish us well.

I will see you soon. I promise.

Love, Jenny

p.s. Please spend the college fund on yourselves. Take that cruise?

p.p.s. I will call you from Charmington.

BEN TURNED ONTO JENNY'S STREET. AN UNEASY FEELING HAUNTED his gut and had for the past few hours. He hoped that nervousness

—or whatever it was—would go away once he arrived and saw her. Slowing the engine, he approached her house, watching the shadows on her lawn. As he pulled up, he turned off the headlights and sat idling for only a few seconds before he saw her.

She raced from the house and jerked open the passenger door of the cab.

His heart pounding inside his chest, he embraced her and exhaled so forcefully he felt lightheaded.

She squeezed him tight. "Oh Ben. You're here."

He pulled back and searched her face, noticing the tears there. "Ah honey. It's okay." He thumbed a few tears from her right eye. "It's all going to be okay."

"I know. Let's go."

He took a breath. "We will. There is one thing I need to do first." That lingering apprehension in his gut started up again.

Jenny looked panicked. "What is it? We need to go before they realize you are out here and that I am gone."

Staring into his beautiful Jenny's eyes, he sensed her panic. But he also knew he had to do what he had to do. He'd had a long drive to think it over and knew that part of the queasy sensation in his stomach came from the anticipation of what he had to do next. "Jenny, listen to me. I'm not leaving here until I talk with your father. It may be a quick conversation, but it's one I need to have."

"What are you talking about?" Her eyes darted.

He grasped her hands. "Jenny, look. I need to talk to him one more time. You stay here. Don't get out. Let me do this. I need to do this."

"Oh Ben, I don't know...."

"I do." He shifted and put his hand on the door handle next to him. "Stay here. I'll be right back."

She nodded, but he wasn't certain she would stay put. He left the truck idling and headed up the driveway toward the porch. It was after midnight, and he was certain Mr. Anders would not be pleased waking up to someone on his doorstep, but he'd decided, and he had thought it through. It was the right thing to do.

He pressed the doorbell. Once. Then twice.

A light came on upstairs, casting a beam across the yard.

Footsteps.

Another light in the entry and then on the front porch. The door swung open.

"What in the world...." Mr. Anders stood in his pajamas and robe, framed by the door casing.

"Mr. Anders."

"It's after midnight, son. What are you doing here?"

Ben swallowed. "I've come for Jenny. I have asked her to marry me, sir. She said yes."

Jenny's father stared. "And what do you expect me to do with that information at this time of night?"

"I don't want to leave without you knowing my intentions. I have a judge lined up when we get to Charmington. We love each other and are getting married. I'd like your and Mrs. Anders' blessing."

His brow arched, and he laughed. Laughed! Obviously, he did not take him seriously.

"So, what are you going to do, kidnap her out of her bed?"

Mr. Anders turned as his wife came rushing down the stairs. "Craig, Jenny is not in her room. She's gone."

Ben braced himself. "No. She's in my truck."

"Oh, Craig."

Ben saw tears in her eyes. It was the first time he'd seen any sort of empathy from the woman. The dreaded sensation in his stomach came back with full force.

Mr. Anders pushed past him and stepped out onto the porch. "Jennifer!"

Ben backed up, stepping slightly in front of him and partially blocking his way. "I'd like your blessing, sir. I love your daughter, and I will take good care of her."

"Hell no." He glared then, sticking his gaze onto Ben.

"I'd like to discuss this, if we could."

Blinking once, he studied Ben, then parked his hands on his hips and looked off toward the truck. "This is ridiculous. Fine. Just take her with you. If you two are hell-bent on getting married, then don't let me stop you. I'm washing my hands of this entire situation. You'll learn your lesson. Stay in Charmington. But you'll never get my blessing, or my support."

Mrs. Anders clutched at his arm. "Craig, please. Have them come in and let's talk about this together."

"No!" His gaze never wavered from Ben's. "Our daughter has made her choice."

Ben hedged a little closer to him. "Sir, if I may ask... I don't understand what you have against me. You've barely let me get to know you. I'm a good man."

Mr. Anders stood and stared at him.

BEN CONTINUED. "SHE LOVES YOU AND HER FAMILY. THIS SHOULDN'T be a choice between me and all of you. She shouldn't have to choose. You are being unfair."

"Unfair! You roll in here in the middle of the night, lure my daughter out of her bed, are prepared to take her off to the woods in some god-forsaken village in the country, and I'm unfair?"

He squared his shoulders. "Yes, I believe you are being unfair."

"Then you are delusional."

Ben stepped in reverse. *I'm getting nowhere.* "Mr. Anders, I have a good, reliable job. I'm a respected member of our community. My family has lived there for generations. When Jenny and I get married, I can support her and our future family just fine. We won't require any support from you, nor will we ask for it. All I ask is that you not alienate Jenny. She loves you and her family. She also loves me."

After a moment of staring, tit-for-tat, Ben turned on his heel and headed for the truck. *Seriously getting nowhere.* He'd thought he was doing the right thing and, honestly, he was, but this scenario hadn't turned out as he had expected.

"Then go!"

"Craig, get back in the house." He heard Jenny's mother coaxing.

Ben made his way down the driveway. During the seconds it took him to walk to the truck, he tried to process the conversation with Jenny's father. Perhaps he needed a minute before telling Jenny anything.

He got in and slammed the door.

"Ben?"

Downshifting into drive, he stared straight ahead and drove slowly down the street. "That didn't go quite as planned, but I did what I needed to do. It's done."

"Bad?"

"Let's talk about it later. I need to think."

"What did you do?"

He turned toward her. "I needed to ask for his blessing one more time. I had hoped he would have had time to think about things and reconsider. I was wrong. I'm sorry, Jenny."

"Oh, Ben. Are you okay?"

He nodded. "I will be. Let's get out of the city. Let me drive for a while, and then I'll probably feel more like talking."

The look on her face made his stomach clench. He reached for her hand on the seat and slowed the truck a little. "It's okay, Jenny. I'm okay. Just come over here and sit close to me."

She scooted next to him and cradled his hand in her lap. "Was he mean to you?"

"He was direct. But I expected that."

"Ben." Her lower lip quivered. "Do you still want to marry me?"

"Ah, hell." He braked, stopping the truck, and reached for her. Wrapping his arms around her, he held her close for a moment. "I can't wait to be your husband, Jenny Anders. I love you so darn much."

She pulled back, looking into his face, beaming. "I can't wait to be Jenny Matson."

"Are you sure? No doubts? No cold feet?"

"Absolutely not."

He grinned. "I had planned to wait until we got closer to Charmington—but, Jenny, I got in touch with the judge. She's able to marry us tonight if we want."

"Tonight? Wait." She glanced off, thinking. Her eyes flashed with excitement when she turned back. "It's after midnight, so that makes it Christmas Eve. We can get married on Christmas Eve?"

"Yes. I would like that. Would you?"

Jenny's eyes twinkled. "Oh, yes!"

The happiness Ben felt deep in his chest right then was practically overwhelming—not to mention the relief flooding his entire body. "Then let's get on our way. If we drive straight through to Charmington, we can be there early morning. That gives us time to rest up before we meet the judge."

Jenny leaned forward, kissing him on the lips. "Oh, Ben. Perfect. This is really happening, isn't it?"

"Oh, yes. It is." Looking down, he fiddled with the engagement ring on her finger. His voice lowered. "And I couldn't be happier, Jenny. You're making all my dreams come true."

She lifted his chin with her forefinger and stared into his eyes. "No, Ben. You're making my dreams come true. I can't wait for a lifetime of dreams together."

CHAPTER 8

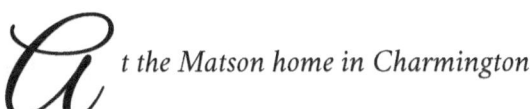

t the Matson home in Charmington

"I THINK THEY GOT THE WEATHER WRONG." CALVIN MATSON TURNED away from the window and caught Ben's eye. That single statement put Ben on high alert. His father never joked about the weather.

"Who?"

"The people on the news."

"The meteorologists?"

"Yes, they're all saying the same thing, but I'm certain their forecasts are bogus."

Ben chuckled to himself, hearing his dad say a word like bogus. "How so, Dad?"

"We're going to get more than a skiff of snow today and tonight. For sure. As cliché as it sounds, I can feel it in my bones. Besides, I don't like the looks of that sky."

Ben and Jenny had arrived in Charmington about eight o'clock that morning. Exhausted when they pulled into town after having driven all night, they went straight to Ben's apartment over the hardware store. They slept through the morning and into the early afternoon. Eager to get on with the plans for the evening, they showered mid-afternoon and proceeded to Ben's parents' home for a short while before heading out to Judge Cameron's farm to get married.

His father's declaration of snow was not in Ben's plans.

"You think we are in for a storm?"

Calvin pursed his lips. A corner of his mouth drew up. "If I were to predict, I'd say we're in for a few inches at the least. That dark blue-gray sky in the west worries me. The wind is picking up too. What exactly are your plans for tonight?"

Ben glanced to the corner of the den where his mother, Charlotte, and Jenny were chatting, oblivious to the conversation he was having with his dad. He lowered his voice. "The Judge says she can marry us at seven this evening. Then after that, we're heading to The Pitcher Inn in the Green Mountains. I got a room after they had a cancellation. It was difficult to find something at this late date."

Calvin nodded. "I'm sure. That's a nice place. Does Jenny know?"

"Where we're staying? No. I wanted to keep that a surprise."

"Well, I'm a little worried about you driving up into the mountains with this storm coming in. I know it's only a couple of hours away, but you can't tell about this weather."

Ben was a little worried, too. He'd been watching the news, and the forecasters were not predicting anything severe—but his father was rarely off with his predictions.

In the background, he heard the phone ring in the kitchen and watched his mom scurry off to answer it. "I'm trying not to worry, Dad. Maybe your bones are wrong?"

With a smirk, Calvin patted Ben's back. "My bones are never wrong, son."

But worry tugged at his gut. "I know."

His mother's head popped around the corner. "Ben? It's Grace Cameron. She wants to talk to you."

The uneasy feeling he'd had last night crept back. This might not be good. Had Jenny's parents somehow figured out who would marry them and would try to circumvent the wedding? Surely not. Still, he hurried to the phone, eager to know what she wanted. "Yes? Judge Cameron?"

He caught Jenny's eye through the kitchen doorway as she started toward him.

"I see. Yes. I understand."

He listened as Jenny approached.

"Of course. We will see you soon. Yes, ma'am. I have all the paperwork."

The judge hung up, and Ben slipped the phone back into its cradle. Jenny reached for his hand. "Ben?"

"Let's step into the den."

"All right."

They did and faced his family. With a heavy sigh, he shared the news.

"Judge Cameron wants to move up the ceremony. Her son's flight was delayed because of the weather, and she has to drive to Montpelier to pick him up tonight. She's afraid that if we wait until later, they'll get snowbound in the city for Christmas."

"Goodness." Jenny looked concerned. "Is it supposed to snow that much? I haven't been paying attention."

Ben caught his father's eye. "I guess your bones are on track."

Calvin stepped up to the couple. "Grace is as good a weather predictor as they come. If the two of us are predicting a storm, then watch out. When can she do the ceremony?"

"Now." He turned to Jenny. "Is that okay with you?"

Jenny glanced around at his family, then landed on Ben. "Yes!" She bounced a little and gripped his hand tighter. "But I want to say something before we leave."

"Of course, Jenny," Maureen offered, stepping closer. "What is it? I've been concerned that something is bothering you ever since you stepped in the door."

Ben watched Jenny take a breath, then draw her lower lip in with her teeth. Her gaze darting, she exhaled, and the words tumbled.

"Thank you for being so welcoming to me from the very beginning. I know Ben and I haven't known each other long—just a few months, actually—but you've trusted in me..." Glancing at Ben, she leaned in closer. "You've trusted us to know that we are making the right decision. That means the world to me. To us. I wish my parents could see what you see in us. That they were more supportive. They had plans for me. Unfortunately, their plans didn't mesh with mine.

"I want you to know, though, that they are good people. And Ben?" Her gaze fully encompassed his again, and he could see the mist of tears forming in her eyes. "I love him so much. He did everything right with my father. He asked for my hand in marriage, and even when my father refused, he went back and braved him again. I'm not sure that went too well either, but I love him for trying."

Ben felt his throat closing at her words. He'd not told Jenny everything about the conversation with her dad, and he needed to do that soon. Now, however, was not the time. "Ah, Jenny. I love you so much."

Maureen stepped closer to the pair. "I think your parents will come around eventually. I hope so, for your sake. And theirs. But as for us? We love Ben, and we love you too. I can't picture my son with anyone else. The two of you are perfect together, and I couldn't be happier."

"I'll second that." Calvin gave Jenny a hug.

Jenny beamed. "I love being part of this family!" She curled into Ben, and he wrapped his arms around her.

Charlotte rose, gave Jenny a squeeze and a smile, and then headed for the front door, talking all the way. "You know I love you, girl, but I gotta run. If the old folks' bones are calling for snow, I need to get the boys from my in-laws, pick up milk and bread, and head home." She kissed Jenny on the cheek. Then to her brother, she added, "Love you, baby brother. Take care of her." She gave him a bear hug and stepped back.

"I will." Ben smiled at his sister and watched her leave. To Jenny, he added, "Well, I guess that's our cue. Ready to get married, Jenny Anders?"

"More than ready." The look on her face then, as her eyes glazed over with love, warmed his heart and soul. *Let it snow. I have everything I need right here.*

JENNY PUSHED ONE ARM INTO HER COAT AND FELT A SUDDEN FLASH of panic. She stopped up short and turned toward Ben. "Oh, no."

Ben finished shrugging into his coat. "What is it?"

"I forgot to call my parents. I was so tired this morning and then got caught up in everything this afternoon. Do I have time to give them a quick call before we meet the judge?" An edgy sensation rippled through her stomach, and she placed a hand on her abdomen.

"Of course, we do." Ben's gaze dropped to her hand. "Are you okay?"

"I'm fine." She smiled then, nervously. "Just nerves. May I call from here? I can pay your parents back for the long-distance call."

"You'll do no such thing." Ben's father stepped up behind them.

"Calling them is an excellent idea. Come into my office, Jenny. You'll have more privacy there."

"Oh, thank you. That would be great."

Her stomach muscles grew taut under her hand. She'd been happy and excited a few minutes earlier, and now she was a nervous wreck. What exactly would she say to them?

The truth. Just tell them the truth, Jenny.

Ben's dad smiled at her, and she found comfort in his gentle, caring ways. She followed his lead as they headed into his office. Ben held back until she reached for his hand and tugged him along.

"Do you want to do this alone?"

Her gaze played over Ben's face. "No. I want you with me if you don't mind."

He gave a quick nod. "Then I'm there. Always."

Calvin ushered them inside, then slipped out the door, softly closing it behind him. Jenny looked at Ben. "I guess it's now or never."

"Jenny, before you call, I want you to know something."

She studied his face, listening. "What is it, Ben?"

He blew out a breath. "You were right earlier. I tried to smooth things over with your dad, and it didn't go well."

"I assumed that, Ben. But what aren't you telling me?"

"I'll just say... Well, your father wasn't very pleased with our plan."

"Did he get angry?"

"He was extremely direct. I wonder... He may not be receptive to your call."

That sounded exactly like her dad. He was an extremely direct person. The lawyer in him, she assumed. "What did he say?"

Ben hesitated.

Jenny sensed he didn't want to have this conversation right now. "Ben?"

"It will take a good twenty minutes to get to the judge's farm," he told her. "We'll talk more about what happened last night on the way there, or maybe it can wait until tomorrow. Right now, I think you should get this call over with, so you can let it go for a while. After all, we have a wedding to get to."

Jenny instantly felt better. Somewhat. "Yes, we do." She angled her head slightly to give him a quick kiss on the lips. "You're right." She moved closer to the desk and picked up the phone receiver. After a brief pause and a deep breath, she dialed the number.

And waited.

On the fourth ring, her mother answered. "Hello?"

"Mom?"

"Oh, my goodness. Jenny? Where are you?"

"Mom, you know where I am. Didn't you read my note?"

"Yes. Yes, of course I did. So, you're in Charmington? Are you married? You know I had hoped that we could have a big wedding. Do all the mother-daughter things that happen when a young woman gets married. Instead, you're…. Eloping." She said the last word with dread in her voice.

Her mother choked up a little and stopped talking.

Jenny's stomach sickened a little at her mother's lengthy sigh.

"Mom, it's okay. Let's do some mother-daughter wedding things later. Like a shower or something."

"Could we?"

"Of course we can."

"But are you married yet? If not, maybe you could hold off?"

"Mom, no. We are getting married tonight. Within the hour."

There was another long pause at the other end. Then, her mother said, "Well, if you are sure."

"I am." Jenny hesitated then, before asking the next question. "Where is Dad?"

Again, another deep sigh from her mother. "He's in the den. I think, maybe, you shouldn't talk to him tonight."

"Why? Mom? What's going on?"

Silence.

"Mom?"

"Jenny, he is not taking this well."

"If he hadn't been so darned stubborn and would only listen, then perhaps he wouldn't be so upset. But you know Daddy…."

"You know he doesn't accept change well."

"Mom, he—"

She heard some shuffling from the other end. "Wait. Craig? I'm talking…."

"Mom?"

Another gap in the conversation. Then, her father's voice came through, louder than her mother's. "Jennifer?"

"Dad?"

"I didn't expect to hear from you."

"But I said in my note I would call. Did you read the note?"

"Your mother said something about that."

"But you didn't read it."

"No. I do not need to read it."

That pained Jenny a little. "But she told you I was going to call. Why wouldn't you think I would?"

"Because you made your choice, Jennifer. You have a new family now."

"Oh, good gracious."

Her stomach muscles clenched, and the queasiness escalated. Lights danced inside her head. Good Lord, she could not pass out… "Dad, I do have another family now. But I also have *my* family, and I love you all. This is not an either-or situation. I get to keep you both."

"Well, that's debatable."

"What do you mean by that?" Pacing away from the desk, she glanced at Ben and pushed away the hurt of those words.

"Think about it."

"Dad? I don't understand." She felt abruptly abandoned. Like her parents had dropped her off at school and didn't come back to pick her up at the end of the day. What was going on here?

"I'm hanging up now, Jennifer. Look. Don't call back. It only upsets your mother. You've made your choice, now live with it. As I told Ben last night, I've washed my hands of this entire situation. You're on your own. There is no need for you to call back here or come back here ever again."

The other end of the line fell silent. A few seconds slogged on, followed by a deep sigh. Then Jenny heard the phone click off.

"What? Wait. Dad?" She turned, catching Ben's eye, and slowly, quietly set the phone back into the cradle. She didn't want to cry, but knew tears were close.

I can't walk out of this office crying... Not on the way to my wedding? How would that look?

"Jenny? Are you okay?"

She nodded. Her chin jutted up. "I'm fine. Let's go." She sniffed.

"How did it go?"

"I don't want to talk about it right now. Maybe tomorrow. We have a wedding to get to." She realized she was echoing his words from earlier, but honestly, her head was swirling right now, and she didn't know what to think. Squaring her shoulders, she turned and grasped the office doorknob and twisted it. She had to get out of this small room—her palms were sweating and her cheeks hot—and then figure out how to quell the conflicting emotions battling inside her heart and her head.

"You're sure?"

She whirled back. "Yes. I'm sure. Don't bug me right now. Okay? I need to process that call, just like you had to process things last night. Which obviously you didn't do very well because evidently, there were some things said then that you have chosen not to tell me. How could you do that?"

"Jenny, let me explain."

She waved him off. "No. There is no time."

Ben glanced at his watch and nodded . "You're right. We need to go."

"Yes. I want to leave. The judge is waiting."

THIS WAS NOT HOW HE HAD PICTURED THE DRIVE TO HIS WEDDING.

Ben squinted at the windshield, trying to see the road ahead. The snow squall had erupted over them about five minutes away from his parents' house. Having slowed the truck significantly, he crept along, trying to keep the vehicle on the right side of the narrow country road, while simultaneously glancing at Jenny to make sure she was all right.

She'd not said a word since leaving the house.

All he'd seen of her since getting into the truck was the back of her head—she seemed determined not to look at him and to stare out the window.

This is ridiculous.

He needed to talk to her and wasn't sure which subject to broach first. Was it safest to first tackle what happened in his dad's office? Or should he attempt to suggest that the snowstorm had likely waylaid their wedding plans?

Neither subject was pleasant. He could be playing whack-a-mole for all he knew. Nevertheless, he had to say something. The quiet in the truck cab was driving him bonkers.

"Jenny, sweetheart... I'm sorry I didn't tell you what your dad said. Okay, maybe I should have, but I thought I was protecting you." Nothing like hitting the nail straight on the head.

"You had no right *not* to tell me." Finally, she spun around to look at him, her eyes flashing, and her hair whirling around her forehead like cotton candy caught up in a swirl of static electricity.

"He doesn't want me to ever come home again? I needed to know that."

"I should have told you. You're right."

"What did he say, exactly?"

Ben cleared his throat and plowed ahead. "He said he was washing his hands of the situation. For us to go on and get married, but that he would never give us his blessing or his support."

Jenny's eyes grew wide, then slowly, she rotated to stare out the windshield. "We were dismissed."

"What?"

"It's what he does. Once he washes his hands of something, or someone, it's over. I've seen him do it with clients, his brother, and a few friends. He pushes them away and never has contact with them again. Remember what I told you? He keeps the circle small. And he just cut me, rather us, out of his life. I am honestly shocked. I never thought he would do that to me."

"Oh, Jenny." Ben's heart was about to burst for her. He reached for her hand.

She pulled it back and shoved it into her coat pocket.

Well. That certainly isn't good. He tried to ignore the fact that he, himself, suddenly felt dismissed. Change the subject?

"This storm is getting worse."

Jenny's right leg started jumping up and down—nervous, he guessed—her foot tapping on the floorboard. "How much longer until we reach the judge's farm?"

"Jenny, to be honest, I've totally lost any sense of where we are in this whiteout. I can't see a darned thing but snow, and I'm getting a little concerned about trying to find her farm in this weather. The lane back to her house is narrow and unpaved, and she lives at the top of a steep hill."

"Are you saying we need to turn back?"

"I'm saying I don't know if I can go on. Or back. I need to find a pull-off."

"Then what?"

"We'll cross that bridge when we get to it."

"Ben? I'm serious. Are we in trouble here?"

He slowed the truck and looked her way. Her eyebrows were knit in worry, and her eyes still held the mist of tears. "Jenny, I don't know. Maybe."

"Great. That's all we need."

Ben sighed. "Look. Maybe we should try to do this another time. This weather is a bear. Besides, I'm not sure either of us are in the right frame of mind to get married today."

She jerked closer to him on the bench seat, tears in her eyes now. "And I'm not sure why you didn't tell me last night my father had practically disowned me. Were you afraid his tactics would work on me and that I wouldn't come with you?"

"That never entered my mind, Jenny. I never doubted that you would come with me."

"Well, I'm doubting right now that we ever will get married."

Ben braked hard. The rear of the truck skidded to the right. He stared at Jenny. "What does that mean?"

She didn't hesitate. "It means I'm not sure we should even get married, Ben. Let's just forget it for now. There is too much going on in my head, and there is the snow, and I need to talk with my mother because she sounded upset on the phone."

He edged closer to her. "Jenny, you're right. There is a lot going on. It's not the time to decide about getting married or not. It will happen. Just not tonight, I fear."

She shook her head. "We can't get married until I figure out this thing with my family."

Nodding, he couldn't disagree with that. "All right. That's fair. I know we can't get married tonight, given the situation, and I'll give you time to figure out the family dynamics... But Jenny Anders, I don't want to wait forever for you to be my wife."

The look she gave him sent his stomach into a downward spiral. Her eyes were narrow, her gaze determined. "Ben, I don't know when I will be ready. It wouldn't be fair to you, or to me, to put a timeframe on this right now."

A timeframe?

Twenty-four hours earlier, she couldn't wait to get out of her parents' house. Now...?

"So, our marriage is off the table?"

Her eyes widened. "Yes. For now. I don't know if I can marry someone who keeps things from me. I need you to always be upfront with me, Ben. You didn't tell me what my father said on purpose."

"And I explained that!"

Ben pushed back and leaned against the driver's side door, staring out at the road ahead of the vehicle. The truck was idling, the wipers pushing wet snow to the sides. He couldn't stay here, parked in the road. That could be a recipe for disaster should someone come up behind him on the highway.

Down the road, between the swipes of windshield wipers, he spotted a mailbox to the right. That gave him a clue where they might be. They needed to get off the road. If there was a mailbox, then there was a lane to the right. Or should be.

There. Shifting into drive, he eased the truck forward, then after several feet, pulled off and parked the truck in the entrance, but kept the engine running. Wet snow pelted the roof and the windshield. He turned to Jenny.

"Look. Let's put the marriage discussion aside for a minute. I didn't tell you what your dad said because I didn't want to hurt you."

"Seriously, Ben? Not telling me *did* hurt me. Can you imagine how I felt when I heard my dad say those words?"

"What did he say? I could hear only one side of the conversation. Yours."

"He said basically what you said. He was washing his hands of the situation. That I was on my own and that I shouldn't call or come back home ever again. He basically kicked me out of the family and suddenly, I feel so lost. I don't know what to do."

"Oh hell. Come here, Jenny."

Ben gathered her close and wrapped his arms around her, tight. "It's okay, sweetheart. We are going to work this out."

"We really aren't getting married. Are we?" She raised her head and searched his eyes.

"Not tonight."

"Ben, I'm having serious doubts. Second thoughts. I'm sorry. I'm a little confused and upset. I guess I'm a mess."

He figured as much. While the thought of that pained him to the core, he had to keep faith in their relationship that it would work out. "It's okay, Jenny. We will work through this. But right now, my major concern is keeping us safe. I'm not sure we can get out of this driveway."

"What are we going to do?"

Ben stared ahead, out the windshield. The wipers were working overtime, shoving the wet snow off the glass. Occasionally, when he got a peek ahead of them in the distance, he thought he could see a light. If he was where he thought he was, this could be the old Holly Hill farm, and hopefully the Petersons, an older couple who owned the farm, were home tonight.

"We're going to walk."

"In this weather?"

"It shouldn't be far. We really don't have a choice. If we stay here, the snow will pile up. We'll run out of gas and, besides, it's dangerous to run the engine if the snow is piling up around the car."

"Carbon monoxide."

"Yes."

"We need to get someplace."

"Yes." He nodded. "I see a light up ahead, off and on, through the snow. We're going to layer up and head toward it before the power goes out and we can't find it again."

"Oh Ben. I'm a little scared."

He hugged her again. "We are going to be fine. I won't let anything happen to you."

Or us.

CHAPTER 9

H olly Hill Farm, Christmas Eve

NEAR TEARS AND EXHAUSTED FROM TRUDGING THROUGH THE quickly accumulating snow, Jenny stumbled up the porch steps of a rather large farmhouse—what she could see of it anyway—while eyeballing the light to the right of the front door. They'd used that light as their beacon, all the while praying that someone was home. Her cheeks felt frigid, and she feared that if the tears in her eyes fell, they would freeze right to her face.

That would be awkward, not to mention ugly.

She had no clue how far they had walked. It could have taken them ten minutes to get this far, or an hour—she literally had no sense of time, distance, or direction. She simply followed Ben in the swirling snow as he tugged her along, his arm securely linked with hers to keep her on the right track and moving forward.

Ben stomped his feet on the wooden porch as they approached the door. Not as much snow had accumulated in that area. He rapped on the storm door and waited. After a moment with no answer, he glanced at Jenny, and then tugged on the outer door handle. It fell open with two jerks.

He knocked again, harder, on the inside wooden door.

A faint female voice came through from the other side. "Who is out there?"

"Mrs. Peterson? Is that you? It's Ben Matson. My truck's stuck in your driveway. May we come in?"

The door creaked open slightly, about an inch, and Jenny could see an older woman hesitantly peeking out in the space between door and frame. "Ben? My stars. Get in here." She opened the door wider, noticed Jenny standing there too, and waved them both inside. "You poor girl. You too!"

"Oh, thank you," Jenny breathed. "We are so cold."

Mrs. Peterson fluttered about in her bathrobe and nightgown, fuzzy bedroom slippers on her feet. Her white hair was caught up in a clip, with tendrils of curls spilling out around her neck. "Get those wet things off, you two. Shoes first. Ben, put them over by the fire. Give me your jackets."

"Oh no," Ben responded. "We'll get you all wet. Just tell me where to put them and I'll take care of them."

They stood in the entryway, while the older woman tottered off toward the dining room, chattering all the while under her breath. Jenny glanced at Ben then followed her as she grabbed a straight-back chair. She suspected Mrs. Peterson was close to eighty years old, but she wrangled the two dining chairs with ease.

"Here," she said to Jenny. "Let's drag a couple of these over into the living room by the stove and we'll hang your wet things on them. It will be fine. These old chairs have seen more wet coats than I could likely count."

Shrugging out of her coat, Jenny thanked her and grasped the top of a chair. "I don't know what we would have done if you'd not been home." She crossed the entryway with her chair and placed it in front of the stove. Turning, she went back to help Mrs. Peterson. "I don't mind admitting I was a little scared. Thanks again, so much, for letting us come inside."

The woman beamed. "Oh, pish. It's what we do. Isn't it? Help each other out in times of need?" She scooted her chair across the plank floor, then glanced toward the stove. Jenny took the chair the rest of the way. Mrs. Peterson pointed to Ben. "There. That's good. Not too close now. We don't want those coats to spontaneously combust!" She laughed.

"Oh my. Would they?" Jenny asked.

Mrs. Peterson shrugged. "I have no clue, but it sounded good, didn't it?"

It was Jenny's turn to laugh.

"So, Ben, is this your new girlfriend? I heard in town that you had one. Been sneaking off to Pennsylvania, I understand, just to see her."

Jenny glanced at Ben, who slowly turned away from the stove to face them. "Yes, Mrs. Peterson. I'm sorry I didn't introduce you when we came in the door. This is Jenny Anders. She is my…" Ben paused, looking at Jenny. She could almost read the question darting across his face. *What am I to him now? Fiancée? Girlfriend?*

"Fiancée," Jenny said. She gave Ben a warm smile, then looked at Mrs. Peterson and fluttered the fingers on her left hand. "See? Ben proposed and gave me this beautiful engagement ring." It was all true, of course. Ben had proposed and given her a ring, and she was technically still his fiancée. That they'd argued and talked about postponing the wedding didn't enter into this equation.

Did it?

We really aren't getting married. Are we?

Not tonight.

Ben, I'm having serious doubts. Second thoughts. I'm sorry. I'm a little confused and upset.

Mrs. Peterson drifted toward her. The action jerked Jenny out of her thoughts.

"Oh my. What a beautiful ring. What a lucky girl you are." She paused, looking into Jenny's eyes.

Lucky? She supposed she was. Then why was she so confused?

Mrs. Peterson continued. "The ring is lovely, Jenny, but I didn't mean you were lucky because of a silly diamond." She looked at Ben then, and Jenny followed her gaze. "Ben Matson is one fine young man. None better. And so's his family. You're lucky to call them your own."

And she knew she was. She just hoped she could still call them her own, in time. Once she'd worked things out. Jenny's gaze drifted to catch Ben's, and he held her captive for a moment with his stare.

"Well, I need to go check on Harold," Mrs. Peterson said, then glanced at Ben. "He's not well, you know. His oxygen and all that. Lungs are just giving out. I need to make sure he's okay."

Ben took a step. "Is there anything I can do to help you?"

At that moment, the lights in the room flashed brighter, then dimmed, flashed once more, then went completely out.

"As a matter of fact," Mrs. Peterson called out in the dark. "There is. The generator is on the back porch. Gas can too. We need to get that thing started up so Harold's oxygen machine will run. We have a few tanks, but they won't last for hours. Now, I need to tend to him."

"Will do," said Ben.

"Mrs. Peterson!" Jenny called out. "Wait. I'll go with you and help."

The woman reached for her, and Jenny took her small, soft hand. "Let's take it easy. We don't want to trip over anything."

"You are a dear. Just as nice as Ben. I'm sure you're going to make a fine couple." She patted her hand and then added, "Please help me get to my husband. He needs me."

I'M SURE YOU'RE GOING TO MAKE A FINE COUPLE.

Ben pushed his arms into his wet coat by the light of an outside security light shining in the window, which somehow was not affected by the power outage. He glanced about the living room for a flashlight or lantern. Finding none, he slowly made his way down the hall in the same direction as the women and called out softly.

"Mrs. Peterson? Do you have a flashlight or two?"

The voice came from just inside the room around the corner. "I have one here," she told him. "But look in the kitchen, in the pantry to the right of the stove. There should be another one, and a couple of those battery-powered lanterns. Could you grab those too?"

"Of course."

He found everything, all the while his brain working over Mrs. Peterson's words about them being a *fine couple*, and Jenny's admission of her being his fiancée. Did she say that just to make things easier for him, or did she really intend to stay his fiancée? Earlier in the evening, he wasn't sure what the state of their relationship was.

Approaching the bedroom door, he saw the soft glow of the flashlight a few feet away. "Here are the lanterns," he mumbled, not wanting to wake Harold.

Jenny tiptoed his way, the flashlight bobbing in the dark as she grew closer. "Thanks, Ben."

The soft light cast a warm glow over Jenny's face, and for a moment, his heart clutched from loving her so much. She was so pretty standing there, looking up at him. Her enormous eyes held an expression he wasn't sure he could put his finger on, yet somehow, he felt everything was going to be okay. Eventually.

"Let me turn one on for you." He fiddled with a switch on the bottom of the lantern to turn it on. More light flooded the area.

"Thanks, Ben."

He grinned. "You're welcome."

"I'm going to take this over by the bed now, so Mrs. Peterson can see her husband."

"Of course. Right."

Her eyes were still big and round and drawing him in, much like they did that day at the beach. But he stepped back. He was pretty sure the attraction was all from his perspective. He still had no clue how Jenny felt about the entire situation.

"I should get that generator going."

Nodding, Jenny stepped back as well. "Be careful, Ben. Please?" Worry crossed her face then and flooded her eyes.

"Always."

He turned and headed toward the door.

Jenny carried the lit lantern closer to where Mrs. Peterson sat beside the bed. The woman fiddled with an oxygen tank and tubes, and some sort of device that sat atop the tank where you turned the oxygen off and on. Mr. Peterson needed the tanks to replace the machine that wasn't working now because of the power outage.

Jenny placed the lit lantern on the floor, handed the flashlight to Mrs. Peterson, and found the switch on the second lantern to light it as well. "I'll set this one on this table over here."

"Yes, please," Mrs. Peterson replied. "Then, can you help me move another couple of tanks closer to the bed? They are over there by the closet. I need to see how many we have to estimate how many hours of oxygen we have left."

Those words panicked Jenny a little. "Of course."

Lifting the second lantern, she searched in the closet area and found several tanks. She did a quick count, then grabbed one to take closer to the bed.

"There are seven there, including this one," she told Mrs. Peterson.

The older woman looked up at her with worry etched across her face. "I worry that won't be enough."

At that moment, Jenny froze. "Enough?"

"To get through the storm."

"But what about the generator?"

She shook her head. "It's old and crotchety. I don't know if Ben can get it going."

"Then what do we do?"

Mrs. Peterson's gaze dropped to her husband's sleeping face. "Pray."

Jenny's heart seized with anguish for the woman. "Is he okay?"

She looked back up at Jenny and shook her head. "He's been sleeping since early this afternoon. I sensed the big storm coming and sent the help home . I knew Harold would prefer to go without nurses hovering over him."

Jenny sucked in a quick breath. "He's dying?"

She nodded and whispered, "Yes. Not yet, but his time is short."

"Is there anything we can do?" Jenny was a bit horrified by the situation.

Mrs. Peterson looked at her with caring eyes. "Just keep him comfortable. The hospice nurse left me with some morphine, and that should do the trick." The older woman looked away then, but the mist in her eyes didn't go unnoticed by Jenny.

"I should leave you to be alone with him."

Mrs. Peterson blinked and reached for Jenny's hand and tugged. "No. Sit with me, please. Bring that desk chair over here and stay e while I sit with Harold. Can you do that, sweetie?"

"Of course." Jenny retrieved the chair and positioned it closer. "If you are sure."

"I am." She laid her hand on Jenny's knee, looked long into her eyes, and sighed. "I thought I wanted to be alone with Harold when the time came, but right now, I want company."

Jenny nodded and placed her hand over Mrs. Peterson's. "I'm happy to stay here with you. As long as you want. I'm honored."

"One day, before you realize how quickly the time has passed, this day will come for you and Ben. One of you will go before the other, and one of you will be alone. You are lucky, Jenny. You found each other when you were young, and you and Ben are going to have a long life together. I know it."

Jenny sighed. "I'm not so sure, Mrs. Peterson."

"Call me Elaine." She patted her hand. "We need to be on a first-name basis here, sweetie. It's going to be a long night. Now, tell me why you are not sure about you and Ben. I can clearly see the love he has for you in his eyes."

Yes, Jenny could see that too.

"I..." Jenny hesitated. "I'm not sure it's the time or place to discuss my problems, Mrs., um, Elaine."

Elaine Peterson studied Jenny's face for a moment, then looked back to her husband. Taking his hand in hers, she brought it up to her lips and kissed it. "There's never a good time to discuss some things."

That statement hit home immediately and tangled with her heart. *Never a good time to discuss some things.* Had she avoided talking to her parents about her feelings? About college? About Ben? Was she somehow at fault with her family issues?

"That's very true. And something I need to think about."

Elaine looked up and smiled. But beyond the sparkle in her pupils, and the thin-lipped grin spreading across her face, Jenny also saw fatigue in her eyes, and the slight quiver of her lower lip.

CHAPTER 10

*B*en had some difficulty with the generator. He figured it hadn't been started for a couple of years. And while it rested on a covered part of the porch, he needed to move it away from the house, where there would be no threat of fumes getting inside. Where to, also posed a problem, with the snow piling up. But he got it off the porch and under the overhang of a shed several feet away. Luckily, the heavy-duty extension cord reached that far.

He'd popped inside once to tell Mrs. Peterson and Jenny that he had to do some fiddling with the starter, and that it would be several minutes more before he would have things running.

He found the pair in the bedroom chatting.

"We'll be fine for a while. Harold has at least four to five hours of oxygen in the tanks," Mrs. Peterson said. "I'm sure you'll have it going before then. I'll only fret if we need to rely on tanks past then."

"I surely hope that is not the case." Ben worried he'd be able to keep his promise. Promises seemed easily broken these days. He glanced at Jenny. "Are you okay?"

She rose and stepped toward the bedroom door, picking up a lantern on her way. She motioned for him to step into the hallway.

He followed her.

She turned toward him. The worry etched on her face frightened him.

"Oh, Ben. This is awful."

"What?"

"Mr. Peterson is dying. She sent the nurses home."

"What? Are you okay in there?"

Jenny nodded frantically. "I'm fine. She wants me to stay with her, and in some small, strange way, I want to be with her too. I don't think she has anyone else."

"They never had children."

Sucking in a breath, Jenny stared into the room. "It's sad."

Ben touched her arm to get her attention. "I'm going back outside. I'll be in as soon as I get that rickety thing running."

"Is it really that bad?"

"Bad enough."

JENNY AND ELAINE TALKED IN WHISPERS WHILE HAROLD SLEPT. SHE was still having a difficult time calling her Elaine instead of Mrs. Peterson.

"Being called Mrs. Peterson just makes me feel damned old," she confessed to Jenny. "Even though I am old. I'll be eighty-two next month, you know."

"I would have guessed you were in your seventies," Jenny teased

Elaine cackled then. "Oh sweetie. You are a hoot."

It was nice to hear her laugh. She wondered if there had been much room in her life lately for laughter.

Elaine looked at Jenny. "You and Ben make a lovely couple."

Glancing off, Jenny studied a picture over the bed, avoiding her comment. It looked to be one of those aerial pictures of a farm—perhaps this farm, she wasn't sure. It was taken some time ago, she guessed. She'd seen one of those before, at her grandparents' home —her father's parents—in the country. They'd not gone there much in recent years, but she remembered the picture perfectly.

"Jenny?"

She looked at Elaine. "I'm sorry. You were saying?"

"Your wedding. When are you getting married?"

Hesitantly, she debated how to respond. "Well, we were on our way to the judge when the storm hit. I guess we've postponed."

"You guess?"

Jenny shrugged. "Well, it can't happen today, that's for certain."

Elaine studied her. "Are you unsure about this marriage, Jenny?"

"Well, of course. No. Sure. It's complicated. I..." The words tumbled out. Jenny knew she wasn't making sense.

Elaine reached for her hand and tucked it between both of hers. "Tell me. Tell me everything."

With a sigh, Jenny dove in. "It's just that... I wish things had gone better with my parents. That they understood."

"They are against the marriage?"

"My father, yes. I think my mother would come around if not for him. But I haven't talked with her...really talked. You know?"

Elaine nodded. "You should find that time."

"I know."

"That said, you are an adult, right? You can make your own decisions. Why do you feel you need their blessing?

"Because I've always strived to please them. Grades, and so on, that's what I've always done. I ache inside thinking that I've done something that will affect my relationship with my parents for the rest of my life."

Elaine studied her. "But is it really what you have done? Or what your father has done?"

Blinking, Jenny stared at her new friend. "I hadn't thought of it in quite that way. Perhaps you are right."

"You're not at fault here, Jenny. All you are doing is following your heart."

And right now, her heart was aching even more. "Oh, Elaine…" she whispered. "You are right."

"And what about your relationship with Ben?"

That statement stunned Jenny a little. "Ben?"

"You love him. Right?"

"Oh, more than anything."

"Then that's all you need. One relationship is not more important than the other. You just need to figure out how to make it work."

"But—"

Elaine laid a finger on her lips. "Sh. No buts. If there is love, true love, you cannot deny it. You can try to push it away. You can try to reason with it. But if it's true, it will refuse to be denied, and it will fight its way back to you."

Jenny thought about that for a minute. "Could it really be that simple?"

"No. It's not simple at all, Jenny. I have some beliefs about love if you want to hear them."

"I do." She nodded. There was something rather serendipitous about this day and evening, and she and Ben landing here at the Petersons. "Please?"

"I don't believe you meddle with first love," Elaine began. "First love is powerfully strong. There is a bond there that I believe never goes away. In fact, I know that firsthand.

"When that love gets disrupted, it affects the rest of your life. Your choices, your subsequent loves, and relationships, and more. I don't think you realize it at the time—until your one true love finally comes back to you."

Jenny watched the older woman wind her fingers with her

husband's as she thumbed his knuckles and then adjusted his oxygen tube.

The way she looked at him... They had something special. Powerful. She could feel it.

Jenny felt like a spectator of a private moment that she wasn't sure she would witness.

She glanced off, and her gaze landed on an old picture on the dresser.

"Were you high-school sweethearts?"

Elaine's gaze lifted from her husband to the picture. It was an old picture of a couple of teenagers, all dressed up in fancy clothes. Made of cardboard, the frame holding the picture was frayed and bent at the edges. Jenny watched a slow smile travel over Elaine's face.

"We were in high school," she started, her voice a mere whisper. "He was my boyfriend, and a year older than me. That year, he was a junior, and I was a sophomore. He asked me out through a friend of his, and I have to say I'd never given the boy a second glance. But that day, I suppose knowing he had some sort of interest in me changed things. We started exchanging notes throughout the day. He'd smile shyly as we passed in the hall. Eventually, we went out, and from then on, it was just the two of us for nearly three years. Then he graduated."

"And you broke up?"

She looked at her. "Yes, but not because of him graduating. My mother came between us. I suppose she was only protecting me, in a way. But she meddled between us until I questioned the relationship and wondered what life would be like without him once he went off to college.

"The breakup was bad. Poor guy, he had quite a time of it. He tried and tried to get me back that summer. Did anything he could think of to impress me. New clothes. New car. Letters. Wanted to take me out to fancy places to eat.

"But I had shut down. I think it was easier for me to shut him out of my life than to deal with my mother. At least that's what I thought back then."

Her gaze drifted off for a moment, then she looked back at her dying husband and stroked his face. "He's unconscious, you know. Not just sleeping. I gave him powerful painkillers and a sedative before you and Ben arrived. That's one reason he is sleeping so soundly—why I sent the hospice nurses home. I wanted to spend time alone with Harold before he passed on. Our last Christmas Eve together."

Jenny stood. "Oh my, Elaine. Really and truly, Ben and I shouldn't be here. We are imposing and I—"

Elaine grasped her hand. "No, you should be here. You and your young man… You are so much in love, I can see it. And I love feeling the power of that between you. It reminds me so much of my own first love. Love is powerful, Jenny. Never forget that. Promise me. With it, you can get through anything."

Tears stung Jenny's eyelids as Elaine stared at her with intent. Nodding, she whispered, "I promise."

"I wish I'd been strong enough to stand up to my mother. In the end, our relationship was never the same either. I always blamed her, and I regret that. Even though I did what she wanted, I always felt I had somehow disappointed her."

Jenny squeezed Elaine's hand. "I understand. I truly do."

"This thing has come between the two of you. Don't let it, Jenny."

"I don't want it to, truly."

"Resolve the issue with your parents. Perhaps that will free up your mind, and you'll know exactly what to do next."

Jenny nodded. "Perhaps." She wondered about that. "You are right. I need to face it head-on."

Elaine smiled. "There are so many things in life we need to face head-on. Don't avoid them. Face them and conquer them."

Leaning in, Jenny gave the old woman a hug. "Thank you, Elaine." Pulling back, she smiled and studied her face. "You didn't finish the story. What happened to you and your high school beaux? Your first, young love?"

Elaine smiled broadly then and looked lovingly at Harold. "Oh, he's right here. Harold was my one true love, Jenny. We went our separate ways. We each married another, but neither of us had children. After several years, I divorced my husband. Harold lost his wife in a car accident.

"We didn't find each other again until nearly forty years had passed—but we've been together ever since. There are days I mourn the decades we were apart. The life we missed experiencing together. A wedding. Children. Growing old over time. But now... I'm only happy we are together. I often wished I had not listened to my mother and had run off with Harold all those years ago, like he wanted me to do."

Jenny's heart swelled as she watched the Peterson couple. Elaine lovingly stroked Harold's face and cooed soft words to him. The strong bond, the love they shared, had carried them through time and would end here tonight. Sniffling, Jenny glanced off toward the young teenage couple in the picture on the dresser.

Elaine spoke quietly. "Having you here right now, Jenny. Well. It helped me to remember how much Harold and I loved each other as teenagers, and how even though we were separated by decades, I'm so grateful we found our way back to each other, and that we will have these final hours together."

She stroked his head again, then leaned in to kiss him on the cheek. "If there is one thing I've learned in life, it's when to hold on, and when to let go. Think about that. Is it time to hold on to Ben with everything you have? Or is it time to let go?"

After a moment, she waved Jenny off and carefully climbed into bed beside the love of her life. As Jenny quietly left the room, she noticed Elaine's damp cheeks.

Time to let go?

In the hallway, she met Ben coming in from the back door, carrying a thick extension cord.

"Ben. Oh, Ben." She rushed toward him. "Where are you going?"

"To plug this into Harold's oxygen machine."

Jenny grasped his biceps, shaking her head. "No, wait. Give Elaine a minute. She…" Her words trailed off, and suddenly, Jenny sobbed, and tears rolled down her cheeks. "She's letting go. Harold is… Oh, Ben. It's so terribly sad."

Ben lifted her chin with his forefinger. "Jenny? What is going on? Are you okay?"

"No. Yes. Yes, I'm okay. Ben, I'm so sorry. I was wrong. I've messed everything up. I love you so much, and I don't want us to be apart. I'm not ready to let you go. Ever. I still want to marry you. I want very much to be your wife. If you'll have me."

Ben dropped the heavy extension cord and grabbed Jenny up into a bear hug that she never wanted to end.

CHAPTER 11

*E*arly the next morning, Jenny blinked herself awake, squinting against a beam of sunlight shining in the window, and pushed herself into an upright position on the sofa. Ben was still asleep, curled up against the sofa arm, a blanket wrapped around his shoulders. She remembered hunting for that blanket the night before and tucking it around them while they slept in each other's arms in front of the stove.

It didn't take either of them long to fall asleep.

A quick glance at the anniversary clock on the mantel told her the time was just after seven in the morning. She stepped toward the front door and peeked out the window—the morning was still and bright, with several inches of sparkling snow blanketing the area. The good news was that the aftermath of the storm didn't look as bad as she feared. The generator was still running outside, and she could hear the hum of the oxygen machine in Harold and Elaine's bedroom. Ben had plugged it in a few hours ago.

She wondered how Elaine was doing.

Ben stirred on the sofa, catching her eye. "Good morning," he murmured. "What time is it?"

"Early. The snow has stopped, and it doesn't look too bad out there."

"Great." Ben rose and stumbled toward the door. "That's a good sign. I wonder if I can dig us out this morning so we can get back home?"

"I hope so," Jenny said. "But I don't know about leaving Elaine."

Ben rubbed his chin. "I know. We will figure something out. I don't like the idea of leaving her alone with Harold in this condition. I wonder when the hospice nurses are coming back?"

"Elaine probably knows."

Gathering her into his arms, Ben peered down into her eyes, a serious look on his face. "Good morning. I love you."

She smiled. "Good morning to you. I love you, back."

Leaning in for a quick kiss, Ben hugged her tighter. "Merry Christmas," he added after a moment.

Jenny pulled back. "Goodness. You're right. It is Christmas day."

"Yep. And we were supposed to be in Vermont today for our honeymoon."

"What? Really?"

He nodded, touching his nose to hers. "If we can dig out early, I'm wondering if we can make it by tonight?"

"To Vermont?"

"Umhm. The Green Mountains. For our honeymoon."

"But..." Jenny searched his face. "But we'd have to get married first to have a honeymoon, and there is the snow, and...."

He silenced her with a kiss. Jenny relaxed and let him nibble her lips for a long, sweet moment. "Oh..."

He spoke softly between kisses. "Marry me. Today, Jenny Anders. On Christmas day. Please? Put me out of my misery."

Jenny reluctantly let go of the last kiss, stared into his eyes. "If anyone can make it happen today, Ben Matson, it's you. We have the whole day ahead of us. Yes. I love you. Let's get married."

Stepping back, Ben cocked his head and studied her. "Do you want to clear things up with your parents first?"

Jenny thought about that, taking a big breath in, and exhaling slowly. "You know, I need to have a discussion with them. Elaine and I talked about that last night. But I also need to do what is best for us. And today? We need to focus on getting married. I'm not procrastinating the inevitable. I'm simply putting our relationship first. I hope that is okay with you?"

A sly grin crept across Ben's face, then burst into a big smile. Reaching for her, he grasped her forearms and tugged her closer. "That, my love, is fine with me. In fact, it's perfect."

Leaning in, he took her lips in another slow and sultry kiss. Breaking away, he gave her a silly grin. "There's more where that came from...later." His eyebrows waggled.

Jenny punched his shoulder and grinned. "Oh, you!"

Abruptly, the humming sound in the bedroom stopped and a strange silence filled the space. Ben and Jenny froze and looked toward the hallway as Elaine stepped from the shadows and into the room.

"Mrs. Peterson?" Ben asked, stepping toward her. "Is everything all right?"

She shook her head. "No. Nothing is going to be right again, for the rest of my life."

Jenny rushed to Elaine and wrapped her arms around the older woman, who suddenly seemed a lot frailer than she had the night before. "Oh, Elaine. I'm so sorry. Come sit over here."

She helped her to the sofa where they sat, side by side.

"I let him go." Elaine leaned her head against Jenny's shoulder. "I finally let go, and he slipped away in the night, and I'm not sure what to do next."

"We'll help," Jenny told her, rubbing her shoulder.

"I mean with my life. How do I live without him?"

Jenny hugged her closer. "I don't know the answer to that. I suppose you have to take it one day at a time."

The older woman turned in Jenny's arms then and whispered. "Hold on to him with everything you have, Jenny, for as long as you can. You won't regret it. Not one second. I promise you."

Jenny saw the pain in Elaine Peterson's eyes. "I promise you I will."

Elaine sighed and leaned into Jenny. She patted her knee and whispered. "You're a good, good girl. I like you, Jenny Anders. I hope you marry the Matson boy." In the background, the lights flickered, and Ben said something about a truck coming up the driveway.

WITH THE HELP OF SOME NEIGHBORS DOWN THE ROAD, BEN DUG THE truck out in a couple of hours. While that happened, a few locals with plows on the front of their trucks worked to clear a path down the country road for traffic. He was amazed that the aftermath of the snow squall the night before was not worse. He supposed that he and Jenny had gotten into the thick of it, and things must have dissipated during the night.

Jenny stayed inside with Mrs. Peterson and waited for people to come and help with Harold. The phone at the house was still dead, but one neighbor helping Ben had service at home, so he called hospice, who then called the funeral home and other authorities.

Ben also asked him to call his parents and let them know they were okay, where they were, and that they would be back home soon.

A couple of hours later, they were ready to leave. Jenny felt terrible leaving Mrs. Peterson alone at the house and wanted her to come with them.

"No," Mrs. Peterson told them. "I'm not going anywhere today. The hospice nurse offered to stay for a while, but I told her no. I'm tired and I want to sleep. I need some quiet time to reflect and think. I will be fine. I have everything I need."

"Except for a phone," Ben reminded her.

"Except for that. And that could be a blessing." She grinned slightly and herded them toward the front of the house. "I expect once word gets out that people will stop by later today. Now, it's time for the two of you to take control of your own lives and get on with your plans." She stared first at Jenny, then Ben. "You do have plans. Right?"

Jenny smiled. "Yes. We have plans."

"Good. Then get to them. I'm going to take a nap."

Ben nodded and put his arm around Jenny. "Someone will be by to check on you later."

"Of course. Now, skedaddle."

"Yes, ma'am," Ben said.

"Don't ma'am me," Elaine told him. "Makes me feel like an old woman."

Ben laughed. Jenny hugged and kissed her goodbye.

THIRTY MINUTES LATER, THE COUPLE PULLED UP AT THE MATSON'S home. An additional vehicle parked in the driveway was the first thing Jenny noticed.

She gasped. "Ben. That's my parents' car."

He slowed the truck and braked. "What?"

"My parents. They are here."

Shoving the gearshift into park, Ben turned to her. "Jenny, look at me."

She did. "Why are they here?"

Ben exhaled. "I don't know. Take a breath. Let's think about this a second before going inside."

Jenny nodded. "Yes."

"Obviously, they are here because they care about you. Enough so, it looks like, to brave a snowstorm and make their way to a place they've never been, and to see people they barely know."

"That's true."

Ben stared harder into her eyes. "The bottom line here is, Jenny, that this changes nothing between you and me. Right?"

She glanced at her parents' car, and then back to Ben. "It changes everything."

He jerked back. "How so?"

"I'm going to fix it. I'm going to make it right. Right now. Today. It's something I should have done long ago, but I need to tell my parents exactly how I feel, that I love you, I hate school, and that I love them too and want to keep them in my life."

"And we are still getting married."

"You bet we are. Ben Matson, I'm holding on to you for the rest of my life. I hope you are ready for that."

He gathered her into his arms. "Sweetheart, I can't wait."

CHAPTER 12

*A*s Jenny walked up to the Matson's home, she wondered what kind of situation awaited her inside the house. Bracing herself for whatever onslaught her parents wanted to unleash, she also hoped her father would be a bit more reserved since he was out of his element, and in someone else's home.

"I can handle this," she said, stepping onto the porch.

"You got this, Jenny." Ben squeezed her hand. "Remember, I love you, and we are in this together."

With a deep breath and exhale—from them both—Ben pushed open the door.

"Jennifer! Thank God." Her father stood in the entry, taking a hesitant half-step forward. Her mother stood slightly to his right, wringing her hands. On the left were Ben's parents. The looks on their faces were of concern.

"Hi Dad. Mom." Tears stung the back of her eyelids. She didn't want to cry. It was the last thing she wanted to do right now, but she feared the tears might spill, anyway.

"Oh, honey…" Her dad rushed forward and swept her into his arms. "I'm so happy to see you."

His big bear hug felt like coming home. She'd not had one of those in a very long time. Holding back her tears was no longer possible.

"I'm sorry, Dad." She sniffled. "I never meant to upset you so, but it seemed it was the only way I could do what was right for me."

"No. I'm the one who is sorry." He pulled back and studied her. "I'm the one who caused all the friction and made it difficult for you and for Ben. It's my fault, not yours. I'm a stubborn old man. I've been on a royal tear for the past few years, mostly because I'm unhappy with myself, but I finally got set straight the night you left."

Puzzled, Jenny glanced from him to her mother. "How? What do you mean?"

He followed her gaze to his wife.

Her mother stepped forward. "Well, I had a few things to say after Ben left the house two nights ago, and we watched you both drive away. Things I should have said a long time ago but didn't. Watching you and Ben drive away and knowing he told you never to come back. Well. I told him I was leaving too. That finally got his attention."

"Mom? Seriously?"

She nodded. "Yes. And I'm sorry I didn't do it sooner. I should have stood up more for you and your feelings. I should have listened, but I didn't. So, your father and I are both at fault here."

She moved closer to Jenny, brushed her fingertips over her cheek, and stroked her hair. "We set out for Charmington yesterday morning and figured once we got here, we would find Ben's parents. We were right—small town indeed—all we had to do was pull up to the gazebo in town and ask the first person who came along. Within a few minutes, we had an address and a phone number. We called and told them we were on our way to meet them, and I must say they have been very accommodating with our last-minute arrival."

Maureen Matson stepped into the crowd. "And we've had a lovely visit, Jenny. I've enjoyed meeting your parents very much. You are a lucky girl."

A *lucky girl*. Elaine Peterson said the same thing.

She supposed she was. "I think I need a moment to process all of this."

"Take your time, honey," her father said. "None of us are going anywhere for a while."

That was certain. "So, you're not here to convince me to go back home?"

Her mother shook her head. "No. We came, hopefully, for your wedding."

"Our wedding? You want to come?"

"We all do," Maureen added, tossing a glance at Calvin, and hooking her hand in the crook of his elbow. "Right?"

He nodded. "We would love to be there. If you and Ben agree."

Ben? Turning, she caught his eye as he stood barely a foot away from her. Just like he'd said he would, he was right by her side. "We do, right?"

"Yes. Definitely." He grinned and put his arm around her.

Jenny's father interjected. "We thought we'd spend a little time in Charmington after the festivities. We hear it's a great little village, and we want to know more about where our daughter is going to live. Besides, we haven't been on a vacation in years, and it's high time."

Her mother edged forward. "But first, the wedding. Just to clarify, there is going to be a wedding, albeit a small one, isn't there?"

Jenny looked at Ben. He put his arm around her. "Yes, Mrs. Anders. There is going to be a wedding."

A few hoots and hollers went up from the parents.

"I'm Katherine, by the way," she said to Ben, then gave him a hug. "I should have done that long ago."

"And I'm Craig." He shot Ben an intense stare and put out his hand.

Ben gave him a slight stare back, then shook it. Jenny noticed the shake was firm, from both men.

She took another deep breath. "Dad, can we talk? You, me, and Mom?" She looked at Ben and reached for his hand. "And Ben, too."

Her father dropped his chin in a nod. "Of course. I'd like that."

Calvin Matson stepped forward. "My office is right down the hall if you want privacy." He pointed. "Jenny knows the way."

Dropping Ben's hand, Jenny gave her soon-to-be father-in-law a hug. "That would be perfect. Thank you."

Ben sidled up beside Jenny. "I have just one thing to say first, though." He glanced at his watch. "If there is going to be a Christmas wedding today, I need to check in with the judge and make sure she's available."

With a twinkle in her eye, Maureen said, "Oh, no worries there, son. She'll be here at six. That gives us roughly seven hours to get ready."

"Piece of cake," Katherine Anders stepped closer to Maureen. "Where's your phone? Let's get moving." She glanced at Jenny. "But after we talk, of course."

"What?" Ben's gaze darted between the two moms. "What have you done?"

Maureen smiled and kissed her son on the cheek. "What mothers do."

Jenny smiled and hugged her mom. Then to Ben, she said, "Let them do their thing. Besides, the train has left the station. It's out of our control."

❄

THE MOOD IN THE OFFICE A FEW MINUTES LATER WAS A LITTLE MORE somber. Jenny leaned against the desk and crossed her arms, hoping she had her parents' full attention. They stood opposite her, their gazes fixed on her.

"Dad, Mom, I'm not really sure where to start because I'm not sure how everything got so tangled up, but I'm glad we are talking."

"We are too, honey." Her mom grinned nervously and glanced at her dad.

Jenny hoped she was on the right track here. Things were finally smoothing over. She didn't want to upset her father again.

Her gaze darted back and forth between her parents. "I should have told you long ago, Dad. I tried many times, but I couldn't get all the words I wanted to say out of my mouth. I don't want to be a lawyer. I have never wanted to be a lawyer. I didn't want to disappoint you, so I sort of went with it."

"We knew that, sweetheart," her mother said. "Deep down. We were just avoiding it, I think. And we will admit we had unfair expectations. Candy was so easy. She knew what she wanted in life. There were times we just didn't know about you."

That was true of her sister. Her ambitions were well known since she was in elementary school. While she was laser-focused on her law degree, Jenny floundered from this to that, entertaining all sorts of ideas about what her future might look like.

"Speaking of Candy… Is she here?"

Katherine shook her head. "No. She has an interview tomorrow, so she is home preparing."

"Oh, that makes sense. I figured she might mourn the fact that I was getting married first."

"Well, that too," Katherine said. "You know your sister."

"That I do." Jenny noticed her dad was pacing a little. "Dad, what do we need to clear up about school? Are you okay with me not going to law school, so I can explore an art career?"

"Frankly, I know nothing about this art business. How do you make money painting pictures? You need to get me up to speed."

Jenny laughed. "Most artists I know are called starving artists for a reason. It's hard to make a living by making art—that's why I want the business minor. But with me, it's not all about making a living. I need to paint. To create stuff. It's who I am. And I want to learn more and more about it and live a creative life—degree or no degree."

Her dad nodded, then looked at Ben. "And since you are going to be a married couple, are you okay with this?"

Ben smiled. "Why not? I'm more than okay, Mr. Anders, um, Craig. I understand what's in Jenny's heart and soul. I make a decent living at the hardware store. One day, it will be mine. Right now, I live in the apartment above it, rent-free. Jenny and I will stay there while we save to buy a house. There is a room at the back that is perfect for a studio. That space is Jenny's, to do with as she pleases."

Her father contemplated Ben's words, then turned to her. "Your mother and I have talked, Jenny, and we will foot the bill for art school, if that is what you want."

Jenny's gaze bounced from her father to her mother. "I may take you up on that, but I need a little time to figure things out. I'll likely do community college or online courses for now. I need to check what is available in this area. Then down the road, we can discuss more." Hesitantly, she moved forward and hugged her father. "Thank you."

Her mother tapped her fingertips on the desktop. "You know, I have things to do. Have we wrapped this up yet? We have a wedding to plan and virtually no time to do it." She turned toward the door.

"Wait. There is one more thing I want to say before we leave here, just for the record. I want to make sure that you both, Dad and Mom, have no qualms about Ben and me getting married. We are getting married, regardless, but I also want to make sure you understand I want you both in our lives, too. I love you, and it's unfair to make me choose between my family and Ben and his family. Are we good there?"

Her dad smiled. "Are you sure you don't want to be a lawyer? That was a pretty convincing speech."

Jenny hugged him. "I learned from the best."

Her father's expression grew serious. "Jennifer, I have a lot of work to do on myself. I realize I was a domineering old man—I was turning into my father, a man I always said I didn't want to be like. I didn't realize how much until I got so angry with Ben the other evening. I'm working on it. Okay? In the meantime, the answer to your question is yes. We are good here. Whatever you want, I want."

Jenny's eyes teared up. "I love you, Dad. One more question."

"Yes?"

"Will you give me away tonight?"

This time, Craig Anders didn't hold back his emotions, choking back tears. "As long as I'm not giving you away forever."

Jenny let go of a long-held sigh. Leaning up on tiptoes, she gave her dad a kiss. "You're not getting rid of me that easily."

Her mother sighed. "Are we finished here, you two? Wedding? Time is short."

Laughing, her father glanced at Ben. "Can you stick around? Let's let the womenfolk do their thing. I think we need a chat, just you and me."

"I look forward to it," Ben said.

JENNY PEEKED AROUND MAUREEN TO LOOK AT THE CLOCK ON THE dresser in her bedroom. In an hour she would be married. "Are you sure Ben is okay? I've not seen him since this morning in Calvin's office."

"He's fine, Jenny. I promise," Maureen said. "Besides, the groom is not supposed to see the bride the day of the wedding, and we've already tempted fate in that regard earlier in the day."

"Well, that was unavoidable." Jenny looked at herself in the mirror, turning this way, and the other. Curling iron in hand, Maureen curled her hair into long tendrils. "That looks pretty, Maureen. Thank you."

"I was thinking maybe we could try pinning some of these pieces up once I get all the curls."

"Oh, I like that idea too. You're good at this."

"I used to work in a salon years ago. You should have seen me during prom week! This curling iron was stuck to my hand like a third appendage. I'm rusty though."

"Well, I like it!"

Her future mother-in-law bent down to look in the mirror too, their faces side-by-side. "You're going to make a beautiful bride. I'm so happy for you and Ben."

Jenny returned a smile in the mirror. "I'm happy for all of us."

Katherine swept in from the hallway. "Well, I made all the calls on the list you gave me, Maureen. You're right. The people in this town are so friendly and giving. Not one person refused to help us out, even on Christmas day. Do you think that would happen in Philadelphia? No. The only thing I had to promise to anyone was a piece of cake to the florist. I can't believe they still had poinsettias."

"What about the bakery?"

Katherine checked something off of her list. "All done. Leslie's Bakery was happy to whip up something. She said it would not be her usual wedding cake fare—because those take a couple of days to create—but she said she could wing a small cake with already baked layers she had on hand."

"Great."

"And the photographer?"

"Out of town. However, when I talked with the florist about the flowers, she told me about a woman who is just getting her business started. So, I called her, but she has little kids and well, Christmas, but she told me to call a man named Rand Carpenter, who lives in another town, I think, but close. Thankfully, he said he could do it and will be here at five-thirty."

"Well, thank goodness. You really had your work cut out for you. I think that's everything."

Jenny cleared her throat. "Maybe not everything."

The women stared. "What? We have forgotten nothing. I'm sure of it."

Jenny looked down at herself. She stood before them in jeans, an oversized navy-blue V-neck sweater, and her Eastlands. "I don't have a dress. Ben and I hadn't planned on anything fancy, just a quickie wedding at the judge's house. I didn't pack a dress in my backpack."

Looking up, she caught her mother's eye, and saw the mist in them. "No worries, honey," she said softly. "I have you covered."

Katherine left the room and Jenny and Maureen exchanged glances. Soon, she returned with a garment bag. Katherine positioned the bag on the bed and unzipped. With a flick of her wrist, she pulled out a cream-colored, sleek and chic wedding dress. No sequins, no ruffles or bows, no lace, no pearls—just a classy, off-the-shoulder wedding dress that looked perfect to Jenny.

"This is your dress, Mom."

She nodded. "It's yours now. Try it on?"

"Seriously? I've wanted to try on this dress since I was a little girl, and you never would let me." Stripping down to her underwear, and with the help of the women, Jenny slipped into the gown. Perfect.

"Well, I wanted to wait for this moment, sweetheart. Oh, my. You are stunning."

Jenny spun slowly in front of the mirror. The women admired her.

"It fits her perfectly."

"It's beautiful."

"Do we need to tuck anything anywhere?"

"No. It's a picture-perfect fit. What do you think, Jenny?"

"I think…" She stood still and looked at herself in the mirror. "I think I'm getting married today."

"That you are."

Katherine took her daughter in her arms and then hugged her tight. Maureen was right behind her. Jenny was pretty sure both women were crying.

The knock came at the door.

"Yes?" Maureen called out.

Calvin answered back. "Grace is here, honey."

Katherine glanced at her watch. "That's the judge," she said to Katherine. "Already? Where has the time gone?"

Jenny escaped the clutches of the two moms and smoothed her dress down while she took one long and heartfelt look in the mirror. This was her wedding day. She was marrying Ben.

Exhaling long, she let the moment wash over her. "You two go ahead of me. I want a minute, and then send Daddy up."

Katherine and Maureen left on a flitter.

"I *am* going to marry that boy today," she whispered, stepping away from the mirror.

CHAPTER 13

*W*hen Jenny stepped down the staircase on her father's arm, joining the family in the living room, Ben thought his heart would literally jump out of his chest. Jenny —his Jenny—was a beautiful bride. Stunning. And wearing a sophisticated wedding dress he'd no idea she even possessed.

Suddenly, he was glad his father had insisted he wear his suit.

Smiling shyly as she turned the corner, she slowly approached him. When she stood by his side and faced the judge with him, he had to remind himself not to lock his knees so he wouldn't get lightheaded and pass out right there in front of everyone.

But his knees were shaking anyway, and so were his hands.

Jenny reached to her right and tangled her fingers with his left hand, casually. He calmed somewhat.

Leaning to his left, he whispered, "You are so beautiful. I love you, Jenny Anders."

She met his gaze back and smiled. "I love you too. Always."

The wedding was small, and that was exactly the way they had planned it, although a little larger than the elopement they thought they were going to get. Jenny's parents stood to her left. His parents stood on his right. Charlotte and her crew sat on the sofa behind them all.

Suddenly, the front door swung open, and a cold whiff of air ruffled throughout the room. Everyone turned to watch Jenny's sister, Candy, stumble in the door.

She blew out a breath. "Whew. Looks like I made it in the nick of time." She approached Jenny, gave her a hug and a smile, then settled into a chair close to her parents.

The judge cleared her throat. She said some words. Ben heard them but didn't comprehend a single one of them. He grasped Jenny's hand tighter with his sweaty left hand.

"Who gives this woman today?"

Craig stepped forward. "Her mother and I, your honor."

The judge looked at Jenny's dad and grinned. "Thank you, but we're not in the courtroom, Mr. Anders."

A giggle or two went up in the room, and Ben relaxed a little. He looked at Jenny, who was also smiling.

The judge grinned and continued. The ceremony was short and sweet.

They exchanged rings.

Both Jenny and Ben said their vows.

"I promise to always hold on to you, Ben Matson, and never let you go. I will love you until our days are through."

"And I promise you, Jenny Anders, that I will love and take care of you, cherish you, and be thankful for you, all the days of my life."

There was a brief pause, and Ben took advantage of the silence and the moment to stare into Jenny's eyes. Six months ago, he could never have guessed this day would happen. His mind drifted back to that day on the beach when he first spotted her.

Her with her big, bronze eyes staring back at him.

Him being drawn to her like nothing he'd ever before experienced, just wanting to know more about her.

"I've loved you from the first moment I saw you," he whispered.

She smiled through misty tears. "That day we met, I went back to the beach house, and told myself that I might just marry you one day. And now, well...."

Ben's chest swelled. He was so happy. So full of love for her. And so ready for the rest of their lives together.

The judge cleared her throat again. "By the power given to me by the state of New York, I now pronounce you man and wife. Ben Matson, kiss your bride before you spontaneously combust or keel over into a quivery puddle of gelatin on the living room floor."

Jenny laughed and threw her arms around his neck. Tears and cheers sounded in the room. Ben gathered her close, leaned in, and took her lips in their first kiss as a married couple. And he enjoyed every...last...second...of it.

Once more, the front door swung open wide, a gust of wind played peek-a-boo in the room, and everyone turned that way. Elaine Peterson slowly ambled inside on the arm of one of Charmington's local police officers, smiling. "Well, looks like I nearly missed it."

Both Jenny and Ben rushed forward.

"Mrs. Peterson. What in the world are you doing here?" Ben asked. "We didn't expect you. It's been such a long day for you."

She grasped his forearm to steady herself, then glanced at the officer. "I'm fine now, Joel. Come back in thirty minutes, if you will."

He nodded at her, then tipped his hat to the rest of the room and left.

Mrs. Peterson scanned the crowd. "He's my neighbor. Hey, it's not every day you can catch a ride with a hunky policeman, right?"

More laughter skittered through the room.

Jenny hugged the older woman. "I'm so glad you are here, but you surely didn't have to come. How are you holding up?" She led her to a chair. "Why don't you sit?"

Mrs. Peterson waved her off. "I'm fine. I had a long nap. It's been both a sad day, and a happy day. But I couldn't let it go by before seeing the two of you were married. You've been on my mind all afternoon."

"I've been thinking of you too, Elaine," Jenny told her.

The older woman smiled and patted her hand. "Before I forget about it, I have something for the two of you." She pulled a manila envelope out of the purse hanging on her arm. "Ben, you're a good man. And Jenny, I just met you, but you are perfect for Ben. I know you will have a long and beautiful life together. Open this later, after I'm gone. I just wanted you to have it today. And let me see those rings, you two."

Ben took the envelope. They showed her their left hands.

Elaine Peterson smiled. "All right. Then this is a good day—a wonderful day—after all."

MUCH LATER, AFTER MRS. PETERSON HAD LEFT, THE CAKE WAS devoured, champagne flowed, and the family wedding pictures taken, Ben and Jenny changed into travel clothes and grabbed their luggage so they could get to the mountains for their honeymoon—a day late.

As they embraced family and gave kisses at the front door, Jenny spied the manila envelope sitting on the table by the door. She gasped Ben's arm.

"Ben? We forgot about the envelope from Elaine."

"Oh, that's right." He stepped to the table and retrieved it. "Should we see what's in it?"

Jenny nodded. "Yes. Let's do."

The family gathered around while Ben opened the envelope. He pulled out several pieces of paper, shuffled through them, then lifted his gaze to look at Jenny. "There's a letter and some legal papers."

Puzzled, Jenny stepped closer. "What?"

Ben began reading the brief letter….

Dear Ben and Jenny,

Thank you for being with me last night when Harold left me, and for all you and Jenny did to help me through the night. The most important thing you both did was remind me how much in love Harold and I were when we were kids—I saw it in the two of you. Last night, I needed that.

Now, I'm an old woman, and I'm not going to be around much longer. As you know, Harold and I had no children. Holly Hill Farm was in Harold's family for a couple of generations, but there is no more family on his side to pass this beautiful farm on to.

So, I am giving it to you. Upon my death, Holly Hill Farm belongs to the two of you. I've managed to get paperwork signed and taken care of today. Yes, even on Christmas Day. It's my wedding gift to you on this very special Christmas. We may need to meet with the attorneys again next week, but this is my intent.

Enjoy the home, the land, and please, please have children and raise them there. It's something I was never able to do. I want to know that one day, children's voices will ring again in the halls of that big house.

Hold on to each other, Ben and Jenny. Hold on until you can't. Only then, do you let go.

I am forever grateful to you both.

Elaine Peterson

EIGHTEEN MONTHS LATER...

"*I* can't believe you would even consider opening the inn while you're in this condition, Jenny." Katherine Anders sat on her knees planting geraniums along the sidewalk leading up to the porch at her daughter's new business venture, Holly Hill Inn.

"Mom, it's just a test weekend. We only have two guests. I'm fine." Jenny pushed soil around her last flower and stood up, brushing the dirt off her hands. "Besides, I'm not due yet for another two months. I've timed things perfectly." Her back did ache, though, but that probably had very little to do with her pregnancy. She'd been working long days lately.

Maureen burst out of the house and onto the porch, the screen door slapping hard behind her as it closed. She glanced back. "That is something you need to get fixed. I'll put that on the list for Ben."

Luckily, she had plenty of help today. Wanted or not!

"Ben already knows, Maureen. He's bringing home new hinges today from the hardware store ."

"Oh, good. I'll check that off." Maureen scurried down the steps and to her car. "I'll pick up the groceries on your list I found in the kitchen while I'm heading into town to pick up scones from Leslie's Bakery."

"But I wanted to do the grocery shopping...." Her words trailed off as Maureen waved, got in the car, and sped off.

Katherine stood. "Let her. She's almost as OCD as I am about getting things done and list making."

"I've learned that over the past eighteen months, for sure."

They turned as another vehicle made its way up the drive and parked.

Jenny smiled as her husband exited his red pickup truck and headed her way.

"I remembered the hinges," he said, holding them up.

"That's good. Your mother was about to call a repairman."

He rolled his eyes.

Katherine headed for the house. "I'm going to go check on some things in the nursery. I'm sure the baby doesn't have everything he or she needs yet. I wish I knew if this was a boy or a girl...."

She scampered off, probably to make another list, the screen door slapping hard again behind her.

Ben winced. "Did you survive the day?"

"With both your mother and mine? Barely." She laughed.

"I'm so glad to be home." His arms snaked around her waist.

Jenny wrapped hers around his neck. "I'm doubly glad you are here, Mr. Matson."

He grinned, planted a lingering kiss on Jenny's lips, and then looked at the house. "The place is beautiful."

"Thanks to Elaine and the extra funds she left to us, we've really spruced the place up."

"It's perfect. When do the guests arrive?"

"Friday evening. I can't wait. I've been testing breakfast recipes today. I know it's five o'clock in the afternoon, but want to sample?"

"Show me the way!"

Jenny took Ben's hand and led him up the porch. On the way in, she gave the sign hanging by the door a tap with her forefingers and smiled. It was her way of saying thank you to Elaine and Harold for their generous wedding gift—a home for Christmas.

CHAPTER 14

MIRACLE AT HOLLY HILL INN

ecember 22

EVEN THE TREES SPARKLE.

Ariana Estrella pushed open her car door and stepped out onto the snow-covered pavement. In awe, she scanned her surroundings to take in the quaint Main Street lined with Victorian shopfronts—each one decorated to storybook perfection with greenery and red bows, a hefty portion of tinsel and holly, and of course, snow.

The snow was real. None of that fake stuff like back home.

Closing the car door, she moved toward the sidewalk, twirling once, maybe twice, still perusing the most precious Christmas village scene she'd ever before encountered—and that was saying a lot. Christmas was her business, her world—and this town just might be Christmas perfection. She was so glad she'd come.

Stifling the urge to lift her face to the sky and catch a drifting fluffy snowflake on her tongue, she sighed with happiness, eager to explore.

Down the street sat the gazebo. She recognized it from pictures she'd seen of the town. It, too, was draped in greenery and ribbons, looking somewhat like a confection sitting atop some sort of pretty Christmas cake—at least one she might bake. It appeared the gazebo was situated within the town square. Beside it was a statue sporting a red scarf billowing in the brisk breeze. Stepping onto the snow-swept sidewalk, she kept an eye on the structure and wandered a few steps in that direction.

There.

Off to the side of the gazebo stood the town square Christmas tree, proudly displaying gold and silver baubles, ornaments of all colors, and more ribbons—all peeking through fresh snow. The annual Charmington Christmas Jubilee tree lighting ceremony happened earlier in the month, and she was sorry she'd missed it—but there was no denying the tree's magnificence.

And, oh? Is that a carousel?

Her insides twittered with glee, bubbling up so rapidly she could barely contain it. She might have let out a quick little giggle.

Pausing her stroll, she spied a colorful sign hanging in the shop window to her right. Her eye traveled over the shopfront—Leslie's Bakes & More—and her tummy rumbled. Another cup of coffee soon, and perhaps a pastry, would be nice.

Her gaze landed on the red and green sign. *Holiday Lighting Event at Holly Hill Inn, Thursday Evening, December 23rd.* With a quick look at the calendar on her digital watch, she smiled. Yes. Today was Wednesday, so the lighting event at the inn was tomorrow—on the eve of Christmas Eve, or Christmas Eve Eve, as she liked to say. Why not stretch out the holiday as long as possible?

That was her attitude, anyway.

Smiling, and immensely happy she'd braved the snowstorm—

even against her family's warnings—she felt silly with holiday cheer. The weather had been dicey the day before, delaying her trip into historic Charmington. While she didn't mind getting stuck an extra night at the small New England B&B she'd booked about in Vermont, she was glad the storm had let up enough so she could get to Charmington.

And *bonus!* Because of a cancelation and a matter of happenstance, she had secured a reservation for three nights at the popular Holly Hill Inn, although she was in no hurry to get there. Too much to explore first in the village. Besides, she couldn't check in until late afternoon—so she had most of the daylight hours left to discover the magic of Charmington at Christmastime.

Charmington just might be the small-town Christmas village of her dreams. She couldn't wait to get pictures and write about it. Her blog readers were going to be so excited.

Reaching into her bag, she pulled out her camera, adjusted the lens, and began walking. As if by magic, the town suddenly teemed with shoppers, milling in and out of the shops, chatting on the sidewalks, and calling out holiday greetings.

Shopping for last-minute gifts before this storm hits again.

Ariana smiled, dizzy with Christmas excitement and filled with the holiday spirit. She snapped pictures, chatted with the townsfolk, and gleefully made her way up Main Street, around the square, and down the other side.

Her heart was happy.

It was Christmas and she was finally in Charmington.

Nothing could spoil her mood. Absolutely nothing.

MATT MATSON PULLED THE BOTTOM OF HIS SWEATER SLEEVE OVER the heel of his palm and rubbed out the smudges his breath made on the old windowpane. Peering out into the street—perusing the local shoppers and visiting tourists—he sighed. His breath, once again, fogged the glass, so he took one more swipe at it and then turned away.

How many more days until Christmas was over? Too many.

Heading back to his cubby-hole refuge behind the old wooden countertop desk, tucked into the back of the hardware store, he traveled the center aisle between time-worn, nearly ceiling-high, wooden shelves which housed everything from plumbing and electrical supplies to household cleaners and associated paraphernalia, some small appliances like electric can openers and hand-held mixers, and tools. Lots of tools.

And where there were tools, there were also items that went along with tools—like fence wire, and tape measures, and replacement doorknobs, and cabinet pulls, and such.

Instead of shelves in those areas, there were small wooden drawers—carefully catalogued by his Great Uncle Herb years ago—where one could select nails or screws or bolts or washers, or an assortment of those and other items that a carpenter, or perhaps a crafty person might need.

Yes. The Charmington Main Street Hardware held all that and more. His family had always strived to provide the town with what they needed, so variety was the mainstay.

What one wouldn't find at Main Street Hardware, however—a store that had been in his family for over a hundred years—was anything to do with Christmas. No tinsel. No trees. No ornaments, holly, wrapping paper, wreaths, or mistletoe.

Ever.

Well, that wasn't entirely true. His parents had stocked quite a bit of holiday cheer and such in the past. They loved the holiday. But Matt? No. He'd done away with all that years ago.

Christmas was not his thing. It was not his busy season. People weren't shopping for hammers or toilet plungers in December. They were out for holly and wreaths. And truth be known, he'd probably be better off next year to close the store the entire month of December and go someplace warm for a while—someplace where the entire town didn't revel in the idea of the holiday or focus eleven months of the year getting ready for it.

Yes. That is a good idea. Some place warm.

Matt settled himself on the stool behind the counter, crossed his arms over his chest, and peered out over the store. At some point soon, he should think about walking down the street to grab some lunch—but did he really want to brave the crowd?

Maybe he'd just close the store early and go home. He could always open a can of soup. "Merry Christmas to me."

ARIANA IMPATIENTLY PEEKED AROUND THE LINE IN FRONT OF HER AT Leslie's Bakes & More, trying to get a glimpse at the counter to see what cookies were hiding in front of a gentleman standing there waiting for his sandwich. She tapped her foot, inspecting the quaint interior of the business. Patience was not her strong suit, so waiting in line for anything was always a challenge. In the meantime, she'd simply busy herself by perusing the Christmas decorations and the people, the confections and pastries, and the deli menu in the small bakery-slash-sandwich shop.

Which was not a bad idea, she surmised, to combine the two types of establishments. The bakery could cater to the breakfast crowd with pastries and coffee earlier in the day, then later, sandwiches and cookies for the lunch crowd. And pie.

Oh, there was pie. She stretched her neck and took a tiny step to her right to ogle the pie case around the corner from the counter.

Leaning more to her right, she watched the gentleman hiding the cookies step away—*were those Snickerdoodles?*—and the line moved forward.

She took a half-step to the right, then another—but someone darted in front of her, taking her spot in line.

Standing there for a moment, a little befuddled to be perfectly honest, she made the best of it.

"Excuse me." She tapped the man's shoulder. "I'm sure you didn't realize you cut in front of me. I've been standing here for a while. But if you are in a hurry, I'm happy to let you go first. Besides, it's Christmas." She smiled.

He turned and looked at her, mumbled something under his breath, and didn't smile back. "You weren't in line."

"Oh, but I was. Am." Her feet planted, she peered back, not about to move.

He stared back at her with his knit cap pulled down low over his forehead, a shock of brown hair poking out, and his arms crossed tightly over his coat at his chest. "I, also, have been standing in line. You, it appeared, had stepped away and were gawking."

Gawking? "I beg your pardon?"

"Gawking," he replied. "You know, gallerwaggling about. Listlessly wandering. You didn't appear to be standing in line. I thought you were, basically, aimlessly perusing."

Ariana squinted, quickly studying the man. He wasn't an old man. He was, perhaps, a couple of years older than her—but his grumpiness gave off an illusion of being much older—and crotchety. Such a shame. He had pleasant features—high cheekbones, a firm chin, and a scruffy five o'clock shadow that was maybe two days overdue.

She stood a little straighter and set her shoulders. *Forget about the sexy five o'clock shadow, Ariana.* "For the record, I do not gallerwag. Nor do I listlessly wander or aimlessly peruse. I'll have you know that should I ever peruse or wander, I do so with intent. And as to gallerwag? You made that up. It's not a word. Perhaps you meant lollygag."

"No. I meant what I said. Look it up." He turned into the line, showing her his back.

Not to be dismissed, Ariana poked him on the shoulder again with her forefinger. "I actually don't carry a dictionary with me. Besides, words are my business and that is not one."

He shrugged. "Got your phone? Google it." He gave her a backward glance.

"I most certainly will." Reaching for her purse and her phone, she paused, then looked at the back of his head. "Later. You are intentionally distracting me."

He half-turned. "You were already distracted."

Sidling up next to him, she made eye contact. Just for the record, she noted to herself, they were deep brown and...well, right now, they were sort of probing hers. "I'll have you know I was not distracted. I'm an observer. A writer. I examine things. You came from nowhere and simply cut in line in front of me."

"Not exactly correct." He took a step forward with the moving line. "I've been standing behind you for a few minutes. You stepped out of line, so...."

"I most certainly did not step out of line." She countered his step and took another one ahead of him.

"Are you cutting in front of me?"

"Just reclaiming my place."

"Oh, no. I'm next."

In exasperation, Ariana clenched her fists and glared at him. "My God. What a Scrooge." She thought she heard someone off to the side snicker. Glancing that way, she realized they'd become the center of attention.

Great.

He made direct eye contact again with her, leaned in a bit, and then said loudly and clearly, "Bah. Humbug."

"Next." The young man behind the counter called out.

Swiftly turning, Ariana blurted, "Medium black coffee and

three of those cookies." She pointed to the Snickerdoodles.

"The usual, Tom," the man said simultaneously.

Tom eyed them both.

Ariana refused to look at the man standing next to her. *The usual?* A local. Suddenly, her impression of the town was slightly soured, but she would not let that sway her.

"Coming right up," Tom said. He turned to the man. "Matt, please try not to run off the paying customers."

"Far be it from me…" the man called Matt said.

She stared at him. He looked down at her.

Ariana broke eye contact and looked ahead, waiting for her coffee and cookies. After several long seconds of drumming her fingertips on the counter, she sighed when he set a cup of coffee and a white bag of cookies in front of her.

"Four dollars and ninety-eight cents, ma'am."

She opened her wallet.

"Put it on mine, Tom," the man next to her said.

Immediately, she protested. "Oh, no. I'll get it. But thank you."

"My pleasure." He nodded to Tom.

"I mean, I'll take care of my bill."

He peered down. "Welcome to Charmington. I hope you enjoyed your stay. Be careful on your way out of town."

Ariana gathered her coffee and cookies, then looked back up at the guy. "Well, thank you, but I'm not leaving. In fact, I just got here and am planning to stay for a few days. I appreciate the warm welcome." The saccharin sweet smile she tossed him almost made her nauseous. But no matter, she decided right then and there, she would not let this single, unhappy incident spoil her mood—or her impression of Charmington.

"Merry Christmas," she said, turning to leave.

He grunted something.

Ariana paused, her gaze straight ahead, then headed out of the shop.

CHAPTER 15

*A*s she stepped out onto the sidewalk, Ariana abruptly stopped. Townspeople and tourists scurried off to their vehicles or into buildings, obviously sent scattering by the blustery gust of wind zipping down Main Street. Snow swirled furiously and fell at a rapidly increasing pace. Firmly grasping her bag of cookies and her coffee, pulling them closer to her chest, Ariana put her head down against the snow and wind and headed to her car parked a few spaces away.

With a click of her key fob, her rental car door unlocked. She slipped inside, and the door shut tight.

"Whew. That came up quick."

She sat for a moment, placed the coffee in the cupholder, and removed her gloves. The smell of cinnamon and sugar tickled her nose as she opened the white bag. *Ah, a little bit of heaven....*

Her shoulders relaxed as she reached for a cookie. About to take a bite, she looked out her windshield—which was quickly piling up with heavy, cold wet stuff—and watched the gentleman from inside the coffee shop eyeball her sitting in her car as he passed. She made eye contact, just as she was popping a

Snickerdoodle into her mouth, and he glanced away. Following him, she watched as he scurried along, his head down, while passing five shops and then turning left, and finally entering a store on the corner. Her gaze traveled up to read the sign over the shop: *Main Street Hardware*.

"Bah humbug to you," she said aloud, and rolled her eyes.

But her gaze stayed on the shop, and she examined it for a moment. Something was...different from the other shops. Odd that she hadn't even noticed before, but the shop practically disappeared into the scene and didn't stand out at all.

Oh. She glanced up and down the street. "Well, that's ridiculous. It's the only shop not decorated for Christmas."

Bah Humbug. The man's words echoed in her brain.

"I believe we have a modern-day Scrooge on our hands here." She pondered that for a moment, watching the shop front—then shrugging, she popped the last bite of cookie in her mouth. "And none of my business."

Pushing the unwelcome experience aside, she grappled in her bag for her phone. After tapping in the Holly Hill Inn address on her GPS map app, she backed the car out and followed the directions. She was still a little early to check in, but with the snow kicking up, it was probably best she got there soon. The inn was located a few miles out of town. Hopefully, the owner wouldn't mind if she waited inside.

It took all of twenty-one minutes to find the inn.

Tucked back off the road at the end of Holly Hill Lane, the inn finally came into view. Ariana could barely see it through the snow squall until she got closer—a splash of red popped through the blowing white, guiding her like a beacon. She maneuvered the circular drive and parked, eyeing the old inn with delight. What she could see of the home sent the giddy in her tummy soaring right up to her heart—red painted clapboards with white trim and a picket fence bordering the front of the property, all dripped with greenery, red bows, and twinkling white lights. There were candles in the windows on the porch. A brick walk—which appeared recently swept but drifting over again—framed the entrance along with a wide lattice-work arch. The brick rambled through a garden area, one that was likely enchanting in the spring, lead to the front portico of the old home.

And there were holly bushes, right and left, lining the brick sidewalk.

Ariana reluctantly left her car, cookies tucked into her purse, coffee in hand, and camera bag over her shoulder. With her head lowered against the blowing snow, she made her way to the trunk of her car and retrieved her rolling bag. It took a few minutes to lug it all up to the porch—the wheels on the luggage kept icing up —finally, she just carried it the rest of the way. Out of the snow and standing in front of a beautiful wooden front door, she shook herself and stomped her feet to remove as much snow as possible, brushed snow and hair out of her face, and headed for the doorbell.

A woman opened the door before she got there, drawing her sweater about her, and stepping out onto the porch. "Ariana Estrella?"

"Yes. I'm early. I hope you don't mind."

"Oh no." Smiling warmly, the woman reached for Ariana's luggage. "It's not a problem. Please, come in."

They shuffled inside. The innkeeper led the way and Ariana followed. She noticed the woman tap the Holly Hill Inn sign to the right of the door as she entered and wondered what that was all about.

"Let me take your coffee," she said, turning back to Ariana. She grasped the paper cup and set it aside. "There's more coffee in the kitchen, or hot cocoa if you like. But let's get you out of these wet things first."

Nodding, Ariana set her purse on a nearby bench. "Anything

hot would be lovely. Thank you."

"Of course." The woman smiled. "You can leave your boots here." She pointed to a large welcome mat by the door, where a few pairs of shoes and boots lined the entry. Then she helped Ariana out of her coat, hanging in on a hall tree by the door. "I'll roll your bag over to the desk and meet you there."

Kicking out of her boots, Ariana placed them on the mat, then turned to peruse the entryway to the inn.

She sighed. *I'm finally here.*

Christmas. Everywhere, there was Christmas. Holly, tinsel, twinkling lights, ornaments, and more lit up the festive entryway. And the spicy aroma wafting down the hallway smelled heavenly. Christmas cookies? Fruitcake? Her heart danced.

A lovely fir tree stood in the corner, decorated with what looked to be handmade decorations. Ariana drifted to it and as she touched and explored the ornaments, felt a strong sense of family. "These are beautiful," she whispered.

"Yes. Three generations of ornaments, all decorated by children," the woman said, and then stepped around the counter closer to Ariana. She put out her hand. "Hi. I'm Kat Hamilton, by the way, owner of Holly Hill Inn. We spoke on the phone. I should have said that earlier."

Ariana shook her hand and smiled. "I assumed. I'm thrilled to meet you. This tree is simply stunning. Do you mind if I take pictures?"

Kat shook her head. "Not at all. If I remember correctly, you're a writer—a blogger—and a photographer. Right?"

"Yes. Blogging mostly, but I'm trying to get into magazine work, too. For the writing, that is. My photography skills are fine for blogging but not for a slick magazine. Christmas is my niche." She glanced back at the tree. "And, I should say I'll need your written permission for photographs. I have a sample release we can look at later if that's okay with you."

"Sure." Kat grinned. "I figure it's all advertising, right? I've no problem with pictures."

Ariana thought about getting her camera out and taking a picture of the tree and ornaments right then but thought better of it. She had plenty of time. She fingered a tree decoration—a wooden cut-out of a nutcracker soldier—rather imperfectly painted.

"My brother painted that one," Kat said. "I think he was ten."

"I love that it's sort of messy. Sort of primitive."

"It lends a bit of charm, doesn't it?"

Ariana noticed Kat staring at the ornament. She shook herself and looked away. "Let's get you checked in. Your room is ready. I hoped you would get here early. I think we're in for a pretty significant snowfall tonight."

"Oh? More?"

"Oh, yes."

"This last gust came up fast."

Kat looked up. "Well, according to the weather people, it may stall over us. Who knows how much snow we will get? The storm pushed through quickly from the west, but some sort of pressure out over the coast might hold it here in the valley for a while. I guess we'll get what we'll get." She studied her. "How do you feel about being snowbound?"

"Seriously?"

Shrugging, Kat went back to writing something on a card. "Who knows?"

A smile bubbled up inside her and burst across her lips—she could feel it—and Ariana had to contain her giggle. "You know, Kat? I almost can't think of anything else I would love more than to be snowbound at Christmas in a lovely place like this."

Kat glanced up, reached for Ariana's hand, and beamed. "What a sweet thing to say. And refreshing. Usually when people get stranded here, they are cranky."

Laughing, Ariana returned, "I assure you I will not be cranky."

"You're a woman after my heart."

"I love Christmas."

Just then, the front door burst open, and Ariana turned toward the commotion.

"Mommy!" A little girl shouted while tumbling inside, slamming the door, dropping a backpack with a thud, and shrugging out of her coat—which landed in a heap in front of the door—while also kicking out of her boots. "We got out of Christmas Camp early. The bus brought me. The big snow is coming!"

She rushed forward while Kat rounded the desk. "Aimee Hamilton." She halted the child with a look and crossed arms. "Where are your manners? Please say hello to Miss Estrella, our guest."

The little girl halted, sighed, and looked at Ariana. "Hello. Sorry. I'm Aimee." She stuck out her hand, much like her mother had done earlier.

Ariana crouched and took the child's small hand in hers and shook it. "I'm Ariana. Nice to meet you. How old are you?"

"I'm six." The little girl beamed, obviously proud of herself.

Smiling, Ariana said, "I thought as much. I have a six-year-old niece. Wow, your hands are like ice!" She rubbed the girl's hands between her own.

Aimee looked up at her mother. "Lost them again."

Kat rolled her eyes. "I'll find you another pair of mittens. Now, go back and hang up that coat, put your boots on the mat, and take your backpack up to your room. The Camp called, so I knew you were coming. Cookie ingredients are waiting in the kitchen, and we have work to do. Now, go on, and don't forget to wash those hands."

Aimee grinned, displaying two missing front teeth. "Awesome. I love baking cookies. Will you bake with us, Miss Estrella?"

Taken aback a little, Ariana glanced at Kat. "Well, I... I don't want to impose. This sounds like a mother-daughter moment."

Kat laughed. "Oh please. I get a lot of those around here. We could use your help if you want to bake. I always appreciate another set of hands. But only if you want to."

"Please?" Aimee jumped up and down, grinning.

With a tip of her chin, Ariana said, "Only if you call me Ariana."

Aimee stuck out her hand again. "Deal!"

"Deal." Ariana hesitated no longer and shook Aimee's hand. "I'd love to."

Kat's fists settled on her hips. "Well then. Let's get you both upstairs. We will meet in the kitchen in fifteen minutes. All right, ladies?"

"All right, Mommy." Aimee bounded toward the stairwell.

Ariana retrieved her purse from the bench.

Kat turned back to the desk. "I just need your signature on this card, Ariana, and then I'll grab your key and we will get you to your room." She pushed the card across the desk, along with a pen.

Ariana took the pen and started to sign.

"Just note that I left the end date open—who knows when you'll be leaving here."

Jerking her head up, Ariana caught Kat's gaze. "You're serious about the snow, aren't you?"

Kat's eyes twinkled as she grinned back. "Anything is possible in Charmington at Christmas, and for some quirky reason, I have a feeling you will be here for a long time."

"Oh, really?" Ariana pushed the card across the counter.

Kat winked and turned toward the stairs.

"WHAT IS YOUR FAVORITE KIND OF COOKIE, AIMEE?"

Shifting around Kat to grab a cooling rack from underneath

the kitchen island, Ariana sidestepped Aimee and placed it on the countertop. Bending to peek into the oven window, she inspected the sugar cookies, waiting for just the right second to take them out. She had a theory—you take them out when they are slightly golden on top, and they will come out chewy in the middle and crispy around the edges, just how she liked them.

"I love Pecan Meltaways." Aimee crouched to look in the oven window too. "But those sugar cookies look so good, I can't wait to get the icing on them."

Smiling, Ariana rose and headed back to the island. "Me too. They will have to cool for a while first, but let's get started on making the icing."

"I know," Aimee singsonged. "Mommy says it too. Ice them too quickly and the good stuff melts right off."

"Exactly." Scooting around Kat again, who was busy layering the ingredients for chocolate toffee bars, Ariana rummaged in a utensil drawer for a rubber spatula when she spied a bamboo skewer and picked it up. "Oh, that's perfect."

She headed back to the oven.

"You sure know your way around a kitchen," Kat told her.

Crouching again, watching for the golden tint to pop up on the cookies, Ariana sighed. "Well, my mom is a baker. She's been big on Christmas baking for as long as I can remember. We still bake every year. Except, well, I'm not with her this year."

"Oh?" Kat wiped her hands on a kitchen towel. "Why not?"

Ariana popped her head up and smirked. "Because I'm here."

Laughing, Kat pointed. "Of course. What are you doing with that skewer?"

"This." Standing, Ariana pulled open the oven door, stepped back for a second as the heat escaped, then carefully poked a skewer into one cookie in the middle of the pan, quickly removed it, and brought it closer to inspect it. "Perfect."

"Clean?"

"Yes. And it's long enough to get to a middle cookie so you don't burn yourself."

"Wonderful tip."

Ariana grabbed an oven mitt. "Yes, and I never worry about the big hole in the middle because that's the one I'll eat first! They need to be taste-tested, right?"

Kat laughed. "Even more brilliant."

Smiling to herself, Ariana reached into the oven. "Let's get these out to cool."

A phone rang from somewhere. Kat glanced toward the kitchen door. "Drat, that's mine. It's on the desk in the entry. Aimee, can you run for it?"

"Got it, Mommy."

"Thanks, sweetie."

Ariana studied Kat, then perused the kitchen. Reaching for the camera she'd set off to the side, she snapped a few quick pictures of Kat working, and of the trays of cookies scattered about the kitchen. After a minute, she stashed her camera back in a cabinet, safe from the cookie makings.

Returning her attention to the sugar cookies, she said, "We've done some serious work here. These need to cool for a minute before putting them on the racks. I'll get started on the frosting." She measured some powdered sugar into a bowl.

"And we've lots more to do, I'm afraid." Kat lifted a spatula and slid it under a cookie. "With the lighting event here tomorrow evening, I like to have plenty of goodies on hand. Who knows how many people will show up?" She shrugged, touching a cookie top. "I think these are cool enough to move now."

"Great."

"Mommy?" Aimee called out. "Uncle Matt is on the phone."

"What does he want?"

Ariana could hear Aimee talking to someone in the other room. Did she say Uncle *Matt*? Second time today she'd heard that name.

She shrugged that off, watching Kat finish up the candy layer on the toffee bars, then retrieved the milk from the refrigerator.

"Says he needs his room tonight. Okay?"

Ariana caught Kat's eye as she stopped what she was doing and glanced her way. Her lower lip curled into her mouth and she bit it. Suddenly, Kat appeared a bit perplexed.

"Everything okay?"

"That's my brother," she said.

"Oh."

"I guess if he needs to stay here tonight, the roads must be closed heading out to his farm. Lord knows you wouldn't catch him here at Christmastime for any other reason."

"Oh." Ariana looked to the kitchen door where Aimee had just appeared.

"Well?" Aimee asked, tapping her toe on the plank floor.

"Of course." Kat told her. "We only have one guest tonight and it's Ariana. His room is clean and ready. Tell him dinner is at six if he wants to eat with us."

"Okay." Aimee ran off with the phone again, chattering with her uncle.

Ariana put a tablespoon of milk into the sugar bowl, added a bit of vanilla, and whisked. She thought about what Kat had just said. "So, if the roads are closed, then probably the businesses in town are closed, too. Right? And the restaurants?"

Nodding, Kat said, "Likely so."

"I see…" She picked up a bottle of red food coloring and tipped it to add two drops to the sugar mix. "I was hoping this would blow over so I could explore the town this evening and maybe grab dinner there." She stirred the color with a wooden spoon.

Kat sidled a look her way. "Where did you say you were from?"

"California."

"Ah. You don't know much about snow. Do you?"

"Well, not really."

Kat faced her, smiling. "Snow just doesn't blow over around here. It whips around and stays with us for days on end sometimes."

"Oh. So, no restaurants or shopping?"

"Probably not happening in your near future, Ariana, sorry to say. Besides, you're having dinner with us."

"Oh no. This is a bed-and-breakfast, not a bed-and-dinner."

Kat laughed and pulled out some plastic wrap to cover the toffee bars. "Not when you're snowbound. We feed whoever lands on our doorstep."

She guessed that made sense. "I'll pay you, of course."

Kat turned back with a stern look. "You most certainly will not. Besides, you are working your tail off here this afternoon. I think you've earned your supper."

"Well, if you are sure."

"I wouldn't have it any other way," Kat said. "Oh, and that frosting you've been stirring is getting a little hard. Think it needs to go on the cookies?"

Ariana, realizing she'd gotten a bit distracted, laughed. "Right. I'm on it."

MATT STOMPED THE SNOW OFF HIS BOOTS, TWISTED THE KNOB ON the heavy front door to the inn, and stepped inside. The house was warm and, as always this time of the year, practically glowing. As much as he despised the season, his sister loved it.

If the road to his farm hadn't been closed, he wouldn't even be here....

No use pondering that. The situation was what it was.

His boots on the mat and his coat on a hook, he ambled in sock feet down the hallway toward the kitchen of the old home. He'd grown up here, so he knew the way by heart. He'd not been here often, though, in recent years, keeping mostly to himself.

His sister inherited the place after their parents, Jenny and Ben Matson, died. She'd been too young then to take it over, but the property was held in trust until she turned of legal age. Same thing happened for him with the hardware store. His father's attorney managed the estates until it was time, then it was up to each of them.

Laughter bubbled down the hallway from the kitchen and when he stepped inside the door, his heart sank. Kat mentioned dinner at six, but with the looks of the kitchen, he doubted that was happening soon. Boxes of decorated cookies, remnants of sugar and frosting, and sparkling decorations were scattered everywhere. Christmas music played from Kat's phone, propped up against a flour cannister. Not a nook or cranny was without a container or two of tasty confections.

The room oozed of Christmas, attitude and all.

"Whoa. What is all this?"

Kat swiveled from where she was talking with someone—a guest, probably—and looked at him. "Hey, Matt. These are for the lighting tomorrow."

"And you think that is still going to happen with this snow?"

She rolled her eyes. "First, as you know, I'm an optimist. Second, it's happening whether there are four people or a hundred. It's tradition, as you know."

"Bah. I doubt you will get four people."

"You don't have to be so negative."

Aimee giggled. "Oh, Uncle Matt. You are so silly. See? We have four people now. One. Two. Three. Four." She pointed to him, her mother, herself, and the guest.

Matt looked at the woman. Her back was to him, but she slowly turned. She was wearing one of his mother's Christmas aprons, which immediately set him on edge. Dusted with flour or powdered sugar or something, she also had a stripe of blue icing on her cheek—which, if he would admit it, looked kind of cute on her. He was certain her shoulder-length blond hair didn't normally sport a streak of green sprinkles—*also cute*—although today, who knew for sure.

But it was the rolling pin she held in her hand like a weapon that wasn't so charming. Plus, she was staring hard at him, and—

"You," she said.

"No, it's you," he countered.

Kat looked from one to the other. "You two know each other?"

He eyed the woman. "We've met. If you could call it that." Then, changing the subject and dismissing her, he glanced at his sister. "Did you say something about dinner?"

Kat looked none too pleased. He would be happy to leave the subject and the festivities in the kitchen alone and find something to eat.

"There's beef and noodles in a slow cooker on the buffet, along with rolls and a salad. Help yourself. We'll be along as soon as we wrap up here."

He glanced again to the woman. What was it about her that pleasantly irritated him?

Abruptly, she stuck out her hand. "I'm Ariana, by the way. We've not been properly introduced."

He stared at her hand, sugar and dough and all, but didn't take it. "Just call me Scrooge." He headed for the dining room.

"I think I already did."

A guffaw burst from his sister's lips, which annoyed him.

He shot her a "that's not funny" look and stopped in his tracks.

Spinning back, he ran his gaze over the three females, then landed on…what did she say her name was? *Ariana?* "And your point is?"

She shrugged. "No point. I just already had you pegged."

"For?"

"A Scrooge."

He held her gaze hostage for a moment. "And what makes you the expert?"

Ariana tipped her head to the side. "Well, to be perfectly honest, I am an expert on Christmas. And you possess all the qualities of a town Scrooge. Doesn't take one long to figure that out. You're grumpy. You don't even decorate your store for the holiday."

Kat looked at her. "Well, you are observant."

Dismissing his sister, he eyed the guest, this *Ariana*. Who in the heck was this pipsqueak of a woman who was hellbent on interrupting his regularly scheduled life? "A lot of details for a woman who hasn't even been in town for a day."

"Like I said, doesn't take long. Besides, I'm a—"

"Writer. I know. You're into details."

"Exactly."

"So, pat yourself on the back, *Little Miss Christmas*. You got it right. I am a Scrooge, and don't you forget it." He turned toward the dining room and the beef and noodles. A thought struck him, and he twisted back. "And don't you go getting any ideas about reforming me. Got it?"

The woman saluted. "Yes, sir."

Suddenly, he was famished. "Are you finished?"

"Probably not."

He stopped at the door. "What the hell does that mean?"

"Matt, watch your language."

He threw Kat a look. "Sorry." Pivoting back, he caught Ariana's gaze again. "Look. I am what I am. You are what you are. We'll never get together on this thing, so let's not try. Got it? Now, I'm tired and hungry, and if you all don't mind, I'm going to eat and then find my bed."

He left the room. His head hurt. He'd already talked more in the past hour than he had all week. People exhausted him. This one woman was worse than ten others.

CHAPTER 16

"*D*on't mind him. He's been in a foul mood for years."

Ariana watched Kat's brother—*Matt was his name, right?*—move around the corner and into the dining room. "I should apologize." She began untying her apron. "I was really out of line."

Kat stilled her hands.

"No. Let him get his dinner. Men are usually less grumpy after they eat. Let's clean up here and we can join him in a few minutes. Or, better yet, let's leave him alone, and we'll eat after he's finished."

Sighing, Ariana agreed. "All right." She re-tied her apron strings.

"So, where did you two meet?"

Blowing out a breath, Ariana faced Kat. "Earlier today. We had a brief encounter in the bakery."

"Leslie's?"

She nodded.

"Great scones." Kat placed a few sugar cookies in a box. "I'm assuming the meet did not go well."

"Let's just say it was…awkward."

"Hm."

"Uncle Matt hates Christmas." Aimee stood on a stool washing dishes at the sink. "I don't get it. He doesn't do presents, either."

"Aimee…" Kat gave her daughter a warning look.

"Well, he doesn't. He just sits in his house all alone on Christmas day and doesn't come eat with us, or anything."

The thought of anyone being alone on Christmas bothered Ariana. "Oh, Kat. That makes my heart hurt."

Sighing, Kat looked her way. "I know." Her voice lowered. "It's his own choice. He's a bit of a hermit. He works and goes home. Holidays, and especially Christmas, are not his best days."

Ariana glanced once more toward the dining room. "Well, I think that's awful. I just can't imagine…."

"There are reasons." Kat sidled around her and reached for a mixing bowl Aimee had placed in the dish drainer. She rubbed a dish towel over it.

"We don't talk about it," Aimee said.

"I can hear you," came a male voice from the dining room.

Ariana knew her eyebrows had probably shot up because she could feel the draw on her forehead from the inside. "I don't understand," she whispered, leaning toward Kat.

"Me either." Aimee shrugged.

Kat leaned closer, too. "It's not my story to tell. But I'll say this. It has to do with our parents and something that happened years ago."

"They died." Aimee whispered the words, then jumped down from the barstool, wiping her hands on a dish towel. "Done, Mom."

Kat bent to untie Aimee's apron strings. "Aimee…."

The little girl looked up at her mother with enormous eyes and whispered again. "Well, it's true."

"I'm so sorry to hear that." Ariana searched for some emotion on Kat's face, finding none.

Rising, Kat took a breath. "It was a long time ago." A tendril of hair slipped out of her barrette, and she swiped it away from her face with her forearm. "But Ariana...?" She paused, searching her eyes, and then said softly, "He really is a good guy."

Reading more into the conversation from staring into Kat's eyes than by listening to her words, Ariana decided she would not press the matter any further. "I'm sure he is, Kat," she whispered. "I just feel for him. And for you."

"All right. Enough." Matt shouted from the dining room. "I'm taking my dinner upstairs so you can talk about me without whispering."

Kat rolled her eyes. "Sleep well, Matt," she called out.

Ariana let out a breath—one she'd been holding forever, it felt like. "Well, that's that."

Kat agreed. "I think we're finished here." She took her own apron off and put her hand out for Ariana's. "Aimee, can you take these and put them in the laundry?"

"Yes, Mommy."

"Good. Let's get dinner."

It had been quite a while since her coffee and cookies earlier in the day. "Great. That beef and noodles dish has tickled my nose all afternoon."

But before they left the kitchen, Kat laid a hand on Ariana's forearm. "I know it's odd, and I'm saying more than I should, but Matt is the way he is because he's never been quite able to get over what happened. And this time of the year...well, it's just worse."

Studying Kat's face, Ariana saw the love and concern she had for her brother. It was clear by her facial expression and the way she touched her just now. "I understand. I wish there were something I could do."

Kat shook her head. "Just be yourself, please? You are bright and cheerful and bubbly and so full life and the holiday spirit.

We've needed a bit more Christmas spirit around here lately, and frankly, I think you may have been heaven sent to us this year."

Ariana stared, a little dumbfounded. "I can't imagine why, Kat. All I see around me is Christmas."

Exhaling long, Kat stepped closer. "Sometimes things aren't exactly as they seem, but we put up a good front."

Her words puzzled Ariana. "But—"

Suddenly, Aimee bounded back into the room. Kat rushed to her and pulled her daughter close. Smiling, she met Ariana's gaze again. "We are happy you are here. Come on. Let's eat."

Aimee looked up and grasped Ariana's hand. "I like you," she said.

Her heart swelled, and she felt so touched. "Oh, my. I like you too, sweet girl."

LATER, AFTER DINNER WITH KAT AND AIMEE, FOLLOWED BY COOKIES and cocoa by the fire in the living room, Ariana happily settled into her bedroom upstairs. She showered and slipped into her favorite flannel Christmas pajamas, pulled her laptop out of her bag, and tucked herself into her warm bed topped with a fluffy red and green quilted comforter. She smiled at the small Christmas tree in the corner of her bedroom. Its twinkling lights added a warm and festive ambiance to the room. It was the perfect atmosphere to jot down some highlights of her day, thinking about tomorrow's blog post.

She switched off the lamp beside her bed and worked only with the light from the laptop and the tree. The night before, she'd posted about her stay down the road. Her readers knew her destination was Charmington, and according to recent comments, they couldn't wait to learn more about the 'Official Christmas Village of New York,' as someone had once dubbed the town. Too tired to write the whole post now, she'd be ready by morning—if she had a few talking points to guide her.

Yawning, she typed a few notes about the town: the square and gazebo, the shops, Leslie's Bakes & More, the snow, and Holly Hill Inn. First impressions—maybe that's the focus of the piece. Her impressions of the town, the welcoming people like Kat and Aimee, and.... Her mind drifted and her eyes closed. When they did, behind her eyelids she saw the hardware store sitting undressed and plain among a town full of shiny balls and glittering tinsel—kind of like a wallflower sitting on a chair in the back of the dancehall, realizing she might never receive an invitation to dance.

And that reminded her of Matt. Her mind raced over all she'd learned about him today, their awkward conversations, and the not-so-positive interactions. Plus, Kat's words about him. *He really is a good guy.* All of it made her heart a little sad.

Kat was right. She shouldn't change who she was because of him. That would only depress her. She had to keep on doing her Christmas thing, as normal.

And Matt?

Well. Maybe she'd just have to ask him to dance.

MATT PUSHED BACK THE CURTAINS AND PEERED OUT HIS BEDROOM window, watching the snow swirl around the security light pole below. It was early, but he was always up early, and old habits died hard. He rarely slept well when he was away from home but being back in his childhood bedroom had lulled him into a deep sleep.

He'd be ready for coffee soon, though.

Before leaving the store yesterday, he'd put a sign on the front door saying he was closed until after the first of the year. Probably shouldn't even have bothered with the looks of things outside. He doubted any of the shops would be open today—unless it would be the Old General Store and Post Office, both run by Hattie Howard, who had lived in the apartment above the store for the past forty years. She felt it her duty to be open every day—just in case someone needed something. Besides, neither snow nor sleet nor rain... Or whatever the saying was... The mail was always delivered.

Small town for sure, through and through.

Enough. Time for coffee.

The stairwell creaked as he descended. The Christmas tree was lit at the foot of the stairs, providing some light as he made his way down. He barely glanced at it as he passed. The only light in the kitchen came from a single under-the-cabinet fixture over the coffeemaker—a coffeemaker, which, to his delight, was on and brewing a fresh pot of coffee.

It didn't appear anyone else was up. Perhaps Kat prepared the coffee the night before and set the timer. Glancing at the clock on the stove, he realized it was barely six o'clock in the morning. His sister rarely slept in, but today, perhaps, she'd indulge herself.

The coffee finished, he reached for a cup, poured himself a mug, and leaned against the counter. One sip and his brain fog cleared.

It was unlike her not to be cooking breakfast, though—this was a bed-and-breakfast, after all—and she had a guest. But she knew what she was doing, and he would not wake her. This was her business. He didn't interfere.

The one guest.

He thought about the vivacious, Christmas-loving tourist he'd encountered yesterday. For some reason, she'd popped into his thoughts off and on since their first encounter. He couldn't imagine why. They obviously had nothing in common.

Hopefully, she would sleep late too. He wasn't up for merry, gleeful delight and unending Christmas cheer this morning.

He took his coffee and ambled toward the sunroom on the east side of the house. The morning sun—should it be able to penetrate the snow—would warm the room nicely on a day like this. He wandered through the family room and down the hall, then turned into the sunroom.

There was one low light on in the room, in the far corner next to the sofa. Someone else was up. The glow from a laptop screen lit up her face, and immediately he knew who was there. Ariana typed furiously and obviously didn't realize he was there until he stepped inside and flicked on the overhead light. No way he was sitting in the near-dark with her. That felt a little creepy and stalkerish—and the last thing he needed.

Her head jerked up, and a hand went to her chest. "Oh."

"Good morning." He took a sip of his coffee. "Sorry. I didn't mean to startle you. I didn't know anyone was in here." Something was different about her. Oh, yes. Glasses.

She bit her lip. "I was trying to be quiet."

"As a mouse, you were. I didn't mean to sneak up on you, either. Working?"

"Yes. Just finishing up, actually."

The conversation was a little stilted, but not necessarily unfriendly. Okay, he could do this. He headed toward an armchair. "Don't mind me. I'll just watch the snow and wait for the sun to come up." He sat and peered out the window, although there was not much to see, other than the blowing snow around the outside lights. Besides, it was still dark, and it appeared unlikely the sun would light or warm up the room today.

"Good luck," she said, maybe with a little sarcasm.

He chuckled a little inwardly. Pulling knitted throw from the back of the chair around his shoulders, he asked, "Are you chilly?"

She finished typing, then peeking over the laptop screen, pushed her glasses back up her nose and briefly met his gaze. "No.

I'm fine. I have coffee to warm me up. Thanks." She gave him a half-smile.

"Hm." He noticed the mug of coffee on the side table to her right, and the small plate of cookies next to it.

Ariana went back to her work.

Closing his eyes, he listened to the gentle and rhythmic tap of her fingertips on the laptop keyboard. She'd feverishly type for a minute, then pause, then start in again. Something like that could lull a fellow back to sleep.

The clatter of her fingers stopped. A soft snap suggested she'd closed her laptop. Opening his eyes, he looked across the room.

She sat staring back, her coffee mug to her lips, and took a sip.

"Cookie?" She motioned to her plate. "I brought plenty."

His immediate reaction was to say no. Christmas cookie? No way. Then he looked at the pile of cookies on her plate and thought, *why not?*

"Sure." He got up and crossed the room. "What have you got there?"

"Pecan Meltaways, chocolate chip, and a fruitcake bar."

He took one of the powdered sugar covered Meltaways. "I always loved these as a kid." He took a bite.

Ariana giggled.

"What?"

"Your shirt."

Looking down, he noticed the sugar dust on his chest. "Well, I look like a Christmas confection. Maybe you'll like me now." Immediately, he stepped back. Why those words came out of his mouth, he didn't know. Stupid. Glancing at Ariana, he caught her blank gaze, and then backed away. "I'll go back over here."

He did, and she scooted to the edge of the sofa.

"I don't *not* like you, Matt. I don't really know you."

Embarrassed, somewhat, he downplayed the situation. "I was

joking, Ariana. See? I can have a funny, upbeat side of me too."
Badly played, but it was an attempt.

"Sure. Hey. I should get back to my room." She began gathering her things. "I need to post this piece to my blog and do some other work stuff." She slipped her laptop into a bag at her feet, followed by a mouse and mouse pad. Then, pulling off her glasses, she snapped them inside a case and tossed them in the bag too. She rose and moved toward the door. "Enjoy your…um, sunrise?"

They both glanced out the window only to see blowing snow.

"Not happening." Matt stood. "I'm off to find Kat. She's usually up by now."

Ariana turned back at his words. "She's sleeping in this morning. I told her I didn't need breakfast. Hence, the cookies. She was exhausted last night."

Matt pondered that. Kat leave a guest to fend for herself? "That's unlike her."

"I insisted. Besides, it's Christmas Eve Eve. Everyone needs a down day occasionally. She's been going a mile-a-minute since I got here, and I have a feeling things will not let up for her until after the holiday."

"Yep. That's my sister." He thought for a second or two. "Christmas Eve Eve?"

"Yeah. It's a thing. In my world, anyway."

"Ah."

Ariana just stood and looked at him. After a moment, she faced him fully. "Matt, look. I want to apologize for yesterday. I think we started off on an unpleasant note. I was, perhaps, a teeny bit rude, and…."

He stopped her by putting up a hand palm out. "No, I was the rude one. I was impatient standing in line yesterday and, in case you haven't noticed, I don't enjoy the holidays, so I was testy. Plus, I was hungry. So, it's all on me."

Still, she stared at him. "Not really. I appreciate it, but I goaded you a bit. Can we call a truce? Start over?"

Now it was his turn to stare. "I can do a truce. But that doesn't mean I still won't be grumpy."

Ariana laughed. "All right."

"But on one condition."

"Which is?"

"I want to like you, Ariana, so just don't push the Christmas stuff on me. Okay? That's going over the line."

Her eyes twinkled as she answered. "Oh, of course not, Matt. I wouldn't think of it."

CHAPTER 17

I would just do it.

Ariana smiled back at Matt. There would be no thinking, she was certain. If she pulled him kicking and screaming into Christmas, she would likely do it without rhyme or reason. She couldn't help it.

Christmas should be happy and spontaneous and giving. And like Kat said last night, she just had to be herself.

"There you two are. I wondered where you'd wandered off to."

Turning, Ariana saw Kat standing in the doorway. "I thought you were sleeping in?"

Kat looked at her watch. "Well, it's six-thirty in the morning and I'm usually up by five, so I say that's a rather good sleep-in. Are you two hungry?"

"I had cookies."

Kat looked at Matt's shirt. "Looks like you did, too."

"And coffee," he added.

"Well, that barely counts. Let's see what we can do. Besides, Aimee will be up soon, and she's cranky if she doesn't get a proper breakfast. Plus, we have tons of things to do today—

baking the gingerbread for the gingerbread house assembly tomorrow, prepping the cookie trays for tonight, and finish getting all the lights up in the house for the lighting—so let's get cracking."

Ariana watched Matt roll his eyes. "Tons of things to do that sound like Christmas—and we don't even know if anyone will be here for the lighting. As much as I would love to help with gingerbread and cookie arranging and the lights, I have some tasks I want to tend to, so…."

Kat stopped him with her glare. "Oh no. Not today, Mr. Pessimist. All the roads are closed, and the officials are telling everyone to stay in, so you're not going anywhere."

"My case in point."

Kat ignored him. "We are moving forward if there is a crowd, or not. It's—"

"Tradition. I know."

"And don't you think for one minute, Matt Matson, that you are going to escape off to the attic or basement or barn to tinker, because today, in this house, it is all-hands-on-deck. Do you hear me?"

"Not sure what I can contribute, Kat."

"You're in charge of lighting."

"What? But you always take care of the lighting, and you are so particular."

"I'm going to be busy, Matt. Can you help, please?" She winked at Ariana.

Ariana truly had no clue what Kat was winking about, although she liked the way she handled her brother, and had rather enjoyed listening to their banter. She wondered if that was her usual modus operandi, or something new.

"I'm in," she said. "Just point me in the right direction. Matt? What do you say? We can do this. Right?"

"Is this a conspiracy?"

Kat shook her head. "No, this is family. Now, let's get breakfast and we can discuss."

Family?

Ariana warmed at the thought. Being part of a family like this would be wonderful. Not that her own family wasn't great—they were. And she loved her parents and sister more than anything. But this family—even with their quirks—just felt like….

Well, like her circle was complete.

How she could feel that way in such a short time—and with people she hadn't even known early yesterday—she didn't know.

About an hour later, Ariana peeked over Kat's shoulder at the list she was making while standing over the kitchen island. The three of them had breakfasted on sausage, eggs, and biscuits, and of course, more coffee. Aimee took sleeping in seriously and still wasn't up yet.

"So, this morning, Aimee and I will make the gingerbread dough and start baking the slabs so they will all be cool later today."

"Sounds good, Kat," Ariana said. "What can I do?" Then she glanced at Matt, who sat perched on a stool at the end of the kitchen island drinking coffee. "I mean, what can Matt and I do?"

He arched a brow.

Kat glanced sideways. "You two are going work on the window lights if you don't mind. I want something in every window."

Matt cleared his throat and glared at his sister. "Seriously? All the windows? Do you know how many that is?"

Pushing upright, she nodded. "Yes, I do. There are forty-two windows. I wash them every spring and fall. Since we can't do much outside other than what we have already done, let's focus on the house. I want a candle or maybe a wreath in every window. There are enough in the attic. Remember when Mom used to do that? Of course, I don't know if all the light bulbs still work so we will have to check them."

"Hm." Matt stared at the list.

"Okay?"

"Of course. What else?"

"I'm not sure," Kat said. "Do you two have any ideas?"

Ariana interrupted with a thought. "We have to be organized about this. I need to get a lay of the land and look at the windows. Where do you store your extra Christmas decorations, Kat?"

"Those are in the attic, too."

Ariana directed her attention to Matt. "Can we go look?"

Matt shoved off the island. "We have to go up there to get the candles, anyway."

"Great."

"What are you thinking, Ariana?"

Of course, she should tell Kat her idea. "Well, I'm just wondering if we can simulate a Christmas tree in some of the random windows, too. It would be more lights and maybe illuminate the house a bit more. But it should look balanced and not randomly chaotic." She watched Matt's face. He appeared to be thinking about that.

Matt crossed his arms. "Mom also used to put a small tree in some of the bedrooms."

"Like in my room! I love that," said Ariana.

"Yes." Kat grinned. "I love it, too. Can you two see what we have in the attic? I've not gone deep into the tree room in years."

The tree room? Ariana felt a little giddy. "Are you kidding?" She looked at Matt, stretching her eyes wider. "You have an honest-to-goodness Christmas tree room? Oh, point me in the right direction, please."

A hint of a smile crept across Matt's face. Ariana wondered if she amused him.

"This way," he said, turning away. Suddenly a crying Aimee appeared in the doorway, and he stopped short. "Aimee? What's wrong, sweetheart?"

She sailed past him and into her mother's arms. "Mommy!"

Her wail startled Ariana as she watched Kat scoop her up.

"Goodness, honey. What is the matter?" She held Aimee in her arms and sat her on the edge of the island. The little girl clung to her mother, her arms wrapped around her shoulders and her pajama-clad legs around Kat's waist.

"Dream," she finally said, hiccupping between words. "Bad. Daddy."

"Oh, honey…" Kat's eyes closed, and Ariana saw a tear escape a lower lid. At once, her heart went out to Aimee and her mom, and she wondered what in the world was going on.

Worried, she looked at Matt for some sort of answer. Instead, he crooked his finger for her to follow him, and then quickly and silently left the room.

She pursued him down the hallway and toward the entry, stopping at the base of the stairs.

"Matt?"

He put a finger to his lips. "Sh."

She nodded and whispered, "Okay."

Then he grabbed her hand and led her up the two flights of stairs to the attic.

TAKING HER HAND HAD BEEN BOLD OF HIM—AND TO BE HONEST, IT was such an impulsive act that had he thought about it, he wouldn't have.

But he was glad he did.

It had been a long time since he'd held any woman's hand, and the feel of Ariana's small, soft palm in his was nice. Very nice. In fact, her fingers laced with his were pleasant enough that he slowed his steps as they approached the landing to the attic and was semi-reluctant to let go when they got there.

But just as quickly as he'd grabbed it, he released it.

The attic door creaked as he pushed it open. Moving past the threshold, he yanked an overhead pull string and light flooded the area. Before he could move farther inward, Ariana grasped his arm and stopped him.

"Matt?"

"Hm?"

"What was going on with Aimee? Seemed like more than a bad dream."

He perused Ariana's face. Her expression appeared full of concern and worry for his niece, and that touched his heart. Who was this woman who had suddenly burst into their lives? Someone who had him in the attic looking for Christmas decorations and felt genuine concern for his family?

"Yeah. Well, Dylan, Kat's husband, is deployed right now. He's on a mission and we know little. He's in the Navy, a SEAL. That is stressful for Kat, as I'm sure you can understand. But right now, we're not sure where he is or when he's coming home. It's unlikely he will be here for Christmas."

"Oh, that's awful for a little girl."

"It's difficult for Kat, too. Although she understands Dylan's commitment. We're all proud of him. Aimee has been having a hard time because it's the first Christmas she won't see her daddy. And they've not been able to video call like they normally do."

"Poor baby."

"I know. I think Dylan being gone is one reason Kat keeps so busy. It keeps her mind off wondering where he is and if he's safe. It keeps Aimee's mind off it, too."

"Then we need to make sure this is the best Christmas ever, for Aimee and Kat." She stared at him, a dead serious look on her face.

Matt paused. "In case you haven't noticed, Christmas is not my forte."

"Really? Well then, it's a good thing it is mine."

He wanted to chuckle at her semi-amused expression, at the one cocked eyebrow and her slightly rounded lips. He couldn't help but grin at the twinkle in her big blue eyes, and had to admit she possessed an alluring charm that was sucking him right in. "All right. I'll make the effort. I can already see a plan forming in your head."

She laughed, but just as quickly, grew serious. Again, she touched his forearm. "No plan. Let's just make it a merry time. Matt, I came here because I wanted to write about the town of Charmington and experience the Charmington Christmas Jubiliee —but suddenly, I feel there is more here for me. I know this probably sounds odd, but I am drawn to your family and this place. And since I know my way around Christmas decorations, I want to help make these next couple of days special. I need your help, though. Please? Let's do this for everyone. Even if it's just us here tonight."

He nodded. "Which is entirely likely."

Ariana blinked, looking up at him. "And that's really enough. Isn't it?"

He supposed it was. "All right. This way." He motioned and turned, still a bit in awe of Ariana. She'd fallen into their lives like a Christmas angel of hope and had suddenly changed the mood of this Christmas season—at least for him.

He led the way deeper into the attic. She followed, glancing about as they wove their way through boxes. "Wow. This *is* what you call a real attic."

Laughing, Matt headed to the right, where he knew the Christmas decorations were stored—or used to be, anyway. "I suppose you don't have real attics in..." He stopped and turned. "Where are you from?"

"California."

For a moment, Matt studied her. "You drove all the way here from California?"

"Oh, no." She began picking through a box of assorted Christmas paraphernalia. "I flew into Boston and rented a car. I've been in New England for a little over a week."

"And you're staying how long?"

She shrugged. "Through Christmas, at least. Longer if the snow doesn't let up." She smiled warmly.

"But what about Christmas with your family back in California?"

"I'll miss it this year—and them—but I need to be here because this is where my writing brought me, and my writing pays the bills. My family understands my obsession with Christmas. Besides, there is no snow in So-Cal, and this year I want to be where the snow is."

"Well, you got that, for sure."

"I did."

"And you don't mind being stuck here for a few days longer than planned?"

"Mind? Oh, no. I'm ecstatic. I've never seen snow like this in my life."

She grinned wide, and Matt smiled back.

There was something infectious about her enthusiasm. He watched her turn back to the box and start poking through it. Matt realized he didn't mind watching her dig through the items. Their conversations were pleasant, too. Seemed they truly had called a truce.

"Oh, look at these..." Ariana peeled back an old quilt, covering the contents of a box, to reveal several wooden ornaments underneath. She picked one up and showed it to him. "These are gorgeous. Are they hand-carved?"

Matt's gaze settled on the intricately carved snow scene on the wooden ball in Ariana's hands. His mind traveled back to a Christmas past, of the tree in the living room, tucked into the corner by the fireplace, and decorated with those old ornaments. When he and Kat were young, his parents had little money—most of what they made went back into the inn or the hardware—so they used what they had. These ornaments had been passed down from his dad's side of the family. He remembered how the lights on the tree would bounce off the wood and provide a warm glow in the room. It was a happier time.

"Yes. They are. My great-grandfather carved them, or so the story goes. I haven't seen these in years." He reached for the ornament and examined it, turning it over in his hands. "They still look good but could use a good polish. I can do that."

Ariana looked up, another ornament in her hand, and made eye contact. She appeared to be studying him now. "Are you okay, Matt?"

"Yes. Just memories." *Just a few ghosts of Christmas past.*

She held his gaze for another moment, then set the ornament back in place. "We could use these on the window trees if we can find them. Or perhaps the sunroom could use a tree. Over in the corner? What do you think?"

It was thoughtful of her to ask his opinion. "That would be great. I've always liked these ornaments. It wouldn't hurt me to enjoy them again."

Ariana drew back, her eyes wide, and her mouth open. "You? Enjoy a Christmas something? My ears. What am I hearing?" Laughing, she softly punched his arm. "Just kidding, you know."

"Of course." And he didn't mind. Not really.

She spanned the attic then. "My goodness. Look at all the stuff in here." Turning, she eyed him again. "And no, I never lived in a house with an attic like this in California. We always lived in a ranch-style home, which only had pull-down stairs in the ceiling that led to a place I never wanted to go. This..." She spun again, "is incredible."

"It's just a lot of old junk." Matt grinned.

"It's a lot of beautiful and interesting old junk. Oh look. I see lights over there."

Matt stood for a moment watching Ariana bounce from one thing to another. He had to smile at the joy she was getting from poking into all the assorted holiday trimmings. From boxes of greenery to a stash of red ribbons and bows to three more boxes of tree ornaments, and finally, to three plastic tubs full of electric candles and two spare boxes of light bulbs.

She was a refreshing beacon of light in his formerly dark and clouded world.

"Ariana? Thank you," he said aloud.

She looked up and caught his gaze. "For what?"

"For your efforts. Helping me see the joy of the season again."

Blinking, she held his gaze, and for once, it appeared she didn't know what to say. "Is it working?"

"Maybe a little. But Ariana, this is still difficult. I...."

She stood and approached him, touched his hand. "You don't have to explain, Matt. I don't want to push. You're welcome, of course, but if my obsessive enthusiasm about Christmas gets to be too much...."

"I will tell you."

"Good." She broke the connection between them and went back to rifling through a box of lights. "Now, if only those bulbs will work, *and* if we can find the little trees."

The serious mood broken, he stepped forward. "Over here." He knew exactly where those were. Leading her to the side of the attic, he opened another door and ducked to step inside. "Watch your head."

Ariana followed. "Wow."

"You keep saying that."

"Because... Wow. Is this the tree room?"

He swept an arm toward the center. "Yes. You asked for Christmas trees, madam? Here you go."

"And all shapes and sizes." She whipped back, her wide-eyed gaze landing on him. "We have our work cut out for us. How many windows again?"

Matt laughed out loud. Watching her was like watching a kid in a penny candy shop—and for some reason, that gave him a bit of joy. "Forty-two. And yes. That, we do. I'm at your command."

She sailed off to inspect the trees. Whether or not he wanted to admit it, he was enjoying this day, and being with Ariana.

ARIANA FELT BOTH OVERWHELMED AND EXCITED. "So, WE REALLY GET to decorate with all of this stuff?"

"Any and all of it. Whatever you want to use," Matt told her.

"I'm hoping I don't bite off more than we can chew… But Matt, I want to use it all."

"All of it?"

"I have ideas running through my head. Brilliantly, beautiful Christmas ideas."

"Oh, boy."

She twisted back. "I thought you were going to say *Bah, Humbug*, and I was about to chuck this ball of tinsel at you."

"Naw. I think my inner Scrooge is still sleeping in today, for some odd reason."

"Good. Keep him there."

"I'll try."

Ariana caught his eye. There he was again, just looking at her like she was this odd character or something. "So, okay, I know I'm weird about Christmas."

He shook his head. "No. You are incredibly bubbly and energetic about Christmas. Nothing weird about it at all. I think I'm the weird one."

"I think you're softening."

"I think you may have something to do with that."

Her heart skipped a beat, and that startled her a little. She turned away, ignoring the heart-thumping thing. "Then my job here is done." *Or maybe just beginning.* Ariana hesitated and looked at him again.

His gaze skittered over her face.

A switch had flipped a minute ago. Why was her heart fluttering wildly in her chest just now? *Not thinking about that.*

"I'd say we're off to a good start."

She nodded and dismissed her wayward thoughts.

"Agreed. Before we drag stuff downstairs, I want to get a look at all forty-two of those windows. Maybe make some sketches and a plan."

"Sounds good." Matt reached for the two boxes of light bulbs and a box of candles. "I'm going to take these with us so I can test out these bulbs."

"Great idea. Let's get started."

He led the way out of the attic. Ariana followed, watching Matt carry the boxes down the stairs, wondering why all at once she felt a little different toward him. Somehow, in such a short time, her feelings for him had done an about-face, swinging from empathy to...

To something different.

CHAPTER 18

*A*riana stepped back and perused the arrangement. It was the last one she'd pulled together, and this one was simple—a single candle, some holly, and a red bow. The window was in a short hall off the entry, leading into the dining room. With all the decorations in the rooms on either side, she didn't feel they needed to go overboard in this spot.

The aroma of gingerbread wafting down the hallway tickled her nose and teased her appetite, leaving her with a warm, cozy, Christmassy feeling. Hours had passed since breakfast, and her tummy was growling, so she hoped to grab something to eat soon. Plus, the scents of cinnamon, nutmeg, and ginger didn't help matters any. She tilted her head to one side, satisfied that the uncomplicated approach was perfect, and nothing else needed to be added.

Matt stepped up beside her. "That looks nice."

"I think so, too."

"I secured all the candles in the sunroom windows," he added. "Thanks for getting the greenery ready there. The sunroom is going to look awesome tonight."

She glanced his way. "I love the addition of the tree in the corner. The colors will pop through the windows. Plus, those wooden ornaments look even more awesome since you polished them. They really seem to glow. I can't wait to get pictures of everything."

He moved closer. "You've done a great job in the sunroom, Ariana. Aimee and Kat are going to love it."

That was certainly her intention. "It was fun. If it's the one place we can keep Aimee out of until tonight, that would be great."

"I was just in the kitchen. I think they will be busy for a while longer."

"Good." She stared at the window for another few seconds, cocking her head to the side, and studying it from all angles. "If I can get a good picture of this, it will be great for my blog post tomorrow."

Matt stood silent beside her.

After a moment, the stillness between them felt awkward. The atmosphere crackled between them a little. She peeked his way. The smile he wore earlier had dissipated. "Matt?"

"Hm?"

"Everything okay? You have a look."

He shook himself and stepped forward to fiddle with the candle. "I'm fine. Glad those bulbs worked."

Ariana wasn't so sure, but she would not push it. "Me too. I can't believe you had all those extras in your truck. I mean, who would have thought?"

He chuckled. "I know my sister. I grabbed those before I left the store, just in case."

Glad to see him smile again, she faced him, crossing her arms over her chest. "So. You actually have some Christmas decorations in that store of yours."

"They were tucked in the back room, left over from when Dad managed the store and Mom had her art studio there. She would create all sorts of Christmas scenes for the inn, the hardware store, and the town. She'd paint the characters and use the lights to illuminate." He stared out the window for a moment, thinking back, perhaps. "The lights were old, that's why I wanted to test them first."

"I see. Makes sense."

He stood for a moment, looking past Ariana. "They've been gone a while, my parents, but both of them have been on my mind a lot today."

Maybe that's why his attention keeps drifting. "That's understandable, Matt. I'm sorry. Kat mentioned yesterday they were no longer living."

He said nothing for a minute. "You know, for a long time I avoided Christmas because it dredged up too many memories, too much emotion. Sometimes, I just couldn't handle all the feelings. You'd think at my age, and after all this time, I'd have dealt with it —but I haven't. Not really. Yet today, I welcomed the memories."

Ariana moved closer and touched his forearm. "That sounds encouraging, Matt."

He made eye contact, and Ariana's heart warmed at the connection. "I hope so."

She held his stare a little longer. "How long have they been gone, Matt?" The instant she said the words, she wondered if her question was out of line. A sliver of panic raced through her abdomen. "I'm sorry. I shouldn't have...."

His gaze moved from hers, now transfixed on the candle. Matt seemed far away again. Ariana waited while he gathered his thoughts—and maybe his emotions—then briefly made eye contact and turned toward the entryway.

"A long time." He took a couple of steps and paused, as if contemplating whether he wanted to continue that line of conversation. He faced Ariana. "I've never seen two people enjoy each other so much—practically inseparable and so much in love.

They shared an incredibly strong bond. And they loved Christmas." He smiled then, for a moment, his gaze back in sync with Ariana's. "They got married on Christmas Day."

Ariana smiled. "I can't think of a more beautiful day to get married."

Their gazes danced then. "Maybe someday I'll tell you their story."

"I would like that."

He heaved a sigh and tossed another glance toward the entryway. "How about we check on the gingerbread girls?"

"Sure."

Ariana watched him move away. His off-and-on somber mood tugged at her heart. She wished she'd not asked that question, but at least Matt had shared something personal. That was positive, she hoped.

Her thoughts wandered back to what Kat had said the night before. *It's not my story to tell.* So, if Matt wanted her to know more, he'd tell her. She just had to be patient.

He turned. "You coming? I'm starved." He reached for her hand.

Instinctively, she stepped forward and met his grasp, and their fingers mingled for a few seconds. "Yes. But I want to run up to my room and get my camera first. I'll just be a few seconds."

She dropped his hand and tore her gaze away as she started for the stairs. A cool draft of air swept down the staircase as she ascended, causing her to shiver. Yet, his touch still lingered warm and inviting on her fingertips.

THE SMELL OF BAKING GINGERBREAD WAS EVEN MORE OVERPOWERING in the kitchen than throughout the rest of the house. Ariana immediately began snapping pictures of Kat and Aimee as they baked. Aimee kneeled on a stool at the kitchen island—a pillow under her knees—rolling out gingerbread dough. She wore a too-big apron wrapped around her waist and tied in the front. She wore flour smudges on her cheeks, dough on her fingers, and a smile on her face. Glancing up as Ariana aimed the camera her way, she smiled a big, toothless grin. Ariana snapped the picture.

"That one is awesome."

Aimee grinned wider. "We've been baking all day."

"I know. I could smell the ginger all over the house." Ariana stepped closer to the island. "Are you tired?"

"A little. Mostly, it's fun."

"She was a big help today," Kat called out from across the room. She peeked into the oven. "Just a couple more minutes on this one. We'll finish soon."

Ariana snapped another picture of Kat. Then, looking around, she noticed all the gingerbread layers cooling on racks. "Goodness. When did you say the gingerbread house assembly happens?"

"Tomorrow," said Aimee. "We always do it on Christmas Eve. It's—"

"Tradition." All voices in the room chimed in at once. Including the male voice coming from the breakfast nook, which was decidedly the loudest.

Aimee giggled. "Uncle Matt. You're funny."

He rose from the table, a sandwich plate in hand, and reached over to pinch Aimee's nose. "And don't you forget it, elf."

"I'm not an elf." Aimee giggled some more and batted at his hands.

Ariana snapped a quick picture of the interaction between the two.

Matt turned to Ariana. "Sandwich fixings are on the table." He dusted the crumbs off his plate into the garbage and stashed the plate in the dishwasher. "Still hungry?"

"Famished. Thanks."

"No problem." Brushing his hands together, he added, "I've got some things to take care of outside—looks like the snow has stopped for a while—I'll be in the barn if either of you need me."

Kat turned. "In the barn? Are the lights finished?"

Matt approached his sister and gave her a peck on the cheek. "Relax. All done, sis. And you can thank Ariana for the expertise. It's going to look great tonight, and I can't wait for you to see it. However, we're requesting no peeking until later. Okay? That includes both you and the elf." He ticked his head toward Aimee.

"I'm not an elf, Uncle Matt!"

"What?" He turned and swept Aimee off the chair and swung her around. "I'm sure your ears are pointed. Let me see." Sitting her back down on the stool, he went about inspecting her ears. "Hm…" he said softly. "I thought I saw points there last year. Maybe they don't come out until Christmas Eve."

Aimee giggled again. "I don't have points."

He shrugged. "Well, let's wait and see tomorrow. I think I see little ear buds starting to grow, though. You better go look in a mirror."

"What?" A wide-eyed Aimee hopped off the bar stool and ran out of the room.

Kat wiped her hands on a dish towel, tossed a quick glance at Ariana, and then gave Matt a long, hard look. "Excuse me. Who are you and what have you done with my brother?"

Matt feigned innocence. "What?"

Smiling, Ariana shrugged. "This guy sort of appeared this afternoon."

Kat faced Matt and gave him a bear hug. "Well, I like him."

Rolling his eyes at Ariana, he hugged his sister back, then settled his hands on her shoulders and gently pushed away. "Let's forgo the mushy stuff."

Kat grinned ear to ear.

Matt's phone binged. He fished it out of his pocket, glanced at the face, and then turned away from the women. "Gotta take this. Later."

"Dinner is at six." Kat called out. "And then the lighting."

Waving with one hand, he headed down the hall, his phone to his ear.

"Well, that's that," Ariana said. She watched him disappear down the hallway. Her heart felt light and happy for Matt. And, for herself. She liked him, despite his quirks, and wanted him to be happy.

"And he's been like this all afternoon?"

"Off and on." She swiveled to look at Kat. "He's had a few nostalgic moments mixed in, I guess you would call them, but he was okay. It surprised me he didn't balk at anything. We worked very well together."

"Great!"

Ariana picked up a peppermint disc. "These look so festive."

"Thanks. I love doing them."

"Matt told me a little about your parents a few minutes ago."

Kat swiveled to look at her, putting down her spatula. "Did he say much?"

"Only that he's having pleasant memories today. Oh, and he talked a little about them, about how much in love they were."

Kat's eyes misted over. "They were incredible." Moving closer, she added, "I told you he was a good guy."

"I know. He is." Ariana gave her a quick hug, then glanced down the hallway where Matt had gone. "I like him."

Returning to her gingerbread, Kat smiled. "I think the feeling is mutual."

Ariana's attention shifted. "What? I certainly didn't mean, well, you know, romantically."

The smile on Kat's face widened. "Why not? Romance has to start somewhere."

"I didn't come here for romance, Kat. I came to work. And

while I'm sure that Matt is a great guy, and he is personable, and I did enjoy spending time with him, I don't feel...." Her words tapered off. How did she feel?

"Well, I think there is something between you two. I can see it."

"Really?"

"He likes you, Ariana. And you said you like him. So, what does it hurt to explore a relationship? Besides, you are good for him."

"He's fine figuring things out on his own, Kat."

Shrugging, Kat faced her. "Maybe. His track record isn't so great. I think it's you. I've tried to pull him into Christmas without success. You pop in here for a day or two and suddenly he's digging into the tree room and hanging garland."

"Oh no. It's not me. I think he's just ready to leave whatever it is behind."

"Maybe." Kat grasped Ariana's hand. "But I still think it's you." Kat squeezed her hand, then headed to the oven. "So, what is this about not looking at the lights in the sunroom?"

"Well, do you mind keeping Aimee out of the sunroom until the lighting? You, too. Okay?"

Kat gave her the side-eye and crossed her arms. "But I need to set up the cookie trays. We always have cookies and cocoa in there after the lighting."

"I'll get everything set up for you."

Kat paused. "Actually, with finishing up here and trying to get dinner on, that would be awesome. Are you sure you don't mind?"

"Are you kidding me? I live for this stuff."

"Oh, that's right. Silly me." Amused, she added, "You know where the cookies are. The fancy trays are in the built-in cupboard in the dining room." She checked the oven. "Oh and check the bottom section of the hutch in the sunroom. I have some decorations stashed there that I've used in the past. Help yourself. Whatever you need."

"Great. I'm on it. Right after a sandwich."

"Mom! Ariana!" Aimee burst back into the room. "Uncle Matt lied! I don't have ear bugs! Look!"

Kat and Ariana burst out laughing.

Aimee parked her hands on her hips. "Stop laughing at me!"

Kat's lips clamped up tight, and Ariana had to swallow a giggle. The little girl was so darned serious that it made Ariana's stomach hurt from holding in her laughter. Finally, she gained control and crouched to meet Aimee's gaze. "I think Uncle Matt was teasing you, sweetheart."

Aimee rolled her eyes and shrugged. "I dunno what's up with him!"

"Aimee Hamilton? I can use your help over here," Kat called out.

"Coming..."

Ariana watched Kat bustle about. "Matt told me about your husband being deployed. I'm sorry to hear that."

Kat's hands stilled, her eyes closed, and she exhaled. "I'm trying not to think about it."

Ariana stepped closer. "And I just made you think about it. I'm sorry about that too. But Kat, you need to slow down. You can't fill every minute of the day with activity just so you don't think about it."

Kat looked ahead for a few seconds, then dropped her gaze to her daughter sitting at the island, busying herself sorting candies. "I know. But it's better than drinking. Right?" She faked laughter.

Ariana touched Kat's hand.

Kat eyes grew misty. "I don't want to upset Aimee," she whispered.

Ariana nodded. "I understand."

THE SUNROOM WAS LIT UP AND GLOWING. THE LIGHTS FROM THE candles and the Christmas tree bounced off the floor-to-ceiling windows on three walls, only adding to the magical effect. From the inside looking out, the reflections amplified the amount of light in the room. Ariana perused every nook and cranny—she wasn't sure she could get more Christmas in the room if she tried.

Trays of cookies sat on end tables and the coffee table, as well as on the buffet top of a built-in hutch to her left. Also there, sat two thermoses of hot cocoa, a pitcher, and assorted candy additions for the hot chocolate, such as marshmallows, red hot candies, candy canes, and other chocolate meltables. She'd pulled fancy dessert plates and cups from the cupboard in the dining room, along with some candlestick holders and candles. She had forks and spoons and stirrers and napkins, too. All she needed to do later was light the candles.

Except. No. Not quite finished yet.

Ariana glanced about one last time.

If she had some glass ornaments, they would go perfectly in the wooden bowl over on that side table. And if she could find some tinsel, she could tie it around the candlesticks. And….

Oh. She snapped her fingers. Kat said there were decorations. Ariana's gaze swept to the bottom of the hutch.

Crouching there, she opened the doors and pulled out a few boxes.

There. Some tinsel.

Oh, this holly will work great.

And some glass balls. Perfect.

Taking what she needed and setting them aside, Ariana set the boxes back on the shelf. When she did, a framed photograph dislodged and fell out. She caught it before it hit the floor.

Turning the frame over, she ran a finger over the dusty glass. The image was several years old, to be sure. The photograph was of a family standing in front of the inn. There was snow on the ground and the house was lit up behind them, as was the picket fence and arch.

There were four people. Two adults, two children. A boy and a girl.

"Kat and Matt?"

She thumbed over them, wiping away more dust. "Yes." And their parents, she guessed.

Kat looked to be in her young teens, Matt a couple of years younger. Everyone was smiling. Happy.

Turning the frame over, she read the words scrawled on the backing. *The Holly Hill Inn Christmas Lighting, 2005. Ben, Jenny, Kat, and Matt Matson.*

Ariana took a deep breath. Glancing into the cabinet, she located a dust cloth and cleaner. Quickly, she swiped the frame and picture, and set it atop the buffet. Then, she went about placing the final touches around the room—some holly on the hutch, tinsel on the candlesticks, ornaments in the bowl.

With one last glance about the room, she made a quick decision to place the picture on the hutch—front and center and eye level— where it would surely be noticed when people got their hot cocoa.

Stepping back, she smiled. What a lovely tribute to this family and the inn.

Her heart felt full, and she was excited for the evening to come. With a lingering over-her-shoulder perusal, she left the room to change for dinner.

CHAPTER 19

"Why can't we go out on the porch?" Aimee looked up at her mom. "Why can't I go in the sunroom? And why are all the lights turned off inside?"

"Because Uncle Matt said so, and he told us to stay here in the entryway and wait for him. Patience, little one."

Ariana smiled at the anxious child. "The surprise will be so much better if you wait," she told Aimee.

The girl rolled her eyes and did a little jiggly dance. "But I am patient...."

"*Impatient*." Kat looked down at her daughter.

"Oh look. I see lights." Aimee jumped and pointed out the door window. "Is that Uncle Matt?"

Ariana watched as a vehicle drove up from barn area, circled the drive, and parked in front of newly shoveled sidewalk. The snow had stopped earlier in the afternoon—which was a godsend —and Matt had shoveled the drive and walks, and then worked in the barn throughout the afternoon. In fact, he didn't even come in for dinner.

"I can't believe it." A wide-eyed Kat glanced at Ariana. "Do you know anything about this?"

"No. I'm as clueless as you."

"I think I'm witnessing a miracle," Kat added.

Ariana noticed tears in Kat's eyes. "Hey, are you okay?"

In the next motion, Kat embraced Ariana and held her tight. "Thank you," she said. "Thank you."

"But I did nothing." Ariana pulled back and looked into Kat's eyes.

"You've done more than you know."

The door swung open. Matt stood framed in the doorway, then glanced to his right, tapped something on the wall outside the door, and stepped inside.

"Uncle Matt!" Aimee excitedly flew forward. "Are we ready now?"

He swept her up into his arms. "We are, elf. Let's go."

Ariana watched as he paused briefly, held Kat's tearing gaze for a moment, and reached out to touch her shoulder. Then, just as quickly, he stepped away.

"This way, folks. Follow me. Watch for icy snow on the bricks."

He carried Aimee and walked ahead. Kat locked arms with Ariana and they made their way down the porch steps and along the brick walk to where Matt had parked. It was dark, the sun had set about thirty minutes earlier, but the porch light and an outside lantern lit their way—plus the outside security lights away from the house. When they were all there, Matt lowered Aimee to the ground and turned to the pair.

Kat stepped forward. "Matt. How did you get this old thing running again?"

He shrugged. "Luckily, with a little tinkering and some good gas, she started right up." He glanced at the truck. "But I didn't want to risk turning her off again, so that's why I left her idling."

Ariana looked at the old pickup truck. She knew nothing about trucks, but as far as this one went, it was charming, to be sure. Red with white wooden side-rails, with the words Holly Hill Inn painted on the passenger side door. "What a cute truck."

"It's a 1956 Ford F100. A classic. I'm just glad she started."

Ariana laughed. "All of those words and numbers mean nothing to me, but I still think she is adorable."

"This was our father's truck," Kat said. "At least the one he bought to showcase the inn. Every truck he ever owned was red. He bought this one in the 90s, restored it himself, then drove it every day until… Well, until he didn't. But on the evening of the lighting, we had a tradition."

Matt nodded, glancing to his watch. "Yes, and we need to quit standing out here in the cold and get to that tradition." He reached for Ariana's hand. "Do you mind sitting in the middle, Ariana? Kat, sit by the door with Aimee on your lap."

They all scrambled into the truck cab. Matt rounded the front and got in beside Ariana. When he did, they made eye contact for a moment. "You're full of surprises," she told him.

He patted her knee, leaned closer, and whispered, "Just wait."

Ariana's heart fluttered at his closeness. "So, about this tradition?" She directed that to Kat.

Matt put the truck into drive.

"Well, before the guests would come for the lighting, Dad would pile all of us in the truck, just like now, and we would drive around the property looking at the house from all angles." She stopped talking and leaned forward to look out the windshield. "Matt, did you snowplow this path today?" She glanced sideways at him.

"I did."

"Just like dad."

Ariana looked back and forth between them.

"Yep. I guess so."

Kat's eyes welled up again. Ariana reached out and clasped her hand. Kat squeezed it tight.

Matt drove toward the back of the inn, circled around, and parked the truck so they could get the full and unobstructed view of the back of the house and the side garden.

"Wait for it." He pushed his coat sleeve back to look at his watch.

"What?" Kat glanced his way.

"Now."

At once, the entire house lit up like a burst of fireworks. Lights twinkled on the trees and holly bushes outside the inn, skittered along the picket fence, and raced up and over the arch. To Ariana, the most beautiful part was the candles dancing in all the windows, like little punctuation marks of prettiness. The sunroom was especially magnificent.

She gasped. "That is splendidly beautiful."

Matt exhaled, and Ariana looked his way. He stared straight ahead, and she noticed that his eyes, too, had grown misty. He turned her way.

"Dad was all about the dramatic," he said. "The flare. He was ahead of his time with electronics and he loved to tinker. Running the hardware store was perfect because he had access to all kinds of gadgets and tools and devices. When there was downtime, he was fiddling with something. One year, he rigged up the lighting system in the entire house—inside and out—to come on and off with a series of timers. I had no clue if it would still work, but by Christmas, it did."

Ariana sighed and looked again at the inn. "By Christmas, you are right."

"Well, it's beautiful," Kat said. "And that sunroom literally pops."

Aimee bounced on her mother's lap. "I see a tree in there." Her eyes grew wide.

"Yes, we added a few trees here and there," Ariana told her.

"It's lovely."

"It's magic." Ariana whispered the words and stared ahead. She, too, felt a little like crying. "Thank you both for letting me be a part of this day." Suddenly, she knew she had found the perfect Christmas, and it wasn't in Charmington—it was here at Holly Hill Inn. Christmas wasn't only about tinsel and snow globes and mistletoe—it was about family and relationships.

While she knew that, being with Kat and Aimee and Matt, and being privy to their family struggles, made her not only appreciate the holiday and her own family but differently.

Matt fumbled for her hand and clasped it tight. He'd taken off his glove, and Ariana welcomed the warmth of his fingers wrapped around hers, not to mention his affection. That warmth and affection traveled from her hand right up to her heart. Slowly turning, she met his searching gaze.

"Thank you," he whispered back.

The moment was suspended for a heartbeat or two.

"Is that a light coming up the road?"

Matt quickly released Ariana's hand and pulled the truck out of park and into reverse, again glancing at his watch. "Crap. Yes, it is."

"We have guests?"

Ariana was confused. "I thought the roads were still closed."

Matt drove slowly to the front of the property. "They were earlier, but there are ways to get through. If there is a will…" As they grew closer, everyone in the truck's cab grew silent.

"There is a way. Dylan always says that. Oh my God. Matt? What have you done?"

Ariana watched him shrug, then catch his sister's questioning gaze. "I just helped Santa a bit."

"It's not a car. It's a sleigh. Is it Santa?"

Ariana followed Aimee's gaze and immediately felt her bouncing excitement. As they pulled up closer to the front of the inn, she noticed a driver—who looked a lot like Santa—help a man get his gear out of the sleigh and onto the ground.

A man who was wearing a military uniform.

Aimee screamed, "It's my daddy!"

"Oh, my God." Kat burst into tears.

Matt parked the truck. Kat's door flew open. Aimee jumped out and ran. Kat let go of a sob, looked again at Matt, and then followed behind her daughter at a slower pace.

Ariana sat in the truck with Matt, tears in her eyes, and watched the reunion scene unfold before her. Dylan Hamilton hugged and kissed his wife, pulling her close with one arm, while holding his daughter with the other. After a moment, Ariana turned to Matt...who was looking back at her.

"You did this?"

He shook his head. "No. Dylan did this. I just helped him set the scene a little."

"You have a good heart, Matt Matson," she said. "You are a good man."

Matt's gaze traveled over her face and landed on her lips. One hand cupped her cheek as he leaned in, searched her eyes momentarily, and then placed a soft, sweet, kiss on her mouth.

Their lips danced for a few seconds. His lingered over hers with featherlike touches. Then he gently pulled back.

Ariana sighed and closed her eyes at his release of her lips.

Matt's arms went around her and tugged her closer. Wrapped up in his embrace, her head against his chest, his heart beating wildly against her cheek, Ariana had never been more content in her life.

WALKING SLOWLY INTO THE INN, HOLDING HANDS WITH ARIANA, Matt felt on top of the world. He paused for a moment at the entrance, tapped the Holly Hill Inn sign next to the door, and glanced at Ariana.

"I noticed Kat do that the other day. And you, earlier. Why?"

He ran his hand over the old sign. The wood was weathered, and the painted lettering had faded, but both he and Kat had hesitated to have it repainted. "Mom and Dad put this sign here the year they opened the inn," he told Ariana. "Since they've been gone, tapping the sign is something we both do, sort of like saying hello to our parents."

Ariana squeezed his hand and stepped closer. "That's lovely." She trailed a finger over the letters and read the words below the name of the inn. "In loving memory of Elaine and Harold Peterson." She looked at Matt. "Who are they?"

"They owned the farm before my parents. Elaine willed the farm to them when she died. There is an entire story about how my parents and the Petersons are connected that I'll tell you one of these days." He looked down at her and grinned. "It's a story about love and commitment, about holding on and letting go."

Ariana's head bobbed up and down. "Oh. Tell me later?"

He leaned closer and kissed the tip of her nose. "I would love to."

They slowly moved inside, following a chatty Aimee into the large entryway. The animated girl engaged her dad in excited conversation, while a quiet Kat clung to Dylan's arm listening to every word her husband and daughter said.

The trio hurried down the hallway and turned right.

"They are so happy." Ariana slipped out of her coat and boots and looked up at him. "I need to run upstairs and get my camera."

"Can't it wait?" His hands lingered on her waist. Her full lips looked like they needed kissing again.

She shook her head. "Oh no. I want to capture their expressions from the beginning when they step into the room." She broke away.

Matt stopped her with a hand on her cheek. "Wait."

Her eyes grew round. "Oh?"

"Your mouth needs nibbling," he said.

"It does?"

Pulling her into his embrace once more, he brushed his lips over hers and then deepened the kiss. His heart sang as her arms went around his neck and she solidly kissed him back.

Pulling away slowly, she peered into Matt's eyes. "More of those later?"

He grinned. "Oh, yes."

"Good. Because right now we need to get in that sunroom."

He dropped his arms. "All right."

"And I need my camera."

Matt frowned a little and watched her fly up the stairs. He wasn't sure he understood this blogging business and the need for pictures, but it seemed important to her. Her feet padded quickly along the carpeted hallway overhead, entered her bedroom, and then reversed. She came flying back down the stairs as quickly as she'd left.

"Hurry," she said. "I want to see their faces when they see the lights."

"Yes. Of course."

They hustled down the hall and burst into the sunroom. Aimee twirled, eyes wide, her gaze shooting about, looking at everything. Matt watched Ariana aim her camera and snap picture after picture as an excited Aimee delightfully chattered with her parents as she took in all the Christmas cheer.

Matt had to admit the room looked awesome—with lights twinkling and reflecting, the cookies, the decorations. Ariana had evidently added a few more touches after he'd finished with the candles.

Dylan and Kat settled onto the sofa. Aimee plopped down with them, looking at the cookies. "I want one of those, and one of these, and oh, one of those too."

"Slow down there, little one. There will be plenty. You don't have to eat them all tonight."

"I know." She turned toward her dad. "We have to save some for Santa tomorrow."

"Absolutely.

Dylan winked at Kat.

Aimee reached for a cookie. "Can I have some cocoa too?"

"Of course, you may," Kat told her.

"I'll get it, elf." Matt turned toward the buffet. "I'm closer."

"Thanks, Matt."

"I'll help," Ariana said.

Matt glanced her way, tossing her a covert grin as she joined him. He liked that they shared this little kissing secret between them, and he wasn't ready to share it with anyone else yet. It was nice that it was just the two of them.

But when he reached the buffet, he halted, their stolen kisses forgotten. His gaze focused on a picture on the hutch—one he knew wasn't there earlier—one he hadn't seen in a very long time. "What is this?" He flipped around, looking at Kat. "Why is this here?"

"What do you mean?"

"You know what." He pointed. "This picture."

ARIANA WATCHED THE UNFOLDING SCENE AS IF IT WERE HAPPENING in slow motion.

Kat headed toward the hutch—her gaze connected with Matt's. Her expression puzzled. "I don't know. What picture is it?"

Then she stopped up short, too. "Oh."

Ariana froze. From the looks on their two faces, she knew she'd made a mistake. "It was me. It's a lovely picture, and I thought it would be nice to display, but I'm sensing I was wrong. I'm so sorry."

They turned and stared.

Ariana took a step forward. "I found it in the lower buffet cabinet. The note on the back said—"

"We know what the note says." Matt snatched the picture off the shelf and shoved it back into the cabinet. Rising, he looked Ariana square in the eyes. "You have no right to butt into our family business."

"Matt!" Kat grasped his arm.

Dylan rose and headed toward the door with Aimee in his arms. "We are going to take an exit," he said. "To see if there are more cookies and cocoa in the kitchen."

"Good idea." Matt stared at Ariana. "Aimee doesn't need to hear what I am about to say."

Ariana was floored. "Matt, please. I thought it was a beautiful family picture and—"

"And it was not up to you to decide to put it there."

"I thought you'd like your parents to be... Earlier today, you mentioned them, and I thought you would be open to having them be a part of tonight's lighting, kind of like with the truck and the lights and..." She stopped talking, searching his face. "But I can see now I was wrong. Matt, I'm sorry."

His expression was stern, emotionless, unmoving. "That's enough. You've come in here with your glitter and sparkle and upbeat attitude, and you think you can make everything all right with a few baubles and some candy canes. You can't. Nothing can change the past, Ariana. Not even an old picture that should never see the light of day again."

"But Matt. It's your family."

"Was my family."

"They are still your family."

He stepped closer. "All you care about is getting your Christmas pictures for your blog or article or whatever. You want to portray the perfect Christmas, the perfect town, the perfect inn, the perfect family. Well, that's not us, so put your camera away. Besides, I hate all this commercial Christmas crap, anyway."

She looked at Kat. "No. It's not like that. It was never like that."

Matt pushed past her. "Oh, I'm sure it is."

"I'm so sorry. I don't know what I've done wrong."

Kat touched her shoulder.

He headed for the door. "I'm going to the farm."

Rushing after him, Kat called out. "Matt, the roads."

"I'll be fine."

Ariana moved past Kat and followed Matt down the hall and into the entryway. "Matt, please. Can we talk about this? I don't know what I did wrong, but I want to understand and apologize and make it right."

He looked up as he grabbed one of his boots and shoved a foot into it. "I've been a fool. Just got caught up in the magic of it all. Magic isn't real. Christmas isn't real. *You and I are not real*, no matter how much I—" He cut his words short and glanced off. "Nothing can bring them back. Not a picture. Not a memory. They are gone, and you can't fix that."

She halted, stunned by his words. *They* weren't real? "I didn't want to fix anything, Matt. I can't. But I believe that you can keep their memories alive in your heart. You just have to believe that, too. Heck, you do that every time you tap the sign at the door."

He glared. "You don't get to talk about that." He shoved his other foot in his boot now and grabbed his coat. "I don't believe in any of this. I told you that from the beginning."

"And I don't believe *that* for a minute." She lifted her chin in defiance.

"Well, you don't have to." He quickly zipped his coat. "Be careful traveling home, Ariana. I hope you got what you came for."

He left, slamming the door a little too hard behind him. She jumped. Tears filled her eyes as she watched his shadow stalk down the brick walk and across the parking area to his truck.

"I didn't know…" she whispered. "I'm so sorry."

Turning, she noticed Kat standing beside her. "You did nothing wrong."

"I need to go after him." She bolted forward.

Kat grasped her arm. "No. Let him go."

Whirling back, she looked Kat square in the eyes. "I need to explain. We can't let him just go off like this. Things just feel…undone."

Kat held Ariana by both shoulders and gave her a little shake. "Ariana, this is Matt's problem to work out. Not yours. And not mine. You and I have both done all we can. He's the one who has to work through these issues."

"And what issues are those, Kat?"

She glanced off and exhaled. "The picture triggered a terrible memory."

"How was I to know?"

"You couldn't. But it *was* in the cabinet for a reason. I put it there a few years ago when he had a similar reaction. I made the same mistake back then."

She studied Kat's face. "Tell me. What happened to your parents?"

Kat let out a long sigh. "The picture… That was the last day we saw our parents alive, Ariana. Right before our lives changed forever."

She could see the pain in Kat's eyes after all this time. "I know losing your parents hurts, and I don't mean to make light of your pain at all, but I have to wonder why Matt has taken this so much harder than you, even to this day?" Ariana wasn't sure how Kat would take the question, but she meant it in the sincerest way possible.

"It's simple, Ariana." Kat stared into her eyes. "He thinks their deaths are his fault."

CHAPTER 20

By the next morning, Ariana had decided. One sleepless night and a gnawing ache in her tummy were the most prevalent indicators for what she should do next.

She needed to head home—and lick her wounds all the way there.

Merry Christmas to me. Bah humbug.

Her bags packed, she parked them by the front door in the inn's entryway. After piling her coat, purse, and camera bag on the bench, she made her way into the kitchen. According to the local news station, the storm had moved out of the valley, heading toward the coast; the main roads and interstates gradually reopening. A quick call to local law enforcement informed her that the county roads were mostly clear between the inn and downtown Charmington, but that she should proceed with caution between Charmington and the main highway.

She could likely make it to Boston easily over the next day or two and then get flight home. She didn't mind taking her time. Having done a little research online for potential accommodations between here and Logan International, she'd jotted down a couple of hotels and their phone numbers on a Holly Hill Inn notepad and tucked the paper into her purse. She'd make her plans once she was clear of Charmington. She was in no hurry to get to California, really, and could use the hotel time to write and upload her blog posts.

Besides, she wanted to be alone. There was a lot she needed to think through. Even though she'd suffered through a sleepless night thinking, she hadn't come close to coming to any sort of resolution about her feelings for Matt, and why his rejection cut so deep.

What she knew was that she couldn't stay in Charmington any longer.

There was no reason to stay at the inn, and every reason to leave. She had experienced Charmington, taken pictures and recorded story ideas, and had a great stay. Now, it was time to go back home and get to work on next-year's Christmas article pitch to the national magazine.

Besides, she had lost the Christmas spirit—and truthfully, that worried her as much as anything. She might just need a Christmas miracle to get her back on track.

Stepping into the kitchen, Ariana noticed Kat glance her way as she stood flipping pancakes. The kitchen clock over her head on the wall said it was just before seven o'clock. *They all must have slept in. Good.* Aimee bounded off her stool at the kitchen island and rushed toward her. Dylan looked up from his coffee.

"Well, there she is," Kat said. "Coffee?"

"I would love some. Do you have a to-go cup?"

Kat stared. "Oh, no. You're not leaving."

It wasn't a question. It was a rather firm statement of fact.

Approaching her, Ariana said, "Yes, I am. I thought about it last night. I made a mess of things, and it's best I go now. I hope you understand."

"But we haven't made the gingerbread houses yet. And tonight

226

is Christmas Eve. You don't want to be alone on Christmas Eve, Ariana."

To be straightforward, she may not have thought her plan through. Tomorrow *was* Christmas. She'd decided. It would be fine, and she could use the alone time to think. She stepped closer to Kat. "If I can be honest, I don't think I have it in me to be festive and cheery today. I wouldn't be good gingerbread house making company."

"Well, I've never seen a gingerbread house making session where people are all doom and gloom. It might do you some good, Ariana."

She shook her head. "No. It's okay. I have posts to write, and I can do that in the hotel room."

"And you can also write upstairs in the room you've stayed in for the past two days. Forget the gingerbread. Just stay. If you leave, you'll wake up tomorrow morning alone in a hotel bed on Christmas Day. I'll not have that."

Dylan stood up and went to the coffeemaker. "It's settled. You're not going anywhere." He poured another cup and then took a sip, looking over his cup at her.

She appreciated their efforts and their words, but she'd made up her mind.

"Thank you both, but I've already made my plans. This is for the best. Besides, the three of you deserve some family time, and I don't want to interfere."

Aimee sidled up beside her and tucked her little hand in Ariana's. "But you are family. I don't want you to go. I have a stocking for you and everything." Small tears formed on Aimee's lower lids.

Crouching down, she searched the child's eyes. "Oh sweetie. That's so nice of you. I would love to share your Christmas Eve tonight, but I'm just not able to. I need to go home to my own family."

"But we are your family, too. Right?" Aimee looked at her mother.

Ariana followed her gaze. "What?"

Kat let out a breath. "It's something Aimee asked for in her prayers last night. For you to be part of our family."

Aimee nodded. "And it's on my wish list for Santa."

To say she was overwhelmed would be an understatement. Ariana blinked back tears and reached for Aimee, holding her tight. "You are such a sweet girl. I love you to pieces."

"I love you back, Ariana," she said. "Please stay?"

Standing, she swiped at her tears with one hand, and held Aimee's small hand with the other. "Aimee, I can't stay this time, but I do hope I can come back and visit again. Maybe next Christmas?"

The girl teared up more. "Okay. Promise?"

It was all Ariana could do to hold back a sob. "I promise."

"But how do I know?" Aimee looked up at her with expectant eyes.

Ariana bent again and whispered. "Just believe, little one. Just believe." *Am I saying that to Aimee, or to myself?*

Aimee nodded and flashed a toothless grin.

"Now, back to your breakfast."

Aimee climbed onto her barstool, and Ariana turned to Kat. "Can you meet me at the front desk? I still need that signed photography waiver."

She dried her hands on a dishtowel. "Of course. I forgot all about that."

Ariana kissed Aimee on the cheek. "Goodbye. I'll see you again." Then she looked at Dylan. "It was so nice to meet you, Dylan."

"Likewise. Please come back again. I mean that."

"I will."

She headed for the entryway. Once there, she turned to Kat. "I left the waiver on the desk. You can sign and return to me by email when you get a chance. But Kat, there is one thing I want to say before I leave."

"Ariana?"

"I am truly sorry. I meant no harm. I wish... I wish I could rewind the whole scenario and make it better. My heart aches that I hurt Matt. And you. I would never intentionally hurt either of you." She paused, glancing away. Words escaped her.

Kat grasped both her hands. "Ariana, it's okay. I understand."

"Matt doesn't."

"He will."

"I'm not so sure."

"Give him time."

Exhaling a breath she'd held for way too long, Ariana squeezed her hands back. "I wish he had given me a little time, at least. We've barely had time to get to know each other. It was over before it even started, it seemed. I doubt that more time will make it better."

"I'm praying you are wrong, Ariana. Secretly, I wished for you to be a part of our family too."

Her heart jerked a little at Kat's words, her cheeks warming. "I'm not sure I believe in love at first sight, Kat. I'm darned sure Matt doesn't."

Kat dropped Ariana's hands and shrugged. "Our parents did. They married young and quickly, and once they did, never looked back."

"They were special. I can tell. But Kat, Matt and I, we are total opposites in the Christmas department. It would never work. And honestly? I can't have his bah humbugish attitude rubbing off on me right now...or anytime."

Frowning, Kat leaned into the desk. "I understand. But Ariana, if he wanted you to give him another chance, would you?"

Would she? How do I respond to that?

"Oh, Kat…."

"Can I convince you to stick around a little longer? I'm sure he'll come back to the inn sometime today, his tail tucked between his legs."

Turning, she pulled away from Kat and reached for her coat. "No. I need to go. And if Matt wants to find me, I'm sure he can figure out how." Leaning in, she gave Kat a kiss on the cheek. "I can't thank you enough for the beautiful stay and for your hospitality. I'll be sure and send you a link to my blog posts, and I assure you they will all be positive."

Kat smiled. "Please do. I look forward to reading them."

Ariana donned her coat, then swung her purse and camera bag over her shoulder. Grasping the handle of her roller bag, she paused, looking at the front door. "Kat, when you see Matt, will you tell him goodbye for me?"

Kat put herself between Ariana and the door, making direct eye contact. "Why don't you say goodbye yourself? I can tell you how to get to his farm."

"You are persistent." She knew what Kat was doing. "No. I'm the last person he wants to see."

"I wouldn't be so sure."

She fished her car keys out of her purse. "I'm sure. He was quite upset. And quite clear." Tears stung her eyes again. "He wouldn't let me explain. I tried to apologize, but he was not hearing anything I said. I feel like things are left undone… But Kat? Now is not the time. I'm not sure my heart can take it."

She turned and twisted the doorknob, not wanting Kat to see the tears streaming down her face.

"I think his heart is broken, too."

She glanced back. "Is that what I'm feeling? A broken heart?"

"That's for you to decide, Ariana."

She sniffed and then nodded.

"Stay around a while and think about it."

Shaking her head, she said, "No. This is not the place for me to wallow in what I did wrong and how I feel. Again, thank you so much."

Moving out the door, she rolled her luggage across the porch and down the brick sidewalk. She was leaving Holly Hill Inn on a much clearer day than when she'd arrived—weatherwise, that is. Her head was anything but clear, however. As she circled the drive and drove away, she watched the red clapboard home fade in her rearview mirror.

What a mess she'd made of things.

MATT PULLED ANOTHER BOX OFF THE SHELF AND SET IT ON THE floor in the back room of the hardware store. This one was full of garland. The one before that was filled to the brim with velvety red ribbons and bows. And the one before that held an overabundance of glittery plastic balls in assorted sizes and colors.

His mother would string the garland across the front of the store and hang the larger plastic balls beneath it. The bows were for the front windows. Somewhere in the backroom, there were several giant wooden cutouts. If he dug deep enough, he might come across a nativity scene or two that his mother had painted for church displays. Or, he might find the elves, Santa and Mrs. Claus, a big red sleigh and all the reindeer, including Rudolf, that used to circle the town gazebo when he was a kid. His mother had painted so many of these Christmas caricatures over the years, he had no clue where many of them ended up.

She had loved every minute.

Her work was featured in various Charmington Christmas displays throughout the years. She'd been frequently touted as the town artist and creator of the "curious and whimsical Christmas cutouts," as dubbed by one writer, in local and regional magazines and newspapers.

His thoughts immediately shot to Ariana. If she'd been around back then, she'd likely have been one of those people with a camera eagerly capturing the quirkiness of his mother's art. Pushing out a sigh, he was suddenly sorry for being silently annoyed with her desire to capture the beauty of the season and the Christmas spirit.

He should apologize.

If his mother were still alive, she would have latched on to Ariana just like Kat and Aimee had. They both loved Christmas and capturing its spirit through their art—his mom with her paints; Ariana with her words and her camera.

Suddenly, his heart grew warm thinking of both Ariana and his mother together in his thoughts. The two of them in his head made him smile, inside and out.

Returning to his task, he pushed aside a couple of old artificial trees, and spied a couple of characters leaning against the back wall. He brushed away the dust.

"Well, hello Santa. It's good to see you again."

And if Santa were here, the other pieces were likely here too. Good.

He'd been up all night. Hadn't even been to bed. In fact, he didn't go home as he'd told Ariana and Kat he would but came straight to the hardware store after leaving the inn. Here, in the back room of the hardware—the place that used to be his mom's art studio, and where she had stored years and years of Christmas paraphernalia—he'd had a come-to-Jesus meeting about Christmas, his parents, and his stubborn Scrooge attitude. It was a serious meeting that included himself, the absent Santa and the missing baby Jesus from the nativity scene, and probably his Maker, about how it was time to get his head on straight about all the above—and about why he'd been avoiding anything to do with the holiday for way too many years.

Oh, he knew why. He kept playing the same tapes over and over in his head every holiday season. And it was time for him to forgive himself.

Time to stop.

Besides, now he had a good reason—and her name was Ariana. While he couldn't rationalize the reality of loving her so quickly, he knew that love was what he was feeling in his heart. And if his parents could fall in love at first sight, so could he. Right?

But could Ariana?

Did she love him?

Could she *forgive* him?

With every box he pulled off the shelf and rummaged through, he saw Ariana poking through the boxes in the attic at the inn. Her smiling face, full of cheer and happiness, graced his thoughts and poked at his emotions.

She was an unending bundle of joy...and he'd squashed her without a backward glance.

He'd been wrong last night, and he needed to apologize. Wanted to apologize. For so many things.

But first, he had a few urgent tasks to take care of, and then he'd head back to the inn. She was staying through Christmas, so there was time. Hopefully, he could make amends with Ariana and see if they could try once more to get off to a better start.

They'd barely had a chance.

But there was one more thing he wanted to locate if he could.

Pushing through the stacks of boxes, he stood back and glanced over the dusty shelves, his gaze spanning the back half of the room. Finally, there, about midway up on a shelf, was the old hatbox he'd been looking for. He pulled it down, dust drifting from the shelf. He blew off another layer of grit from the top and set the box on a nearby table. Carefully removing the lid, he then pulled out a handful of old photographs.

He sat on a nearby chair, suddenly exhausted, but determined. One by one, he looked at every picture in the box of Christmases past. Remembrances flew by through tears and even some laughter. He could only hope that by facing some of the happy Christmases he'd experienced in the past, he could somehow carve out happier Christmases in the future.

EVEN WITH THE CHAOS OF LAST EVENING, ARIANA COULDN'T RESIST one last visit to downtown Charmington. Her heart was heavy, and maybe another look at Charmington would soften the hurt she felt inside—just a little. After all, she'd come all this way. Right? Even though the situation with Matt was weighing heavily on her, there was something about the town, some sort of magnetic pull, that drew her in.

Perhaps a small bit of Christmas cheer would help.

She parked near the gazebo this time, rather than at the other end of town, like before. Pulling into a parking spot, she glanced about the square and focused on the holly-draped wooden structure off to the side. Town workers had been busy clearing snow from the sidewalks and the gazebo, and she decided she needed the perspective of looking down Main Street from the gazebo steps for her blog. She had not taken that angle the other day.

Removing the camera from its case, she changed out the lens and exited her car. She approached the gazebo, climbed the few steps up to the landing, and turned around to look down Main Street. A few people were milling about—last minute, after the snowstorm, Christmas Eve shoppers, she suspected. Taking a deep breath, she inhaled both the sights and smells of the day. Fresh coffee was brewing somewhere. The air was crisp. The sky clear. And the day was just beginning.

Ariana raised her camera, focused, and took the first picture, aiming straight down the street. She angled herself a little to the right, shifted perspectives slightly, and snapped again. Moving the camera along the street, she focused on a man and woman heading into Leslie's Bakes & More. She snapped another picture. Then past the pastry shop, she panned the camera lens down the street, rounded the corner and grazed over a couple of shops at the end.

Wait. She backed the camera up and looked again, focusing on the shop near the corner. Pointing the lens a little higher on the building, she pulled the camera away from her face and blinked.

"No. It couldn't be."

She brought the camera to her eye again. *Yes, it is.*

Main Street Hardware popped into sight, all decked out for Christmas with Santa, his reindeer, and more.

"Well, I'll be."

A little giddy with excitement, Ariana lowered the camera and examined the hardware store's facade. In the night, Santa had done a little magic on the storefront. Had he also done a little magic on the man who owned the hardware?

She bit her lip. "Should I try to find out?"

Without hesitation, she grasped her camera tighter and made her way down the freshly swept steps of the gazebo and got into her car. As she started the engine and backed out, she wondered if she was doing the right thing.

If Matt were there, would he want to see her? Would he send her on her way, embarrassing her one more time about her innocent miscue? She didn't know.

But she had to try. Didn't she? One last time?

She pointed the car down the street, rounded the curve, and headed for a parking spot in front of the hardware store . After parking, she faced the structure and studied the wooden cutouts propped in front.

She blew out a breath. "Matt Matson, you broke my heart last night. Hurt me really bad. And on Christmas Eve, no doubt. I don't know what these decorations mean, but I know they weren't here a couple of days ago. Have you changed your tune so quickly?"

Not likely, a voice in her head said.

But there was proof. Right? In the decorations?

Ariana opened her car door and slowly stepped onto the pavement. She stood for a moment, looking at the front door, wondering if Matt would open it and pop his head out any second.

He didn't.

Gently, she closed the car door with a click. She ambled toward the front of the building and took a long moment to stare into the big display window. She couldn't see much. It was dark inside.

"Store's closed."

Ariana jerked to the right. "Oh?"

A man wearing a puffy jacket and a knit hat pulled down over his forehead stopped in front of her and nodded toward the hardware. "He always closes this time of the year. Wish he wouldn't because sometimes you just need stuff, but he does." The man shrugged and continued. "Of course, I guess he has his reasons." He peered directly into Ariana's eyes.

"I suppose so. I thought perhaps...."

"Naw, see? He even has a sign on the door."

"Oh?" Ariana took a few steps closer to the door. She saw a piece of paper taped to the inside of the window:

CLOSED UNTIL THE NEW YEAR

And then she spied the tiny letters beneath and peered closer:

bah humbug

Ariana stepped back, turning to say something to the man, but he was already down the street. She glimpsed him heading into the wine shop about three doors down. Lowering her eyes, she grasped the doorknob on the hardware store door and jiggled it a little.

Locked tighter than a drum.

"Who am I kidding? Matt must have put out the decorations before he left the other day."

Without a backward glance, she got into her car and headed for Boston.

CHAPTER 21

*T*he butterflies inside Matt's gut were an unusual thing for him. He was not the nervous or anxious type. He didn't have bodily or physical reactions to emotional things. But the closer he got to Holly Hill Inn, the more his stomach quivered.

He had to apologize to Ariana, and he had no clue how she would react, or if she would even talk to him. What he knew was that he didn't want another hour to go by before he told her how sorry he was for acting like an ass, and for saying the things he had said.

And on Christmas Eve, of all days.

He'd surely ruined her Christmas. Ironic, huh? That he'd be responsible for ruining the thing she'd come to Charmington and Holly Hill Inn for? To experience the magic of Christmas?

Magic. Bah. He'd killed that.

When would he learn?

Pulling onto the circular driveway to the inn, he braked hard. "I have to get the magic back. Now."

He took a deep breath, exhaled, and stared at the red clapboards framing the inn. "Now or never."

Exiting the truck, he slammed the driver's side door, jogged up to the porch, and grasped the doorknob. As he twisted it, the door jerked open, the knob out of his hands.

"Uncle Matt!"

He grinned. How could one not believe in magic with this beautiful child around? "Hey ya, elf!"

"I told you, Uncle Matt. I'm not an elf."

Inside now, he lifted her up and swung her around in his arms. "You know, you're right. You're not an elf at all. Those points I saw on your ears the other day? I don't think they were just any old common elf points."

Aimee grew wide-eyed as he talked. "They're not?"

He shook his head. "No, they're not. I think…" He leaned closer to her ear and whispered. "I think they were Santa's special helper elf points. That makes you special."

Aimee pulled back and grinned at Matt. "I want to be a reindeer."

Her toothless smile made him laugh. "I love you, Aimee Hamilton."

Aimee grasped his face in her two hands. "I love you too, Uncle Matt!"

They stood at the entrance to the kitchen now. Matt put Aimee down. He glanced at Kat and Dylan drinking coffee at the kitchen island. He felt giddily happy and scared out of his wits at the same time.

Their faces fell the moment he stepped into the room.

"Where's Ariana?"

Kat glanced at Dylan and sat up straighter in her chair.

"You're about an hour too late, Matt. Sorry."

His happy place was skidding off. "What? She's supposed to be here through Christmas. Where is she?"

"Gone home." Dylan rose, coffee cup in hand, and headed for the coffeemaker. "If you haven't a clue about that, man, you need lessons in women...and perhaps, relationship building."

Matt stepped forward. "I know I was a little harsh last night, but I didn't think she would leave. I've been working through things all night, and I need to see her. I don't understand why she left so soon." The butterflies in his gut had left by now, and in their place suddenly dropped a gnawing, empty ache.

Kat stood beside Dylan. Quietly, she said, "You broke her heart, Matt. She was hell-bent on getting out of here."

"But tomorrow is Christmas!"

"And she wants to spend it alone."

Frustrated, he paced and raked his hands over his head. "But no one should be alone on Christmas."

He stopped pacing and exhaled, looking at Kat.

"You're right," she said. "And we've been telling you that for years, Matt, but you haven't listened. Until now."

"Have I ruined things?"

"For whom? You? For her?"

"For us."

Kat shook her head. "Maybe. I don't know. I guess it depends on what you do next." She paused, looking him over. "The one thing she said was that she didn't need your negative Christmas attitude in her life, so if you expect to get her back, you're going to have to come to some sort of resolve with the past, Matt."

He agreed. "Yes. And I already had that come-to-Santa meeting last night."

"What?"

He waved her off. "Never mind. I'm good in that department. I just need to find her, but I have no clue what to do next."

Dylan piped up. "What do you want to do, man?"

He caught Dylan's gaze. "I want to apologize. I can't lose her." He suddenly felt frantic inside and a little out of control. "I think I'm falling in love with her."

"They go get her. Find her."

"How?"

Kat stepped up to him and grasped his forearm. Reaching into the pocket of her sweatpants, she pulled out a slip of paper. "Here. I found this on the floor next to the nightstand in her room. I think she forgot it, or it slipped out of her things."

Matt glanced at the paper. On it were the names of a couple hotels and some phone numbers. He snatched the paper from his sister and drew her into a big bear hug. "Thank you."

About an hour out of Charmington, Ariana pulled into the parking lot of a big-box store, just off I-89. She needed a minute just to gather her thoughts and work out the kinks in her shoulders. She'd done a bit of white-knuckle driving between Charmington and the main highway. The interstate was mostly clear in the right lane and was much easier to navigate than the two-lane roads. Still, she hadn't expected the drive to be as hazardous as it was.

"Geez. You're from California, Ariana. Kat was right. What do you know about snow?"

Nothing. Absolutely nothing.

At the other end of the parking lot, someone driving a pickup truck with a plow on the front cleared the snow, having already moved piles of the white stuff in the area where she had parked.

Leaving the car idling and the heater going, she stared ahead at the store. It was closed, but there were a few cars besides hers— some with people inside, engines running, exhaust puffing. Early-riser customers, she guessed. Last-minute Christmas shoppers.

The others were empty, engines off, likely vehicles of workers already in the store.

Glancing at the clock on the dash, she realized the time. She'd left Holly Hill Inn around seven o'clock that morning, and now the hour was creeping up on nine. Sitting there, she let a moment of peace and quiet waft over her, closing her eyes and breathing deep. Within seconds, tears stung and rolled over her lower lids—the first cry she'd let herself have since Matt got so angry with her—and she didn't stop them from falling.

As she cried, the tension in her neck and shoulders dissipated. She'd been driving with her arms and shoulder muscles taut the entire time—partially because she couldn't relax and partially because of the roads. It felt good to let go, with no one around to see her, hear her, or ask questions.

Lord knew she'd questioned herself enough over the past several hours.

Why she would assume, after knowing Matt and Kat only a few days, that it would be okay to do something as personal as pull that picture out and place it front and center, she didn't know.

But she also didn't know—and no one had told her; everyone had skirted the issue—why there was so much secrecy around their parents' deaths. Maybe it wasn't secrecy as much as an unwillingness to dredge up the past.

And she'd put the past right in front of Matt's face. Stupid.

Swiping at tears with the back of her hand, she pulled her bag closer and rummaged for a tissue. Finding none, she turned to the console where she had tucked a few napkins from a fast-food restaurant a few days ago. There. Success.

After blotting away lingering tears and blowing her nose again, she poked through the items in her big purse. "What in the world did I do with that note paper?"

Not finding what she was looking for, she sat back in the seat and stared at the store again—which had obviously opened because people were leaving their cars and heading inside.

"Darn it," she murmured. "I must have left that list at the inn."

Well, no matter. *I'll do a quick Internet search for hotels on my phone.* But when she picked up her phone, she quickly noticed the battery was nearly nonexistent. Plus, there was a voicemail. Why hadn't she heard the phone ring?

Low battery, likely.

"But I charged you last night! Why are you dying?"

This wasn't good. She needed her Wi-Fi, and she needed her phone. She dove back into her bag, searching for her charger and again, coming up empty. Next, she dug deeper into the console between the seats. She had brought her car charger. She knew she had—she had used it on her trip up to Charmington from Boston.

This was getting ridiculous.

Hotspot. She'd purchased a hotspot from her cell phone carrier just for this trip, having been warned of spotty internet service in some of the rural areas she would travel through. She'd not used one prior to this, so she'd almost forgotten she had it. But if memory served correctly, she could charge her phone with the hotspot device plus get Internet, of course.

She emptied her bag onto the passenger seat. Out plopped the hotspot device. "There you are." Sighing, she grabbed the thing and sat back in her seat. She pressed the button to turn it on and waited.

Cord. She needed a cord to charge her phone. Glancing at the seat, she saw none there. She knew she hadn't spotted one in the console. Had it slipped between the seats or under? She was going to have to get out of the car to look underneath the seat.

The hotspot blinked on in her hand. Then off. Then on again. She saw the lit face long enough to see the red line on the battery icon, the power at only two percent. "You're dead, too?" In disbelief, she tossed the device at the pile of paraphernalia on the passenger seat, then sat back in her seat and laid her head against the headrest.

"I can't believe this." Tears stung again. "No. I will not cry over this. This is not a thing to cry over."

I'll figure it out. No phone. No hotel numbers anyway. No internet. And no GPS map app to guide her to Boston. And tomorrow is Christmas.

Not how she had planned to spend Christmas Eve and Christmas Day. What happened to her sparkly, tinselly, and sugary holiday world?

Ariana exhaled so forcefully her cheeks puffed out, and condensation billowed up on her windshield. Sitting up taller in her seat, she stared ahead for a few minutes, thinking. Then quickly, she pulled the shifter into drive, accelerated, and pointed the car back toward the interstate.

"Just. Keep. Moving. Forward."

Ariana navigated around the plowing truck and the snow piles and a few cars entering the parking lot as she left. Once she was back on I-89, she breathed a little easier—until less than a half-mile down the highway traffic slowed significantly, and she came to an abrupt stop.

"Now what?"

The state police had blocked the road with their official vehicles, lights flashing, and were turning cars around. She eased up closer, following the line of traffic—basically because she had no choice—until she pulled up next to a trooper. Stopping, she rolled down her window. "Good morning, officer. What is going on?"

"There is a major accident up ahead, ma'am," he said. "You'll need to turn around and find an alternate route."

"But I'm heading to Boston."

"Not this way. The interstate will be closed for some time. There are fatalities."

Ariana sucked in a breath. "Oh, my."

"Can you move along, ma'am?"

"Yes. Of course."

Ariana followed the traffic and turned around, guided by the troopers directing traffic toward the other side of the road. Once she was heading north again, she just drove, not really knowing what to do next. She supposed she could stop at the big box store and gather her thoughts again. She could go in and buy a charger there, and maybe a map, so she could find another route to Boston.

Or she could not waste time and simply head back to Charmington.

And what would she do once she got there? She couldn't go back to the inn. That was out of the question. She was certain there were no other hotels in the area—she'd searched before she'd booked at the inn. So, she really *couldn't* go back to Charmington.

Could she?

On the console, her cell phone buzzed and jumped. Ariana glanced down to see the caller: Holly Hill Inn.

Quickly, she snatched up the phone while watching the face turn black. "Hello?"

But no one responded. Apparently, that call has sucked the last bit of juice from the phone.

It was dead.

MATT DROVE AS FAST AS HIS TRUCK AND THE ROADS WOULD LET HIM. He'd called all three numbers on the paper Kat had given him and learned that Ariana had not made reservations at any of those hotels—and that they were all full up for the holiday, anyway. All he knew was that she was heading to Boston, so he supposed that's what he would do, too.

He shook his head. Needle in a haystack.

He'd never find her.

Snatching his phone out of his jacket pocket, he drove on and called Kat. She answered within a couple of seconds.

"Matt? Did you find her?"

"No. Not yet."

"I tried to call her just a few minutes ago. No answer."

Matt sighed. "I don't know why she wouldn't pick up a call from you. It's me she's mad at. I can understand why she hasn't returned my call."

"You called her?"

"Yes, and I left a message earlier."

"I hope you were nice."

"Kat. Do you think I'd call and yell at her again? I feel terrible about that. No, I apologized and asked her to reconsider and come back so we could talk."

He heard Kat blow out a long breath. "Well, that's good. Hey Matt, be careful. There was a report of an accident on I-89. A couple of semis tangled with a car or two. I guess the roads are still a little slick down that way."

The second Kat mentioned the accident, his gut seized. "Oh, my God. Ariana."

"Oh no. Matt. Surely she's not involved."

"Try to call her again. If you get through, let me know. I see lights up ahead. I'll let you know what I find out."

He ended the call and tossed the phone onto the passenger seat. Gripping the steering wheel so tight his knuckles hurt, he sped up, heading toward the roadblock, an ache in his stomach the size of New Hampshire.

No. This was not happening again.

SHE'D SAT PARKED IN FRONT OF THE GAZEBO IN CHARMINGTON FOR at least an hour now. Maybe longer. She'd sort of lost track of time. Ariana knew she had to make some sort of move, and soon. She couldn't sit there all day. Had to find a place to stay the night. And she needed to get her phone charged so she could communicate with people. Glancing about, she wondered if any of the shops around the square carried phone chargers.

Maybe the hardware. Yeah, right.

The hardware was closed. There had to be some other place.

"Just get out of the darned car and go look," she mumbled. "Stuff will not happen with you sitting here."

She'd sat there entirely too long anyway, but at least she felt comfortable in Charmington. Until she'd arrived back in the friendly town, she felt nervous and unsure and, well, rather lost. At least in Charmington, she felt good. If only she could bring herself to go back to the inn, she might feel even better.

Her gut ached to talk to Matt. She had so much to say. So much to apologize for. She hated the undone feeling that had encompassed her entire body. Maybe she should try to get in touch with Kat. She would know what to do.

"Okay. Move it, Ariana."

She pushed open her car door, grabbing her wallet off the seat, and locked the car. Spanning the landscape around the square, her gaze landed on a drugstore next to that yummy bakery with the Snickerdoodles she'd visited a couple of days ago. The drugstore looked to be her best bet.

She headed that way.

Over the next fifteen minutes, she secured a car charger for the phone and grabbed a scone and coffee from the bakery. She put the phone on the charger in the car and let it charge while she took up residence in the gazebo.

Leaning on the rail, she sipped her coffee and looked down the square to where the hardware store stood. She eyeballed the big Santa figure, the garland dripping with tinsel, the Rudolph flanking Santa's side.

"When in the world did he do all of that?"

The smell of coffee suddenly became stronger. "Took me a

while to find old Santa, but once I did, the others weren't far behind. I figured better late than never."

Ariana whirled. "Matt?"

He strolled toward her from the other side of the gazebo, carrying a steaming cup of coffee himself. "Hi, Ariana. Thank God you're here."

A bit dazed, she shook her head. "What are you doing?"

"I was about to ask you the same question. I thought you'd gone. I've been trying to find you, and you've been here all along?"

She shook her head. "No. No. I was headed to Boston, but the interstate was closed, and I didn't know what else to do but come back." Pausing, her stomach trembling a little, she eyed him. "I thought you were at the farm."

His gaze drifted off, looking down the street. "Naw. I never made it to the farm. I came into town last night instead. Spent the night at the store."

"And decorated, it looks like."

"Yes. And that."

He shuffled his feet, glancing lower, and then looked back at her. "I had just got back into town when I saw you park your car. I've been out looking for you. Kat said you were going home."

"That's right. I am. Was."

"But you're here. In Charmington."

She nodded. "I, uh… Came back." She wondered if what she was about to say would sound superficial to him, then figured she'd deal with it if it was. "I'd like to say I came back to see the town one more time, and well…to take some more pictures. I know you think that's weird and commercial or something, but Matt, it's my business. It's how I pay my bills. And frankly, it's my passion. Besides, other people enjoy my writing and my photography."

"But it's not why you came back?" He stepped closer.

"No. Not really."

"It doesn't matter. I'm glad you did. Ariana? I'm a jerk. To be honest, I don't remember everything I said to you last night, and if you could spare me a few minutes, I'd like to explain a few things."

Stepping back, Ariana shook her head. "Wait. Matt. What I just said wasn't entirely true. I was halfway to Boston when I got turned around because of an accident and, well, other stuff, and I just headed toward Charmington. I have no clue what my next move is. I didn't even plan to come back. I just sorted of pointed my car in this direction and ended up at the gazebo. I suppose I just wanted to be here."

Matt's expression was a mix of seriousness and relief.

"Ariana. I saw the roadblock too. I feared it was you until I talked to the trooper. He described the vehicles, so I knew then you weren't involved, but I have to tell you, it scared me to death to think you could have been."

She stared at him. "I guess it's a good thing I pulled over earlier. I took a moment in a parking lot."

"A parking lot?"

She nodded. "Yeah, I needed to… Well, I needed to cry and get my act together. The past twenty-four hours have not been my finest hours."

Matt moved closer and grasped her elbow. "Ariana, I want to apologize."

"No. I'm the one who needs to apologize, Matt. There is a lot I don't understand. And to be honest, you don't owe me any kind of explanation. I'm just some girl who happened along one Christmas —I don't need to get mixed up in your life."

"What if I want you to get mixed up in my life?"

"Do you?"

"I would like to see what happens."

"Oh, Matt. It would never work. You are Scrooge. I'm Miss Christmas. I don't think—"

"What if I kill the Scrooge act?"

She stared at him. "Can you?"

He took a moment before answering—still, his eyes never left hers. "Yes. I can. But there is more. Can we talk? It's just a short walk down to the store. Do you have the time? Can you make the time? I'd like to share a few things with you."

Ariana bit her lip. She had all the time in the world, so why not?

"Matt, I don't know…."

He took one step closer and reached for her hand. "Please?"

CHAPTER 22

$\mathcal{M}$att unlocked the front door to the hardware store and stepped back to let Ariana go inside first. Blinking as she moved into the building, her eyes worked to adjust to the absence of light inside, then Matt flipped on a switch and overhead lights flickered to life.

"Wow. What a neat old building," she said, looking around and turning to Matt. "Like something you might see in a movie." Her gaze drifted up from the aisles of old shelves and drawers to the exposed wooden beams and rafters above.

He glanced about. "It is rather cool. There are days I'm sure I don't appreciate it enough."

Ariana eyed him, wondering what he meant.

"Follow me." He took her hand and led her through the center aisle.

Her boot heels made only a soft sound on the worn wooden floor planks. Still fascinated by the store and its contents, she took in as much as possible as they approached the rear of the store.

Matt opened a door and led them into another room.

"It's a mess. Sorry about the dust. I hope you don't have allergies."

"I'm fine." She followed him to a table. Matt pulled out two chairs and motioned for her to sit. She did, and he sat in the opposite chair.

For a moment, he just sat there looking at her, then reached for her hands and held them. With a lengthy sigh, he peered directly into her eyes.

"I might need to just talk for a while."

Ariana slowly nodded. "Okay, Matt."

He gave her a little smile. "First. Last night... I said some things, and I didn't mean any of them, but I didn't know how to react, so I reverted to old behaviors."

Pausing, he watched her face.

"I actually have grown to like your glitter and sparkles and Christmassy attitude, Ariana. I never meant to say I didn't. I was hurting and my words came out that way too, I'm sure."

Ariana moved one of her hands over his. "It's okay, Matt. I understand."

"And I don't want you to think I don't appreciate who you are, or what you do. I know your writing and photography are important to you. And you love sharing the joy of Christmas with others. I want you to know that I get that."

She scooted closer to him. "Matt. We all say things when we're scared or hurt that we don't mean. It's okay. I understand. But Matt...?"

"Yes?"

Sighing, she grasped his hands tighter. "I am sorry about the picture. It was wrong of me to assume it was okay to display it. Had I realized, I never would have placed it there."

"I know."

"My heart aches just thinking about the pain I caused."

"My heart aches thinking of you leaving here because of me. Of your not enjoying Christmas because of me. And of me not getting a chance to make things right."

Ariana felt his worries and hurt. She watched Matt's eyes dart back and forth, then his gaze shifted, looking just off her shoulder.

He motioned to the table. "I want to show you these."

"Pictures?"

"Yes. A box full of them. Mom often stored things she didn't have room for at the house here. This back room was her studio for many years. Sometimes she'd come here on slow days and work on putting the pictures into photo albums or categorizing them. Dad was a camera buff," he looked at her, "like you, I guess. He took a lot of pictures."

Ariana picked up a few and looked through them. "These are Christmas pictures."

"Yes. The entire box. I went through them all last night."

Ariana lowered her hand with the pictures to her lap. "Matt. Will you tell me what happened?"

She waited.

"I was eleven," he began. "Kat had just turned thirteen. It was the day before Christmas Eve, and I rushed home from my friend's house to change my wish list for Santa. All I could do was rave about the new Razor Scooter my friend's uncle had brought him for Christmas. I wouldn't shut up about it."

Stopping for a moment, he searched her eyes.

"So, of course, that was the day of the lighting and everyone was busy. The picture you found? It was taken that day. Dad set up the tripod and the timer on the camera and took it. Years later, my grandmother found the camera and had the film developed and framed the picture. I had the same reaction then when I saw it.

"But it wasn't really about the picture. It was about the damn scooter. Early on Christmas Eve, Mom and Dad left for the city. They told us they'd be back by early afternoon. When five o'clock came around and they weren't home yet, Kat called our grandparents, who lived a few miles away. They didn't answer, but after a while, they pulled into the drive. That's when we learned both Mom and Dad were killed in a car accident."

"Oh, no, Matt." Leaning closer, Ariana gripped Matt's hands tighter. "I'm so sorry."

He lifted his chin. "Yeah, me too."

"It wasn't your fault."

"I've been told that many times, Ariana. But when I found out that they had gone to get the damn scooter, all I could do was blame myself."

Ariana exhaled a breath she'd been holding for too long. "If that's true—if that is why they were going, Matt—they did it because they loved you."

He dropped her hands and stood. "I know. But I sure as hell would have rather had them in my life the past fifteen years than a scooter that would have lasted until the new wore off."

"That's the adult you talking now, Matt. Not the kid, you. Be easy on yourself."

He nodded. "Yes. You're right."

"So, you've been avoiding Christmas ever since?"

"I tolerated it as a kid and through my teens, but the guilt always ate at me. Our grandparents—my dad's parents—did what they could to make things better for Kat and me. Our Mom's parents did too, but they lived in Philadelphia, and we didn't see them as often. Mostly summers. But I could never really shake the guilt, especially during the holidays. As I became an adult, I just avoided it altogether, and before I realized it, that guilt became a part of who I am and made me one sour sucker to get along with during the holidays."

"Did you go to live with your grandparents?"

He shook his head. "No, they moved into the inn. They wanted to keep things normal for us. Kat inherited the house eventually, and the inn business. The hardware store came to me on my eighteenth birthday. Grandpa Calvin died a year before that. Grandma Maureen stayed on for a while, then she moved back to her place. We lost her a few years ago, and their small farm became mine."

He stopped talking and focused on her. "I'm sorry, Ariana. I've ruined your perfect Christmas."

"Oh, Matt. No." Reaching for him, she put her arms around his shoulders and hugged him. "Nothing is ruined. And nothing is ever perfect. We just have to believe everything is going to be better from here on out."

He pulled back, peering into her eyes. "Is that all it takes? To believe?"

"I'm sure it also takes time—but believing in the magic of Christmas never hurt anyone. I do believe in that." She paused. "And sometimes, it helps if you don't have to do it alone."

He sucked in a breath. "I have time," he whispered. "I want to believe."

She grinned. "Me, too."

"And to be perfectly honest," he added, "not doing it alone sounds very nice, too."

Ariana whispered, "I like the sound of that."

Matt leaned closer. "Ariana, will you stay a few more days? I feel like there is so much more I want to share with you. So much I want to learn about you. I know I have no right to ask you to stay, but will you consider it?"

Tilting her chin, she peered into his deep brown eyes and tipped her face up to brush a soft kiss across his lips. "Yes, Matt. I want to stay."

ARIANA FOLLOWED MATT BACK TO HOLLY HILL INN. ON THE WAY, she pressed the button on the side of her cell phone, now fully charged. Immediately, her notifications popped up.

A call from an unknown number.

A call from Holly Hill Inn.

A call from her parents.

She punched the password for her voicemails while observing the road.

You have three messages. The first message was sent at seven-thirty-five a.m. from an unknown caller, lasting forty-two seconds.

"Ariana, it's Matt. I know you don't want to talk to me, but please listen. Okay? I'm going to take one more shot here and ask you for some time to talk. I know I was ugly last night. I behaved badly and I want to apologize. Hell, I'm sorry, Ariana. You don't deserve what I dished out. I have no excuse. I screwed up and I want to make amends. Please? I'm heading to the inn now. I hope you will find it in your heart to see me when I get there. Please." A silent moment passed, but the message didn't end. Then quickly, he added, "Ariana, I'm falling in love with you. Please let me apologize."

Matt was falling in love with her?

Message number two, sent at eight-twenty-nine a.m. from Holly Hill Inn, lasting twenty-one seconds.

"Ariana, this is Kat. Please call me when you get this message. I'm worried about you. There is a wreck on the interstate, so the roads aren't so great. If you get this, turn around, please, and come back. Besides, Matt was here. He's a mess. And he's trying to find you. Please come back and talk with him."

Message number three, sent at nine-forty-five a.m. from Doris Estrella, lasting eighteen seconds.

"Sweetheart, it's Mom. Just checking in. Hope you are having a wonderful Christmas Eve. We saw the weather on the news, so let us know how you are faring. Call us please? Love you."

End of messages.

She called her mother first, assuring her she was alive and well and safe from the storm. Ariana shared she was indeed having a wonderful time, would send pictures soon of the magical Charmington, and that she would call her again in the morning, on Christmas Day.

Since they were just a few miles from the farm, she wouldn't call Kat back. And Matt? She would see him soon.

Smiling, she tailed his truck, feeling like she was following him into their destiny.

MATT PULLED INTO THE CIRCULAR DRIVE AT THE INN AND PARKED. Immediately, he pushed open his door and jumped out of the truck, looking back to where Ariana was parking behind him. Her door popped and she rushed forward. He was at her side in seconds.

"Oh, Matt," she breathed. She took one look up at him with her big blue eyes and then wrapped her arms around his neck and hugged him. "I think I'm falling in love with you too."

He cocked an eyebrow. "You got my message?"

"Yes. Finally!"

"Why just now?"

She rolled her eyes. "Long story. Tell you later?"

He grinned and tugged her closer. "I'm hoping we have all night." He paused then, a little panicked by having said that. "Not that I'm expecting… Well, you know what I mean. For you and me to talk and—"

Ariana silenced his bumbling words by putting her lips on his mouth. "Kiss me," she whispered.

He fully embraced her, wrapping his arms around her small, compact body, and pulling her even closer. "Yes, ma'am."

The kiss was exquisite. As their lips pressed together, all tension melted from Matt's body. Her mouth nibbled and teased. Groaning, he clutched the back of her head and came up with a handful of soft, silky hair. Inside his chest, wacky, wonderful things were squeezing his heart.

Letting go and letting himself fall in love her was so much better than holding onto the guilt and anger.

Ariana deepened the kiss, and he was a complete goner. Breaking away, he whispered, "I think I've already fallen for you, Ariana. My gut ached so when you were gone. I thought I'd lost you."

"I thought you didn't want me."

"I didn't know what I wanted. I was hurt and angry and wrong."

"Matt, I'm so sorry I caused you all the pain."

Stroking his face and peering down into her eyes, he said, "That's all gone now. No more of that. Okay? I love you, Ariana."

Her mouth turned up in a cute, pert grin. Her eyes may even have twinkled. His Ariana was back. "I love you too, Matt."

He leaned in again for another kiss when a door slap sounded behind them on the porch door.

"They *are* back! Mommy! Daddy! Ariana and Matt are here!" Aimee skipped down the porch steps toward them.

"Where in the world is your coat, elf?" Reluctantly letting go of Ariana, Matt turned to scoop up Aimee.

"Elves don't need coats," she said. "They are used to the cold."

"Well, that's only when they've become acclimated to the North Pole," he told her.

"Accli...what?"

"Never mind."

Kat rushed from the porch and took Aimee. Dylan stayed on the top step, watching, and sipping from his coffee mug.

"Oh, my goodness, child. Come on, let's all get inside." Kat paused and motioned them toward the house. They all moved forward. Kat stared at her brother, then sidled a glance at Ariana. "You're back. Both of you."

Matt nodded. "We are."

"And all is good?"

"All is fine."

Kat blew out a breath that fanned out in puffs on the cold air, stopping at the steps to face them.

Aimee piped up. "Ariana, you did come back. Just like you said. Only quicker."

Matt turned to Ariana and noticed some misty dampness in her eyes.

"I told you I would someday, Aimee."

"I know. But I really didn't think it would happen."

"You didn't?"

Matt touched his niece's cheek. "I didn't either, sweetheart, but this past day I kept telling myself that I had to keep believing it could happen." Glancing to Ariana, he grasped her hand and tucked her into his side. "Sometimes all you need is to believe."

"The magic of Christmas," Ariana added.

Matt cocked his head and looked deep into Ariana's eyes. "My parents married on Christmas Day. They believed in the magic, too—but they almost didn't get married."

"What happened?"

"They were on their way to elope when they got caught in a snow squall. They ended up at the Peterson's—remember the names on the sign? The story goes that Elaine Peterson shared some Christmas magic with Mom, and she and Dad patched things up that night."

Ariana smiled. "There truly is magic at Christmas, isn't there?"

"I believe that now."

"I think it's this place," she told him. "And the people who live here. Holly Hill Inn seems to be a place for Christmas magic...and perhaps a miracle or two."

Matt touched his forehead to Ariana's. "You are my miracle."

She smiled. "You are my magic."

Matt grinned and kissed her lips.

"Come on! Enough kissy stuff. We have presents!"

Matt glanced up at the porch, saw his toothless niece waving frantically, and clasped Ariana's hand. As they walked up the steps, he thought about the turnaround his life had become in such a short time. As he and Ariana stepped up to the front door, he tapped the Holly Hill Inn sign, Ariana's fingers entangled with his.

"Merry Christmas," he whispered. "I love you all."

ONE YEAR LATER...

"*O*kay, everyone. Hold those positions and say cheese!"

Ariana looked one more time through the lens of the camera, made sure all members of her family were in the picture, and checked the timer. Eight seconds.

Racing around the tripod, she took her place at the far end of the group, leaned in, and said, "Smile."

Everyone froze.

The camera finally flashed.

Then, the group broke into a cheer, and Ariana rushed back to make sure no one would trip over the tripod. "That's the last one for a while. I promise."

"It better be." Matt leaned in, gazed into her eyes, and kissed her lips. "Here, can you take him? I'm going to help your dad get their gifts out of the car."

"Of course." Ariana took Little Matt out of her husband's arms. "Can you stash this tripod and camera somewhere safe on your way out?"

"I can."

Little Matt tangled his fingers in her hair.

"Hey, sweetie." She rubbed noses with him.

"Aunt Ariana? Can I hold him now?"

She glanced down at Aimee, and then at the chaotic scene in the sunroom. Cookies were everywhere. Her mom, Doris, was sitting on the sofa chatting with Ariana's sister, Claire. Her sister's two kids were playing with a toy train under the tree. Dylan and Grant, Claire's husband, were watching a football game. Why they all wanted to gather in one room, she didn't know.

"How about you sit by Grandma Doris. I'll hand him to you."

Little Matt was barely two months old, but he was still a chunk and a handful to carry around. Best Aimee was sitting when she held him.

Doris looked up as Aimee plopped beside her. "I get to hold the baby," Aimee told her.

"And Grandma Doris will be right here if Little Matt gets fussy. Okay?" She made eye contact with her mom. "I need to help Kat in the kitchen."

"We're fine here, darling." She waved her off. "Go get dinner on the table."

Standing, Ariana smiled, then headed for the kitchen. Before she left the sunroom, however, she turned back to take in the scene. Even with all the chaos, her heart was full and happy.

Kat snuck up behind her and whispered in her ear. "See, I was right."

Ariana turned. "What?"

She winked. "I told you the first day you got there that you would be here for a long time."

Ariana stepped back and eyed her. "That you did. Who would have thought I would never leave?"

Kat grinned. "I need to get back to the kitchen."

"I'm behind you." Ariana turned to follow her and felt a small hand tuck inside of hers. She looked down. "Aimee? I thought you had the baby?"

"Grandma Doris wanted him."

"Oh, I see."

"Aunt Aimee?"

"Yes?"

"I really did get my Christmas wish, didn't I?"

Puzzled, Ariana crouched down and met Aimee's gaze. "What's that, sweetheart?"

"I got you for my family. And baby Matt, too. And Grandma Doris. And Aunt Claire. And—"

"Whew! Aimee," Ariana interrupted. "Yes, you have all kinds of new family now."

The little girl nodded. "You told me to believe, and I did."

Not being able to contain her tears, she tugged Aimee close and hugged the child. "Oh, honey. I love you so much."

"We both just needed to believe, didn't we, elf?"

Ariana looked up into Matt's eyes. Then standing, she put her arms around her husband's neck and kissed his lips. "And I love you," she whispered. "Believing can be contagious."

"You are contagious…" he said, nibbling at her lips. "Merry Christmas, Mrs. Matson."

"Merry Christmas to you, Mr. Matson."

CHAPTER 23

THE LAST CHRISTMAS AT HOLLY HILL INN

"What time is your mom's flight?"

Ava Cohen looked up from her coffee cup and frowned at her husband, Will. It was too early on a Sunday for conversation, and given that, why was she even awake at—she glanced at the kitchen clock—eight-twenty-nine in the morning? Sleeping until noon on the weekends was her usual modus operandi. Plus, the performance ran long last night, and then there was the after party….

Oh, right. My family. And his.

They would all arrive today—her mom and brother flying in from Indiana, and Will's parents and grandfather driving over from Connecticut. They would gather at Will and Ava's Brooklyn apartment, then head out in the morning on the train north to Charmington, where they would spend their Christmas week together. Taking the Christmas train, as they sometimes called it—because it was often full of Christmas shoppers and holiday vacationers—was just the start of their holiday week. It's the only time all year that the families got together.

It was a sacred week, and a tradition was born a dozen years earlier when Will and Ava were in high school. The two had grown up best friends in northern Indiana, and their families had always been close, but when Will's dad transferred to Hartford, the families separated. That first Christmas, the families spent the holiday week together at Holly Hill Inn, near the famous upstate New York Christmas village of Charmington. The tradition began.

Ava yawned. "I have to look at the email. I don't remember."

"Well, check on it. If they took an early flight, we should head to the airport soon. JFK or LaGuardia?"

"Newark. I remember that. And I'm fairly sure they arrive this afternoon."

"Fairly sure?"

She rubbed her temples with both forefingers. "Yes, Will."

"Can you check?"

Ava blinked and sat back in her chair. "Yes. Right after I finish my coffee. My phone is charging in the bedroom. What's the hurry?"

"We have things to do, Ava. I still need to get a couple of gifts. Have you packed?"

He was anxious as an old hen, as her Grandma Rosie used to say. Ava huffed out a quick breath, guarding her impatience. "No. I've not packed yet, and I still need to get a few things too. We have all week. Christmas is six days away. Remember, we always shop in Charmington for some of our gifts. That way we don't have to carry everything on the train."

"I know. I want to get a little something for the Halls at the inn. They are almost like family this time of year."

"Of course. I haven't shopped for them yet, either. And I still need to find something for your grandpa, but let's wait until we get there. Okay?"

"Sure." He eyed her for a moment. "That's unusual."

"What?"

"You, agreeing with me. Especially lately."

Ava rolled her eyes and brought her coffee cup to her mouth.

Will didn't sit on that subject for long and headed in another direction. "Big party last night? You got in later than I expected."

She shrugged. "The usual suspects. It went long. Last production before the holidays and all. You know?"

"So that's why you're hungover."

Ava scowled and sipped her cooling coffee. What was it with this third degree? "Good God, Will, I thought you were working the night shift, so I didn't think it mattered what time I came home. Or, if I'm hungover."

Closing his eyes at her words, Will turned away.

"And for the record, I'm not *that* hungover. I had a couple of drinks. I'm tired. This fall has been a long haul after not working for months."

"Got it."

She eyed him. "Why didn't *you* work last night?"

"They didn't need me. I came home early."

"Excuse me? Since when does Belview Medical Center not need its top emergency medical physician within arm's length? Especially on a Saturday night before the holidays?"

"Last night was surprisingly slow." He moved closer to the table, took her coffee cup, and filled it at the coffeemaker. He set it carefully back before her with a quick glance, then stepped away. "I was on call in case they needed me. They didn't."

Ava watched him. That kind of gesture was one reason she had fallen in love with him so many years ago. He always thought of others' needs and sometimes neglected his own. Sometimes.

"You're always on call, Will."

His gaze narrowed. "Touché."

She didn't acknowledge her minor victory. "So you came home early."

He nodded. "I'm off until after the new year. Remember? I'm getting a break before—"

Before you start your new position. Ava knew why he had cut off his words. He didn't want to go there, and honestly, right now, she didn't either—so she ignored them.

"Of course. Me too."

The Gershwin had closed for the holidays after last night's production of *Wicked*. While she was stellar playing Glinda in the play—at least according to reviews—at home lately, she more accurately personified the Wicked Witch of the West. Why she couldn't be nice to Will, she didn't know.

Well, she did know. And so did he.

She'd had only a few nights off since Broadway reopened in September after the pandemic closures, and she was ready for a break. But she wasn't looking forward to spending it with the family this year, especially after the decision she and Will had made a few weeks ago.

"I hope we don't kill each other before the end of the week."

Will turned. "That's the spirit, Ava. Can we wait until the family leaves before we kill each other? Or should you put me out of my misery now?" He punctuated that statement with a long, hard look, and then left the room.

"You know what I mean, Will. When do we ever get seven days together?" she called out. "Once a year, and it usually only takes three days before we are on each other's nerves."

"What about our honeymoon? Did I get on your last nerve then too?"

Ava felt the delayed chill of his words and, for whatever reason, felt like crying. *Crying for what?* For their lost love? For the loving couple they used to be? For the future they would no longer share? The children they wouldn't have? For all the plans made when they were younger and stupidly in love, which would never materialize?

Or for faking it these past months and cheating themselves out of a happy life?

No crying. Buck up, Ava.

She pushed away from the table and stood. After one more sip of now-cold coffee, she followed him into the living room. "If you want to sign the papers today, perhaps that will put us both out of our misery. Let's just do it." *I need things final.*

His back to her, she studied him. Will stood looking down onto the street below outside their brownstone in Brooklyn, likely watching the Saturday morning dog walkers and grocery shoppers. Even though she couldn't see his face right now, she knew he was tired. His shoulders were rounded and slumped; his dark brown hair tousled, like he'd slept restlessly or had been raking his fingers through it.

"No," he said.

"Why not?"

"Because we agreed, and we have a plan. Let's not let that go off the rails at this point. Besides, the families are on their way."

"We can still go to Charmington, Will. We'll just go with everyone knowing." Sighing, Ava stepped into the center of the room and stretched her arms toward the ceiling. She'd slept curled into a ball, evidently, her body wound tight. Her brain was still not fully engaged. Yes, she'd probably had one too many martinis. "But perhaps you're right. Let's not stray from the plan. Heaven forbid."

He whirled to face her. "Is that what you want? Are you so hellfire sure that signing the divorce papers is what we need to do? What about the plan?"

"The plan to go to Charmington wasn't to save our marriage, Will," she reminded him. "Going to Charmington for Christmas one last time was for the family."

"And not for us?"

"Well, indirectly, I suppose."

"But not to save our marriage."

"No. Our marriage cannot be saved. We've hashed this over

repeatedly. We want different things. And if you recall, the whole separation thing was your idea to begin with."

"Yes, initially, a separation. But things snowballed when the subject of divorce came up, and…."

"Let's just get through the week, Will. I am not in the mood to rehash all of that now."

"So, we'll fake it the entire week. Can you do that?"

"Well, that's what you are proposing, isn't it?"

"Yes, but can you do it?

"I'm an actor. I think I can manage it. Can you?"

"Of course."

"I just don't get it. Why pretend all week that things are okay, and then turn around and tell them at the end of the week that we are splitting? They are going to figure it out."

Will stared. "Because we won't let that happen. We said we wanted to spend one last Christmas together at Holly Hill Inn like normal. We didn't get to go last year because of the snowstorm. I want us to spend one last family time together, Ava. And I want one more Christmas with you before our lives change forever. Can you do that for me? Please?"

Ava studied him, heaved a lengthy breath, and then let it go slowly. "Even though I'm cranky and not even sure I want to do it?"

His gaze connected with hers and held. His deep brown eyes had never looked so intense. "Yes, Ava. Even though."

WILL COHEN LIKED TO THINK HE WAS A MAN WHO COULD HANDLE about anything. He'd been through medical school, had faced some tough challenges there, and had come through unscathed. He'd survived countless tragic nights in the ER—most recently with the

Covid pandemic—when too many people had died, and he and his staff were physically pushed to their limits.

When he was twelve, his ten-year-old sister, Camille, died. He'd toughened up and held his emotions in check that day—even though his world was collapsing around him. When his parents couldn't wake her that morning, he'd watched his dad cry out like a wounded animal and hit the wall repeatedly with his fist. His mother wailed and withered into a fetal position on the floor. Will called 9-1-1, telling the dispatcher to hurry, because he was afraid for his parents. He knew his sister was dead, and that there was nothing anyone could do for her. And even though her dying brought a bottomless ache to his gut, he was more worried about his parents.

All of that was tragic. But splitting up with Ava was ripping him apart in ways he didn't know he could be ripped. The hurt was emotional and, at times, physical. They'd been together since they were sixteen. Their families were close even before then— essentially, they'd grown up together. But as adults, they couldn't come together on certain things, and neither would budge on what they wanted.

Did he know how to live without her?

"How did we get here, Ava?"

He'd stared out the window of their brownstone for more minutes than he realized, because when he turned around for Ava's response, she wasn't there.

Par for the course. Every time his heart ached enough that he wanted to talk, and needed answers from her, she wasn't available —either emotionally or physically. Was it because she had a sixth sense about these things and instinctively knew when to leave to save herself some agony? Or did he seek the answers to the harder questions when he sensed she wasn't there to answer them.

Either way, the questions remained unsaid, and at this point in the game, he hadn't a clue if they would ever warrant a response.

It was probably too late to turn things around anyway.

Ava bustled into the living room about an hour later. She'd showered and dressed, fixed her hair, and talked herself into what had to happen over the next six days. She wondered if she could do it.

Will looked up from the sofa where he was reading on his iPad. "You look nice," he offered.

"Thanks. Their plane lands at twelve-thirty-five."

Will looked at his watch. "Perfect. We'll pick them up, and if you want, we can meet my folks somewhere for dinner. They are running late. Snow in Connecticut. I just got a text."

"Would it be easier to get takeout and eat here?"

Will stood. "Maybe. Let's think about it."

"I'm sure they are all tired from traveling. Especially your grandfather."

"True."

Will stood, looking her over. "That's the sweater I got you last year. I don't think I've ever seen you wear it."

Because I've never worn it. Ava wasn't sure why she hadn't, other than it wasn't her usual style. Still, when she slipped it on minutes ago, she liked it better than she thought she would. Glancing down at herself, she said, "I kept forgetting about it. I like it, Will. Thanks."

His broad grin stretched across his face, and Ava smiled back. She was attempting to be normal. She supposed she had to practice a little. Right?

"That wasn't so bad, was it?"

"What?"

"Smiling. Being cordial. Acting human."

Ava tossed back her head and rolled her shoulders. "My God,

Will. Yes. I'm trying, for whatever good it will do. But please stop making it a big deal every time you think I'm being nice. Okay?"

"I was just pointing out—"

"Well, stop then."

"All right, Ava." He glanced at his cell phone. "We need to go."

Turning, he headed for the front of the apartment. Ava drifted off in the opposite direction. Sudden doubt swept over her, and she questioned the sanity of their situation. She twisted back. "We should just tell them tonight, Will. Please. We can still have the week, but let's just get it out in the open."

He ambled back toward her. "We've been over this, Ava. No. We are not telling them until we get on the train coming home."

"I really don't think it's a good idea."

"Not a good idea for us, or for you?"

"Just not a good idea. Period. I can't fake my way through the holidays just to make our families happy. We both know our happily-ever-after is a farce."

"Then can you do it to make me happy. Just this one last thing, Ava?"

His words gave her pause, and she studied him. "You make it sound so final. One last thing."

"Well, isn't it?"

"I don't know, Will. I just don't know if I can do this."

He stared. "Maybe it's because you really don't want a divorce."

Her eyes flared. Her mouth opened to speak, then closed again. Finally, she blurted out, "That's ridiculous. We've discussed it and agreed."

"That doesn't mean you still want it."

Ava turned away. What did she want? He was confusing her. Or was it she who was confusing herself? Without turning back, she said, "I want the divorce. I can't do this week."

"You could if you tried. It's not that difficult to be nice to each other. We used to do it all the time."

"We used to be in love."

"We still could be."

Ava stared at him. "What? Do you want to be in love again? Not sure you can just turn love on and off like a faucet. Is that what you are saying?"

"I'm saying I don't think we are through, Ava. Not yet. Give us the week."

The week? "What are you asking, Will? Stop screwing with my head. We agreed to divorce. You are the one who upset my entire world by coming home one night saying you thought we should separate. Now, have *you* changed *your* mind? Be plain and clear, please, because I'm a bit befuddled. What do you want?"

"If you're confused too, then it's a good reason not to upset the families prematurely. Wouldn't you agree?" He huffed out a breath while stepping closer, then grasped her elbows as if to steady himself. "Ava, I'm not ready. I know it was me who started all of this. And I know we discussed. I want this week, you and me, together. With our families. Can you try, please? If it doesn't work out… If it all blows up in our faces, then fine, we will tell them. But in the meantime, let's give it some effort."

Ava broke away and stared out the window, her arms crossed over her chest. Outside, snowflakes floated to the ground, blanketing the Brooklyn sidewalks and street below. "That ship has sailed, Will. And you know it."

"No. The ship is still at the dock. It's not too late, Ava. Give me the week. That's all I'm asking. Even if you have to fake it."

She turned, met his gaze, and swallowed something hard in her throat. She *was* confused. Her head spun with what they'd discussed, how she felt, what he had said, and more. But what Will said now was crystal clear. He wanted one more week together. With her.

What *did* she want?

She'd righted her world once already after he'd tipped it on its axis. Could she risk having to do that again?

Sighing, she wasn't sure possessed the emotional capacity to pull it off. She could give him the week, she supposed. They'd shared five years together as a married couple. Six years going steady and engaged before that. She could certainly give him the week.

"All right, Will. All right. One week. I'll do it. But if this gets emotionally taxing for either of us, let's agree to reconsider the plan. Okay?"

Will nodded. "Agreed."

CHAPTER 24

The next morning, Ava sat back in her seat on the train and closed her eyes. The day had been hectic enough so far, but they were finally on the train and settled in for the trip. Perhaps she could doze until their stop.

The morning comprised endless cups of coffee, pastries from the bakery down the street, and seven people attempting to get ready for the train in the small, one-bathroom, two-bedroom apartment. It was like this every year. Will and Ava slept on the pull-out sofa bed in the living room, while the parents occupied the two bedrooms. Will's grandfather, Zachary Cohen—Grandpa Z to the families—claimed the recliner in the den. He announced every year that he slept more in his recliner at home than in his bed, so he'd be fine. Ava's younger brother, Alex, crashed on an air mattress and a pile of blankets on the den floor. When you are seventeen, you can do that.

By eight o'clock, they had secured a couple of cabs to take them to Penn Station, or more accurately, the Moynihan Train Hall, to catch the Christmas train. And by nine-forty-five, they were heading north.

The train route didn't go all the way to Charmington. In fact, the Christmas village was about a thirty-minute drive from the closest stop, so Will's dad always arranged for someone at the inn to pick them up.

It was snowing by the time the train pulled into their drop-off station, and about half of the people on the train got off, carrying shopping bags with Christmas presents and bustling toward loved ones.

As soon as she stepped off the train and felt the snow on her face, Ava's heart felt lighter than it had for months. Smiling, she put her face to the sky and let the flakes drift over her.

"Earth to Ava." Will leaned in and whispered in her ear.

She opened her eyes to see him smiling down at her. "It's Christmas," she said.

"So, it is." He nodded and took her arm. "I think I see Dylan Hamilton over there." He waved toward the man standing beside a shiny red SUV with the Holly Hill Inn logo on the side door.

His hand on her elbow felt comforting. As they strolled toward the vehicle, she caught a side glance at Will, who stared straight ahead with a slight smile on his face.

Maybe I can do this after all. It's Christmas. Right?

"Dylan! It's good to see you, sir. How has your year been?" Will put out his hand and Dylan shook it.

"It's been an interesting year, to be sure. Business has been decent this fall, despite everything. We took advantage of the pandemic break for a few months to spruce up the place. You'll see the improvements when we get there."

Ava stepped forward. "I can't imagine the inn being any prettier than it already was. Dylan, It's good to see you. How's your family?"

"And you, Ava. Kat and Aimee are great. They can't wait to see you. Especially, Aimee. She's fascinated about you being on Broadway."

Ava smiled and suddenly felt happy all over. "I can't wait to tell her all about it."

"She has something to tell you too."

"Well, I doubly can't wait then!"

Dylan pointed to his left. "You know Matt. Kat's brother?"

Ava nodded to Matt.

Will piped up. "Of course. You own the hardware store in Charmington, right?"

Matt tipped his head. "That I do. My wife, Ariana, and I have a little farm over the hill from the inn. I help Kat when needed. Ariana works for her now part time, doing marketing and decorating—whatever Kat needs help with—when she's not working on a writing project. It's a family thing. You know?" He paused, looking over the gathering crowd.

Ava glanced behind her to see that the family had all moved in. "Well, I guess we're all here now."

Dylan nodded toward the SUV. "I can take five of you in my vehicle," he said, "and Matt can take two in his truck. That work?"

"Perfect." Will grasped Ava's hand. "We'll go with Matt. The rest of you go with Dylan."

Before she could protest, Will tugged her toward Matt and his truck, opened the passenger side door, and helped Ava into the center of the truck cab, sitting on the bench seat.

Matt put their bags in the smaller back seat of the cab, then got in on her left, slamming his door.

Will moved in on the other side. "Cozy, huh?" He winked and threaded his fingers through hers again and squeezed.

Ava glanced down at their clasped hands, then back up at Will, who appeared to be waiting for a response. "Yes, definitely."

"Sorry about that, folks. All the other family vehicles were being used, except for the 1950s model Ford pickup and I didn't think that would work well at all."

Ava turned his way. "Oh, Matt. No worries. This is fine."

Will leaned forward and gave Matt a wink. "I'm not complaining. Anytime I can get close to my wife, I'm happy." He dropped her hand and put his arm around her shoulders, pulling her closer. "Besides, she can't get away from me so easily." He squeezed her shoulder.

Matt laughed. "I understand. My wife is so busy I'd love to get her in a tight space one of these days soon just to make her slow down. Glad to accommodate."

"Ava, slow down? Ever played whack-a-mole?"

"Your wife too? Girls these days."

Ava cleared her throat. "In case you two haven't noticed, I'm sitting right here between you. Can you talk about me later during some man-cave time or something?"

She caught the look on Will's face and realized she'd embarrassed him. *Well, sorry.*

"We were just teasing, Ava."

"Teasing me? Or just digging at women in general?"

"Ava, please don't start."

Matt interrupted. "You know, that was a little rude. I apologize Ava. We meant no harm or disrespect."

Ava glanced at Matt. Bringing him into the ongoing battle between Will and herself was not fair. "No. I know, Matt. I overreacted and I apologize."

"It's not a problem, Ava. Truly."

Lowering her voice, she faced Will. "Just don't poke fun at my expense this week, okay? I know it's something you and your family like to do, and you all think it's harmless and great fun, but this is not the week to make me feel foolish. Got it?"

Will's arm went lax on her shoulder and, after several seconds, he pulled it closer to his body. "Got it." He stared straight ahead.

Silence filled the cab of the truck for about ten minutes.

Darn it. Ava mentally kicked herself for her blunt reaction.

She'd apologize to Will again once they got to their room. Now was not the time.

Matt broke the silence by making the obligatory reference to the weather. "So, we're getting some flurries this afternoon and evening, and the forecast tells us we should have a couple of inches on the ground by morning."

"Perfect," said Will.

"Great," Ava added.

"The snow should be light all week, they say," Matt continued. "It shouldn't interfere with any of the festivities or shopping, and as far as I know, all the events are still a go."

The festivities. The lighting at the inn. Shopping, of course, and the holiday scavenger hunt sponsored by all the shops. Ice dancing at the pond. Caroling throughout the town. Visiting the tree farm. If there was anything to boost her spirits this week, these were it.

"The gingerbread making competition still on?" Ava had always wanted to do that but had never made the time. Maybe this was the year.

"Oh yes. Ariana has already entered and so has Kat. The inn didn't sponsor it this year. The Chamber of Commerce took over. They are holding it down at town hall. You need to sign up by tomorrow afternoon. Kat has some sign-up forms at the inn."

"Hm."

"You should do it."

Ava studied Matt's profile. "I just might."

"You need a partner, you know?"

"Ah." Ava stared straight ahead for a couple of seconds, then strictly on impulse, looked at Will. "Well? Partner?" She was trying to extend the olive branch here. Would he take it?

With the eye twinkle of a skeptic, Will immediately responded. "No. Not your guy. Perhaps try Grandpa Z."

Ava blinked, and her mouth gaped. She couldn't believe he'd said no. Well, not in so many words, but the message was clear.

Well, so be it. "Perfect. The man knows his way around the kitchen. This will be fun." Narrowing her gaze at Will then, she glared a little, and then looked ahead.

"We're nearly here," Matt said. "Right around the next curve."

"Good." She was more than ready to exit the cab of this vehicle.

THE LAST THING WILL WANTED TO DO THIS WEEK WAS TICK AVA OFF. He was barely holding it together himself and secretly wondered if she was right about telling their families their plans. That she wanted to do so, however—get things in motion—cut him deeper than he'd imagined. Telling the family made everything that much more real. He had been having second thoughts lately and wondered if they had been too hasty in deciding to separate.

Never mind. Not thinking about that now.

Ava had morphed into a chatterbox beside him. She and Matt were having quite the conversation about downtown Charmington, the local arts and entertainment landscape, and the upcoming festivities.

"The house lighting at the inn is still on Christmas Eve," Matt mentioned. "We should have a sizeable crowd this year, not to mention the drive-by traffic browsing the lights. It's become quite the show the past year or two."

"Are you in charge of that?" Ava asked.

He nodded. "Yep. Kat assigned that task to me after Ariana came into our lives. She dragged me kicking and screaming, but, hey, it's Christmas magic, right? And speaking as a reformed Scrooge, I believe in the impossible."

Will glanced to his left and saw Ava smile. "Yes, you're right. It is Christmas."

"Oh no. Not just Christmas, but the magic of Christmas. It's the magic that makes the difference this time of year."

Could there be magic this Christmas?

Ava shifted in her seat and looked at Will. He caught her stare and held it.

"I guess anything can happen," she said. "With magic."

Will's heart fluttered at her words.

MATT'S VEHICLE FOLLOWED DYLAN'S AS THEY PULLED INTO THE circular drive of Holly Hill Inn.

"Well, there she is," Ava remarked. "Just as beautiful as ever. Maybe more."

The red clapboard farmhouse sprawled before them. Ava's gaze followed the white picket fence adorned with holly and poinsettias and greenery. Her vision trailed up and over the arch that framed the entrance to the front lawn garden area and guarded the brick walkway to the large sweeping porch. She could see Kat's touch everywhere with the Christmas decorations.

Or perhaps that was Matt's wife's touch, too?

There were recent additions as well. Things she hadn't remembered from all their years here before. A small gazebo graced the garden area to the left of the house, with the picket fence extending beyond where she remembered. A new bench sat next to a young tree. And beyond, she noticed a new patio and outdoor kitchen area.

Matt put the truck into park; she glanced his way. "I see some of the sprucing up you've done around here." She pointed toward the side of the house.

"Sure is. That's part of it. The addition of the outside kitchen was Kat's brainchild and has turned out to be a real draw for people staying here in the summer. They like staying out on the patio watching the stars and having an adult beverage. We didn't expect, though, that it would go over just as well in the fall and winter."

Ava was surprised at that too. "Oh?"

"Yes. We can light a fire in the brick oven to warm up the area, and we added a fire pit recently. Keeps the stone pavers warm and the atmosphere toasty and cozy. A hot toddy and you're set for the night."

"We may have to try that later."

Grinning, he agreed. "That's the plan."

"I'm ready."

Leaning her way, Will added, "Ditto. Matt, it looks great. Can't wait to try it out."

"Oh, and wait until you see inside. Kat has completely overhauled the kitchen too. It was time."

"I can't wait to see her," Ava said.

"Well, you won't have to wait long. There she is."

Ava shifted her eyes and looked toward the porch. "And little Aimee!"

"Who is growing up way too fast!"

"I can see that."

"Well, let's go." Will lifted the door handle latch. He exited the truck, turned back, and offered her his hand. His steady gaze held hers for a moment. She studied him as he stood there watching her, waiting. Expectant.

Hesitating only a couple of seconds, Ava lifted her hand and placed it in his.

CHAPTER 25

While the family spilled from the two vehicles, Kat Hamilton and her daughter, Aimee, skipped down the porch steps while pulling on jackets, dodging snowflakes, and calling out to his family. Will had to smile at the pair. It was certainly good to see them. Aimee was growing up. She'd been five, the last time they were here. What a difference a couple of years makes.

One reason he loved coming to Holly Hill Inn was because of the family who ran the inn. He truly considered Kat and Dylan Hamilton to be close friends.

He absorbed the scene quietly, as a passerby might, watching everyone exchange greetings and hugs. Seconds later, a woman carrying a baby slipped out the front door and quietly waited for them. By now, the crowd was moving in mass toward the porch, bags and luggage in tow. They took the steps, crossed the wide porch, and stepped inside the inn. He brought up the rear. Ava had moved ahead of him, talking with the women and Aimee. The entry was crowded but no one seemed to mind.

Kat moved to her desk and faced them all. "It's so good to see everyone. Especially since we were snowed out last year. We missed you! Now, I have everyone's keys and rooms ready. I need someone from each room to fill out this card and sign it. Let's get you all checked in so you can relax in your rooms before dinner."

She started passing out the cards and handed one to Ava.

"Oh, surely you are not planning dinner for us. Are you?" Ava asked. "We can eat in town."

Kat batted the air. "Of course, I am. I know you people like I know my kinfolk. You've had a long day traveling. Relax here tonight, and you can join the holiday festivities in Charmington tomorrow."

Ava touched her arm. "You are amazing. Thank you."

"It's nothing fancy. I made a ginormous pot of chili this afternoon, and there is a cheese board and crackers. Sandwiches, if you want. Later, we can do cocktails on the patio—that is, if the snow lets up. If not, we have a couple of fireplaces inside."

"That all sounds lovely."

Matt stepped forward with the woman and baby. "Hey everyone. We have a couple of additions to the family this year. Meet Ariana, my wife. We met during the Christmas holiday last year, got married before the snow melted, and were blessed with this little dude in October—our son, Matthew."

"Yes, it was a whirlwind." Ariana grinned and waved. "We call him Little Matt."

Will watched Ava rush forward. "Hi Ariana. I'm Ava. Oh, he is so adorable!" She stroked little Matt's cheek with the back of her knuckles. "And so soft," she whispered.

"Would you like to hold him?" Ariana shifted the baby in her arms.

Ariana's eyes lit up. "May I?"

"Of course." Grinning softly, Ariana handed her son to Ava.

Will did a double take. He'd never seen Ariana so eager to hold a baby before. Her face lit up as she cradled the young boy and instinctively, her body started weaving back and forth in a slow rocking motion. He'd never seen her do that before, either.

They'd talked about having children back in the beginning. For a while, they'd agreed that children for them would come later in life. The past year, they'd discussed whether to have children. If he remembered Ava's words accurately, they were simple and to the point. "Maybe we are just professional, career people, Will. Not baby people."

He'd shoved any desire or dream of a future family away at that point and hadn't thought about it much again.

Until now.

Watching Ava hold the baby... Seeing the smile on her face... Taking in her mannerisms as she cooed and rocked and touched the infant... All of it suddenly made him long to see her that engaged with a child of their own.

Ava stared into the baby's face for another few seconds, her soft auburn curls sliding over her shoulder. She tossed her head back to swing the locks out of her face, glanced up, and briefly caught Will's eye. A longing came over him as he probed the contented depths of her azure eyes. Had some sort of feeling come over her as well? After a few seconds, she carefully handed the baby back to his mother. "He is so sweet," she said, looking at Ariana. "I know you love him so."

"He is definitely our pride and joy. I'm a lucky woman."

Ava smiled and stepped back. Briefly, her gaze skittered over Will's again, then she slipped into the crowd while Kat moved throughout the room.

"Here are your room keys." Kat gathered up the completed cards and handed out small envelopes with keys and room names on them to both sets of parents, to his Grandpa Z, and to Ava's brother, Alex. Turning to Will, Kat whispered, "The Christmas suite is open this year. The Campbells, who usually book it—do you remember them?—canceled last week. I thought you and Ava might like it. The upgrade is on the house." Smiling, she ticked her head toward Ava. "I hope the two of you enjoy it."

Will thanked Kat. He looked down at the key envelope in his hand—the words "honeymoon suite" were written across it. Lifting his eyes, he found Ava staring at him.

THE CHRISTMAS SUITE WAS LOVELY. AVA WAS CERTAIN SHE'D NEVER been inside the room before, even with all her years of coming to Holly Hill. Previously, it had always been occupied by other guests. Her understanding was that they called it the Christmas Suite only during the holidays. The rest of the year, it was the Honeymoon Suite, and part of the inn's Adirondack wedding destination package.

Great. She and Will were going to be stuck in the honeymoon suite for the entire week. She felt a *bah humbug* trying to gurgle up in her throat and then choked it down.

No. I will not be the bah humbug. At least I'm trying hard not to be. Attitude adjustment, Ava!

Instead, she focused on the beauty of the room and vowed never refer to it as the honeymoon suite—but always the Christmas suite, as Kat had said, when she'd whispered the information to Will.

It was like Kat knew something. Did she?

The bedroom area was extensive, with a small sitting area in an off-set part of the room. She thought that might be part of the octagonal turret that ran up the north side of the large Victorian farmhouse. Someone had spent a bit of time exquisitely decorating the suite for Christmas. A fire gently rolled in the fireplace on the opposite wall from the bed. In the corner stood a vintage silver Christmas tree with sparkling mini lights and with one of those rotating color wheels, also vintage, splashing revolving colors on the tree. A bedside table held mints and books and an old-fashioned wind-up alarm clock.

A tea and coffee service sat against the wall between the fireplace and the sitting nook.

Candles and wreaths in the windows added to the low-lit ambiance.

Ava wandered about the room, touching furniture, and inspecting artwork and holiday decorations. Turning a door handle, she stepped inside a large master bathroom. All the amenities were there—double sinks, commode, walk-in shower, and a huge garden tub with jets. There were bath salts that smelled of holly and cranberry, soaps galore, and huge puffy towels hanging on the towel rack beside the tub.

Sighing, she eyed the tub in longing. What she wouldn't give for an hour alone soaking in that tub. Stress relief? Maybe later.

"Some place, huh?"

Ava whirled, almost startled. She'd nearly forgotten Will was in the room. "You've been quiet," she said.

"Just watching you. Nice of Kat to give us this suite. Wasn't it?"

"Yes. I'm surprised, though. One of our parents would have enjoyed it."

"And then we'd hear the others debating why they didn't get it."

Ava grinned. "You're right. And yes, it is nice."

They headed back into the bedroom. Will glanced at the king-size bed. "I suppose that's big enough for us to camp on either side." He stared at the bed and turned back to look at her.

"I suppose it will work."

"Are you sure? We haven't shared a bed in weeks. Are you okay with it?"

Ava nodded. "Yes, Will. I assumed we'd be sharing a bed. We've never had a room here with two beds. It's fine."

"All right. I'm good with that too."

"Great."

She eyed him, thinking about their exchange in the truck. "Will. I'm sorry about what I said earlier with Matt there. I shouldn't have said any of that. I didn't mean to embarrass you or upset you. And I promise that will be my last bit of grumpiness for this entire week."

Will cocked a brow. "Really? I would like to believe that, Ava, but to be honest, I'm not sure I do."

"I promise. This week… I'll make the effort. For the family, for us."

"You're sure."

"I am."

"Well, that's good news."

Glancing off to the side, Ava watched the fire flicker in the fireplace. "Would you reconsider something?" Slowly, she turned and made eye contact with him. "It's not a big deal, but I wondered if you would reconsider being my partner for the gingerbread house contest this week."

"I thought you were going to ask Grandpa."

"I haven't yet."

Angling slightly to face her, Will crossed his arms and eyed her. "I'm not a cook."

"No, but you can read and follow directions. Right? Besides, it might be fun."

Again, he stared. "What's the ulterior motive here, Ava?"

Goodness. Had she terrified him that much with her inappropriate behavior? She must have been a real bitch the past few weeks. Honestly, she wasn't sure how else to act. The weeks had been long, and she'd done a lot of thinking. When Will approached her to separate, it had thrown her for the proverbial loop. The only way she'd known how to react, to respond to his query, to protect herself, was to fake it and tell him she'd been thinking the same thing. She couldn't let him know how hurt she was, could she?

And evidently, that hurt had manifested itself in bitterness.

"No hidden agenda," she breathed. "I just thought it would be fun for us and perhaps get us out of this doom and gloom." Breaking his gaze, she sat on the bed and took off one boot. "Don't worry about it. I get it. That's taking the faking a little too far. Isn't it?"

She fiddled with her other boot, her gaze cast downward. Will hadn't said another word. After a moment, she looked back up to find him staring at her.

"Okay. I'll do it."

"You don't have to."

"I want to."

"You're sure?"

He nodded. "Yes."

Ava grinned, her chest fluttering. When she looked at him standing there, the flicker of candlelight reflecting off his face, her heart warmed. She could do this. After all, this was Will. The boy she fell in love with as a teenager, and the man she still loved a little bit—even though he'd fallen out of love with her. She'd worried so much that if she faked this week like he wanted, that she'd fall back in love with him—a lot.

But perhaps it was worth the risk.

"Thanks, Will. I'm glad."

LATER THAT EVENING, THE FAMILIES SHARED A CHILI DINNER, laughter, and conversation in the newly renovated kitchen with the Holly Hill Inn crew—the Hamilton family and the Matsons. Afterward, they sipped hot cocoa outside by the fire pit, wrapped up in quilts and blankets against the dropping temperature, but enjoying the crisp evening and the vast night sky lit with flickering stars. Shortly after, Will and Ava retired for the evening to the Christmas suite.

Ava lingered in the tub, letting her mind wander and relax, while Will read up on the latest literature in a medical journal he'd brought with him. His brain was always on medicine, and Ava understood that. But perhaps he would also benefit from an hour with the tub and jets this week, too.

Hm. And the tub *was* big enough for two. How far was she to assume they were taking this "faking" holiday?

Not going there, Ava.

After the lights were out—except for the twinkling ones on the tree and the candles in the window—Ava and Will lay quietly on opposite sides of the bed. She could hear the soft whir of Will's breathing, and listened, staring up at the ceiling. It had been a while since she'd heard that gentle snore of his, right before he fell fully sleep.

"Ava," he whispered.

"Hm?"

"I've been wondering."

"What is it, Will?"

"Well, I assume you'll want the apartment," he said. "I'll start looking for a new place as soon as the holidays are over."

Where did that come from? Ava blinked and fixed her gaze on the light fixture above. "Why are you bringing this up now?"

"I'm not sure. Just lying here, my mind wandering… It came to me we've never talked about where we each would live…after."

"I supposed we'd figure that out."

"You can keep the apartment. I'll find someplace close to the hospital."

"Will, I'm not sure what I am going to do. We don't have to make any plans tonight, and we shouldn't."

"What do you mean?"

She turned onto her side and faced him. "I might not stay in the city after the divorce. Since I'll be on tour for most of the year, I really don't need to keep a home base in Brooklyn. I can live anywhere."

Will didn't turn her way but still lay looking up. "So, are you really going through with it? The tour."

Had she not officially told him that? To be honest, she wasn't certain if she had. "I signed the contract last week. I'll be leaving the second week of January."

After a minute, he responded. "Oh."

"I thought I told you."

"No. No, you didn't."

"I'm sorry, Will. We haven't exactly been conversing normally lately. Basically, we've been two ships passing in the night."

"For way too long."

"Probably."

"So, it's a done deal. The tour, I mean."

"Yes. It is." Ava lay back on her pillow, staring up at the ceiling again. What did he expect? "You know, I signed before you said you didn't think we were through. I have to tell you, Will, this back and forth is killing me."

"I understand. Can you pull the contract?"

"No!" She looked at him. "Will, you know I can't. And honestly, I don't think I should. I may need the income. Besides, it's still part of the dream. I want to see this through."

Again, he went silent. "I never considered you would leave New York. Is that really what you want to do?"

"Maybe. I'm not sure."

"But where would you go?"

"Home maybe?" She shrugged. "I haven't decided."

"But what about after the tour? Won't you want to be back in the city? Back on Broadway? Why Indiana?"

She shrugged. "Why not?"

"Because we..." He paused. "Because it's what we talked about years ago. Remember? After we made it big, we'd settle down back home. Or a small town somewhere. You know I've missed Indiana and...."

She stared. "Yet, you're the one taking the big new job coming up that is going to keep you here in the city for years."

"And that makes you nervous?"

"Yes, yes, it does."

Will eyed her. "And yet, you're the one going on tour."

"What am I supposed to do, Will? I have to support myself."

"I didn't think you were anywhere near thinking about going back home. I assumed you would stay in New York. That we'd still see each other occasionally... Friends, you know?"

What was he saying? Ava propped herself up on an elbow. "Seriously? That's a lot of assumptions. If you're expecting that we can be chummy exes... I just don't know what that looks or feels like right now. Not saying it couldn't happen, but it's too soon for either of us to assume."

"You're right. I just never envisioned your leaving. I thought you enjoyed the city life."

"I do. Most of the time. But there will come a day when I'll grow weary of it. Besides, I'll be traveling for months. I'm sure I'll be ready for peace and quiet when all that is through."

"I don't understand why you gave up the Broadway show for the tour. I figured after landing Glinda, you'd be ready to chase the next one."

"I'm still Glinda, Will. And it's still Broadway, just taking it on the road." Ava stayed silent for several heartbeats, then added, "To be honest, I'm actually tired of chasing the big roles, Will. I'm having the time of my life with *Wicked*. The tour opportunity presented itself, and I thought things might be easier between us if I was out of the picture, traveling. We could each have space."

That statement had Will turning toward her. "Why would you think that?"

"It will just be easier. You'll get the separation you want so we can both think about things, and then after a few weeks, perhaps we can move forward with the divorce."

"Easier for whom?"

Ava sighed. "For me, Will. I can't go on like we are. The tour will be a nice buffer between being together and… Well, not being together."

"And then you'll go home."

"I might. My family could benefit from my being there. It's not been a wonderful year, as you know."

"But I can't believe you'd give up the nightlife that you so desperately need and want."

Ava searched for his eyes, but it was difficult to connect directly in the dark. "Desperately need and want? You really don't know me as well as you think you do. No, I will not miss the chaos of the city. That's you. Remember? You're the one who gets all jazzed up by the hustle. You're the one who wanted to move to New York to begin with."

"That's not true. You always dreamed of being on Broadway."

"I dreamed of being on Broadway. Yes. I was a kid then. I never gave a thought about living in the city or what that means. Think about it, Will. Ever since you moved to Hartford, you talked about living in the city. It's why you chose Columbia for medical school."

Will didn't respond.

Let him think about it. She rolled away then and faced the sitting area. There was a lone candle in the window, and she focused on it. She'd be just like that candle one day again, single and hopefully still flickering.

"I'm not ready to discuss the apartment yet, Will. Let's get through this week first."

She guessed his lack of response was her answer.

CHAPTER 26

*A*va tip-toed out of the Christmas suite early the next morning, careful not to wake Will. As she headed downstairs to the kitchen, a rich coffee aroma teased her nostrils. Someone was up already and busy. She sniffed and descended the stairs, the coffee luring her like a siren song. Not the typical early riser, it thrilled her that someone else beat her to coffee making this morning.

Of course, she expected nothing less. She often suspected Kat Hamilton lived in that kitchen. She was always there ready to serve her guests. Yet, had she been sleeping in, Ava felt comfortable invading her space and getting the coffee started.

After all, coffee was life. Right?

She noticed her mother sitting with Kat in the breakfast nook as she entered the kitchen. Hunched over their coffee cups, they shared a plate of scones and quiet conversation. Ava hated to interrupt their chat, so she quietly made her way to the coffeemaker, chose a festive mug, and poured herself a cup.

She loved the Holly Hill Inn coffee. The brew was festive, for lack of a better word. Kat would only confess to adding cinnamon sticks to the brew for a subtle hint of spice, but Ava could swear there was another secret ingredient—something sweet and earthy —that Kat would not divulge.

She was happy to see her mother, Carol, smiling and relaxed. Ava's father had died earlier in the year, an unexpected heart attack. None of them were prepared, of course, and they all struggled the past few months—which was an important reason she had said nothing to her mother about the situation with Will.

Her mother loved Will. And Alex had thought of him as an older brother for most of his life. Alex was only seven when she and Will started dating seriously in high school. What she and Will did with their relationship was going to effect people than just the two of them.

She hadn't quite thought in those terms yet, and it bothered her.

Her mind wandered to Will's family, too. How could she simply walk away from his parents, and especially Grandpa Z? They were as much a part of her life as her own family. She wasn't sure she knew how to separate herself from them.

Worried, she turned and pressed the small of her back against the countertop. Her mother sat back and glanced her way. "Ava, honey. Come join us." She waved her over.

Pushing away from the counter, she moved toward the pair. Carol scooted to her left on the banquette seat, and Ava sat beside her.

Her mother tucked a stray strand of Ava's hair back over an ear and smiled. "I'm surprised to see you up so early."

Ava sipped her coffee. "You know me so well."

"That I do." Carol nodded and gazed into Ava's eyes for a moment. "You're tired."

She nodded. "I am. While performing on Broadway this fall has been a dream come true, it has exhausted me to no end. But it's a happy, satisfied tired."

Sighing, Carol nodded. "Oh, but darling, what a dream come true for me too, seeing you up on that stage. Oh my, Broadway! Your father would have been so proud."

Ava dropped her gaze and stared at the tabletop. Thinking of her father made her feel warm inside. "Yes, he would have loved it."

"I'm sure he knows."

Ava lifted her gaze and smiled at her mother. "I'm sure too."

Carol patted her hand. "I'm glad you're getting some downtime this week."

"Me too." She leaned closer and kissed her on the cheek. "I'm glad we're all here. We all needed it."

"Yes." Carol broke off a corner of her scone. "I've not mentioned it, but Alex is having some trouble in school. I was just picking Kat's brain."

Ava glanced at Kat and smiled, thinking about her brother. "He was quiet on the train."

"He didn't want to come. I made him."

That worried Ava. "Oh, Mom. That's ridiculous. He always loved coming here!"

Kat reached across the table and tapped Ava's hand. "I know a couple of kids his age in town. Maybe I can hook him up. Might give him something to do."

"That would be great," Ava said, then turned toward her mom. "But Mom, what kind of trouble is he getting into?"

Carol signed. "Well, he's skipped school a few times, and I can't get him to come clean about where he went when he did. He argued with a teacher and punched out a kid who Alex said was bullying him."

"Oh dear. Should I talk with him?" Suddenly, Ava was worried about her brother. Ten years younger than her, Alex sometimes seemed so moody and distant. They'd not spent much time together the past few years.

For a moment, a pang of regret rippled across her chest. Had she neglected her family?

"Let's see how it all plays out, honey," her mom said. "He might reach out to you."

"And that would be better."

"Yes."

A door closing and shuffling noises in the entry caused all three women to look in that direction. Footsteps sounded down the hallway.

Kat sat up in her seat as a man entered the kitchen. "Matt? Good Lord. What are you doing here so early?"

Matt grinned as he strolled into the kitchen, tugging at his gloves. "Oh good. Coffee. May I? I came to pick up Alex." He headed for the coffeemaker.

Ava glanced at her mother, whose eyes flashed wide, and then back to Matt. "Why?"

Matt filled a cup, then scooted a chair to the end of the table and sat. He plucked up a scone from the plate. "Orange?"

"Yes," Kat said.

"Yum. My favorite."

"Matt?"

"Oh, yes. Alex. Well, we were talking last night, and it seems he likes mechanical things, so I asked him if he wanted to help me tinker with the old train set Dad used to have. I've got it set up in the back of the hardware store, in Mom's old studio. I fiddle with it when I have downtime. Alex said he'd like to see it and maybe tinker a little, too." He glanced back and forth between the women. "That okay with you, Carol?"

"That's perfect, Matt. I mean, if you want. Lately, he's been a moody seventeen-year-old teenager."

"Oh, that's all? I can relate. I was once seventeen."

"And definitely moody," Kat interjected. "In fact, my brother was moody for about twenty years until he met Ariana. I think he's got moody covered." She turned to Matt. "I was thinking of calling Michael Dodson and Lynn Cook—they are about his age—to see if they want to hang out this week with Alex. Okay if they come by the store to meet him?"

"Fine with me." Matt broke off a piece of the scone and popped it in his mouth. "The more, the merrier. Maybe they can help clean up that track."

"Great."

More sound erupted from the entryway as someone bounded down the stairs. Alex burst into the room. Ava was glad to see a little zip in his step. "Hey, Matt. You're here already."

Matt nodded. "I follow coffee."

"Well, you've come to the right place." Ava looked at Kat. "Best coffee in all the Adirondacks right here. Love the cinnamon."

"You figured me out." Kat smiled.

"I love it. I just need to know the other secret ingredient."

One corner of Kat's mouth turned up.

Alex cleared his throat. "Hey, Mom. Okay if I go with Matt today? He invited me last night. I forgot to tell you."

"Of course. Matt already mentioned it. But Alex, don't give Matt any trouble."

"Mom...."

"Promise?"

"I won't."

Matt stood. "We should get going. Ready, Alex?"

Kat rose and headed toward the kitchen island. She filled a paper bag with four more scones. "Here. It's early. These should hold you two over until lunch."

Matt shrugged and looked at Alex. "Maybe until we get to town, I'm thinking."

Alex nodded. "Yes, sir."

The men left, and the women turned back to their coffee. Kat rose and grabbed the carafe. "More?"

"Yes, please."

"What's on your agenda today, ladies?"

Ava caught her mother's eye. "Shopping?"

Carol shifted in her seat. "Oh yes. You know I love shopping in Charmington. Oh, by the way, Kat, I shipped a box here last week. Did it arrive yet?"

Kat snapped her fingers. "Yes, it did. I forgot to grab that for you. It's in the storage room off the entry."

"Great. I'll pick it up later. Just a few gifts, you know."

"Well, you two ladies have a wonderful day in Charmington. Ariana is coming over in a bit and we're planning our strategy for the gingerbread house building competition later in the week."

Suddenly, Ava perked up. "Oh, that's right. I need to sign up. Will and me. Where can I do that?"

"I have the sign-up sheets on my desk. I'll grab one for you. I think you can also sign up online."

Kat scampered off.

Carol put her hand over her daughter's on the table. "Ava, look at me."

She angled her gaze toward her mother. "What is it, Mom?"

Her mother's face grew serious, and the look in her eyes immediately worried Ava. "I'll just be blunt. What in the world is going on between you and Will?"

Stunned, Ava sat quietly for a couple of heartbeats. She had no clue that her mother had witnessed anything between her and Will that would signal trouble. "There is nothing going on. What do you mean?"

"There is something going on, Ava. You two barely spoke to each other yesterday, and on the train you sat apart most of the time. The tension is almost palpable. And it's okay if you don't want to talk about it now, but know I'm here whenever you want to share with me."

Ava didn't know what to say, so she said nothing. Just nodded and covered her mother's hand with her own.

WILL MET HIS FATHER, MARCUS COHEN, AND HIS GRANDFATHER, Zachary, on the landing outside their bedrooms. He'd had coffee in his room after he showered, waited for Ava to come back, and when she didn't, gave up and headed downstairs.

His dad gave him a nod. "I've lost your mother."

Will chuckled. "I've lost my wife."

Grandpa Zach sidled up to them both. "Sounds like a personal problem to me." Brushing past them, he headed down the stairs, muttering. "Dang boys can't hold on to their women."

Will looked at his dad and shrugged. There was more to this entire conversation than either his dad or grandpa realized.

Marcus followed his father down the stairs. "Pot calling the kettle black, old man? Mom left you twenty-five years ago."

Grandpa Z turned on the stairs. "And you don't see me getting attached again, do you? I have enough to keep up with. I don't need a woman to lose. Already lost one." Turning, he took a couple of steps, then halted and twisted back. "You two either need to put a leash on those women's necks or set them free."

"Grandpa! What a thing to say." Will followed the older two down to the entryway landing.

"Well, it's true. These days, women have too much freedom."

Will rolled his eyes. "Grandpa, please don't say that in front of the—"

Grandpa Z whipped around and finished Will's sentence. "What? In front of the woman? Henpecked, that's what you two are. Henpecked. It's a shame. Man should rule the roost. What he says goes. Women should look pretty and obey."

They approached the kitchen door. "Hush, Grandpa," Will told him. "No wonder Grandma left you."

But Grandpa Zach would have none of it. He ignored Will and rushed over to the table where all the women sat in the banquette —Ava, Carol, Kat, and Will's mom, Dorothy, along with Ariana— and started up conversation.

"Good morning, ladies!"

"Well, good morning, Zachary." Kat stood. "Coffee?"

"Oh now, now you sit down there." He placed a soft hand on Kat's shoulder. "No need to wait on me. I can take care of myself. It's the twenty-first century, you know. Men should take care of their own needs." He glanced about the banquette. "How are all you beautiful women this morning? Oh, my goodness, every one of your coffee cups is empty. Let me find that coffeemaker." He tottered off toward the counter.

Will exchanged an eye roll with his father.

Zachary retrieved the full carafe of coffee and filled each of the women's coffee cups. "There now," he said. "Everyone is full up. Can't let these cups get too low now, can we?"

Marcus crossed the kitchen and pulled down a couple more coffee cups. "How about over here, Dad?"

His father glanced at him and set the carafe aside on the kitchen island. "Help yourself, son. There you go." He turned and gave the women another broad smile.

"Oh, Zachery, you are such a kind soul," Kat said to him. She stood and kissed him on the cheek. "I just love when you come to visit. Now, have a seat right here, and I'll get you a scone. Or would you prefer an apple fritter?"

Will watched his Grandpa Z in awe as he sat across from Ava and Carol and then looked up longingly at Kat. "An apple fritter would be lovely, darling, if it's not too much trouble. A pretty thing like you shouldn't be toiling over a hot oven, though."

"Toiling? Oh, good Lord, Zachary. Food is my love language." Kat skittered off.

Zachary Cohen sighed happily, then glanced at Will and winked. Sidling a gaze over to Ava and Dorothy, he added, "Just so you know, your men have been pining away for you upstairs. Lost souls. Total wrecks without you. Were about to call in the missing people folks."

"Oh, heaven's sake, Zachary." Dorothy Cohen shook her head and looked at Marcus.

Ava gave Will a shy smile.

He stepped forward. "Now, Grandpa...."

Zachary winked again. "Keep them guessing, boy." Then he faced the women. "Anyone up for a game of euchre this afternoon? I play for money."

Kat sat a warm apple fritter in front of him. "Well, we usually play for cookies around here." She gave Zachary a teasing smile. "I'm game, but later this afternoon. I have my usual B&B chores this morning. Dylan will be back by two. He busted out of here early this morning to run errands. Hopefully, we can find a fourth."

"I'll play," Dorothy said.

"Splendid."

Ariana signaled to Ava that she was ready to get up and scooted around the table. "Kat, what time do you want to discuss our project for this week?"

"How about three? Will that work?"

"Perfect."

"Mom and I are going shopping." Ava stood to let all the women out of her side of the banquette and caught Will's eye. "Did you want to go to Charmington with us?"

He nodded. "I need to shop, but if this is a mother-daughter thing, I can go another day."

"No worries. Come with us. We will all go our separate ways in town, anyway. At least for part of the time."

Ariana scooted out after Carol. “I have errands to run in town, too. My folks are here for the holidays and staying with little Matt at the farm, so it’s the perfect time for me to get my last-minute shopping done. I can drive us all into town in my minivan. Who else? Dorothy?”

Will’s mom shook her head. “Not today. I have a book waiting for me beside that fireplace in the sunroom.” She cocked her head toward the hallway.

“Aimee and I may join you for lunch if I can get my morning work finished on time.” Kat glanced at Ariana. “Text me where you’ll be. Okay?”

“Sure thing.”

Zachary sat back, chewing his fritter. “I’m perfectly fine right here in the kitchen with this lovely lady of the food language.”

“I’ll stay here and keep the old man in line,” Marcus added.

Will blew out a thin breath. His grandfather was a piece of work. But he loved him. “Good. Well, sounds like a plan. When are we leaving?”

Kat took his arm and led him toward the table. “Not until you have breakfast. Have a seat, Will. You too, Marcus. Fritters or scones? Or are you men up for a Holly Hill Inn breakfast special with the works?”

Zachary raised an eyebrow. “Is bacon involved?”

Kat nodded. “And sausage. You game?”

He patted his stomach. “Game on, darling. Give us the works.”

“Same for you two?” Kat looked at Will, then Marcus.

“Bring it on.”

“Ditto.” Will glanced at Ava and winked.

She grinned and gave him a slight finger wave. “See you soon.”

He nodded. “Yup.” If he made it through breakfast with his pop and grandpa.

❄

Lunch at Kringle's was on the agenda for the entire group, with plans for all to meet up there at one o'clock that afternoon. Kringle's was an experiment by a new local chef. Ariana shared the details as she drove to Charmington. Ava could tell she was excited to try out the new Christmas-themed restaurant—being the self-dubbed Christmas Queen, and all that. Ava also learned that Ariana was a Christmas blogger and writer, who was eager to cover the venue for her blog. The diner-style, pop-up restaurant would only be open for the holiday weeks.

If it went over, Ariana told them, the chef might seek a permanent location for Kringle's in Charmington. Which, according to her, would be simply perfect and wonderful.

At any rate, after their arrival, Ava, Will, Ariana, and Carol scattered off to different stores to do their shopping. They planned to meet for lunch at one, then head back to the inn.

Her shopping nearly finished, Ava wandered the streets of Charmington for several minutes—window shopping and simply enjoying the snowy, sunlit day. She paused at the bakery, ogling the pastries, and then at a dress shop, admiring a couple of handbags in the window. She strolled by an abandoned building, looked up to see the time-worn marquee above the entrance, and then stepped closer to the windows to peer inside. An old theater!

A sign on the door—one that obviously had been there for some time—said it was closed until further notice. She reminded herself to ask around about the theater's history sometime this week. Odd that she'd never noticed the old building before now.

Glancing at her watch, she stepped away, moving down the street toward the restaurant.

She still had about twenty minutes before they were to meet, so she ducked into a gift shop next door to Kringle's. In the shop, she perused the Christmas decorations, glittery balls and holly-twined wreaths, and such. She sniffed cranberry-scented candles, savored the aroma of dark chocolate fudge, and admired a couple of hand-painted snowy scenes by local artists.

Turning a corner, she discovered an entire section of snow globes against the wall, all sizes and with different themes, each one crafted to perfection, waiting for someone to pick it up and shake it.

These weren't your average gift shop snow globes, Ava noted, but something a bit more special. They were hand-carved and hand-painted, according to the sign above the display. Locally made. The glass looked clear as ice, and the characters and scenes inside were beautifully whimsical.

Unable to resist any longer, Ava studied the display until she found just the right globe and picked it up. Turning it slightly over and lifting it, she noticed a signature across the bottom. She held it closer, examining the scene inside, delighting herself by shaking the globe and watching the snow spin around the tiny house with the wreath on a red door, and the picket fence surrounding the house draped with holly and ivy, and the decorated pine tree in the front yard. The swirling snow slowed and revealed three tiny people standing in the yard—a man, a woman, and a child. Oh, and a dog. Was that a cat in the window?

So much detail.

Ava smiled. She loved this so much and wanted to buy it. She rarely bought anything impromptu and whimsical—she was a practical, no-nonsense buyer. Impulse purchases were not her thing. No, she wasn't out shopping for herself, she was still looking for a gift for her mother. Shaking the globe one last time, she sat it back on the shelf, feeling a little melancholy.

"That's a beauty, isn't it?"

Ava turned as Ariana approached. "Yes. I love it."

"You should totally buy it."

"Maybe, but not today. I'll think about it."

Smiling, Ariana touched the globe. "He's a local artist—the man who makes these—living just out of town a bit on a small farm. He makes only a limited collection every year, and each one is different. Unique. You won't see another one like that one."

Ava stared at the glass orb and the people inside. *Maybe I should buy it.* Turning to Ariana, she said, "I'll think about it over lunch."

"I'm heading there now," Ariana said. "Coming?"

"Yes. In a minute. I want to look around a little more." But Ava stood staring at the globe display again. "You know, I bet living in Charmington is kind of like living in a snow globe. The village and the snow are beautiful and perfect, and protected by this beautiful glass bubble from all the issues of the outside world."

"Oh, believe me," Ariana told her. "Charmington has its share of troubles."

"Really? Like what?"

"Well, a couple of kids broke into the ice cream shop the other day and stole the whole tub of rocky road."

Ava laughed. "That's all you have?"

"I heard one of our local attorneys is having an affair, but that's unfounded."

Ava cocked a brow. "You gotta give me more dirt than that, Ariana."

"Dirt? Sweetie, I hear the town is so safe people don't lock their doors at night." She laughed.

Ava gasped. "Seriously?"

"I'm afraid so. Yep. I guess we live in a glass bubble."

Smiling, Ava perused the display again. "Might be nice, though."

"What? To live in a small town like Charmington?"

"Umhmm. I think it would. I grew up in a small town. I probably didn't appreciate its merits then, but I think I do now."

"But you have all the excitement of the city at your fingertips in New York! The hustle and bustle, the nightlife, your career...."

Ava nodded. "Yes, all true. But it's not all it's cracked up to be."

"Are you thinking of moving? Making a change?"

Suddenly, tired of all the secrecy, Ava felt like just blurting out the truth. "Yes. I am. Will and I are... Well, we are likely separating."

Ariana sucked in a breath. "Oh, no, Ava. I'm so sorry. I've just met the two of you, but I can't imagine." She touched Ava's arm.

Ava felt and appreciated her compassion. "Thank you. And it's all okay. But please don't mention this to anyone. We haven't told the family yet."

"Of course. But Ava? Perhaps there is still a chance?"

Suddenly, Ava felt pulled toward the snow globe again. She gazed at the house with the picket fence inside the glass bubble and shook her head. "No, it's a lost cause. I think it's time for me to go out and start making my own happiness."

With a concerned smile, Ariana squeezed Ava's forearm, then tugged her forward for a hug. "I'm heading over to the diner now. See you in a few." After a moment, she walked away, stopping at the exit to glance back and give her a quick wave.

Ava smiled and waved back. Then turning back to the snow globes, she frowned.

Is that really what I want? To live inside a bubble, protected from all the chaos and mess of the outside world? Or am I just trying to figure out my place in life now that it's been disrupted and uprooted?

Honestly, living in a glass bubble sounded perfectly fine to her. As if that were even possible.

Leaving the snow globes behind, she headed for the diner.

CHAPTER 27

*W*ill stepped out of Charmington Hardware and onto the bustling street. The town was teeming with shoppers and Christmas tourists. Charmington was a great destination place this time of year. With every shop decorated and lit up with holiday splendor, shoppers were delighted with the magic of the holiday and enticed to purchase their Christmas wares. The holiday events schedule featured festive happenings every day through Christmas Eve. A children's choir serenaded shoppers from the gazebo, which was festively draped with garland and red ribbons. So far, he'd heard bits of *Oh Holy Night*, followed by *Rudolph the Red Nosed Reindeer,* and then a shortened version of *White Christmas*. He supposed a variety of holiday music genres was appropriate.

Earlier, he'd popped in to see Matt and Alex at the hardware store and ended up staying over an hour helping them tinker with the toy train. It was a cool old train set—a 1980s Lionel that had belonged to Ben Matson, Matt's dad, when he was a kid. Matt had uncovered the train in the attic at the inn a few months ago and brought it to the hardware to see if he could get it running.

While Will was there, no fewer than six local men, and a couple of teenagers, came in to see the train and check on Matt's progress with the thing, so obviously, it was a conversation item around town. He was happy to see Alex enjoying himself, too. They had fun examining the train engine, trying to figure out why it wasn't making contact with the track. They decided that parts of the track needed cleaned. With a little steel wool and elbow grease, they went at it.

He was glad he'd stopped by. *I should spend more time with the boy....*

Alex. He loved the kid like he was his little brother. He'd filled a void years after losing his sister, Camille. It was nice having a sibling, of sorts, in the family. But what would happen to their relationship if he and Ava split? Would he still be able to see Alex and Carol? How would Alex feel about him then? He had to wonder what Carol would think of the divorce, too.

He spotted Ava across the way as he strode across the circle. She entered the gift shop next to Kringle's, the diner where they were to meet—he glanced at his watch—in fifteen minutes. He took his time crossing and lost sight of her after entering the store —until he heard her voice.

Will stood at the end of the aisle. He'd rounded the corner and halted when he saw her, reversing his steps.

His first thought was to sneak up behind her and embrace her or place a light kiss on the back of her neck. He would have done something like that a couple of years ago and she would have turned warmly and planted her lips on his. Didn't matter if they were in public. Kissing wherever was always good with them.

But then he caught the pensive look on her face as she gazed at the wall of snow globes. She picked one out, turned it over, and even mumbled a little as she shook the thing and watched the snow swirl. Then, he caught sight of Ariana moving toward her in the aisle and he ducked out of sight—not that he didn't want her to see him, but….

He'd not intended to eavesdrop on the conversation between the two women. He supposed he shouldn't. Eavesdropping was not normally something he did, nor was it something to be proud of. But as the women continued to chat, the conversation became a bit more intriguing.

A growing ache in his belly gnawed away at his insides as he internalized the conversation.

What? To live in a small town like Charmington?

Umhmm. I think it would. I grew up in a small town.

But you have all the excitement of the city at your fingertips in New York! The hustle and bustle, the nightlife, your career....

Yes, that's true. But it's not all it's cracked up to be.

Are you thinking of moving? Making a change?

Yes. I am. Will and I are likely separating.

Will heard little after that. He knew that Ava and Ariana were still chatting softly, then he watched Ariana move away and exit the store. But Ava stood there for a while longer, staring at the snow globes. Reaching out, she touched one of them again softly, then dropped her hand.

The pang in his chest rivaled the thud that landed deep in his gut. Suddenly, it felt like there was so much about Ava he didn't know or had assumed he knew. How had they become so distant from each other—or was it he who had grown distant from her? Had she been telling him all along what she needed, and he wasn't listening?

He didn't know. But he had to find out.

Will watched her take a deep breath, then let go of a lengthy sigh. Turning, Ava took the same path as Ariana through the store and exited. Will waited until the bell on the door stopped tinkling before he moved closer to the snow globes and tried to determine exactly which one had held Ava's attention for so long.

❄

"Ava! Over here!"

The second Ava crossed the threshold into the diner, she heard her name called. Glancing about, she saw her group at a large corner table. Aimee Hamilton, Kat and Dylan's daughter, sat on her knees on her wooden chair and motioned for Ava, grinning widely. "Will you sit by me, please? Pretty please?"

Ava smiled and wove her way through the tables. "Of course! I've been wanting to talk to you."

"You have?"

"Oh, yes." Ava pulled out the chair next to Aimee and sat. She stuffed her purse and packages under the table at her feet. "Ever since I heard you had a part in the Christmas pageant, I've been dying to talk to you."

Aimee flipped in her seat and sat on her bottom, leaning closer to Ava. "Ever since you got here, I've been wanting to talk to you!"

Leaning closer to Aimee, Ava whispered. "We actors have to stick together. Don't we?"

"Yes!" Aimee's grin was infectious.

Ava laughed, then patted Aimee's knee. "So, I want to hear all about it and your part. But first, let's look at the menu. Okay?"

"Okay." She turned to her left. "Mom, what can I get?"

Kat glanced at Ava but spoke to Aimee. "Anything that isn't pie, cake, or ice cream."

"Cookies?"

"That either."

Aimee pursed her lips. "Muffins?"

"That's on the breakfast menu. Look at lunch, please, Aimee."

Ava pointed to the lunch section on Aimee's menu. "Oh look. They have a small Cobb salad. I think I'll get that. Lots of protein and vegetables. All good to keep our energy up. What about you, Aimee?"

The girl's lip curled. "You eat vegetables?"

Ava nodded. "Every day. They are good for me. Actors are busy people, and we need to eat right. I need the protein too, from the turkey and eggs and cheese. Good for the muscles."

Giggling, Aimee said, "You don't have muscles. Muscles are for boys!"

Ava whispered in her ear. "Let you in on a little secret. I lift weights too."

"You do?"

"Yes."

"Wow."

"We actors have to take care of ourselves."

"Right." Aimee returned to the menu. "I'll have the small Cobb salad, Mom. Okay?"

Kat's eyes widened. "Okay by me." To Ava, she mouthed the words, *Thank you.*

Grinning, Ava took one last look at the menu, decided for sure that she wanted the Cobb salad, then lifted her gaze to span the table. When she did, her gaze connected directly with Will's. He was staring at her with an odd expression on his face. How long had he been there? She and Aimee had gone on for a while, she imagined.

Will looked worried and concerned. But the look in his eyes spoke something else. Caring? Questioning? Adoration?

"And for you, Miss? What can I get you?" The server interrupted her musing.

"Cobb salad, please, small. Blue cheese dressing on the side. No croutons." Ava smiled and handed the woman her menu.

The server then looked at Aimee. "Same thing!"

"Alrighty."

Ava waited until the server had taken everyone's orders, menus were collected, and conversation ensued about purchases, and so on, until she asked the question burning a hole in her brain. "Who can tell me the story of the old theater down the street?"

Spanning her friends sitting at the table, her gaze landed on Will, who sat up a little straighter at her question. "Anyone?" Ava asked.

"It's been here for like, a hundred years or more," Kat told her. "And I'm sure we could dig up some history on the old building at the historical society, but the short answer to your question is that we don't know much anymore."

Frowning, Ava said, "That's too bad."

"What we do know is that it was part of the old Markey estate that was sold in the 1990s. Whoever bought it lives out of state and has little contact with anyone in town. I've heard that the town council has the details but that they agreed to keep the owner anonymous in exchange for being able to use the space occasionally for town events. But that's been rare."

"Hm. I see." Ava's wheels were spinning off in a direction she wasn't sure she wanted to go, and she worked to rein them in. "What a shame." She glanced at Aimee. "It would have been cool to have seen a play there back in the day. Wouldn't it?"

Aimee's eyes lit up. "Like the Christmas pageant!"

"Exactly." Ava grinned at the girl, and they resumed their chatting about the Christmas pageant, *Wicked*, and more.

"I love being on the stage with everyone looking at me," Aimee said. "I'm good with the acting parts, just not as good with the singing and dancing."

"Oh, I so agree with you, Aimee. I get the jitters every time I sing. But don't you worry about that, okay? Take some lessons and with every performance, you'll feel more confident."

"Like you?"

Being on stage was the one place Ava always felt confident. She was herself, but she wasn't. She was someone else. "Yes, exactly. Let me tell you about this time...."

They chattered on. The crowd hummed around them, merrily conversing, happy with their morning finds, and ready for lunch. Occasionally, Ava would glance over at Will, and not once, it seemed, had he taken his eyes off her.

"ARE YOU SURE YOU DON'T WANT TO SOAK IN THE TUB, WILL? IT HAS jets."

Ava busied herself at the bathroom sink after brushing her teeth and hair, contemplating whether to indulge in a bath again tonight or take a quick shower. Standing in her bathrobe, looking at herself in the mirror, she leaned closer to study the lines on her face she hadn't noticed before.

Goodness. She was twenty-eight, not forty-eight. Where had those come from? Shaking her head, she stepped back. *I'll think about those lines another day.*

She supposed she shouldn't hog the tub in case Will was interested. But the warm-hot, swirling water was heavenly last night, and she was certain it would do wonders to ease the tense kinks out of her back and shoulders. She might even try the cranberry-lavender bath salts.

Will sauntered into the bathroom from the bedroom. "Did you say something?"

She caught his reflection in the mirror. "Do you want to try out the tub tonight?"

"With you?" He arched a brow.

"That was not my thought. I just thought you might be interested. If not, I might."

Sighing, he shook his head. "I'll take a shower later. Feel free to indulge if that's what you are getting at."

"I wasn't getting at anything, Will."

"Then why don't you just be direct and say what you mean?"

Goodness. Turning, she faced him. "I thought I did. What's wrong, Will?"

He shook his head and backed out of the room. Ava watched him disappear into the bedroom. Something was eating at him.

She decided against the tub bath and would take a quick shower instead. She'd linger too long in the tub to avoid the inevitable nightly discussion with Will. The two of them were barely together during the day, so they'd had little time to interact and talk. By the time they were back at the inn after lunch, she was ready for a nap. Later, the family had all gone out for pizza in Charmington, and she'd ended up talking mostly with her mom. Will seemed to take extra time with Alex, and she was glad about that.

Now, after changing into her gown, she stepped into the bedroom. Will sat dozing in a chair in the sitting area, another medical journal open on his lap. He'd have a crook in his neck if she let him sit like that for long.

Ava approached him and softly shook his shoulder. "Will? Wake up. Your neck."

Slowly, he lifted his head and blinked, looking at her. "Hi, sweetheart. Thanks." He shifted in his seat. The journal slipped to the floor.

Sweetheart. That endearment hadn't come from his lips for some time.

"Your turn for the shower."

He grasped her hand and tugged her forward. Caught off guard, Ava stumbled toward him. Will clasped his hands around her waist and hauled her into his lap.

"Ava."

"Will," she breathed. "What are you doing?"

His hands cradled her face, and for a split second, their eyes made contact, and Will kissed her lips. "Oh, Ava...." he breathed.

It had been too long since she'd felt the pressure of his lips on hers. Ava savored the sensation for several seconds as he nibbled and kissed. Will's kisses had always left an impression on her. And if she were honest with herself, she'd missed them.

But not enough to let this go on. Pushing back, she stood, her spinning head aching to grasp hold of exactly what she was feeling and what he was doing.

"Will. No."

"Sweetheart."

"No, Will." She stepped backward. "No. I can't."

Her heart fluttered wildly against her chest wall, so much so she thought it might burst out of her flesh. A large part of her wanted to give in, wanted to wrap her arms around him and kiss him silly, and then make long, passionate love with Will in that big king-sized bed.

The other part screamed for her to retreat, and that seemed the part she was listening to the most. All her brain could think about, could settle on, was that night months ago—the night that changed everything.

Six months earlier

The lock jiggled on the front door. Ava heard the sound from her bedroom. A quick glance at the clock told her it was two-forty-five in the morning.

"Will?" she called out.

"It's me, Ava."

"Okay, good."

He moved into the bedroom. "Are you awake?"

"Partially."

"Could you stay awake for a few minutes? There's something I want to talk to you about."

She rolled over. "God, Will. I just got to sleep. Can it wait until morning?"

"No. No, it can't."

The tone of Will's voice caught her attention. Sitting up in bed, she switched on the bedside lamp, blinked, and squinted at him standing in the doorway. "You look like hell. What's wrong?"

"There is something I need to get off my chest."

Panic settled behind Ava's breastbone, causing her breath to catch in her throat. "Will, sit down. What's going on?"

He hesitantly moved closer to the bed and sat on the edge near the foot—like he was afraid to come any closer. Ava let him gather himself for a minute before speaking. He looked visibly shaken.

"I want to have the baby discussion."

That came from left field. "What? Now?"

"Because I have some decisions to make, Ava."

"Decisions? What decisions. Will, I'm not awake enough to speak in puzzles and riddles. Can you be direct, please?"

"I'll try."

"Go on."

"I..." He faltered over his words...glanced off to the floor, avoiding looking at her. "I want to have children."

"And I imagine we will. One day."

He shook his head. "A few months ago, we were heading in the childless-for-life direction—you and I both said we weren't sure if children were in the cards for us—but I've changed my mind. Been thinking about it for a while. I want to have a family. Soon."

"Soon?"

"Yes."

"Why now? We've always talked in terms of the future."

"That's the problem. The future never gets here."

Ava leaned forward, shifting her legs to the side of the bed. "Why is that a problem now, Will?"

Slowly, he lifted his gaze. "Because the timing is better."

She sat back against the headboard, contemplating his words. "For whom?"

"For me."

"And what about for me?"

"You can always postpone your career. I can't, Ava."

"Well, if that isn't the most sexist thing I've heard in a while. Good God, Will. I just landed a significant role in Broadway play—something I've been working toward for years, as you know—and you want me to postpone my career because the timing is better for you?"

He stared straight into her eyes. "Yes. Indirectly, it affects you, and is better for us both."

"Puzzles and rhymes again." Ava pushed off the bed and stood, pacing toward the window and back. Abruptly, she turned toward him, her voice rising. "There's something else. What is it? Why is this timing better for you now?"

He exhaled. "I'm going for the chief medical director promotion. If I get it, I'll start first of the year. The application process will be intense, and if I get the promotion, even more intense. I'll probably see you less than ever."

"What position, again?"

"Chief Medical Director, over Emergency."

"Which means you will practically live at the hospital."

"Yes."

"And you thought it convenient that we shoot out a baby now, for what reason? You don't start for six months, so that gives you ample time to impregnate me, then roll off on your merry way to doctor land. Oh no, Will. What do you suppose I will do all day, and all night long, with a baby, when you are not even around to be a father?"

He continued to stare. "I supposed you would be a mother and do the things mothers do."

"But not work."

"Not for a while. I'll make plenty to cover your salary."

She turned away, not wanting to look at him any longer. "So, I just give up my dream for you, because you want a baby."

"Women do it all the time."

"They have help."

"We'll hire a nanny."

"What about emotional support, like from a husband? You will be no help."

Her back still to him, she heard him exhale. "There is a woman at work...."

Panic raced across her chest, shot through her heart, and traveled down her spine. She whirled. "Are you having an affair?"

He stood then. "No. I'm not. But she is coming on strong and wants to."

"You're kidding me. What did you tell her?"

"I haven't told her anything."

"Did you talk to her about us? About putting off having children? Are you sharing our personal lives with another woman, Will?"

He hesitated, then looked away from her. "Yes."

"What the—" Ava's heart skipped a beat. Maybe two. "Let me guess, she wants to have your baby?"

"Something like that."

"Oh. My. God."

"It was just casual conversation at first. Someone to confide in. But then..." He didn't finish the sentence, staring off into the night.

"Have you kissed her?"

He still didn't look at her.

"Oh, my God, Will."

"Ava, I want to have a family with you. I want you to have my baby. And I'm crazy mixed up in my head about all of this because you keep pushing it off. I'm not getting any younger, and neither are you."

"We're only in our late twenties, Will. There is plenty of time. Who the hell is this woman?"

"You don't know her." Will looked back.

"Because you have a whole different life at the hospital than you have here with me. Well, maybe you just want it all to be hospital life. Is that it?"

"Maybe. Wouldn't you prefer your whole life to be theater?"

It didn't take Ava even a second to think about that. "No. I definitely do not want my entire life to be theater. I want the balance, and you know what? That work life/home balance has surely been lacking for quite a while. What are we doing with our lives, Will? Are you seriously considering having a relationship with this woman so she can give you a baby?

"I think we should separate, Ava. I've done nothing wrong. I've not cheated on you."

"Maybe not physically."

He ignored that.

"Will?"

"I'm afraid I'm going to have an affair with her. Ava, we are not here for each other anymore."

You're afraid *you are going to have an affair?* "And she's there for you."

"Yes. At times. As friends."

"I see."

"Look, Ava. I need our lives to change. I need more of you than I'm getting. Please, can you make this sacrifice now, and I promise you I'll make it up to you down the road."

Ava perused him standing there for a minute. His face flushed, his demeanor disheveled. Will also had worry lines etched into his face. Chasing professional careers had obviously been hard on both their bodies.

"So, you suggest I quit my job and have a baby to keep you from wanting to have an affair. Can I get a written guarantee on that,

Will? Some sort of warranty, so I know for sure that after I give you a baby and halt my career, that you will not want to go off and get in her panties, anyway?"

"Good Lord, Ava. Stop it."

"Well?"

He paced left, then right. "I'm going to sleep in the other room. Let's give us some time and space to consider this before the new year."

"Consider what? The baby? A separation? Your potential affair? Will, are you insane?"

"No, I'm not. I'm trying to be fair and let you make this decision."

"Me?"

"Yes. Either we are a family or we're not."

"You mean, either we have a baby or you're leaving?"

"That's not what I said."

"That's exactly what you said."

"You're twisting things."

Ava took a couple of steps closer to him. "No, I'm not, Will. You're already twisting things in your head. You've not had downtime from work for months and months. It's playing with your thinking. Take some time off."

"I don't want to take time off, Ava. I want you to take time off, so that when I come home, you are here for me. Do you know how much I hate coming home to an empty house at night? Do you know how lonely that is?"

"Actually, I do. It's the same lonely that I come home to, Will." She sat on the side of the bed. "You know this really isn't about a baby, or about a woman who says she wants to have your baby— which I don't even want to get into why you two even had that discussion. This is about you and me growing apart. Sailing in opposite directions, ships in the night, so they say. This is about me being as career-focused as you. And maybe we're just not going to make it."

The pain she felt at that instant saying those words cut deep into her heart. Will looked at her, studied her face for a moment, then headed for the bedroom door.

"Will, where are you going?"

"To the spare bedroom. I need to sleep."

"Now?"

"I'm done, Ava."

"With this discussion?"

He shook his head. "No, I'm done. We're done. You've painted the picture clearly for me with your words. I want a divorce. Until we make that official, let's consider ourselves separated."

He left and softly closed the door behind him. Ava tumbled onto the bed in a crying heap.

CHAPTER 28

Will lay on his side of the king-sized bed and Ava on hers. Meeting in the middle was not something that either attempted. Ava glanced at the old wind-up clock on the nightstand and wondered if she'd wound the thing before going to bed. She didn't remember doing it, so probably had not. Given that, the three-thirty time the clock showed was likely inaccurate. All she knew was that it was dark outside, and that neither she nor Will had had a decent night's sleep.

They both lay there, and tossing and turning, not a lot of sleep happening, and definitely not touching. As she looked up at the shadow of the light fixture—a popular spot for her gaze to land these days—she heard Will's deep sigh.

"I didn't kiss her," he said. "I never kissed her."

Ava's breath caught in her throat. He'd never addressed this before now, even though she'd asked. He'd always refused to answer, and she assumed he had kissed the woman.

"How did you know that was what I was thinking?"

His breathing deepened. "Instinct, perhaps. I sensed it the moment our lips touched."

"You have to admit that was out of the blue."

"I know, Ava. It was impulse more than anything."

They lay there, the room quiet. Night noises flittered in the still atmosphere of the room. "You never kissed her?"

"No, Ava. I didn't."

"All this time we've been separated, and you still didn't?"

"No."

Ava remained silent, unsure what she was feeling now. Elation that Will's lips had never touched the other woman's. Anger that he'd let her believe for such a long time that he might have? Relief that things weren't as bad as she had originally thought?

"It's complicated," Will offered.

"Then explain it to me."

After a moment, Will responded. "I'll try. I'm not sure it will make sense to you. Not sure it does to me."

"Well, I definitely can't understand it if I don't know what is in your head, Will."

He turned on his side. "I was wrong, Ava. On so many levels. And I'm sorry about that."

It was the first time he'd offered an apology. "Thanks for saying that. Go on."

Will sucked in a breath, held it, and then exhaled for several seconds. "We had dreams. Goals for our lives. You and me. We both got crazy caught up in achieving them. Please know I'm not blaming you for any of this. When I say 'we' it's just the way it was for both of us."

"I understand that, Will. I got caught up in the rat race as much as you. When the pandemic hit and I couldn't work, I was miserable for months. I tried to get involved in other things, and I found activities I enjoyed, somewhat, but I was so lonely at home without you while you were at the hospital."

"And then there were those weeks I didn't come home at all. I didn't want to risk getting you infected with the virus."

Not that she hadn't thought about those weeks because she had. "Was that when you... Well, when the woman... When you became...friends."

Will was slow to respond. "Yes."

"Oh."

"We had this joke. Everyone was doing it. She was my work wife. I know it's weird and corny, but it was something people just started saying and doing—not just me and her—but everyone jokingly had someone at work to rely on, lean on, share meals with, talk and cry with when we lost another patient. It was harmless, but it was also the strangest time of my entire life, Ava. Almost like living in an alternate universe. Everyone at the hospital—we needed each other emotionally. Some took it to a physical level. I didn't."

"But she wanted to." Ava was direct.

"Yes. I told her no. But she was persuasive, and it was difficult, I'm sorry to say."

Ava tried to picture him sharing his tough days with her. She couldn't really picture the woman—and didn't want to know what she looked like at all. What she saw in her mind's eye was a woman's blank face—and for some reason, she pictured her as a redhead. That made no sense, but it was how she saw her.

"Meanwhile," she told him, "I'm back at home in isolation, piddling with recipes trying to learn how to cook chef-worthy meals for a man who never came home."

"Oh, God, Ava. I'm so sorry."

"It's all right, Will. The freezer is full of meals. But I hope you can understand that after those weeks and months when everything stopped but you and your work, when the auditions slowly started opening again, I had to jump. I was going stir-crazy in isolation."

"I understand that."

"Did you at the time?"

He paused. "I'm not sure I did. My life was so busy I never stopped to think about yours."

"Yet, you confided every night about your day to a work-wife. What is she, a nurse? Never mind, I really don't want to know."

"She transferred to another hospital three months ago."

Ava looked at him. "So, what does that mean?"

"It means I've not spoken with her for three months. There is no work-wife. It means that I've been trying to get my head back on straight now that this pandemic is waning. It means, Ava, that even though we met with the attorney and had papers drawn up, I'm faltering here because I'm not sure what I—we—went through back then was the clearest thinking on each of our parts."

"Will, we have a lot of work to do, if…" She couldn't finish the sentence.

"I know that."

Neither of them said anything for a while.

"Ava, what do you want in, say, five years from now? Where do you want to be in life?"

Her brain suddenly went to the snow globe she saw earlier in the day. Yesterday. For the first time in quite a while, she was going to be honest with herself, as much as with Will. "In five years, I want to live in a house, not an apartment. In a town, not the city. I want kids, and I want my family."

"What about the career?"

"I don't know how that fits in. Not yet anyway. Not in five years." She paused, thinking. "What do you want, Will? Where do you see yourself in five years? Still climbing the ladder to who knows where?"

He shook his head. "No. I see myself with you. I have always seen myself with you in my future. I know nothing else. What happened weeks ago was wrong and weird and I'm sorry. Ava, I can't imagine my life without you in it."

"Today, you can't. But six months ago, you could."

"That was a different time. I was in a different place."

"Well, like I said. We have a lot of work to do if we are ever going to get there." Ava pulled the covers back and swung her legs over the side of the bed. "I need coffee. I hear people downstairs. I'm heading down after I get dressed."

She padded away toward the bathroom.

"What's on the agenda today?" he called out.

Ava turned back slightly. "I'm not sure. At some point, however, you and I need to talk about gingerbread house building. We need to have our house ready by tomorrow afternoon."

"I KNOW I DON'T HAVE TO SHARE THE TRADITION WITH ALL OF YOU— you've been here for Christmas for years," Kat reminded most of the Cohen family members, "...but just a reminder that the official Christmas lighting at Holly Hill Inn is tomorrow night and I hope you all will be here. In the meantime, I could use help with decorating the Christmas trees in the house, so if anyone is interested in helping with the last-minute Christmas prep—it's fun, I promise—see Ariana, our resident Queen of Christmas." She pointed to Ariana, who was hanging garland over the drapery rods at the bay window.

She smiled and waved. "Hey everybody! Welcome to Christmas Eve Eve!"

"Huh?" Alex shrugged his shoulders. "What's Christmas Eve Eve?"

"Today!" Ariana grinned at him. "Any excuse to celebrate, right?"

Kat stepped into the center of the room. "In Ariana's world, the day before Christmas Eve is Christmas Eve Eve."

Alex slowly nodded and reached for the garland to help Ariana. "Cool. Makes sense."

"I'll second that," said Grandpa Z. "What can I do?"

Ava glanced around the sunroom, which was almost too small for all the people standing in it. Breakfast was over. Marcus and Dorothy Cohen had caught a ride into town with Dylan, so they could do last-minute shopping. Ava's mother hadn't made it out of her room yet and had texted earlier that she was sleeping in an "taking a day" which meant that Carol wanted to be alone for a while. She'd surface later in the day, Ava was sure.

That left Grandpa Z, Alex, Will, and herself. "Looks like Ariana, Alex, and Grandpa have this room covered. What can Will and I do?"

Kat parked her fists on her hips and glanced about. "Well, there are a couple of smaller trees in the windows on the stairwell landings. The one on the second floor and the other one leading up to the attic. Those could use some decorations."

Ava looked at Will. "You game?"

He grinned. "Of course."

"Rifle through those boxes of decorations and use whatever you like," Kat told them.

The two tentatively looked through the items, chose lights, garland, and shiny gold balls, and placed them in an empty box. "Let's see how this looks," Will said.

Ava agreed, then, turning to leave the room, ran straight into Matt. "Oof. Sorry, Matt!"

"Hey Ava. No worries." He steadied her by grasping her biceps. "I wasn't paying attention. Looking for Kat. Seen her?" Matt moved on into the room. "Oh. There's my sister."

"Hey little brother. What brings you here this morning?"

"Well…" Matt drug out the word. "I was wondering if there was anyone here who would like to help me with a minor project. It would involve heavy lifting followed by pizza and beer for lunch."

Alex stepped forward, raising his hand. "I'm in."

"Alex, no you aren't." Ava gave him a motherly look.

He rolled his eyes. "I'm seventeen!"

"And still under the drinking age."

"Geez."

Grandpa Z twisted back from where he was hanging garland and patted Alex on the back. "Let a man handle this, son." He faced Matt. "So, Matthew Matson, I'm up for the beer, but I'll pass on the pizza—the cheese, you know, at my age—as well as the heavy lifting. Capiche?"

Matt shook his head. "No dice, Zachary. Sorry. I gotta have the package deal."

"Well, I'll be." Grandpa hung his head and sidled up to Alex. "Either too young, or too old. Look what you've got to look forward to, son."

Alex put his arm around Grandpa Z's shoulders. "Let's just stay here and eat cookies on Christmas Eve Eve."

"Ah. My kind of solution."

Ava shook her head at the two, then caught Will's eye. He gave her a questioning look. Ah, capiche to borrow a phrase. "We have to plan the gingerbread house today, Will. And we need to do our grocery shopping. "

"We can do that later today."

"That's cutting it close, but..." Looking at Matt, Ava asked, "You'll be back this afternoon?"

He nodded. "That's the plan."

"I promise, Ava. I'll be back in time to shop."

Ariana, still on the stepladder, cleared her throat and turned toward her husband. "Matt, you have to be back by two o'clock, remember? I need you to watch the baby this afternoon so I can get the gingerbread supplies."

Matt grinned. "I remember, and we will be back."

Ava glanced from Matt to Will. "All right. Go on. Have fun. I'll see you later."

"You're sure?"

"Of course."

Moving toward Matt, Will said, "Lead the way. What are we doing?" He glanced at Ava as he left. She could hear them talking all the way out the front door.

"Boys." Ariana smirked.

"Yeah. Boys." Ava lifted the box. "I'll go work on those trees."

"You know," Ariana said, stepping down a step, "I'm going into Charmington to do my shopping for both Kat and my gingerbread house as soon as we finish here. If it helps, I can pick up supplies for you too. Unless you are fussy about what you want."

"I'm definitely not fussy. There are some candies I know I want, but other than that, standard gingerbread recipe stuff."

"Are you baking tonight? Kat and I are. We could make it a huge group project." She smiled and jumped down the last step.

"Oh geez. I guess we should, right? I need to do a little Googling to get this process down."

Smiling, Ariana touched Ava's elbow. "You're fine. Kat and I have discovered shortcuts, and we are happy to share. Plus, there are tons of tutorials on You Tube. Just give me a list of what supplies you need, and I'll take care of the rest."

"Bless you, Ariana. I'm most appreciative."

"Happy to do it." Ariana glanced at Alex and Grandpa Z. "Can you two handle this room? I'll help Ava."

Zachary Cohen sidled over to Ariana and took her hand. "Of course, pretty lady. This room will be splendidly Christmastized by the time you get back." He lifted her hand and kissed the back of it.

"Oh, Zachary. What a lady's man you are!"

He winked. "And don't you forget it, sweetheart." Patting her hand twice, he dropped it and returned to his work.

Ariana stepped closer to Ava, glanced down at the boxes, and gave them a stare. "You know, these will never do. There are more in the attic. I think we'll find more variety."

Ava nodded. "Great. Let's get to it."

Tucking her arm into the crook of Ava's elbow, Ariana led her out of the room and down the hall. "I want to go check on little Matt first. He's sleeping in one of the spare bedrooms."

"Oh? I thought he was with your mother."

"My parents had some errands to run."

"I see."

They ducked into one of the two downstairs bedrooms, where they found an awake and babbling baby Matt.

"Oh, he is so precious." Ava rushed over to the side of the crib, looking over at the squirmy bundle. Glancing around, she noticed the room looked more like a nursery than a guest room. There were toys, a changing table, and a couple of rockers besides the crib. "Did Kat give up one of her sleeping rooms?"

"Yes. For the time being. I should pay her rent, but she insists not." Ariana lifted him out of the bed and cradled the boy in her arms. "Let's sit over here. I need to breastfeed him if you don't mind."

"Of course not. Do what you need to do."

They were quiet for several minutes. Ava watched little Matt, her brain memorizing the curvature of his head, the squishy wrinkles on his forehead, teeny-tiny little fingernails... She could smell the softly scented baby lotion and, well, the practically new baby smell. Ariana simply glowed—a pure look of joy on her face. Ariana watched how she traced a forefinger over his little cheek and listened to the soft-spoken words she cooed to him, and her intermittent hum. Like only a mother could, Ava thought.

Could I do that? Be that comfortable, serene, content, and happy?

Ariana met her gaze. "How are you doing, Ava? I mean, this week, with everything that's going on with you and Will..." She paused, waiting. "I mean, after what you told me, I've been a little worried about you."

Ava glanced off, looking out the window. She could see Matt

and Will heading out toward the barn, all bundled up against the cold. "I see the men. Is it colder out today?" *And am I avoiding answering your question? Of course, I am.*

"Yes, I believe it is."

Ava fell silent, and she sensed Ariana was simply going to wait her out. "It's been surprisingly easy in some ways, and others, not so much."

"Is there anything I can do for you?" Ariana offered. "I'm a good listener."

But Ava didn't want to talk. Did she?

She watched Matt and Will step into the barn, out of sight. The notion that Ariana and Matt had planned this scenario so she and Ariana could talk crossed her mind. She really didn't know her all that well—would she do that?

And if so, did she mind?

While she pondered that, Ariana interrupted her train of thought. "I'm finished. Do you want to hold Matt for a minute before I change him? I need to run to the bathroom."

Should she? Could she? "Oh… Sure, Ariana. You trust me to hold him with you out of the room?"

Smiling, Ariana stood. "Of course, I do. Here. Get your arms ready."

Ava reached for the baby. Ariana laid him gently in her arms, then said. "I won't be gone long."

She stepped out of the room, and Ava shifted in her chair to better cradle little Matt's head. Suddenly, she exhaled, letting go of a breath she hadn't realized she'd been holding. As she did so, her shoulders relaxed, and she settled in, holding the infant.

Little Matt looked up at her with wide, navy-blue eyes.

"Hey, little man," she whispered, then touched his cheek with her knuckle. "You doing okay?"

He cooed and babbled, then did something amazing. A smile

shot through the baby babbling, brightening up his face as he made eye contact with her.

"Geeeeeeee!" The boy gurgled.

Ava laughed, and her heart filled up with...something. What? Wonder? Joy? Amazement that this tiny human being would grow up to be an adult human one day. He jerked then, his arms waving, and giggled a little.

"Oh! You like to laugh, little one?" That warm feeling in her heart burst over her entire body.

Cradling him closer, she leaned down and kissed his little forehead. So soft. Smelled so nice. So cuddly... Closing her eyes, she imagined for just a minute that he was hers.

"I'm back."

Ava jerked. "Oh, Ariana. He is just so... I don't know how to describe it."

"Incredible? Wonderful? Magical? Perfectly lovely?"

"All that and more." She handed Matt back to his mother. "Thank you."

"You're welcome." Ariana settled back in the other rocker. "Do you want children, Ava?"

Glancing back out the window, searching the landscape for Will but not finding him, Ava blew out a long breath. "One day. Will and I need to figure out other things first, I guess. Our lives are too busy, too involved, too...distant. I don't know what is in the cards for us, but yes, I want children one day. Just not now. It's impossible right now."

"I'm sure you know what is best. Sounds like it may be complicated."

"A bit."

"So, you might not separate?"

"I don't know. I think Will wants us to try again. He says we're not done. I guess this week is sort of about that."

"Do you?"

Ava met her gaze. "Can I be honest with you, Ariana? I'm tired of trying to figure it all out. Second-guessing him and myself. I need time, which is why I'm glad I'm going on tour in January. I think the separation will do us both good."

"What does Will think of you going?"

"He wavers. That's what we both do. We don't just come right out and say how we feel, we him-haw around over everything. It's insane."

"And you? What do you want, Ava?"

Good question. "I'm weary of the lifestyle Will and I have shared the past five years. Of course, it was fun for a while—you know, the nightlife, the constant busyness, and so on—but I'm exhausted. Most of the time I feel lost in the shuffle of our lives, the comings and goings, ships passing in the night thing. Secretly, I sometimes long for a house in the country, away from the crazy, with a picket fence and a garden with roses, metaphorically speaking."

"Like the snow globe."

"Yeah. Sappy, huh?"

"Oh, Ava. Not one bit. I feel for you, darling. Can you turn back time somehow and grab onto what you really want?"

Ava shook her head. "No. The problem is that we want different things. That's my secret dream, not Will's. Will thrives on the chaos and a hectic lifestyle. There aren't enough hours in the day for him to save people."

Cocking her head to the side, Ariana studied her. "Is that healthy?"

"Probably not. He saw his sister die when he was a kid. He's been trying to save every person and everything thing that he can since that day. Everything, that is, except our marriage."

"But you said he wants to try again. Something about not being done yet?"

"Yes. Will says all those things, but he's not willing to do what needs to be done to save our marriage."

"Which is?"

Ava stared at her. "I need Will to commit to me, Ariana. I need to know I'm always going to have him. Thirty minutes in the evening and brushing shoulders in the bathroom in the morning doesn't cut it. He wants kids. I do too. But not how we are right now."

"You're great with little Matt. And with Aimee. Someday, when the timing is right, you'll make a great mom."

Those words nearly brought Ava to tears. She blinked back the sting. "I hope so. I'd love to be a mom, but not with Will until he can guarantee he'll be a father. I can't do it alone."

HOURS LATER, WITH ALL THE FINAL CHRISTMAS DECORATIONS UP, Ava sat in the sunroom soaking up all the Christmas aura she could. The cup of mocha with peppermint she was sipping did a lot to put her in the holiday mood. She savored this rare moment of quiet to reflect on her day and the conversation she'd had with Ariana. The room held a soft glow, the day moving into late afternoon. Candles flickered in the windows, the tree twinkled with lights and glitter, and the room smelled fabulous, like pine and cranberry. Alex and Grandpa Z were natural decorators, it seemed.

A knock came softly on the doorframe. Will poked his head in the door. "There you are. I've been looking for you."

Ava glanced at her watch. "Hi. You're back."

"Yes. Am I interrupting anything?"

"No." Ava shook her head. "Just resting, thinking. How did you and Matt get along?"

He sat in the armchair across from her. "Fine. We moved things from the barn to his workshop at his farm. Some large, painted Christmas characters that belonged to his mother. He wants to refurbish them. You should see the small farm he and Ariana have. Very New England. Quaint and homey. Like back in Indiana. You'd love it."

She smiled. "Sounds really nice."

"So, about the gingerbread thing. Are we going to wing it, or what?"

"Sort of, but not really. I've been doing a little research on my phone while sitting here. I think I have the construction part down in my head. We may wing the decorating. Ava's gone to the grocery to pick up supplies for all of us. Tonight, we bake."

"Tonight? Can't we just whip up the cake in the morning?"

Ava laughed. "Um, no. It's not a cake, it's a house. There is no whipping to this. We bake the gingerbread pieces tonight, let them cool and harden, and tomorrow we assemble. We must get the house to the Charmington Chamber of Commerce by four o'clock tomorrow afternoon or we are disqualified. According to the rules."

"Wow, there are rules?"

"Yes, there are rules. They were on that application form I signed and gave to Kat. Pretty simple though—everything must be edible, no moving parts, no lights. Those are the main things, I believe."

"Sounds easy enough."

"I hope. We are not going the elaborate route—that's for experienced gingerbreaders. We are going for the simple cottage style."

Will sat back in the chair and studied her. "A cottage with a picket fence and a rose garden?"

Ava blinked and stared back. He'd just described the house in the snow globe, which was always her favorite style house. "Maybe. I can't believe you remembered. It was so long ago."

"Of course, I remember. We used to talk about it all the time when we were dating. You know, The Grand Plan, we used to call it."

The Grand Plan. She hadn't really, consciously thought about that in years. "Refresh my memory." She remembered the plan vividly, but she had no clue that he'd remembered.

Will leaned forward, his elbows on his knees. "Everything we did back then was for our futures, steppingstones toward a bigger plan. We'd get our degrees. Move to the city. Taste the nightlife. Advance our careers. We'd save a pile of money and then retire early to a small town somewhere."

So, he remembered. "Yes. A Victorian cottage with a picket fence, either in a small town or in the country somewhere. A garden with roses, and kids running about. Plus, the dog and a cat and perhaps even, chickens." She laughed at the memory. "Can you imagine me with chickens? You'd be the country doctor, and I'd open a local theater group. Goodness, but we were naïve. Weren't we?"

"We were kids. It was an unrealistic dream, Ava."

"Why? It's what we wanted then. Dreams are dreams, and why not go big and go for what you want? And look how far we have gotten in that grand plan. Degrees, job success, the city. Heck, we even have a pile of money in the bank."

"Think about the chickens, Ava. You're not cut out for chickens." Will chuckled, then grew serious. "It was what we thought we wanted back then. And it wasn't a terrible plan. It's not what I want now, though. I'm not ready to retire to a small town. Nowhere near it. Maybe in ten or twenty years."

"Yet, you want the kids part. Just not the rest of the picture."

"Yes. Look. I'm not trying to be difficult, or chauvinistic, or anything of the sort. I'm trying to honestly convey my feelings."

"We could make it work if you really wanted. Maybe a small farm, like Matt and Ariana's? Maybe not Indiana, but right here in

Charmington? Just a train ride away from the city. What do you think?"

He stared at her. "It's great for them. And maybe someday. But I just can't turn off the switch like that, Ava. I'm embedded in my work."

"Yes. That's obvious."

He stood. "What do you want, Ava? That house in a small town and a local theater group?"

"That actually sounds pretty good to me right now." She paused, studying his profile as he looked away. "Do you know what you want, Will? Really? Because I'm not sure you do."

He took a few steps toward the window, stared out into the darkening afternoon, then swung around. "Yes! I want a family, Ava. I want you. But I also want my career. I am hoping we can compromise on all of this soon."

Ava slowly stood and moved toward him. "But Will, what are you willing to give up to get that?"

"What?"

Her gaze connected with his and held. There was an anxiousness in his eyes she'd never noticed before. "Will, you tell me you can't imagine your life without me. That you want me in your life. Yet, on the other hand , you're not willing to make the changes needed to keep me in your life."

Will stared at her. "What do you mean?"

Facing him, she squared herself. "If you really loved me, you'd do whatever it takes to keep me."

"And I could say the same for you."

"That's right. But I can't make that commitment until I know you will too."

"So, we really are at a stalemate here, aren't we?"

"Will, we've been at this same place for months. Maybe it's time for us both to move on."

"Or we could do the opposite."

"Which is?"

"Something radical. Don't go on tour, Ava. Stay home. Let's get pregnant."

She laughed. "Sure. I'll do that when you don't take the promotion."

Will moved in closer. "Is that what it takes? Is that the bargaining chip, Ava? If I refuse the promotion—which I remind you will be professional suicide for me—then you'll not go on tour, and we work on getting pregnant? Is that the deal you want?"

Ava blinked twice and huffed out a breath. "Deal? Are you serious? Can we call it a compromise? Otherwise, it feels like there is something to lose here."

"We both are going to lose something, Ava. It's inevitable."

"I suppose that depends on attitude. That's not what we are shooting for here. The last thing we want to do is go into this feeling like one of us has lost a deal."

"That's not what I meant."

"But that's how it sounded."

"Then how would you put it?"

"Like this. I have another idea. What if we both quit our jobs, pull the money out of the bank, sell the condo, and head back home to Indiana. Or wherever. I guarantee you we will survive, and we will both be happier in the end."

Will held her gaze for several heartbeats. "You can't be serious. That's an incredible risk for both of us. We can stand to lose one income, but not two. The best scenario is for you to quit, and I keep on working."

"But I don't like that option, Will."

He acted like he didn't even hear her. "I'll be making a lot more money and we can afford for you to stay home."

"You don't get it, do you, Will? Are you listening to me?"

Will threw up his hands. "I'm trying to Ava. What don't I get?

Most women would love to be home and not have to work. Why not you?"

"Because for one, it's not the 1960s, Will. For two, I like my job and want to keep doing it on some level. And three, I'd be stuck in the apartment all day long with a baby, day after day, with no help because you will be working. No thanks, Will. As much as I would love to have a child, I know I can't do it alone. I need you as a partner in the baby department. Unless that happens, until I have a very firm commitment, until you are making some sort of sacrifice too, I'm out."

"And that commitment is?"

"You are giving up as much as I am."

They stared at each other for several seconds, as if they were both out of words. Suddenly, Carol's voice cut through the icy silence. "Honey? Ava? I've been looking for you. Are you in—"

Her mother halted at the door. Ava could see her slow entry out of the corner of her eye. She didn't break eye contact with Will. "Yes, Mom. I'm here. What did you need?"

Carol slowly approached the pair. "I was just going to tell you that Ariana is back from the store… She could use a hand bringing in the groceries… But what I really need is for someone to tell me what the heck is going on between the two of you."

Will broke eye contact with Ava, glanced at Carol, and muttered on his way out, "Ask your daughter," he said. "I'm done."

CHAPTER 29

"You might as well bake gingerbread, Ava. It will get your mind off things."

Kat glanced at Ava, gave her a knowing look, and then turned to monitor her mixer. Ava rolled her eyes a little and hunkered over her steaming cup of coffee.

After a long talk with her mother—a conversation that went nowhere, her mother had a tough time processing it all—she'd finally confided in Kat and then filled Ariana in on what happened late this afternoon with Will. Now, she sat at the kitchen island and watched both Kat and Ariana flit about the kitchen, measuring and stirring and breaking eggs and such. They looked like pros. She was such an amateur and felt like it—even with the online cooking and baking classes she'd taken last year.

"I can't compete in the contest, so no need for me to bake. I put on the form that Will and I were a team. Ha! Team."

"I think you can still enter the contest if you want. Just scratch his name off."

Ava groaned. "If only it were that easy…"

"I don't think we're talking about the same thing, Ava." Kat moved to the microwave to melt some butter.

"Probably not. But ladies, I do not have the energy to swirl around this kitchen tonight like the two of you are doing. My brain is spent. My body is tired. Emotionally, I'm drained."

"Well," said Kat. "I may have a remedy for all of that."

"Oh?"

"Oh, yes. Just a minute."

She scampered off to the refrigerator and returned with two bottles, one in each hand. "Give me your coffee cup."

Resigned, Ava pushed it forward. Kat delivered a four-second squeeze of chocolate syrup into her coffee. Then, from the other hand, she poured in a couple of glugs of Irish Crème. "There, that should do it."

Ava looked up. "What? No bourbon?"

Kat cocked a brow. "One second." She whooshed off to the dining room and returned with a bottle of amber liquid. Smiling, she said, "Here you go. One-hundred percent Kentucky bourbon." She poured a healthy splash into the coffee. "Bottoms up, darling."

Ariana rushed forward. "No, wait!" She peeled the paper off a candy cane and stirred the beverage with the sugary cane. "There."

"My goodness, you two are nothing short of geniuses. If sugar, chocolate, and alcohol will not get me through the night, then nothing will."

Ariana placed both hands on her hips. "Tell you what, you drink that, and you'll be up baking in no time. And if you are good, we'll fix you another."

Ava gave them a smirk. "Are you two having one?"

Both Kat and Ariana lifted their coffee cups, sipped, then smiled.

"You betcha," Kat said. "It's the only way to bake."

"Pass the measuring cups, please." Ava pushed away from the bar.

A couple of hours later, the women had successfully mixed dough, cut out the house pieces, and had baked enough for at least three houses.

"Is this our second or third cup of Christmas coffee?" Ariana asked, slightly slurring her words.

"Third. Definitely third." Ava bumped into the kitchen table as she rounded the island. "Or fourth?"

"No, it's the third," Kat said. "I never go over three in one baking."

"Okay. Good." Ariana poked a slab of gingerbread. "It's getting late. I think I'll call Matt to come get me soon."

"That's good because you're not driving."

"Of course not."

Kat turned to Ava. "Do you know where Will went this afternoon?"

One corner of Ava's mouth turned up, the other down. "Will who?"

"Your husband."

"Oh, him."

A male voice interrupted. "Yes, him. I'm right here." Will stepped into the kitchen.

Ava turned toward the voice. "Oh. You're my husband? I forgot what you looked like."

Will narrowed his gaze and glanced between all three women. To Ava, he said, "Are you drunk?"

"No, Will. I'm baking."

"Right." He turned. "I'm going to bed. I'll see you soon."

"Wait. No. You can't."

He turned. "I can't what?"

"Go to bed. Not in our room, at least."

"Why?"

Ava gave him a saucy grin. "Because you're done. Right? That means you no longer sleep in my bed."

357

"Your bed? I think it's mine too."

"No, it's mine." She took a step toward him and took a defensive stance.

Will's lower jaw dropped, he glanced at Kat—who obviously gave him no signs of help on her end—and then back to glare at Ava. "Then what am I supposed to do?"

Ava shrugged and turned away. For once, she didn't care. "You're smart. Figure it out."

WILL JIGGLED THE DOORKNOB TO ALEX'S ROOM. LOCKED. INHALING deeply, he glanced across the hall to the room where his grandpa was staying. Should he? He knew what he'd be in for if he bunked with Grandpa Z for the night.

Questions. Advice. Unsolicited solutions to problems he didn't want to face. Or things he didn't want to admit. He stared at the door, then lowered his gaze. Light spilled out from underneath.

After crossing the hallway, he tapped on Grandpa's door.

The older man jerked open the door, grabbed Will by the shirt front, and hauled him into the room.

"Wha—?"

"Get in here, boy, if you know what's good for you."

"Grandpa, let go of me. I'm not twelve." Will pulled his grandfather's hands away from his shirt.

"Well, you're acting like it." He leaned in and smelled his breath. "Have you been drinking?" Then he sniffed his neck.

"No! What are you doing?"

"Checking for perfume. Have you been dancing with wild women?"

"Oh my God." Will pushed back. "Grandpa, what in the world are you talking about. What are you doing?"

Grandpa Z eyed him. "That's my question to you. What are you doing here? You're screwing up your life."

"I'm doing nothing of the sort. I was going to ask you if I could share your room tonight."

"No." Grandpa turned away and walked toward the bed. "No room at the inn, huh?" He whipped back to look at Will. "This bed isn't big enough for two men."

"I'll sleep on the floor."

"You'll sleep with your wife."

"Grandpa, you don't understand...."

"Oh, I don't, don't I? Look, the rumor mill flies fast in this family. Ava's mother is upset. Your father and mother are in denial. And I know the truth."

"Which is?"

"That your head isn't screwed on straight."

"Mine? Why do you assume any problems that Ava and I have are my fault?"

"Tell me one thing she's done wrong in the past five years, boy."

Will thought about that. If Ava had done something 'wrong' so to speak, it should roll right off his brain. Right? But he couldn't think of anything truly 'wrong.'

"That's what I thought. It's your fault."

"There are two sides to every story, Grandpa."

He shook his head. "Not in a marriage. There aren't sides. There should never be sides. Sit down, boy, and let me tell you a story...."

"Grandpa, I'm tired. And I'm not in the mood for a story."

"Sit." He pointed to an overstuffed chair near the window. Will sighed and did as he was told. Suddenly, he felt like he was seven years old.

His grandfather sat on the edge of the bed. "Do you remember when your grandma and I used to be married?"

Will thought back. "Of course, I do. You lived over on Maple Street in Appleton."

"That's right. Do you remember anything else about us?"

Thinking back, Will tried to place himself back in that time frame. He was in preschool, and he'd often go to his grandparents' house after school for a while—a small bus dropped him off there—and his Grandma Alice would wait for him. He shared that memory with his grandpa.

"Yes, you did. Do you remember anything else?"

"That was a long time, Grandpa."

"Think about it."

Will stared at the carpet for a moment. A memory suddenly flashed through his head. "I remember the day when the bus dropped me off. Grandma was crying and had a suitcase sitting on the porch. She hugged me, told me she loved me and that she would see me soon, and then she left." Will looked up and caught his grandpa's eye. "You and I had pizza and ice cream that afternoon for a snack. I remember Mom wasn't too happy about that."

His grandfather sighed. "You remember more than I thought."

Will's brain settled on that scenario for a minute. "Why did Grandma leave?"

"Because I made the biggest mistake of my life."

"What did you do, Grandpa?"

Zachary Cohen stood and moved closer to the window. Will watched him stare out of it for a long moment. "It wasn't what I did, Will. It was what I didn't do."

"I don't understand."

Grandpa Z turned and faced him. "I didn't give her the attention she needed. I worked too much. I played too much with the guys. I left her alone too many nights."

A pang of familiarity lanced through Will's chest. He saw where this was going. "Did you have an affair?"

Shaking his head, his grandfather quickly responded. "No. I didn't. But your grandmother did."

Will's brain spun a little. Grandma Alice had an affair? She had married Mack Kramer after she and Grandpa divorced. "Wow. With Pop Kramer?"

"No. Another man. You wouldn't know him."

"So, you made her leave that day?"

Grandpa Z stared at the floor, his head swaying side to side. "No. In fact, the opposite. I begged her to stay. I forgave her for what she'd done. And believe me, it took a lot for me to forgive her. I told her I would change. But unfortunately, I had told her that too many times in the past. After twenty-five years of marriage, she left me. She said if she could do what she had done, then the marriage was obviously over. She was tired of being ignored, tired of playing second fiddle to everything else in my life. I realized—too late—what a huge mistake I had made assuming that 'until death do us part' meant I didn't have to nurture the relationship."

Will inhaled, then let it out slowly. A cord of tension eased in his chest. "Why are you telling me this?"

Zachary stepped closer, caught his gaze, and held it. "Because I don't want you to make the same mistake, Will. I'm not saying Ava is not at fault. I don't know the circumstances of what is going on with you. But I know I've been concerned, as has all the family, about your long nights at work, and leaving Ava to fend for herself."

"She fended for herself quite nicely. She's landed a big job and is going on tour next month."

"So, one day, you'll come home from work, she'll have her luggage packed, she'll kiss you on the cheek and tell you she'll see you soon, and then she will walk out the door. Let me tell you something, Will Cohen. You may have to let her go, but you also need to examine your own role in all of this. Are you driving her away? Can you change anything? Because you and Ava have shared too much for too many years to throw it all away."

"We've tried, Grandpa. We're at a stalemate."

"No. That's not what it is."

"Then what is it?"

"That's both of you unwilling to budge. Well, one of you must take the first step. The other one must follow. And you have to do this thing together. I wish, for all my days, that I were smart enough and mature enough to see what was happening before my eyes, when it was happening. I wish I had taken the risk and that first step."

He paused for a moment. Will watched his grandfather stare at the floor, misty tears in his eyes. "I have regrets. I didn't try to win her back. I simply let her go. Then after she married again, I always thought I'd find a way, after time had passed, to tell her I was sorry. She died before I could do that."

Will didn't know what to say. He remembered how broken up his grandfather had been at Grandma Alice's funeral. Now, it all made sense.

"I'm sorry you went through all of that, Grandpa."

Zachary Cohen straightened his back and shoulders and looked Will straight in the eyes. "Go back to your room, Will. To your wife. And don't come out until you and Ava have talked. And I mean really talked."

AVA DIDN'T LOCK THE DOOR TO THE SUITE.

She wasn't really drunk, and it wasn't careless. Basically, she just wanted to see if Will would attempt to come to her tonight. And if he did? Well, at this point in the game, she figured she'd let the chips fall where they may.

She was irritated with him for his reaction this afternoon, but by evening, she'd let it all go. All of it. If he was done, then so was she.

What will be, will be.

No, she wasn't drunk, unless she was high on sugar and caffeine and adrenaline. Of course, the bourbon and Bailey's kicked things up a notch, but enough time had passed since she'd left Kat and Ariana, plus her lengthy soak in the tub, for the alcohol buzz to subside.

Still, when she'd come into her room, she wondered if leaving the door unlocked was akin to an open invitation. How would he perceive that? Would he try the door handle to see if she had truly locked him out? Would he tempt fate and choose door number one to see which Ava was on the other side?

Bitch Ava?

Confused Ava?

Drunk Ava?

She lay there in bed thinking about it, about Will, about their conversation—wondering where she'd made her wrong turn in their relationship. Was there anything she could have done differently to make Will want to be home more and not at the hospital? No, there wasn't. She knew from the get-go that he would be married to his work. So, what was it?

It was the baby thing, wasn't it?

Was she being too hard-nosed about it all? Was she really scared to have a baby and practically raise it by herself? Was she afraid she couldn't do it? Worried about the responsibility? Afraid she'd never get on stage again?

Good Lord, Ava. You have some soul-searching to do, my dear.

The doorknob jiggled. Ava's body jerked to full alert. The door opened, releasing pressure on the hinges, cracked open a few inches, and then someone slipped inside. Ava's gut jittered and jumped in anticipation. As he approached the bed, she could see him in the candlelight.

"Will?" she whispered.

"Ava, I want to stay with you tonight. Please?" His voice quavered a little and possessed a semi-begging tone—one she rarely heard from him.

"I don't feel like talking and arguing tonight, Will." She sat up a little, propped on an elbow.

"Me, either. Can we just sleep?"

Ava really didn't think about what she was going to do next. Gripping the side of the covers, she pulled them back and invited Will in.

He kicked off his shoes, shrugged out of his shirt, and removed the rest of his clothing. With one knee on the edge of the bed, his body followed and he nuzzled her back into the bed.

Ava groaned as the heaviness of his body met hers and suddenly, parts of her that felt dead for so long were humming along nicely in anticipation of more.

Good gracious… Did she want more?

His face hovered over hers. His fingertips grazed the side of her face. "Ava…"

"Kiss me, Will. Now."

He rolled over and took her with him to the center of the bed. "No," he whispered. "You kiss me."

Ava lay on top and watched the reflection of the candlelight in his eyes as she slowly leaned in closer and met his lips. In the next instant, her gown soared across the room, and their bodies aligned, skin to skin.

It was the first time in months.

There'd be no sleeping on opposite sides of the honeymoon suite, king-sized bed tonight.

CHAPTER 30

*W*ill untangled himself from the sheets and Ava's legs. Letting her sleep, he tiptoed around the bed and into the bathroom, where he took a long, hot shower. It didn't seem to matter how steamy he got the shower, he still couldn't clear his brain enough to wrap it around the consequences of what he and Ava had done last night.

They'd not slept together since the night he came home and told her about the scenario at work. And this morning, he had no clue what sleeping together meant—for either of them.

It solved nothing. They'd dove into bed with reckless abandon. No thought. Just action. And he supposed that was the only way they were going to cross that fence, because trying to reason it out —whether or not to sleep together—wouldn't have gotten them anywhere.

He dried off, brushed his teeth, and dressed. Before he left the room, he stood beside the bed, watching her sleep. She was deeply under, sound asleep. He supposed it might be the best night of sleep she'd had for a while. Of course, how would he know?

She had been drinking last night. He didn't know how much, of course. But she didn't appear drunk when he came to bed. He certainly hadn't taken advantage of her—she had invited him.

Dammit. Would he come to regret this? What would be her reaction to their night of lovemaking when she woke up?

He supposed he could wait to find out, but somehow it felt it more appropriate not to be there. Maybe conversation with Ava was not the best thing right out of the gate, as soon as she woke. Of course, waking up and him not being there could also send a message.

Okay, I'll leave a note.

He found a Holly Hill Inn notepad on the desk, scrawled a quick message, folded the paper, and put Ava's name on the front. He left the tented note on the nightstand closest to Ava.

He wasn't at all sure it was the right thing to do, or if his reasoning was sound, but he moved toward the door anyway, slipped out quietly, and headed downstairs.

The kitchen was dark. A glance at the clock showed the time at five-thirty-two in the morning. He was certain it was fine for him to get the coffee started and flipped on the kitchen lights. Gingerbread stuff was everywhere—on the kitchen island, and the dinette table, and on the dining room table. He took a quick tour and noticed that each area was labeled with a sticky note. One for Kat, one for Ariana, and one for Ava. Hers was in the dining room.

So, this was what she had finished last night. It looked like she'd baked slabs of gingerbread for the sides, front, and back of the house. Also, the roof, chimney, and some windows. In addition, he noticed star, bell, and sleigh-shaped cookies.

Ava had laid out all the candies and other food items for decorating, along with printed directions for making a gingerbread house. Will glanced over the directions. Easy enough. But he needed royal icing. Did Ava make that last night?

Back in the kitchen, he opened the refrigerator door and

peered inside. Three bowls with plastic wrap covers sat on the top shelf. He took out the one with Ava's name on it.

"All right." Will straightened and headed back to the dining room, the bowl of icing in his hands. "All I need now is coffee and a little time." He secretly wished hangovers on the other two women, hoping they would stay out of the dining room for at least an hour, or so.

AVA ROLLED OVER, INHALED DEEPLY, THEN LET OUT A LONG, SLOW breath. She lay on her back, looking up at the ceiling as her brain and body became more aware. Suddenly, she blinked, and frantically sat up, looking to her left.

"Oh, no."

Where was he? She glanced about. The bathroom door was partially ajar. Was he in there?

Getting up, she pulled on her bathrobe and took tentative steps toward the bathroom door. She listened and heard nothing, then with a forefinger, eased the door all the way open.

Nope. He wasn't in there. Stepping in, she found the damp shower and towel. He'd not been gone long.

What does this mean?

What is he thinking?

She had no clue. How could she wonder what it all meant for Will, when she didn't even know what their sleeping together meant for herself? Were they back together? No. They hadn't discussed one thing that was tearing them apart. There was no mention of a reunion. There *was* an intensive lovemaking session that was, obviously, long overdue. An impromptu roll in the hay would not solve their problems.

Was it?

It meant nothing.

Did it?

No. It couldn't mean anything other than that they were both feeling a little carefree and frisky and possibly horny… That's all it meant.

Right?

Ava sat on the side of the bed. *Oh, hells bells*. What now?

Her gaze darted about the room, then landed on a piece of tented paper sitting on the bedside table. It had her name on it, written in Will's cursive scrawl.

She blew out a breath. Stared at it. Then finally picked it up.

I hope you slept well. Talk soon.

That was it. All it said. She supposed it was all she could hope for, actually.

Talk soon. That meant he expected they would talk. And after months of talking, of thinking about talking, and talking about thinking, she really didn't even want to anticipate what Will wanted to talk about.

She was going to wing it.

What will be, will be.

"Well, you can't hole yourself up here in the honeymoon suite all day, Ava. You've got things to do, a gingerbread house to decorate, and errands to run in town." That's right. Time to quit pining around about what things mean and get out in the world and enjoy your day.

She set the note aside, dressed quickly, then glanced at the clock, only now realizing that she'd slept half of her morning away.

"Oh crap! My gingerbread house!"

Ava raced down the stairs, through the entryway, and into the kitchen—where everyone in the house appeared to be gathering—and then into the dining room. With one look at the dining room table, she gasped.

"All of my house parts. They are gone!"

She whirled, looking back into the kitchen.

"No, they're not. They are over here, Ava." Ariana smiled and pointed toward the island where three gingerbread houses sat in the center. All decorated. Ready to take to town.

"But what...?"

"Come here." Kat rounded the island and reached for her hand. "Look."

She did. There was Ariana's house. And Kat's. And a third one. A small cottage with a picket fence and a rose garden....

Her stomach turned kind of giddy and jumpy.

"Who... Who did that? Who did my house?" She spanned the room, looking at each person. Not Grandpa Z. Not Will's parents. Not her mother. No, none of them would have... Who? "Where is Alex? Did he do my house?"

Kat stepped forward. "Oh no. Alex left about an hour ago to go snowmobiling with a couple of kids down the road. They dropped by this morning."

Carol looked at Kat. "I didn't know that. He didn't tell me."

Looking a little alarmed, Kat touched Carol's arm. "Oh, I'm so sorry, Carol. He told me he had permission from you."

Ava saw the worry cross her mother's face. "I'm sure it's okay, Mom. He needs to engage with kids his age. But if Alex didn't do it, then who?"

"Who do you think, darling?" Grandpa Z sidled up next to her. "I think there is a note." He picked up a piece of notepaper and handed it to her.

She hesitantly took it, searching his face.

"Read it," he said.

She unfolded the note, the same kind from upstairs. Again, in Will's scribble, the note said: *Ava, I hope you like your house. Will.*

Good gracious. She could apply all kinds of means to that sentence. What did he mean by that?

Hope you like your house—meaning, *See you later, alligator, hope you like your house.*

Or, *Hope you like your house*—meaning, *I made this special for you because I want to give you a house just like it.*

Or, *Hope you like your house*—meaning, sarcastically, *You got the house, now are you happy? Too bad I can't be there too.*

What. Did. He. Mean?

Folding the note, Ava slipped it into her pants pockets. "Where is Will?" She looked over at the crowd of people in the kitchen again.

"We don't know, honey," her mother said. "He was gone before any of us got up."

"Gone?"

Grandpa Z put his arm around her shoulders. "It's okay. He'll be back. I'm sure of it. Just take one gift at a time, darling. One gift at a time. Enjoy and be happy in the meantime."

She looked up into Zachary Cohen's knowing eyes and smiled. He grinned back.

His advice was not much different from what she'd told herself moments earlier.

"I will, Grandpa Z," she said. "I will."

But Will's being gone worried her. "Did anyone else leave today? Dylan? Maybe he went with Dylan."

"Sorry, love." Dylan gave her a wave from the dinette. "I've been here all morning."

"Matt?"

"He's home with the baby. My parents left for Philadelphia earlier."

Her heart was getting panicky. "But where would he go? Why would he decorate the house and then leave? He doesn't have a vehicle, and he can't just disappear. Where is he?"

"Ahem."

Ava swirled at the familiar voice. "Will? Oh, my God."

"I took a walk, Ava. What's going on?"

"What's going on is…" *Is that I'm out of control.* "Nothing." The crowd in the kitchen scattered. Ava noticed Grandpa Z shuffling people out of the space.

"You sleep well?"

"Uh-huh. Will, you did the house."

"That I did."

"Why?"

"I thought we were a team."

That gave her pause. "I thought we were too."

Will nodded. "It was time I started acting like it."

"Oh."

He stepped toward the island, inspecting his handiwork. "Does it look okay?"

She nodded. "It's perfect. Almost."

"Almost?"

"Chickens."

"Ah. Well, next time. When do we take it into town?"

She glanced about, avoiding eye contact with him, and she wasn't sure why. "Anytime. I think a bunch of us are going soon."

He nodded again. "Me, too? I mean, may I come?"

"Of course, Will. You are part of the team."

He smiled.

"But not because we slept together last night. That has nothing to do with this."

Will cupped her cheek in his hand, tilting her face up. "Of course, Ava. Sleeping together has nothing to do with… gingerbread houses."

"No. It doesn't." She studied his face for a moment. "But what does sleeping together have to do with?"

"Well…" He slowly shrugged and then ran his hands deep into his pockets. "Making babies?"

Ava's eyes flew wide. "What?"

"Making babies. Making love sometimes makes babies."

"But I'm—" She slapped a hand over her mouth. *No, I'm not.* She'd been off birth control for weeks, and they hadn't used protection last night—she was pretty sure. "No."

"Ava?"

"How did you know?"

"Know what?"

"That I went off the pill"

"You did? When?"

"Weeks ago."

Will tried hard not to smile. Ava could tell he was trying *very* hard not to smile, but he couldn't pull it off. "I didn't know, Ava. I swear to you. I did not know."

"You're sure?"

"I'm positive."

"And am I correct in thinking we didn't use protection?"

Slowly, Will shook his head. "Neither time."

"More than once?"

"How many drinks did you have last night?"

Ava turned away. "Oh my God. Too many, obviously. It's all my fault."

Will grasped her shoulders and turned her toward him. "Sweetheart, it's no one's fault. And we know nothing for sure."

"But Will, don't you see? This could change everything."

He nodded. "And it could be the answer."

Sighing, Ava felt her shoulders slump. "Maybe. Have we just complicated our lives?"

Will tugged her closer. "I don't think so, honey. Let's just—"

A door slammed at the front of the house, followed by the sound of someone running. They jerked toward the sound.

"Will! Ava!"

Kat burst into the kitchen. She grasped Will's arm. "Hurry. There's been an accident."

Ava watched Will's face switch from tender to intense, from husband to doctor mode immediately. "What happened?" he barked.

Kat caught Ava's eye. "It's Alex. A snowmobile accident in the woods."

CHAPTER 31

*A*va's heart somersaulted.

"Show me where." Will and Kat rushed toward the front door.

Ava followed, her head swimming. As they burst onto the porch, she found her mother weeping in Grandpa Z's arms. She touched her mother's shoulder tenderly, then left her with him for a moment while she raced down the steps, hoping to gain more information. A teenager stood beside a snowmobile in the driveway talking with Dylan. The rest of the family gathered around.

She tailed Will until he got to the boy.

"Tell me what happened," he clipped.

The boy recounted the accident. Ava heard bits and snatches. *Alex on the back. Not driving. Went off the trail. Too fast. Thrown off. Trees. Rocks. A small ravine.*

Will went into action. "What's the terrain like there?"

"Rough, snow-covered," the boy said.

"Location?"

"Up on Wilson Ridge, behind Lake Charm."

Will turned to Dylan. "Will EMTs know where that is? Do you have life-flights around here? Helicopters?"

"Yes. All the above."

"Dylan, call 911. Tell them the general location, that we need life-flight, possibly two injured. Do you have a first-aid kit? Bandages? Tourniquet or similar?"

Kat jumped toward the house. "Yes. I'll get them."

"And bring me a heavy jacket. Boots if you have them. Please. Oh, and what about a powerful two-way radio set?"

"Yes, yes. I'll go grab them. We always keep them charged."

"Good."

Kat ran to the house. Ava went with her.

"Get him a coat and whatever he needs from that closet. I'll get the medical supplies."

Ava did as Kat said.

Both raced back out of the house at the same time.

Will shrugged on the coat. Leaning against the snowmobile, he changed into the boots, then directed his attention to the kid. "Get on. Take me there. You have enough gas?"

"Plenty. We'd not been out long."

Kat interrupted. "Here's the medical kit. I put one radio in the bag. I have the other." Kat handed the bag to Will. "Keep us informed if you can."

"Will do." He got on behind the boy. "Thanks, Kat. Dylan, find out what hospital they will take them to. Ava, wherever they take him, I will meet you and your mom there."

"I'll find you, Will. Please help him."

He put his arm through the bag's strap and held onto the teenager driving the snowmobile. The last thing he did was look at Ava. "Don't worry. I'll take care of him."

In the next instant, they raced down the driveway.

Ava knew he would do just that.

WILL HELD ON TO THE TEENAGER AS BEST HE COULD. ONCE THEY got off the trail, he worried about what he would find at the accident site. None of them had any business out in the snow in this rough terrain.

"Are we close?" He yelled to the kid.

"Not far."

Will held on as the snowmobile shimmied to the left, then straightened out.

"Over there." The driver pointed.

He saw the overturned vehicle. Alex sat leaning against it and waved to catch Will's attention. The other boy lay on the ground beside him, semi-propped up against the snowmobile seat.

Will jumped off and went to the other teen first and pushed back a knit toboggan that had fallen over her eyes. Not a boy. A girl!

He looked at Alex. "Has she been out long?"

"Ever since we flipped it. I pulled her over here."

"Good." Will felt for her vitals. A low pulse. He kept his eye on Alex. "Tell me where you hurt."

"My ankle is busted, Will. I can't stand up on it."

Will glanced at his lower leg. It looked big and misshapen. "Don't stand on it at all, Alex. It might be more than your ankle. What else with you?"

"Just my head."

"Did you have on a helmet?"

"Yes."

"Did she?"

He shook his head. "She wouldn't wear it. I told her she should."

"You were right." Will looked down at the girl and examined her head, neck, and looked at her eyes. "She probably has a head injury. Maybe just a concussion, but I don't like her being unconscious this long."

The teenager who brought him crouched beside Will. "What can I do?"

Will looked at him. "Your name?"

"Michael."

"Well, Michael, your friend here is in bad shape. Can you wrap her up in your coat and hold her close to keep her warm? And talk to her."

He nodded. "I can do that."

"Then do it. I'm going to check out Alex." He looked at Alex's pupils. Dilated, one bigger than the other. "How are your ears?"

"Ringing."

"Are you nauseous?"

"A little."

He was also pale. "You've got a concussion, Alex. I'm sure you feel a little fuzzy-headed. It's normal. Your symptoms will subside in time." He ran his hand down his leg toward Alex's ankle.

The two-way radio in the bag crackled. Kat's voice came through. "Will. Can you hear me?"

He hit the button. "Kat. Yes."

"Did you find them?"

"Yes. Do you have an ETA on EMTs?"

"Confirm your location?"

He looked at Michael. "Off the trail at Wilson Ridge. About a quarter mile from the start of the trail. Should I go back up and lead them here?"

Will looked at the girl. Michael had wrapped his coat around her. "Yes. Go, and get them here ASAP." Then he returned to Kat. "Michael will meet the EMTs at the head of the trail. What about the helicopter?"

"On its way too."

"Good."

"What about Alex?"

"He'll live."

"Who else?"

"A girl. Not sure her…" *Crackle, crackle.* He lost connection with Kat. Tucking the radio back in the bag, he looked at Alex. "You okay?"

He nodded. "I'm worried about her."

Will reached for Alex's hand. "She'll be fine, and so will you."

"Is Mom okay?"

"Bawling her eyes out, of course, but Grandpa Z is with her, and Ava too. She's fine."

The girl beside him moaned.

"Alex, what's her name?"

"Lynn."

Will leaned closer and called her name. She mumbled something incoherent. Up above, he heard the *whump-whump-whump* of a helicopter. He lifted his gaze and searched the morning sky.

THE CLOSEST HOSPITAL WAS IN CHARMINGTON, SO AVA AND CAROL waited there with Kat and Grandpa Z, hoping they wouldn't have to drive anywhere else. The next closest hospital was over an hour away, two towns over. Ariana went back home to relieve Matt of baby duty. Marcus and Dorothy Cohen stayed back at the inn, so someone would be there if needed.

They waited in the parking lot until they saw action. Ava sat in the front seat with Kat, watching the sky for the helicopter. Carol sat next to Grandpa Z in the back seat, sniffling a little. He cradled her in his arms, and she leaned into him.

They made an odd sort of couple, but Ava was glad that he was there to comfort her.

Ava reached over the seat for her mother's hand. Carol grasped it and held on tight.

"He's going to be fine, Mom. Will is taking care of things."

"I know. But until I see Alex and know what's going on, I'll be a nervous wreck."

Grandpa Z patted her shoulder. "There, there now. It's all going to be fine, Carol. Will is a smart man. He will take care of your boy."

"I'm so grateful for him."

Ava looked back and met her mother's eyes. "Me too, Mom. Me too."

"Helicopter!" Kat sat forward in her seat.

They all watched as the aircraft softly landed on a helipad to the side of the hospital, snow and dust billowing up around the aircraft. The platform was about a football field length away from the parking lot. They waited as hospital staff rushed out to meet them, carried a gurney off the helicopter with a patient, and the EMTs spilled out to follow them all inside.

"I don't see Will," Ava said.

"Me either. Let's go in and see what we can find out."

The four made their way through the emergency entrance. All the staff at the desk could tell them was that one person came in on the helicopter, and another was coming in my ambulance. A nurse suggested they wait in the adjacent waiting room until more information was available.

Ava stepped up. "My brother is one of the injured people. Can you tell me if he was on the helicopter?"

The person shook her head. "The patient on the helicopter was female. Your brother must be in the ambulance. We expect them soon."

"Okay." Ava looked at her mother, then back at the woman behind the desk. "I don't suppose you have any information about him?"

She shook her head. "No, I don't. But if you will wait, as soon as I know something—"

Flashing lights caught the corner of Ava's eye, and she looked toward the ER staff entrance. She eased that way while watching through the sliding glass doors. The back end of the emergency vehicle flew open, and simultaneously an ER crew from the hospital rushed toward the doors.

Will jumped out of the back, shouting things she couldn't hear. They pulled the stretcher out, and the wheels locked in place. She saw Alex on the stretcher and took a step forward. Someone grasped her from behind and pulled her back.

"Stay here, Ava. Out of their way." It was Grandpa Z.

She nodded and glanced at her mother, standing to her left. Kat brought up the rear.

The sliding glass doors burst open, and the ER team pushing Alex swept inside. Will shouted over the chaos to a man in hospital garb. She quickly assumed he was the attending physician.

"Suspected concussion," Will told the doctor. "Eyes dilated, ears ringing. Balance issues. Suggest an MRI ASAP. May be in shock. Sight disorientation. Probable right ankle fracture. Visible swelling and bruising. The patient complains of throbbing. I'd order an X-ray. No other visible broken bones but complains of rib pain. Possible dehydration so fluids were administered in route."

"Thank you, Dr .Cohen." The ER physician nodded. "We appreciate your help, and we can take it from here."

"He's my wife's brother. My brother-in-law. Take good care of him, doctor."

He gave him a thumbs-up. "Will do."

Will stepped back, and Ava stood watching him as the team and Alex headed down the hallway. They disappeared behind a pair of double doors with the words EMERGENCY PERSONNEL ONLY painted on them.

"Will?"

He turned. "Ava? I didn't see you there."

"You were busy." Both Ava and Carol rushed to him. "What happened?"

Carol clutched his arm. "Is he okay? Why didn't they let you go with him?"

"He's okay. It's protocol, Carol. Not a bad thing."

"But he's hurt?"

"A concussion, likely. Broken ankle. The team here will assess him, and we will know more soon. Let's go sit down."

Ava led her mother off to a bank of seats and sat. Will followed behind Grandpa Z, then sat beside Ava.

Kat scampered off to get water for everyone.

Ava took his hand in hers. "Your hands are cold." She placed her other hand over his to warm them. "Was it bad?"

His eyes met hers. "Will is lucky. He wore a helmet, which saved him from a severe head injury. The girl with him was driving and not wearing a helmet. She'll pull through, but I'll feel better when she's conscious. She looks to have a broken wrist and maybe an elbow."

"Oh, good Lord. The poor girl. What happened?"

"Driving too fast. Will said she lost control. They flipped."

Ava cringed. "What about Alex's ankle?"

"Will he need surgery?" Carol looked around Ava at Will.

"I imagine so."

"Here?"

"That I don't know. Let's wait to hear from the doctor working on him now."

"Can I go back with him?" Carol, again.

"I'd wait. We will hear soon. The important thing is that it could have been worse but wasn't."

Kat returned with water bottles for everyone, then took a call on her cell phone. Ava somehow got the idea from listening to

Kat's side of the conversation that she was talking with someone from the girl's family. She sure hoped the girl would be okay.

They all fell silent. Ava sighed. Carol laid her head on her shoulder. Will kept one hand in hers, and the other wrapped around her shoulders. Grandpa dozed in the seat across from them. She wasn't sure she hadn't dozed for a while, herself.

"Mrs. Barrett? Is there a Carol Barrett here?"

Ava's mother jumped. The ER doctor stood close to the desk. She went to him. "That's me. Is it my son?"

"Alex?"

"Yes."

"I'm Dr. Baird. I've just come from him and can give you an initial update."

Ava and Will moved next to Carol. Grandpa Z snored softly in the chair.

"Yes. How is he?" Carol pressed.

"Mild concussion, as I know you suspected, Dr. Cohen. We want to monitor that overnight. The ankle appears to be broken, as you assessed in the field. We're waiting for X-ray. Our technicians are short-handed right now. As soon as we get them, we'll send off to an orthopedic surgeon to evaluate."

Will interrupted. "You don't have someone on staff who can look at them?"

Dr. Baird shook his head. "No, we're a small country hospital, and we have to rely on the surrounding network to fill in the gaps for us. As soon as I get a tech to get the pictures, I'll send them off. Seeing that it's close to the holiday, I hope we can get them read soon."

Ava glanced at Will. She could tell by the look on his face that he didn't like the response to his question.

Dr. Baird continued. "The ankle will probably require surgery. He's quite swollen right now. We'll put you in touch with an orthopedic surgeon here if you want, Mrs. Barrett, or we can refer you to someone closer to home. You're not from around here though, right?"

"No," Carol told him. "We live in Indiana."

He frowned. "I see. Did you fly here?"

"Yes."

Will stepped forward. "Look. Let's figure out the coordination later. I'd like to call a friend of mine, an ortho surgeon, to examine him or the films. Do you mind? I think I can get it done sooner rather than later."

The doctor agreed. "Of course, I don't mind. Let's work out the details, Doctor."

"Perfect."

Dr. Baird stepped toward the desk, giving instructions to a nurse standing there.

Carol turned to Will. "Please do whatever you think he needs, Alex. I trust you to the moon and back with him."

Will smiled and gave Carol's shoulder a squeeze. "I'll handle everything, Carol. No worries. It's what I do."

Ava's heart swelled watching Will with her mother. He was in his element, and it was the first time in a long time that Ava realized just how important Will's job was—and how good he was at doing it.

Carol gave Will a hug and then drifted off to sit by Grandpa Z again. The older gentleman startled as she sat, then glanced her way and reached for her mother's hand. Carol smiled at him and patted his hand.

Will slowly rotated toward her, making eye contact.

"Thank you, Will," she said. "I don't know what we would have done without you." Suddenly, tears stung her eyes. "Oh, Will...."

"Shh..." He gathered her up in his arms and held her tight. "It's okay, sweetheart," he whispered close to her ear. "He's going to be fine."

"I don't know if ever truly appreciated what you do every single day, for hours on end."

"Oh, Ava. Of course, you did."

"I'm not sure about that."

He pulled back and studied her. "You know, I never realized what it must have been like for you home alone, handling everything on your own. I'm sorry about that and hope to make it up to you."

Ava shook her head and searched Will's eyes. "Let's make it up to each other. I love you, Will Cohen," she whispered. "I never stopped. I was just too afraid to admit it."

"Ah, sweetheart." A slim smile broke his face. "I love you too, honey."

CHAPTER 32

Christmas Day

Alex stayed at the hospital in Charmington for one
night, and most of the second day. When the swelling went down
some in the ankle, they let him go home—or rather, to Holly Hill
Inn—with the promise of a first-floor bedroom and no climbing
stairs.

Kat said she could make that happen.

There were additional stipulations from Dr. Baird that he and
Will worked out as well. He could only travel by car—not by plane
or train—and had to keep the foot elevated because of the swelling.
With the goal of surgery in a week, they needed to get the swelling
under control as quickly as possible. Alex was to follow up with
Will's orthopedic surgeon friend within a couple of days of
returning to New York. Carol and Alex would stay with Ava and
Will until Alex had recuperated well enough after the surgery to
travel back to Indiana.

Dr. Baird's nurse handed over the discharge instructions to
Carol. "Everything is here. Get the painkillers filled as soon as

possible, but since it's a holiday, we've provided enough for a couple of days. Don't hesitate to call if you have questions."

Carol glanced at Will, who nodded, and said, "We're good to go."

Will rented a large SUV and had it delivered earlier in the day. It was barely twenty minutes from the hospital to Holly Hill Inn, but it was good practice to see how easy it was for Alex to maneuver getting in and out of the vehicle with minimal effort and not re-injuring the foot. The trip back to New York might be a long one, if he had difficulty.

The plan was for Carol, Alex, Ava, and Will to head back to the city the day after Christmas by car. Marcus, Dorothy, and Grandpa Z still held their train tickets back to Connecticut and would leave as planned.

In the meantime, they all had one more day and night together at Holly Hill Inn.

Would it be their last?

THE HAMILTON'S PLANS FOR CHRISTMAS WERE TO SPEND THE DAY with Matt, Ariana, and little Matt at the Matson's family farm. They left out very early—not long after the excited, eight-year-old Aimee woke up and ripped through her Christmas presents. Before leaving, Kat had laid out an enormous spread of breakfast foods, breads, and pastries in the dining room for the guests. Omelets and breakfast meats lay snug in the warmers, and coffee dripped steadily into the carafe as Ava and Will came downstairs about nine o'clock that morning.

"I think we're the only ones up," Ava told Will. They quietly slipped by Will's room in the hallway and then into the kitchen.

He leaned over to sniff the coffee. "Hurry, brew. I need you soon."

"I think you can sneak a cup with that machine and it won't drip."

"Oh good. I'm doing it."

"One for me too?"

"Of course, darlin'."

Ava smiled. "I can't believe we slept so much the past day or so. The accident took its toll on all of us." She watched Will pour the coffee, then hand her a cup.

"Stress can do that. I sure hope your mom got some rest last night."

"Are you kidding? She slept in the same room as Alex in a chair. You think any of us could have talked her out of it?"

Chuckling, Will took a sip of coffee, closed his eyes, and sighed. "Man, I hate to admit how much I need caffeine, but I do."

"I totally get that, Will. I remember days when that's about all both of us lived on."

"That's the truth."

Drumming her fingertips on the island, Ava noticed a folder paper with child-like drawings of a Christmas tree lying on the countertop. "What's this?" She pulled it closer.

"Looks like a program."

"That's exactly what it is. Oh, my goodness. The Christmas pageant. I missed it."

Will looked over her shoulder at the list of performers. "There's Aimee's name. I'm sorry, Ava."

"It's okay. Can't be helped. It's bad enough that the Holly Hill Inn lighting was canceled, and we missed Christmas Eve entirely. But I had promised Aimee I would see her in the pageant." Her heart was suddenly sad. She hadn't spent enough time with the little girl this year and she had wanted to. Ava traced the outline of the Christmas tree on the program.

"We'll see her next year." Will touched the tip of her little finger with his. The current that jumped between them was palpable.

His words gave Ava a bit of a start though, and she turned away, thinking. Pretending to examine the ornaments on a small tree on the banquette table, she let her mind drift.

Was that a big assumption on his part, that they would be back next year?

They hadn't discussed their relationship since the accident. Perhaps Will felt they didn't need to. He seemed happy. He told her he loved her. And she'd said and felt, the same. They shared a bed the past two nights, holding onto each other like they never wanted to let go.

Yet, they'd resolved nothing. Or had they?

Ava knew only that she *had* made a decision that would affect the two of them. The night of Alex's accident, she'd done a lot of soul-searching and mentally tying up loose ends she'd left dangling. She guessed she'd learn Will's reaction later today.

"I hope we get to see her next year," she finally said.

Will came up behind her, grasped Ava around the waist and turned her around, pulling her close to his chest. Tilting her face up with his forefinger, he lightly kissed her lips. "Merry Christmas, Mrs. Cohen."

Smiling through the kiss, Ava returned, "Merry Christmas to you, Dr. Cohen."

He cradled her in his arms. "I have gifts for you."

"Gifts? Oh?" Ava's eyes widened. "I may have one or two for you, as well."

He leaned in, touching his forehead to hers. "Want to open them before the rest of the folks get up?"

"Well…"

"Too late for that, grandson!" Grandpa Z bustled into the room and slapped Will on the back. "Now, got a cup of that java for me, boy?"

Will smiled at Ava and released her, stepping back. "Of course, Grandpa. I'll meet you in the dining room."

"Where I'm already heading. Oh goody, chocolate scones. I do love that woman."

Ava touched Will's arm. "I'm going to check on Mom and Alex. I'll meet you for breakfast in a few minutes."

Will bent closer for a kiss.

She ducked away and teased out a smile. "See you in a few, Will."

Ava passed Will's parents in the hallway. They said their Merry Christmases and gave hugs before they sleepily stumbled into the kitchen. Ava noticed Alex's door was open this time as she passed. Inside the room, he darted about on a one-legged scooter while her mother scolded him for going too fast. Ava decided not to become part of that conversation.

She had one more gift to put under the tree. This year, she had two gifts for Will. One of them she had been holding back, unsure for the longest time whether or not to give to him.

Now, she knew what to do.

"Zachary and Alex, this room looks awesome. So Christmasy! I just love it."

Will watched his mother flit from bauble to bow as she swept through the sunroom, landing in front of the Christmas tree. His mother loved Christmas, but ever since Camille died, it wasn't as happy a time as when she was alive. It was good to see her enjoying the holiday, as she always did at Holly Hill Inn. Getting her away from home for Christmas was a good plan on his dad's part.

"I heard you two were the decorators," Marcus said. "I never knew you had it in you, Dad."

Zachary shrugged. "Well, a man of my age, my talents are many, and some of them are hidden. They come out to play occasionally, you know. You just witnessed one of my many moments of splendor."

"Grandpa, you are full of it." Will laughed and nudged his grandfather's shoulder.

Zachary cackled. "Well, let's open these gifts. Shall we?"

Will sat back and watched his family and Ava's as they exchanged gifts. It was customary just to share a gift or two, nothing extravagant or overboard. They wanted to celebrate being with each other and not necessarily how many gifts they brought home.

He anxiously awaited giving Ava her gifts, and truth be told, was slightly nervous about giving them to her. Both gifts held significant meaning for him, and hopefully for her, too. He trusted she would understand without him having to explain too much.

Glancing her way, he watched her content and joyful face as she observed the gift giving.

Carol gave Alex a music subscription for his Apple phone. He gave his mom a fancy new cell phone cupholder for her car.

Will's parents gave each other the same thing every year—a week in Hawaii at their favorite condo. Every year, they broke the extravagant rule.

Grandpa handed a small package to Alex, which turned out to be a money clip complete with gift cards to restaurants. To Carol, he gave a sweet bracelet with a heart on it. Will would have to ponder that one—later. Alex rummaged around and finally produced a gift for Grandpa Z—a pair of fuzzy socks with Rudolph's red nose on the big toe.

Grandpa laughed and immediately kicked off his shoes and put on the socks.

Will moved closer to Ava and handed her a large box. Looking up at him with wide eyes, she took it and laid it in her lap. "Thank you, Will."

"Open it," he told her.

"In a minute." Reaching behind her, she pulled out a long, thin rectangular box. "Here you go, Will. Merry Christmas."

"You first," he told her.

"Let's do it together," she said.

Alex shouted, "Just open the presents, you two!"

"All right, all right." Will slowly started tearing the tape off one end of his. The paper fell away to reveal an elongated white box. He looked at Ava. "Go on. Look at yours."

Ava did the same, pulling the paper away in one motion, and revealing the picture on the outside of the box. Will noticed her breathing grew heavier and quicker. She stared at the box without opening it, a puzzled look on her face.

Not the expression he expected.

After a moment, she looked up and into his eyes. "Thanks, Will. Luggage?"

He nodded. "Yes. It's an exceptionally nice carry-on bag."

"I see that." She ran her hand over the box.

"Open it, Ava. Let's take a look."

But her hand was shaking. When she looked up at him again, there were tears in her eyes.

Will set his box aside and moved closer to her. "Honey, what's wrong?"

"You got me a carry-on."

"Yes. For your tour. I wanted you to have something nice for traveling. Don't you like it?"

Ava blinked away tears and nodded. "I'm sure it's wonderful. Probably the best they make." Then she sniffed and sat up straighter. "There's just one problem."

"Ava, what is it?"

Shaking her head, she swiped at her tears. "Never mind. It's lovely and very practical." She finally made eye contact with him again. "Open yours, please."

Puzzled, Will reached for the white box. He looked at Ava again while he peeled away the tape around the edge. She was obviously disappointed with the luggage, and he was distracted by that, but what could he do about it now? She didn't want to say anything in front of everyone, he assumed. Maybe it was one of those stupid gift mistakes that men make.

Hopefully, his next gift would make up for this one.

The end of the box he was unwrapping fell open, and something hard and metal poked out.

"Slide it out, Will."

He pulled out a shiny metal object.

Ava sniffed again. "It's for your new desk."

Will's head shot up. "My...what?"

"Your desk, Will. Read it."

Blowing out a quick breath, Will read the engraving on the name placard: *Dr. William Cohen, Chief Medical Director.* Swallowing hard, he gripped the nameplate and looked deep into Ava's misty eyes. "Thank you."

It was a subtle yet poignant message. That was what he was thanking her for. She was telling him she supported his new position, and even under the circumstances they shared right now, which meant the world to him.

Ava reached for his hand and gripped it. "Will, thank you for the luggage. It's beautiful. But I will not need it."

"Ava?" What did that mean?

"I backed out of my tour contract yesterday. I'm not going."

Will wasn't sure he'd heard her correctly. "You're not going on tour?"

"That's right. I'm not going."

"Why?"

"Because I have other plans."

"Oh." Will sat back and studied her. "That's odd."

"Why?"

A quick glance around the room told him everyone else was

waiting to hear what was coming next. He cleared his throat. "I've been thinking along similar lines. In fact..." he picked up the nameplate and handed it to her. "This is very thoughtful of you, and it's a beautifully engraved piece, but I hope you can get your money back."

"Well, I'm not sure about that... But why, Will?"

"Because I resigned from the hospital this morning."

Ava gasped. "From the promotion?"

"From the job. I am no longer employed."

"Oh, Will. Why?" She set the nameplate aside and reached for him. "You worked so hard to get that promotion."

"And you worked hard to land the role on Broadway."

"But what will we do? We have no jobs. Are we crazy?"

By now, everyone else in the room had leaned in closer. Will smiled at his family, and then finally, longingly, at Ava. "I have ideas."

"Such as?"

He pulled another gift out from under the tree. "For you." He placed it in Ava's hands. She gazed at him. "Will, what in the world?"

"Open it, Ava," he whispered. "Please?"

"Good God, Ava," Alex pleaded. "Would you put the man out of his misery?"

"I second that." Grandpa Z added his two cents.

Will's eyes were only on Ava, though. She gave him a quick nod, then ripped into the Christmas paper surrounding a square white box. She opened the top flap and pulled out the object.

"The snow globe," she breathed. "Will, how on earth did you...?"

He leaned in and captured her lips in a kiss. "I saw you the other day, before lunch at Kringle's. I bought it after you left."

"But that was days ago!"

"Yes. Ava, I want to give you that cottage in the country, or small town, wherever you want it."

"But how? We have no jobs."

He grinned. "I have a plan, but of course I want your two cents on that. Seems there are rural areas all over the country, just like Charmington, which are lacking in local medical care, especially in specialty areas. I want to remedy that, if only in one community."

"You'd be a small-town doctor?"

"I believe I could definitely give it a shot."

"And you'd live in a small town? Or in the country? Maybe a farm like Matt and Ariana's?"

"As long as you and I are together, loving each other, I am fine with either." Peering into Ava's eyes, Will felt his heart swelling. He loved her so much. "Ava, I just have one request."

"What's that?" She batted her eyes in expectation.

"Call the tour company and see if you can get your job back. Hopefully, they have not had time to replace you. I want you to use that carry-on bag. Finish out that obligation for the year. See this part of your dream to the end. If you want, of course."

Her eyes grew misty, and she sniffled. "Oh, Will. Are you sure?"

He nodded. "I'm positive. I want you to do this."

"But what will you do in the meantime? While I am gone?"

Will pulled her closer, onto his lap, and wrapped his arms tight around his wife. "Well, I was thinking I could go out and find us that cottage. Or farmhouse. Close to a small town. We have enough money to get started on that. I could do some medical writing while I'm home for a little extra income. Basically, I want to get a place ready for you to come home to, and then, perhaps, we can think about adding to our family... That is, if you want."

One of Ava's brows arched. "You mean, like, chickens?"

He laughed. "No, I mean—"

"Will, wait." Ava bit her lip. Turning, she reached behind her and grasped hold of the last gift under the tree and handed it to Will.

"What's this?"

"I bought this earlier in the week. For you."

Puzzled, he unwrapped his last gift. Lifting off the lid, he pushed away a layer of tissue paper. "It's a Christmas ornament."

"Yes. Read it."

He did. "Baby's First Christmas." Speechless, Will laid the ornament carefully aside, and then cradled Ava's face in his hands. "Sweetheart, what? Baby's First Christmas?"

Gasps went up from Carol and Dorothy.

"Are you? I mean, it's too soon because of the other night, right? You can't be..."

Ava put a finger on his lips. "There is no baby yet, Will. At least I don't think so. But I'm hoping by next Christmas, or maybe the following one, we can hang that ornament on our tree, in our own cottage, in a small town somewhere."

"You are going to be an incredible mother."

"And you an equally incredible father."

"Thank you, Ava." He exhaled deeply, like the weight of a thousand years suddenly lifted. He kissed her softly. "You've just given me the greatest gift."

Tilting her head back, Ava whispered, "I think we've both given each other the greatest gifts of all. Ourselves. Merry Christmas, Will."

"Merry Christmas, Ava."

TWO YEARS LATER...

"*A*imee, darling, move up to your mark on the stage, lift your head and open up your chest, then belt out those lyrics. You can do it. Project!"

Ava stood slightly in the shadows in front of the stage and waited a moment for Aimee to take a couple of deep breaths, blow them out, and shake off her nervousness from her shoulders down to her fingertips. It was a technique she'd learned early-on in her own career and one she taught her students.

"Let's just do the chorus." Nodding at the pianist to play, Ava took a deep breath—for herself, as much as for Aimee. "Let her do this," she whispered.

The music started.

Aimee opened her mouth. *The sun will come out....* She belted out the song from *Annie*.

Ava waited until she finished before showing any excitement, then stepped out of the shadows and into the light in front of the stage, clapping wildly. "Bravo, Aimee! You nailed it!"

Beaming, Aimee skipped to the edge of the stage, plopped onto her bottom and sat, then jumped down and into Ava's arms. "I did it!"

Ava lifted her in a hug. "You sure did. Feel good?"

"Absolutely."

"Now just remember what we talked about when you get stage fright like that again, and everything will be fine."

"Got it." Aimee looked past her when a door at the back of the theater opened, and a triangle of light lit up the area. "Oh look. The babies!" Aimee ran off.

Ava turned to see Will coming down the aisle between the rows of seats, pushing the stroller. She turned fully and walked toward him as he approached.

"How's the play practice going?"

Shrugging, Ava said, "Better. We are on our way. I'm glad we still have two weeks until opening night. We are a little rusty in places, but I think that will work itself out. How was your day?"

Will blew out a hard breath. "Goodness, Ava. I don't know how you do it all day long by yourself. These guys are a handful."

Smiling, Ava crouched in front of the stroller. Her smiling twin baby boys, just six months old, cooed back at her. She tweaked a couple of toes, then leaned in to kiss them both. "You munchkins giving Daddy a hard time today?"

"The one on the left was cranky."

Standing, Ava gave Will a look. "The one on the left? He has a name, Will. It's Jonah." She laughed. She had trouble telling them apart herself. "I guess that spot of fingernail polish on his left-hand fingernail has worn off, huh?"

"I suppose. I forgot to look. And by the way, Jamie was practically perfect."

"Of course!" She smiled. "Well, anyway, looks like they are happy and content."

Aimee interrupted. "Can I push them around inside the theater?"

"Sure, Aimee. That would be fine." Will gave over the stroller to Aimee, then reached for Ava. "I know one thing for certain. I'm happy and content."

Ava cocked her head to the side a little. "Are you, Will? I hope so."

"Definitely. You?"

"Happier than I've ever been in my life. I love our farmhouse. I love that we have chickens in Charmington, and a pair of boys who are only going to be more of a handful as they get older. And I love you."

Tilting her head up, she kissed his lips. "Not to mention, I'm loving my job. I am so happy to breathe some life into this old theater."

"If anyone can do it, you can, Ava."

Grinning, she hugged him again. "Thank you for your confidence in me."

"Well, sweetheart..." He stepped back. "I could say the same about you. I heard from the hospital."

"And?"

"The board approved the new hiring plan. I'll be coming on board at the Charmington hospital in a couple of weeks." A slow smile traveled across Will's face.

Ava's heart tingled with happiness. "Dreams do come true."

He nodded. "Big, small, and sometimes in pairs."

Ava moved into Will's embrace. "I'm so happy."

"I'm happier."

"No, I'm happier."

"Okay, we're both happier...."

A NOTE FROM MADDIE

Friends,

I hope you enjoyed reading *A Charmington Christmas*. I loved putting together this special edition book. Every time I revisit Charmington, I want to write more stories set there!

If you enjoyed these books, then please consider sharing with others. One of the best ways to tell others about the book is to leave a review at **Goodreads,** or at the bookstore where you purchased the book. You can also leave reviews at my website, **maddiejamesbooks.com.**

Ready for another Charmington romance story? Turn the page to read the first chapter of *Charming the Prince*—a Charmington Royal Romance!

Can a small-town girl charm the prince into a happily-ever-after that started decades earlier?

CHARMING THE PRINCE

A CHARMINGTON ROYAL ROMANCE

Krissy Kringle's dream of owning her own business and settling into a community with her daughter, Merry, came alive when she moved to Charmington—the small Christmas village in the Adirondacks. Hard work, sacrifice, and a bucket-load of luck make her dream come true—Kringle's Diner exists, business is booming, and above all else, she and Merry are happy. She's also weary beyond words doing the work of three people.

So, she hires a man who wanders into the diner. He needs work, or so it seems. He comes with a huge Bernese Mountain dog named Prince, who takes up residence in the diner corner booth every day with Merry. Krissy can deal with it—help in the kitchen trumps dog germs. Right?

Contrary to popular belief around Charmington, Max Alexander (aka Alex Maxwell) is not homeless. In fact, he is royalty. Alexander Henrik Vincent Maxwell III, Prince of Beldova, heir apparent to the throne, is searching for something. Incognito, of course.

That "something" is Krissy.

Twenty years earlier, as awkward pre-teens, the two shared a magical summer vacation on a lake in Wisconsin. The next year, circumstances cause both of their lives to change forever—and they never see each other again. Years later, finding Krissy becomes a mission for Alex—before he takes the permanent step toward becoming King.

Krissy and Alex work together for several weeks. Their attraction for each other grows, but Alex never tells Krissy he is the boy from the lake. He understands her need for community with the security of home, and he doesn't want to disrupt her happiness. Besides, his future is uncertain. Will he become King? Or not?

When Alex must suddenly return to Beldova, a rapid unraveling of entangled truths reveals his reality to Krissy. Can they untangle the omissions and half-truths, and recover the magic of that one special summer for the holidays?

CHARMING THE PRINCE -
CHAPTER ONE

Summer, Wisconsin

"You can't hide here forever, Alex."

Ignoring his sister, Alexander Maxwell shifted on the sofa and stared at his laptop screen. *I don't need the reminder, Anja.* Instead, he turned up the sound on the news report streaming through his computer. "I want to hear this."

"You should. Things are heating up."

"I keep up with what is happening at home."

"Do you? Beldova needs you right now."

The tone of her voice made him turn and face her, making full and direct eye contact. Not that he'd been avoiding doing so. Well, perhaps. "I do. It's my responsibility and duty, and I take that seriously."

Anja Karin Maxwell Nilsson, his younger sister and self-appointed protector, smirked and crossed her arms over her chest, slouching slightly to one side. The slouch was unlike her. Royals don't slouch. Even if they were tired.

He'd not expected her—but that was just like Anja, to do the unexpected. She wasn't convinced that anything he'd done in the past six months was for the good of family or country. But she didn't understand everything, didn't have all the pieces to the puzzle—did anyone, truly?—so he took her tone with a grain of salt.

"Get settled in your room?"

She nodded. "I did. It looks the same."

"Everything is the same."

"Here, perhaps. But not at home."

"Let's not go there, yet."

She ignored that. "Have you spoken with anyone the past two weeks?"

He had. "I speak daily with Saskia."

"Anyone else?"

Saskia Johansson, the prime minister of his small European country, was his primary contact, and the only person he needed to deal with during these challenging times. Too many cooks spoiled the soup, or so he'd heard his father say on more than one occasion. He'd also exchanged several emails with a few members of parliament who had reached out, but he gave them less precedence.

No need to worry. He was up to speed. And he wasn't going to discuss it yet with Anja. "Saskia keeps me informed."

The streaming newsfeed droned from the computer. Anja was concerned, but there was no need. He was fine. Things at home would settle down. They always do. After a moment of tit-for-tat, brother-sister staring, he changed the subject. "Did Mother send you?"

"She did not. I came of my own accord." Anja broke the stare then and settled into a soft, overstuffed chair in the corner. She picked at a crocheted doily. "Did you have someone clean?"

"I did."

"It looks good in here." She glanced about and nodded. "It feels good here. Comfortable. Familiar. Safe." Her eyes held a faraway look.

"It's where I need to be right now."

"But what about this pilgrimage, or such, you are talking about? I don't understand. Why?"

Shrugging, Alex sat up a little, his back straighter. "I'm feeling hemmed in, Anja. What with everything that's happened the past few months, and the uncertain future... Well. You know when that happens, I need to be outside, in the wilderness."

She studied him. "But why here? You can hike the mountains all you want at home. And who hikes in Wisconsin, anyway?"

"Plenty of people do." He shifted in his seat. "I needed to come here first to ground myself somewhat. I'll set off on a walkabout in a week or so."

"It's kind of risky here in the States, don't you think? It's not like going for a walk in Europe."

"It's a little trickier, but I'll be fine."

Anja said nothing. He watched her peruse the living room and all the knick-knacks he had painstakingly washed and dusted over the past six weeks. A slow smile traveled her face, and her jaw visibly relaxed. "I used to love coming here."

"Me too."

She rose and crossed the room to a row of built-in bookshelves. Gingerly, she traced the titles on some of the old leather-bound volumes. "Pops loved his books."

"Yes. That he did."

"And Nana loved her kitchen."

"It still looks the same."

"I'm sure the breakfasts aren't the same."

Smiling at the memory of big country breakfasts, Alex could almost smell the food in the kitchen. Sometimes there'd be eggs, sausages, potatoes, biscuits, and gravy. Other times, pancakes with berry toppings or apple fritters. "No one cooked breakfast like Nana."

"Not even Eloise."

At that, Alex guffawed. "Truth!"

Anja turned, her face animated, and burst out in laughter, too. "Soft-boiled egg, wheat toast with jam, and orange quarters. The Eloise Special."

"But it's what Dad wanted, and so we all had to eat it."

"Because Eloise didn't want to make breakfast to order. What was it she said once when you asked for pancakes?"

Alex snickered. "Oh yes. I was being prickly. I think I was twelve, and we'd just returned from spending a few weeks with Pops and Nana, where of course, we'd been spoiled by them. Remember that pancake house up in the northern part of the state? Near the lake house at Butternut Falls?"

"Pops loved going there. You asked Eloise that next week for blueberry pancakes with real maple syrup and a side of butter with mile-high whipped cream on top." Anja grinned. "Do you remember that little upturn of Daddy's mouth at the look on Eloise's face?"

"I believe that was a royal inward snicker, my sister. And yes, I remember."

Anja rushed closer and sat beside him on the sofa. "And do you remember what she said?"

"Vividly." Alex cleared his throat and straightened his back, mimicking her. "Master Alexander. I am not a short-order cook." He chuckled. "Then she muttered something as she left about the children running feral while they were in the States. Pancakes, indeed!"

Anja giggled. "Then she returned with The Eloise Special for everyone. Except you didn't get jam. The look she gave you...."

Slouching back on the sofa, Alex sighed. "And by the next

summer both Nana and Pops were gone, and we've been doomed to a soft-boiled life ever since."

Anja sighed. "That last summer was the best one."

"Yes. In so many ways." Alex gave in to the memory. His throat closed a little. It was the best, by far. He sometimes wondered if he'd known it would be the last, would his awkward preteen self have done a few things differently. "I'd had no clue at the time that it would be the last one."

"I miss those days. All of them. Life just isn't the same anymore."

He sat there staring at the computer screen, seeing nothing, really. "No. No, it isn't." The newsfeed had stopped, so he shut the laptop. He'd catch up with things there later. With a sigh, he turned to Anja. "I should fix you something to eat. You must have been flying for days."

She shrugged and jerked a quick nod. "I took the last flight out of Stockholm to London the night before last, and then on to New York yesterday morning. The flight to Chicago last night, and the drive up here this morning. I've not had a good meal in a couple of days—so yes, I'm famished."

Alex stood, picking up his laptop. "Blueberry pancakes? I'll drive."

Anja stood, ready to go, it seemed. "Absolutely." She hugged him hard. "It's so good to see you, Alex. I've missed you. We have lots to discuss."

Alex hugged her tight, then set her at arm's length. "You, too. I suppose it's time to talk. I'm glad you are here. And thank you for not bringing Mother."

The expression that raced across his sister's face then startled him.

"Is something wrong?"

"No, no. Not wrong. Not really. Mother has been very preoccupied lately, and all, but…."

"Is she okay?"

Anja bit her lip and didn't answer.

"Anja?"

"Can I tell you over pancakes? Please? I'm too tired now to get into it, and would like to nap in the car, if you don't mind."

He grasped her hand. "But she's okay?"

She nodded. "Yes. I think so. Yes."

"But something is wrong."

"No, Alex. Not wrong. She's okay. But something is…different."

Learn more about *Charming the Prince* on my website, or purchase at your favorite bookstore.

www.maddiejamesbooks.com

LOOKING FOR MORE SMALL-TOWN ROMANCE?

Welcome to Sweet Hart Inn!

Cozy up at the inn where the heart of the Blue Ridge beats strongest...

Welcome to Sweet Hart Inn, a charming bed and breakfast nestled along the peaceful shores of Falls Lake, at the foot of Falls Mountain. At the center of it all is chef and innkeeper Suzie Hart, whose kitchen is always warm, and whose heart is always open. Together with her husband Brad, Suzie serves up matchmaking advice and comfort food, along with second chances, and a generous helping of happily ever after.

THE SWEET HART INN BOOKS

All of My Heart
Take My Heart
Match My Heart
Tame My Heart
The Dating Game
Miss Matched Hearts
The Husband List
Chase My Heart
No Sweeter Match
One More Kiss

THE FALLS MOUNTAIN BOOKS

Welcome to Falls Mountain, and the quaint town of Harbor Falls.

Tucked deep into the Blue Ridge Mountains, bricked streets, lakeside views, and charming local shops set the scene for small town romance.

In this standalone-but-interconnected series, you'll meet bakers, bookstore owners, chocolatiers, school teachers, and more —all trying to run their businesses, chase their dreams, and keep their hearts in check. But in Harbor Falls, love has a habit of showing up unannounced...

From second chances to secret babies to grumpy-sunshine pairings, each book brings a satisfying happily-ever-after and a cast of characters you'll want to visit again and again.

Falls Mountain Romance is a companion series to the Sweet Hart Inn Romance books by Maddie James.

Dance into My Heart
The Christmas Nanny
The Heartbreaker
Star Crossed
Not This Christmas
Convince My Heart

I hope you'll check out these books, and my other series, on my website at:
www.maddiejamesbooks.com

ABOUT MADDIE JAMES

Romance with a pulse—small towns, big love, and a dash of drama.

Maddie James writes small-town romance with heart, heat, and the occasional haunting. Her stories range from sweet to spicy, suspenseful to supernatural—happily-ever-afters guaranteed! From stand-alone love stories to binge-worthy series, Maddie delivers love next door, some cowboy kisses, an occasional hint of danger, and just enough drama to keep things interesting.

Get all the drama delivered to your inbox when you sign-on to Maddie's VIP reader list!
Free books, sneak peaks, bonus content, giveaways, and more...

Learn more: maddiejamesbooks.com/pages/newsletter

www.ingramcontent.com/pod-product-compliance
Lightning Source LLC
Chambersburg PA
CBHW020413030726
47495CB00006B/1492